Monster Haunter

Blue Moon Sacramento

Alex Gates, Steve Higgs

Contents

Awakening.
Tuesday, July
25th. 0213hrs.

Samantha Graves woke in a state of severe nausea. She refused to open her eyes and realize her situation. Rather, she remained prone, eyes squeezed shut, mentally battling the sickness slithering throughout her body.

Despite the clammy cold heavy in the air, her face flushed with heat. Sweat formed on her brow. Acidic saliva filled her mouth, dribbled off her lip, and ran down her chin. The world lurched, the floorboards rolled, but Samantha remained static among the chaos. She turned her head to the side, awaiting the inevitable sickness.

Two or three years back, Samantha's father had chartered a deep-sea fishing tour out of the San Francisco Bay.

Two years ago, she thought as hot saliva spilled over her jaw. *A present for Wade's twelfth birthday.*

That would have made Samantha fourteen on the day of their voyage — a time and age before their life had changed forever, and for the worst.

At four in the morning, the Graves family had met the ship's crew on the docks, along with the other patrons who paid (for some god-awful, unexplained reason) to fish on the uneven ocean. A handful of older men in rain boots smoked cigarettes and drank coffee, huddling near the frayed rope railing; a bachelor party of six young men shivered against the chilly morning, their breath pluming before their stoic faces. Most of them had their chins resting in their chests, sleeping as they stood, most likely suffering an early morning after a late night.

Samantha and her mother were the only two women to load onto the thirty-eight-foot long fishing boat. Immediately after stepping onto the boat, Samantha felt a jolt of disorientation. Not wanting to spoil her brother's birthday, though, she bit her tongue and swallowed back her immediate sickness.

A deckhand, a large, hairy man wearing a bright yellow beanie and yellow waders, provided a tour around the charter ship. He used a lot of maritime words Samantha didn't know or care to learn. During the tour, he had highlighted an area below the deck where the passengers could sleep.

Without a second thought, Samantha descended the slightly sloped ladder.

From floor to ceiling, two cubbies high and four cubbies long, was a shelf of cheap mattresses and thin pillows. She hadn't cared about the lack of comfort. Samantha crawled into the farthest bunk from the door and closed her eyes.

Samantha awoke four hours later, shivering and beyond nauseous. She stumbled out of the bunk, staggered across the narrow walkway and into the other honeycomb pattern of beds. For a second, she leaned against the frame of the cutout and breathed. Her mouth filled with hot saliva; her skin flushed with a surge of heat.

Once the sensation faded, Samantha lumbered up the steps leading to the deck. For a sensational second, the sharp ocean breeze cut through the nauseating fog covering her body.

"Sammy," her dad called from across the deck. He leaned over the bow, gripping the steel railing. He wore jeans, an old sweatshirt bearing the image of a turtle swimming through clouds, and a black beanie. "You're awake. Perfect timing, too." He walked across the ship with ease, somehow navigating the lurching, erratic surface. "We're about thirty minutes from casting our first line. You want some breakfast? They have a kitchen right through there." He pointed toward an open door. "Wade's in there with Mom."

Samantha white-knuckled a grab bar on the wall behind her and stared across the empty horizon.

No land anywhere in sight.

Only ocean everywhere.

It was simultaneously a terrifying and sickening sight.

She burped, and a sour pool of saliva filled her mouth. "I want to go home." Tears stung her eyes. "I don't like this."

Her dad chuckled and touched her shoulder. "Sammy, the captain makes his living catching fish. What we pay him, that's just icing on the cake. He won't turn around for a while yet, and we're at least four hours from the docks."

Her father's truth broke the barrier that sealed in her sickness. Samantha turned her head and retched onto the deck.

Throughout the rest of the day, she vomited, at least until she only spit up hot strings of bile.

To combat her sickness, she slept.

It was the single most miserable day in her entire life.

The worst until waking to that lurching, rocking, nauseating feeling once again. Except now, in the dark bowels below deck, Samantha didn't know where she was. That absence of knowledge made everything so much worse.

Samantha burped, nearly relieving herself of her last meal.

My last meal was dinner on the riverboat, she thought.

She had thrown a sixteen-year-old tantrum about attending the magic show for Wade's fourteenth birthday. Her parents, as always, had insisted she come along.

Why did they always force her to join Wade's ridiculous birthday adventures? Why did Wade deliberately choose hobbies that Samantha outwardly despised? Magic? Boats? Fishing?

As Samantha planted her palms on the ground to assist herself to her feet, a dull pain creaked up her arm.

Chains rattled.

Her eyes bolted open. In the bowels of the ship swayed a single, dangling lightbulb. It offered little light, but it shed enough on the right swing of the pendulum arc for Samantha to see her wrists. They were bruised, bloodied, and chaffed from the handcuffs clamped on them.

Ice formed over her heart. Chills racked her body. She had never felt so cold or lonely in her life—not even as she lay below deck on Wade's twelfth birthday, crying as she tried to sleep the day away. At least her family had been there. Who was with her now?

That question deepened her terror.

"You're awake," came a high-pitched voice from behind her.

Samantha startled and twisted to face the source.

A boy no older than seventeen sat on the ground, hugging his knees to his chest. He had shaggy hair that covered his eyes, wore a dirty T-shirt and torn jeans, and didn't have on any shoes or socks.

The boy must have noticed Samantha's stark fear. He raised his hands to show he meant no harm, to show he, too, wore handcuffs. "Party with friends," he said.

"What?" Samantha gasped the question in a barely whispered tone. The light in the center of the room swayed away from them, pitching them in momentary darkness.

"I went to a party with some friends on the river bank."

Samantha didn't have the slightest clue what the boy went on about. The light returned, exposing the boy's dirtied, bloodied face and light-blue eyes.

"I'm Rhett," he said.

Samantha pulled in her lips and closed her eyes, a weak effort to prevent herself from crying.

Who was Rhett? Why was he handcuffed? Why was she handcuffed? Where were they?

"What's your name?"

"Sammy," Samantha said.

Rhett offered a broken smile. "That's when they grabbed me. I went off to piss out my eighth beer, but I have this condition—stage fright." He snickered. "So, I probably went off a little too far to find some privacy. They snuck up behind me. Next thing I know, I'm waking up here."

"Why?"

Rhett pouted out a lip. "I haven't seen anyone to ask them. You showed up last night. I was sleeping at first, and when I woke, whoever

I needed to talk to had left already." He sniffled. "Sex trafficking, though."

"Huh?"

"My guess to your why. Sex trafficking. It's a lucrative business, especially for two attractive youths such as ourselves."

Despite the situation and dark possibilities it held, a shock of heat curled around Samantha's cheeks from the throwaway compliment. She couldn't help but blush. "Where are we?"

Rhett glanced around their hold and shook his head. "Some kind of ship. You get seasick?"

As if his question prompted the sickness to rear its ugly face, Samantha turned her head and lost the previous night's dinner across the wooden planks. When she finished, she kept her head lowered. Her tangly hair covered her features. She wanted to cry, to curl into a ball and go back to sleep, to wake up and have the nightmare end.

"Kids go missing all the time," Rhett said, his tone matter-of-fact. "We're just another statistic now."

Samantha wiped her arm over her mouth.

"Isn't it obvious?"

"Huh?"

"We were kidnapped." Rhett snorted a blunt laugh. "If not for sex trafficking, then to serve another person's sick, depraved fantasy until they want someone new to fulfill it."

"You're not scared?" Samantha spoke in a whimpering tone.

Rhett turned and stared at her, studying her face with his piercing eyes. He boasted a light-hearted nature, one that Samantha may have found attractive in any other circumstance. "I'm a leaf in October."

As if incapable of saying anything else, Samantha repeated herself. "Huh?"

"I'm quivering. Holding on for dear life, knowing that at any second, some stiff wind will break me off and send me far away from the comfort of my home." Rhett bubbled with laughter. "Never mind the terrible—what's it called again? An analogy? It doesn't matter. I've already been taken away from the comfort of my home by a chilly wind. So, I guess I'm not scared anymore. I'm riding the breeze and hoping I land somewhere soft."

Samantha lay back down on her side. She hugged her knees to her chest and stared at the single bulb swaying back and forth with the rhythm of the water. The darkness and the light constantly shifted, adding to Samantha's nausea and disorientation.

Where are we going? She thought, over and over, hoping sleep would grab hold of her once again.

Arrival. Tuesday, July 25th. O542hrs.

Incapable of sleep, Rhett and Samantha spent most of the night discussing their lives. Small talk, really. Samantha did far less talking than Rhett, as she battled against seasickness. She desperately wanted to sleep, had even closed her eyes and not responded to Rhett's constant chatter as an attempt to force herself into sleep. However, her fear and adrenaline kept her awake, which lent way to her continued sickness.

"I'm starving," Rhett said. He ran a hand through a mess of his sand-brown hair long enough to cover his ears. To Samantha, he looked like a football player—broad, rugged, and arrogant, though he had an artist's sensitivity about him. "Also, does it feel like we have stopped moving?"

The rocking and lurching had calmed as the hours ticked away. The swaying light bulb no long moved back and forth, but settled into a subtle circling motion. A semblance of Samantha's vitality and color returned. Still, whether they had steered into more serene water or her body had acclimated, her equilibrium remained mostly out of alignment.

"I don't know," she said.

Rhett climbed to his feet and wandered toward the closed doorway. Samantha remained seated on her assortment of threadbare, stained blankets, watching as Rhett tiptoed to the door. He wrapped his long fingers around the knob and twisted. The door popped out of the frame and creaked open an inch. Rhett hopped back and raised his manacled hands toward his face in a defensive gesture.

Samantha held her breath until her lungs grew tight and her chest compressed. She exhaled.

Rhett glanced over his shoulder at her. "I swear," he said, "on God, on my mother, on my grandma, on Baby Jesus, that door was locked when I tried it last night."

Samantha ran the blade of her hand across her eyes and forced herself to stand. Her legs wobbled, despite the ship having moved into stable water. "Before I showed up?"

"Yeah."

"Maybe after throwing me in here, they forgot to lock it." Samantha shivered at the thought of creeping out the door and attempting to escape. Would that only make things worse?

"Go on," Rhett said, nodding at Samantha. "I have your back."

"What? No. No way. You go first."

Rhett pushed the door fully open with his foot. A flood of bright yellow light spilled into their sleeping quarters.

Samantha raised her arm and squinted against it. After a second, her eyes adjusted, and the deck of the fishing charter appeared. A terrible thought wrapped around her throat, choking her.

It's the same charter from Wade's twelfth birthday.

Except, of course, it wasn't.

The below-deck quarter where she had spent her entire trip differed from where she and Rhett stayed. Also, what she could glean of the deck from her vantage showed an older, more weathered vessel than the fishing charter.

Samantha swallowed terror, bile, and uncertainty. She stepped forward on uncertain legs. They held, though, and they continued moving, one foot in front of the other, to the steep stairwell leading upward.

"Ladies first," Rhett said. "I have your back."

All the charm Rhett originally exuded, and any interest Samantha may have entertained, evaporated as the kid prompted Samantha to explore the unknown. Cowardly behavior trumped any physical or emotional attractiveness.

Samantha gripped the steel railing and ascended one cautious step at a time. As she came level with the deck, she half-expected to see her father leaning over the bow and scanning the ocean-blue horizon. Instead, a sharp wind whipped against her. The ocean gusts carried a cool mist. Samantha wore a fashionable outfit for a summer night in Sacramento—white jeans now stained in dirt and grime, a black tank top, and a light denim jacket—but nothing to protect her against the bitter elements. Samantha shivered on the deck of the ship, hugging her arms to her chest. Dark clouds filled the sky, and dark water filled the horizon.

The ship had come to a stop at a rocky shore, one which sat at the bottom of a large, heavily forested and steep hill. Atop the hill, above the marine layer and overlooking the entire ocean, stood a stone-faced castle like something from a storybook. Samantha had lived in an immense estate for almost two years, but not even her home compared to what overlooked the island.

"What am I seeing?" Rhett asked. "Is that a castle?"

Samantha glanced at him. He wore ripped jeans, a thin T-shirt, and no shoes. Yet, no goosebumps prickled on his skin, not the slightest tremble of his shoulders from the cold air. He seemed immune to the conditions.

"Where is everyone?" Samantha asked.

"What do you mean?"

"Like the boat's crew, where are they? We can't be the only people on this ship, right? How did it get here? Someone had to drive it?"

"Maybe," Rhett said, stepping forward, turning around, and looking at the wheelhouse. "I mean, we're washed onto shore, you know? We didn't dock." He returned his attention to Samantha. "Can you operate one of these things? Maybe we can navigate back home."

Samantha chuckled at the idea of her operating a boat. Though sixteen, she hadn't ever driven a car on the road. If they had no other choice, if their only means of escape meant she had to steer the ship, could she do it?

"Do you think it's like driving a car?" Samantha asked.

"I don't have any idea. I've never been on a boat. Can't even swim that well." Rhett looked up at the steep grade leading to the castle. "Should we see if the castle has a phone?"

Samantha didn't know what they should do. She only knew she wanted the manacles off her wrists. The two of them said nothing for a few minutes. The constant tides crashed onto the pebbly beach, and the wind cut across the craggy shore.

After some time, Samantha explored the ship to find a key that would unlock her restraints. She climbed into the wheelhouse. A small desk was built into the wall. A stack of papers and a leather-bound book sat atop the wooden surface. Samantha investigated the drawers and found a handcuff key in the top one. She called for Rhett, freed his hands, and then he released the manacles from her. She rubbed her wrists.

Rhett reached for a radio, fiddled with the dials and knobs until he heard static, and spoke into it. "Hello? Mayday. Mayday. Hello? I'm Rhett Jensen. I've washed ashore an island. I repeat, my name is Rhett Jensen, and I've washed ashore. Hello?"

As he continued with the radio, Samantha grabbed the leather-bound book on the desk and opened the front flap, hoping to glean their location. The journal bore neat handwriting. The first and only entry inside of it read:

Greetings,

I'm sure you have many questions, and I'm sorry to inform you I have limited answers. You are on a remote island, one not pinned on any map, but one set aside from the world, as if it is a world of its own.

On this island lives a monster—a bloodthirsty creature. It requires the flesh and blood and bones of humans.

You have been chosen.

There is no escaping this island. The ship's operating system has been thoroughly destroyed, and upon inspection, you will find an unre-pairable gash along the port-side. If you return it to the sea, it will fill with water and sink.

Escape is not an option from this island.

The monster's name is Asterion. He is an ancient creature with an insatiable appetite. Only through me regularly feeding him will he remain away from civilization and stay on this island.

Consider yourself a contributory, a meaningful sacrifice to appease a great evil.

I wish you an expedient death.

TG

Samantha read the entry to herself. When she finished, she stared at the initials. TG. Her hands trembled at the dark possibilities in those letters. Her father, Terry Graves, had found his success shortly after their fishing trip off the coast of San Francisco. He had befriended the two older men, and the Graves' lives had rapidly changed after that.

"Find something?" Rhett asked, dragging her back to the present.

Samantha licked her lips and read the passage aloud to him. Once she finished, Rhett mulled the words over for a few seconds, rubbing his ear and saying nothing.

"What do you think?" Samantha asked.

"This is all crazy."

"The rest of the pages are blank. These papers here," Samantha lifted the stack of papers, "there's nothing on them."

"You expect me to believe someone kidnapped us and sent us to this island as a sacrifice to an evil monster?" Rhett shook his head and laughed. "No way. It's ridiculous. First off, we're on an island. If they don't feed the monster, guess what? It starves to death."

"Unless it doesn't. Unless it gets hungry, like the note says, and leaves the island. Right here." Samantha read from the note. "Only through me regularly feeding him will he remain away from civilization and stay on this island." She looked up at Rhett and shrugged.

"So, what? We're trapped here with some monster who eats humans?"

Samantha bit her lip.

"It's insane." Rhett turned his back to her and pulled at his hair. "Listen, I'm not the smartest kid in the world—I never graduated high school, believe it or not. Dropped out to pursue a life of medicinal drugs and music. But not even I buy into the idea that a monster roams this island and stays put as long as someone feeds it. I mean, come on. Who feeds him humans? How did they stumble upon that job? It's all so... so—" He threw his hands in the air, unable to think of the word.

Movement in the forest caught Samantha's attention. She stared out the window, leaning forward and narrowing her eyes to focus on the quick blur she had noticed.

Rhett yelped.

Samantha turned to him. Her hand rose to her lips, covering her mouth.

Rhett held a hand over the side of his neck.

"What—?" Samantha's question was interrupted as something bit into her neck—something fuzzy and sharp.

From the fog of the forest, a creature stepped onto the rocky shore. It bore an incredible stature—broad and tall and rippling with muscle. It walked upright like a man, possessed thickset black fur over its entire body, and it had a bull's head with two wide, sharp horns.

Samantha leaned against the desk and slumped to the floor. She wanted to scream and run, but she only closed her eyes and fell asleep.

Indiana. Tuesday, July 25th. O842hrs.

ALINA WIGGLED HER FINGER inside her ear, working out a pestering itch before returning her attention to the computer screen. She sat at August's desk, a simple gesture that would silently annoy him. She couldn't wait for him to enter the office, subtly ask her to move, and watch him open drawers and lift papers to find what Alina had messed with.

Nothing.

The art of innocent torture, she thought. *I should teach a class.*

August's laptop lay closed at the corner of the desk. Though Alina knew his password, her intrusion of privacy only went so far. She left his computer alone, opting to operate on her buggy, lagging, dinosaur of a device.

August had mentioned providing Alina a contract where she earned a salary and full benefits. As a signing bonus, he would buy her a projection screen and a projector to put into the spare bedroom at his house—the room she could escape to when needed; the room currently occupied by Gerald. As she punched the sticky keys of her outdated computer, Alina thought twice about the projector. She strongly considered asking for a new laptop instead.

I can still watch movies on the laptop... just not as epically.

An explosion of tabs showed on the current screen. It took her approximately three minutes to switch between each one as the computer revved and overheated.

Alina leaned back in the chair, stared out the window, and thought about the night before. After the magic show and the interviews with police officers, Alina's father, Stephen, had dropped her off at Maya's house. Instead of making her way to bed, though, Alina had called an Uber to drive her to the Blue Moon office. She spent the rest of the night researching locally missing children from the past year.

Currently, that list showed thirteen children, not including Samantha Graves—Samantha who had vanished before everyone's eyes during the magic show.

The magician, Iniduoh (Houdini backward, because he had a severe lack of creativity) had called for a volunteer. Specifically, he had nudged for Alina to volunteer. When she refused, more than once, Samantha had raised her hand. The street-level magician stuffed the sixteen-ish-year-old girl into a coffin and made her disappear. After performing his hand-waving motion to summon her, he opened the coffin.

The crowd gasped... with fear.

No Samantha.

Iniduoh had tried again to bring Samantha back. He again failed.

Samantha's father thundered from the table and bolted to the stage. He grabbed the portly magician by his cheap button-down shirt, and an audible honk emitted from where Stephen had grabbed.

"Where is she?" Samantha's father demanded. He was slim and of average height, yet he towered over the short magician.

Iniduoh averted eye contact with the man and stared directly at Stephen, or so Alina had believed. At the very least, he stared directly at the table where Stephen and Alina sat. "I don't know," he stammered.

Unless the magician had reached beyond the limits of Earth and tapped into an arcane power to vanish Samantha from reality, only one possibility seemed plausible. A dark and nefarious plan to kidnap the young woman (*to kidnap me*, Alina thought) had unfolded before a few dozen people.

When Alina settled into August's seat, at August's desk, and powered on her antique computer, she typed Iniduoh in the search engine. Alina's aunt, Maya, was an investigative journalist, and she knew about every research trick and hack in the book, and some too unethical to record in a book. Maya had taught her niece a few tricks of the trade. It didn't take Alina long to find Iniduoh's real name.

Victor Pemberton.

Though he had no obvious connections to any other missing children, he had a checkered history of dangerous addictions, mostly involving gambling, drugs, and alcohol. The unholy trinity.

Alina spent some time digging into his illicit activities outside of poor magic, but his trail went cold after she had learned his name and habits.

At around 0300hrs, Alina had shifted her focus and investigated the current missing children from Sacramento County. Thirteen of them, ranging from ages five to seventeen. She combed through whatever online information she could find, looking for a connection to Samantha. Not finding a one.

In the comment section (a cesspool for conspiracy minds to prove their un-intelligence) of a YouTube video on missing children in America, Alina learned through a vast array of opinions why so many people go missing every year, never to be found again, especially in the National Parks.

Stairs that lead to nowhere, cannibals, satanic cults, monsters, aliens, democrats, republicans, or gateways into other worlds.

The gateway theory sounded halfway plausible to Alina, at least during the witching hours of the morning in her exhausted head. Samantha had disappeared from the coffin in front of nearly a hundred witnesses. The riverboat had immediately docked. The police had filed onto the ship, not allowing anyone to leave as they searched for the girl. They had scoured every square inch of the boat, not finding a single trace of Samantha. Maybe Iniduoh had tapped into the arcane arts and accidentally launched her into another plane of existence. Entertaining the idea of such a ludicrous conspiracy theory had forced Alina to focus on more concrete leads.

She returned to Victor Pemberton.

Plunging further into the magician once again, Alina located his childhood home—Indianapolis, Indiana. Her spine tingled at that revelation, though her sleep-riddled thoughts prevented the revelation from creeping to the forefront of her mind. She kept reading. Victor moved away from home for college, where he attended Purdue University, an hour away from his mom and dad.

Once again, Alina paused her investigation into Victor and sidestepped to the missing children. However, she went about with more direction. She focused her search on any missing children's cases during Victor's tenure in West Lafayette. Alina created a timeline, beginning when Victor turned thirteen. She made a list of all the missing children, and she pulled open a new tab for each one—a tab that took far too long to load on her ancient, hand-me-down computer.

The awareness of time slipped away as Alina worked restlessly.

"I'm early for once!" Fred Rogers, August's secretary and oldest friend, burst into the room, breaking Alina's concentration. He brandished a broad smile, and he threw his hands in the air as if signaling a touchdown. The small giant paused as he stepped inside the office, glancing around. His wide grin wavered, shifted into a deep-set frown. After a second, it sprouted again, broader and brighter than ever. "I did it!" He grabbed his head and bellowed laughter. It slowly died away, replaced with a look of utter confusion. "Did I do it? Wait, what's today? Don't tell me it's the weekend."

Alina blinked a few times and rubbed her eyes, wondering about the time. "Did you do what?"

"I beat August to the office." Fred looked at the ceiling and sighed with relief. "Has he come in yet?"

"No."

"It's Tuesday, right?"

"Mmhm."

"So, I did it!" His goofy smile split his face again. "Why aren't you more excited? Did you ever hear about our deal?"

Alina rolled her eyes. "Yes."

"If I ever beat him to the office," Fred said, sharing anyway, "he must go on a date of my choosing, with the person of my choosing." He rolled his shoulders and stretched his neck from side to side. "I never actually believed this day would come. How early am I? Why am I here so early? I could still be sleeping. Or better, I could have indulged in seconds for breakfast." He stared at Alina. "Why are you here so early?"

Alina glanced at the clock at the top corner of her computer screen. "You're not early, dimwit. You're forty-two minutes late."

The excitement, the raw expression of victory, drained from Fred's face. A frown formed and remained, pinching his features into a state of deep worry. "What do you mean, I'm late?"

"You're not early," Alina said. She yawned and glanced over her shoulder at the coffee table. A bunch of bruised bananas sat beside the coffee machine, and her stomach rumbled.

"I get that I'm not early, but I don't understand," Fred said.

Alina pursed her lips. "I don't understand what you don't understand."

"How can I be late?"

Alina looked around the office. "Are you recording me right now? Is this some kind of prank? Did you create a TikTok account? Fred, I told you not to get involved with TikTok."

"Huh?"

Alina rubbed her eyes, pushing away the headache sharpening behind her brow. "You're forty-two minutes late to work, which means you're late by forty-two minutes, which means you're not early. I'm not sure how else to explain the situation in a simpler, more straightforward way."

"No." Fred shook his head. "No, no, no." He leaned out the office door and into the hallway. "No." He stepped across the hall and opened the door to Sarah Herling's private law office. A few seconds later, the giant man returned. "I'm confused."

"Me too," Alina said. Had she fallen asleep while compiling the list of missing children? Was she experiencing a waking dream?

"How long have you been here?" Fred asked.

"Since one last night."

"This morning," Fred said.

"0100hrs," Alina said. "That's why August insists we use military time, so you don't make ridiculous, unneeded corrections."

"August hasn't come through at all since one this morning?"

Alina stood and stretched. "Nope." She shuffled to the table and prepared the coffee.

"You're telling me that August is late for work?"

"I guess."

"You're telling me August is late for work?" Fred asked again, but with more urgency.

"Fred, are you drunk? High? Sober? What's wrong with you?"

Fred dug into his front pocket and fished out his cell phone. He tapped the screen a few times and placed it to his ear. After a couple dozen seconds, he ended the call. He tried again, to the same result. He attempted the call a third time.

"Alina," he said.

"Fred." Alina peeled the bruised banana peel and bit into the browning fruit.

The mammoth man paced to the reception counter and leaned against it. He covered his mouth with a hand, then he grabbed his phone and dialed. Instead of placing the device to his ear, he tapped the speakerphone icon.

Maya answered the phone on the second ring. "What, Fred? I told you to stop calling me this early in the morning unless it's an absolute emergency."

"I beat August to work," Fred said, his voice flat and defeated.

A moment of pregnant silence, followed by rustling blankets, and a piercing, "What?"

"I'm at work before August."

"Okay, hold on. You woke me up, so I need a second to process. Let me break this down. It's after eight, which makes August late for work, which means you won the bet."

"Exactly," Fred said.

"No. No, no, no," Maya said, eerily responding in the same way Fred had.

The coffee beeped. Alina grabbed the carafe and poured a mug for herself, desperately needing the caffeine and four packs of sugar to process the situation herself.

"Fred, where's Alina?" Maya asked. "Her bed is still made. I don't think she slept here last night."

"I'm right here," Alina said. "I've been here all night."

"You haven't seen August at the office?" Maya asked.

"Nope."

"You solved both cases, right?" Maya asked, now speaking fast. "The Vampire of Sacramento and the golem?"

Alina mentally pieced everything together about the same time Maya cursed loud into the receiver and Fred's face stretched into a mask of desperate concern.

"He met with Daniel Quinn, didn't he?" Alina asked. "Why wouldn't he tell us?"

"Wait a second," Fred said, raising his hand in the air. "Hold on. Slow down. Just, everyone, keep your cool and stay calm."

"Fred, shut up and say what you want to say," Maya said.

"That's confusing. How do I shut up and say—"

"Fred," Alina said.

"Right." He moved closer to Alina and leaned his shoulder against the wall. "What if August had a sexy, successful date with Lauren, and she was so calming and relaxing that he overslept?"

"Not possible," Maya said.

Fred sighed. "You're right."

"It's also not possible you beat him to work."

"Well, it is, because I did."

"Fred, Quinn did something to him."

"And when we find him and confirm he's okay, I'm going to make him pay up on the bet. A loss is a loss, no matter how it comes along."

"Oh, God, help us all," Maya said. "August is missing, and we have Fred on the case."

"Should I call Kim?" Fred asked.

"What—Why? No, don't call his mom, nimrod. What's wrong with you?" Maya vibrated her lips, blowing air into the receiver. "Do we know where he met Quinn?"

"No," Alina said.

"Alina, how are you?" Maya asked.

"Tired."

"How did it go last night at the magic show?"

"A girl went missing."

"Come again?"

"Well, we saw this magician, and he asked for volunteers from the crowd. My dad volunteered for me to…" Alina trailed off, her mind returning to the previous night. Her father had insisted she volunteer, and she had refused. He had practically begged her to go onto the stage. Did he know what would happen? Had he planned for her to go missing? Alina closed her eyes and recalled Samantha's dad grabbing the magician, the magician staring directly at Alina's father.

"Alina?" Maya asked.

Stephen Moore had moved out of California to Indiana a few months ago, only recently returning to take Alina back with him. Why now? Why so suddenly? Alina returned to her computer. She typed Victor Pemberton and Stephen Moore into the same search.

Had her father known the magician? How? What evil secrets did they share?

"Alina," Fred said, breaking her concentration.

She looked up at him. "What?"

Maya spoke from the cell phone. "Your dad did what?"

"Volunteered me to go on stage," Alina said. "I refused, and the magician used another volunteer. Samantha Graves. She disappeared during his act. Vanished without a trace. Gone. The security guards scoured the riverboat for her, but they found nothing. Police found nothing when we returned to shore."

"Do you think he used real magic?" Fred asked. "Did he send her into, like, a shadow realm or something?"

"Yes, that's exactly what happened," Alina said.

"Really?"

"No, he didn't use magic. He spoofed the crowd and the security, and he kidnapped Samantha. It should have been me, too." Alina scrunched her face, pushing back tears—not for the missing girl, but from suspecting her dad knew and had volunteered her. "I don't know what happened to her, but she didn't look like she had too much fight in her, you know? I could've fought back. I could've escaped them."

"It's not your fault," Maya said.

"I know that. It's my dad's fault."

"It's also the police's responsibility to find her. Not ours. We need to find August, and we need to save him from Daniel Quinn."

Alina breathed. Maya waited silently on the other end of the line. Neither spoke for a few seconds.

In their rare combined silence, Fred cleared his throat. "This counts, right? I beat August to work?"

Lost. Tuesday, July 25th. 1123hrs.

I PACED A DINGY bathroom. One, two steps before I reached the claw-foot bathtub. An opaque curtain wrapped around the basin, and a shower head dropped straight from the ceiling. I pivoted, turning away from the bathtub, and faced the door.

To my left squatted a short toilet and a single vanity. A broken, scratched, smeared mirror hung above the brown-stained sink. In that dirtied mirror, my reflection was a distortion of a myriad of faces and colors and shapes. Ironically enough, it probably showed the reflection of August Allan Watson more truly than any other mirror ever had—bruised, dirtied, ragged, broken.

One, two steps and I reached the locked door. It had a lever handle that didn't budge, no matter how much weight I put into it. I drove my shoulder against the door, and it barely moved. Someone had gone to the trouble of reinforcing the bathroom exit.

When I first awoke in the strange, tiny bathroom and found the door locked, I knew Quinn had imprisoned me there. I searched my person, searched every drawer, searched every inch of the bathroom for my phone, never finding it. Anger poured through my body, and I had attempted to snap the lever off the door, to break through the wood paneling.

To no avail.

I pivoted, turning away from the door, and I took two steps back to the bathtub.

After unsuccessfully attempting to escape my odd prison, I sat on the edge of the bathtub and stared at the brown-rusted, moldy tile covered in glass fragments, dirt, and hair. The stains in the bathtub, on the floor, in the sink, the smears on the ceiling were more than the long-term effects of poor maintenance. They were the remnants of past prisoners. I couldn't confirm that, but I knew it in my soul. Those before me had bled and signed their soul to this purgatory.

With little thought, I reached for the twist-knob in the bathtub to turn on the bath water. It sputtered, choking air for a second before spritzing and spraying onto the dirty porcelain in black rivulets. It stank like death liquified.

I gagged and threw open the toilet seat. A bloated, soggy rat floated in the brown water. I gasped and inhaled gushing saliva, throwing myself into a fit of coughing and choking.

When I caught my breath, I returned to the locked door and banged on it with both fists. "Quinn!" The single word erupted from my lips like a roar, a challenge. It demanded that he open the door and meet me face-to-face to settle our differences once and for all. "Quinn!"

Repeatedly, I screamed his name, beckoning him to the door, but he never showed. I yelled until my voice fatigued and quit on the job, but I continued to assault the door with my fists—at least until each successive rap left a light stamp of blood. My signature in this bathroom prison.

Then I paced.

How long?

Does time exist in purgatory?

Do seconds string into minutes and evolve into hours in eternity?

During whatever passage of time expired within my captivity, my thoughts grew mushy, malleable like clay. Impressionable. A single errant idea might explode, create an unstoppable avalanche in my mind.

My only escape from the mental destruction was fleeing through pacing.

One, two and turn. One, two and turn. One, two and turn.

Aaron Brooks shot across my dizzied mind. I thought of the darkness that had overtaken me after shooting and killing him, of how I had allowed the darkness to swallow me whole that summer day six years ago. Miraculously, I was dragged out of it. People had fought tooth and nail to help me find light once more.

Maya.

Alina.

Fred.

Daphne.

My parents.

My siblings.

Glacia, who Quinn had taken.

Cambria, who Quinn had killed.

They all shone like stars, leading me, guiding me, keeping me from getting lost again.

In the two-stride bathroom, I had to keep my eyes on them, on their lights and the hope they provided. I had to fight to save Glacia, to avenge Cambria.

How, though?

One, two and turn.

How?

One, two and turn.

How did I fight back?

How did I escape?

I was stuck, locked inside a bathroom in an undetermined location by the machinations of a madman. I couldn't predict what came next, so I would never gain the upper hand to fight back. I needed a foothold, a wedge, an opening. I needed something to grasp and run with.

I stopped pacing, gripped the countertop, and stared at the broken mirror. My thoughts reverted to the night (*last night?*) when Quinn and I met in the parking garage.

I closed my eyes and reimagined the scene.

He had arrived in a windowless white van, similar to the van used by the Vampire of Sacramento. He had parked along the ramp, had stepped out of the driver's seat, had walked around the hood at a leisurely pace. The man wore a wicked smile on his chiseled Hollywood face. The lights in the garage had shone a dull yellow, and the distant sounds of Sacramento buzzed. Quinn stood before me, arrogant in his demeanor.

My memory gummed up right there, right when he appeared and leaned his back against the passenger door of the van. The images in my head burned at the corners, crinkling into black flakes, hazing over in dark smoke.

I opened a palm and tapped my skull, hoping to jar the memory loose. My act of frustration didn't provide clarity to any conversation Quinn and I may have had or what had happened after our meeting. It didn't help to answer the singular question careening through my head. How had I arrived in the bathroom?

However, the impulsive smack released one blocked detail. A smell that still lingered in my nostrils, even as I paced the bathroom.

A smell that smells like nothing.

Gerald had described the odor he noticed before he fought the giant chickens in the library—the giant chickens that were nothing more than children. I had chalked his olfactory observance to the acrid stench of books in an old library.

Now I smelled it, though it didn't smell like nothing. It smelled like... like old dust; like opening a window on a hot day and breathing in a whiff of the accumulated debris from the old screen; like the smell of an old, cracked dashboard; like a storage closet long forgotten.

Had Quinn released some toxin into the air, infecting Gerald's mind to see giant chickens, inciting him to attack the children? Had he deployed the same or a similar toxin when meeting with me in the parking garage, preventing my mind from storing memories? If so, what had happened after Quinn leaned against the van and greeted me?

I growled in frustration. I hadn't touched alcohol in over three years, but my foggy head sure felt comparable to a morning after blacking out.

"The smell." I focused on what I could control, on what I knew. "The smell that smelled like nothing." That's the last I remembered before my memory seemed to drift into oblivion.

Gerald had smelled it and temporarily lost his mind. He saw giant chickens and fought them off. Except Gerald had remembered his trance. I smelled it and lost my memory.

It was as if the stench sent me into a fugue state.

Worry knotted my stomach as I considered the possibilities. What if Quinn had controlled me during my amnesia? What had he forced me to do? The innumerable and horrific answers weighed me down. I slunk to the moldy floor and hugged my knees to my chest, staring at the locked door, waiting for it to open.

Instead, a bright light ignited from the countertop, accompanied by an aggressive buzz.

I glanced over and saw my cell phone. "What?" I asked, muttering in disbelief. I had scoured the entire bathroom upon waking in search of the phone. A chipped, scarred bar of soap had been where the phone now rang. Glancing over the counter, I saw no sign of the soap.

How had I mistaken one for the other? It made zero sense.

The vibrating quieted, only to begin again immediately.

I snatched it and answered without looking at the Caller ID. "Hello?"

"I'm calling for Mr. August Watson of Blue Moon Investigative Agency," said a familiar voice, one I immediately recognized. He didn't even try to disguise himself.

I ground my teeth, incapable of forming words.

"My name is Daniel Quinn, and I need your... unique services."

"Where am I?" I asked. "What did you do to me?"

"I'm afraid I'm not sure what you mean. This is Mr. Watson, correct?"

"Quinn! No more games. What do you want?"

"I want your help. I'm willing to pay handsomely, as well. Can you help me?"

I breathed through my mouth, panting with rage, wanting to lash out at him over the phone, knowing I needed to listen and play along with his games to save Glacia and all the others he had abducted. However, that didn't mean I had to entertain him with a response. I remained quiet, apart from my labored breathing.

"I have a friend who went missing," Quinn said.

I closed my eyes and held my breath and clenched my free hand into a tight fist, employing every trick to keep my poise. If I somehow grew more irate, I would bash my split and swollen knuckles into the mirror.

"A gaggle or a herd or... or a horde, I guess... I'm not sure what they're called when grouped together. I saw three of them, though, and I'm sure there were more in the shadows. A group of zombies abducted my friend. He, that is my friend, was moving to his new home when he noticed something strange. He stopped his vehicle. When he stepped out of the car to investigate, the zombies swarmed him."

I licked my lips, hating myself for what came next, but knowing I had to play his game. "You saw this happen?"

"Dash-cam video," Quinn said.

"What did the zombies look like?"

"Like zombies."

"What do zombies look like?" I asked. "Pretend I've never seen a movie before."

"Like their human selves, but partly decomposed from death," Quinn said.

"You saw that in the dash-cam video?"

"Yes."

"I want Glacia back."

"Solve my case," Quinn said.

"What's your friend's name?"

Daniel Quinn hung up the phone, and the line went dead.

I held the phone to my ear, speaking into the silent receiver. "How do I get out of this bathroom? Where am I? Where did your friend go missing?" The unanswered questions popped off my tongue. As I rubbed my temples, pressing into my budding headache, the phone vibrated again. I glanced at the Caller ID, seeing Detective Ted Wilson's name flash across my screen. "Hello."

"Watson," Wilson said, his voice low, as if attempting to prevent those around him from hearing. "Where are you?"

I glanced around and shook my head. "Bathroom."

"Where were you last night?"

I don't know, I thought, worry replacing anger. I made a bad habit of never lying, so I said nothing at all.

"You there?" Wilson asked after a few seconds.

"Here."

"We need to meet somewhere private and safe. Not your house. Not your office."

"What's this about?" I asked.

"Your midnight activities. I have a few questions that need answering before someone else gets to ask them."

My tongue felt too big for my mouth. What had Quinn forced me to do? Also, how did I escape the bathroom to meet with Wilson? If he suspected me of any crimes, I couldn't avoid meeting with him. That would make me look guilty. I needed a few hours to sort everything out.

"I haven't had lunch yet," Wilson said. "Want to meet at a diner?"

"I'm not hungry right now. How about dinner?"

Wilson chuckled. "I'll give you until 1300hrs. Anything after, my questions won't happen over a shared meal. Understand?"

"Yeah."

The detective sucked on his teeth, and a slurping sound slapped through the receiver. "We'll meet at the sandwich shop a few blocks from your office. You know which one—" Wilson's voice cut into oblivion.

I pulled the phone from my ear and glanced at the screen. It had gone blank. The battery must have died.

Glancing at the ceiling, I reflected on the past two conversations. Quinn had called, needing my help, though he most definitely played some twisted game with me, which somehow had something to do with why Wilson had called.

The detective—an old friend from the police academy—wished to speak with me about an incident last night, supposedly one I was involved with. He offered to meet privately with me, before any other officers or detectives had the chance, because of our history. That meant whatever happened leaned toward the not-so-good side of behavior.

I dropped my attention and stared at the locked bathroom door.

Except something had changed. I no longer stood inside a moldy, stained, decrepit bathroom, but inside the bathroom of my old apartment—the one that sat empty since I had moved out of it a couple months back. The lease didn't expire until the end of July, and I still had the keys.

Had I, after the misadventure last night, hid in my apartment? Maybe, but that didn't explain why it had been so dingy seconds before.

More confused than ever before in my life, I stepped to the closed door and tried the handle. It twisted, and the door opened without incident.

Desperate Times.
Tuesday, July 25th.
1151hrs.

I STEPPED AWAY FROM the now unlocked door, pacing backward. One, two steps before bumping into the side of the bathtub and sitting on the ledge.

I closed my eyes tightly, rubbed them as if rubbing away the lingering sleep after a heavy slumber, and opened them again. With the heel of my palm, I smacked the side of my head, hoping to pound clarity and sense back into my mind.

Every detail within the bathroom had changed. It wasn't just my apartment bathroom's shape and design. It was my apartment bathroom to the last iota. Dingy, but not rotted and decayed as it was two minutes prior. The floor, though dirty, no longer possessed a collection of dirt, hair, grime, and mold, but only a thin layer of shavings from the last time I had trimmed. The mirror, now intact, bore the stains of water droplets and toothpaste rather than the red smears laid across it moments before.

When I moved into my new home, I had purposefully left a few items in case I needed to sleep at the apartment. Hand soap, body soap, shampoo, a toothbrush, and an old, ratted towel remained where I had left them.

How was that possible, though? How had everything in the bathroom changed from one minute to the next? How had the door unlocked? I had struggled before to bust it open, and I had failed. That led to the more pressing question at the moment. What waited beyond the door? Most likely my apartment, or so I assumed.

Did Quinn also wait to ambush me? I chewed on my cheek and shook my head, and then I stood. I took one, two steps to the door.

Quinn wanted to play a game. He wanted to compete—to pit our wits against one another. Leaving me stashed in a bathroom prevented that, and blindly ambushing me ruined it.

As Gerald had seen the giant chickens after catching a whiff of the smell that smelled like nothing, so I had perceived my bathroom as something dark and terrifying. The locked door had only been in my head. Whatever toxin Quinn had used on me last night had faded, and I saw things as they were again...

Or so I hoped.

As I crossed the bathroom, I paused and glanced at my reflection in the mirror. Blood speckled my face. More worrisome, blood covered my shirt in a stiff, matted stain. It stank, too. My jeans had dirt stains and a tear across the knee up to the thigh.

I slowly pushed open the door, peaking through the narrow crack. Despite my suspicions, I didn't care to rush into a dangerous situation. The coast appeared clear from my vantage.

Pushing the door fully open, I stepped into the kitchen and scanned every corner, shifting my eyes with a hunter's alertness. Everything appeared as I had last left it—mostly empty apart from a few necessities, just in case. Except, in my rush to move, I had somehow overlooked leaving a charging cord for my cell phone. Without a charger, I couldn't charge my phone. With my phone battery dead, I couldn't make any calls.

I glanced at the time on the oven. 1157hrs.

I cursed under my breath and hoped my Honda Civic had made it to the apartment's parking lot. If not, I would have to call an Uber... which required a phone... and money.

I patted my back pocket for my wallet, finding it empty.

I had no wallet. No money. No identification. No phone.

To my credit, I had a change of clothes in the bedroom. I also possessed the hope that my car was in the parking lot, along with my wallet and the phone charger stashed in the console. If not, I had to complete the two-hour walk to downtown Sacramento in fifty minutes to meet Wilson.

I highly doubted I could run the seven miles that quickly.

"One thing at a time," I said.

I headed into my bedroom, grabbed the spare outfit off my blow-up mattress, and returned to the bathroom, where I showered as fast as I ever have, cleaning the blood (who's blood? How had it spattered onto me?) off my body.

The rinse and the change of clothing had me feeling more optimistic about my situation, though less than hopeful.

During my two-minute shower, I had strung together an idea to get me to downtown Sacramento in case my car wasn't waiting for me.

Turned out, it wasn't.

I first looked in the assigned stall I paid for each month. After that, I spent about five minutes wandering the parking lot, clinging to hope that I parked in a random location. After convincing myself I no longer had a car, I jogged to the administration building.

The cool interior air hit me like an icy fist. Rita Lemos sat behind a desk, typing on her computer. She worked in management at the apartment complex, and she had an open and obvious liking for me. Rita was ten-ish years my elder, and divorced with three children ten-ish years my youth.

The door jingled, signaling my entrance.

Rita glanced over her laptop screen and smirked. "Well, well, well. Mr. Watson. I knew you wouldn't leave me without saying goodbye. Have you finally come to show me around your apartment before you end your lease?"

"Rita, I need your help. I—"

She raised a pudgy finger to cut me off. "Uh, uh, uh. Not so fast, Casanova."

"If I scratch your back," Rita said, "you're going to have to scratch my back. And boy, it is itchy."

"What's your price?"

"Dinner."

"Deal." Desperate times and all that.

"At my house."

I swallowed. "Okay."

"I'll cook."

"Sure."

"Dessert, too." She bit her lip and batted her fake eyelashes at me.

"Of course. Dessert, too. We have a deal." I barely registered what she proposed. My mind fixated on learning what Wilson knew about last night, on Quinn, on saving Glacia.

"This Friday night," Rita said.

"That's perfect. Now, since we're squared away, can you help me? I need a ride to downtown Sacramento. Can you call me an—"

The woman nearly capsized her chair from the speed, the power used to leap from it. "Say no more." Rita slammed her laptop shut, collected her purse, and marched toward me. She looped an arm around my waist and leaned in, kissing me on the corner of my mouth.

I stood frozen, though my cheeks burned.

"Maria," Rita said, glancing over her shoulder, "you're in charge while I'm gone."

Another woman, one so small and quiet she sat nearly invisible in the office's corner, shyly smiled in confirmation.

Rita grabbed my hand and dragged me to her car—a beat-up Highlander that had seen its share of soccer tournaments. Rita cleared off a mountain of papers and clothes and empty water bottles from the passenger seat.

"I would clear the backseat." She winked. "But given your state of hurry, we'll wait until Friday night."

"Speaking of my state of hurry," I said, staring out the dusty windshield with a spiderweb design breaking across the dead center, "we need to go." I spied a cell phone cord from the corner of my eye. Grabbing it, I plugged in my phone to pilfer some juice.

Rita started the car. The dashboard clock blinked awake. 1223hrs.

I'm not sure how I had managed it, but I would make the meeting with time to spare.

49

Case Closed. Tuesday, July 25th. 1223hrs.

THE CONTRAST BETWEEN THE outside heat and the blasting air conditioner chilled Alina as she stepped inside the McDonald's dining area. She stood a foot inside the entrance and scanned the booths, spotting Detective Kyle Vanek near the window overlooking the road.

Alina's Doc Martens thumped against the floor as she marched to him. She slid into the booth across from the detective.

He was rail thin, skeletal, and his pallid skin stretched around his face, presenting it with the appearance of a skull having a thin layer of flesh wrapped around it. He had a burger halfway into his wide-open mouth. Showing no sign of surprise at Alina's presence, he chomped off a bite, chewed, drank out of a straw, and leaned back in his seat, adjusting the gun on his hip.

"Who are you?" he asked.

"Alina."

Detective Vanek rubbed his sleep-swollen eyes. "You need to call my office and set up an appointment, see if I have the time to meet with a kid. Based on my memory, it's unlikely." The detective leaned forward and ripped free another bite from his burger. Ketchup smudged across his upper lip.

Alina tapped her fingers on the table and sucked on her cheeks. After a second, she reached over and stole a fry from the extra-large carton lying on his tray. She folded it into her mouth.

"Help yourself," Vanek said. "I can do without the calories."

Vanek had a boyish charm about him, a gentle charisma opposite most of the cops Alina had experience with. They usually possessed a bullish personality. If she had grabbed a fry from any other cop's tray, she had little doubt they would have found reason to arrest her on the spot. Not Vanek, though. Despite his angular physique and piercing blue eyes, he had a softness and warmth about him. Alina pictured him working as a teacher more than she saw him as an officer of the law.

Alina chewed, smirking as she glanced at his slight frame. "You're in charge of the Samantha Graves case?"

The detective narrowed his eyes.

"I was on the riverboat last night."

Vanek placed his burger on the red tray and patted his mouth with a napkin. "How did you find me here?"

"I exhausted every donut shop and Taco Bell in Sacramento." Alina stole another fry from the carton. "These things aren't even that good. They're just addicting. I don't want to stop eating them."

"That's why I always get a large." Vanek reached out and grabbed a few for himself. "What do you know about Samantha?"

"She took my place," Alina said.

"Took your place?"

"The magician called on me as a volunteer, but I refused his summoning. Samantha took my place on stage."

Vanek drank through the straw, rattling ice and slurping what remained of the liquid.

"Information is information, right?" Alina leaned back in the booth and stared out the window at the slow-moving lunchtime traffic. "Do you know anything about her disappearance?"

"Nothing I'm going to share with a little girl."

Alina chuckled, amused by his slight. "Who's the primary suspect?"

"Sorry, kid, but this isn't how these run-ins work."

"I know all about how these run-ins usually work. You, the badge and gun, barge in on someone enjoying their meal, harass them for a while, maybe arrest them if you're having a bad day, just because you can. I'm all too familiar with how it works." She reached for another fry. "It's no fun sitting on the other side of the table, is it?"

"At least you don't have a badge and a gun to threaten me with," Vanek said.

Alina snickered, finding herself charmed by the detective. "Listen, Vanek, I'm in a hurry, and I'm sure you don't want me wasting your precious time. So, let's make this mutually beneficial, yeah? I'm looking into Samantha's disappearance as a private investigator for the Blue Moon Investigative Agency."

Vanek enjoyed another bite of his burger and chewed it thoughtfully, taking his time. He slurped his beverage again, finding it empty. The detective cleared his throat. "Excuse me." He stood and ambled to the soda machine to refill the soda. When he returned to his seat, he adjusted the gun on his utility belt. "I'm sorry. What were you saying? Something about you being a private investigator?" He spared a light chuckle. "What are you, kid? Sixteen?"

Alina grimaced at his accurate guess at her age. "Does it matter?"

"I've heard of the company. Blue Moon, right? I didn't think a little girl ran it."

"I wouldn't call August a little girl," Alina said. "He's over six-feet tall and weighs close to two-hundred pounds in rippling, statuesque muscle. I told him to cool it with the weights. His physique is impressive, sure, but also too much. He's neurotic, though, and he insists that working out helps him sleep."

"August Watson." Vanek scrunched his face and nodded. "I've heard of him, too. He specializes in the supernatural, doesn't he?"

Alina clenched her jaw. "Yes."

"Who would hire him to solve this case? Does it involve the supernatural?"

"A magician made Samantha disappear. That's seems a little supernatural to me, don't you think?"

Vanek took another bite and nodded his head. "I can see the connection." He licked his teeth. "I'm curious who hired you, though."

"Does it matter?"

"Samantha's parents asked for us to cede the investigation."

The floor fell out from beneath Alina's feet. If she weren't sitting, she would have fallen. "What do you mean?"

"You don't know?"

"Know what?" Alina asked.

"Samantha Graves returned home earlier this morning. Her mother called my supervisor and informed her not to waste any more taxpayer money on finding her daughter."

Alina's mind spun, attempting to grasp something solid but failing to do so. "What happened then? You spoke with Samantha, right? How did she go missing? I mean, the security detail scoured the boat for her and found nothing. The police found nothing. What did she say happened?"

Vanek set his burger back on the tray and glanced out the tinted window. "I don't know. Ferneau, my supervisor, wasn't too candid when I asked similar questions. She said it didn't matter. The girl was with her family. Case closed."

Alina reached to the end of the table and removed the square salt and pepper packs from their rack. She fiddled with them, shuffling them around the table like a deck of cards as she processed Vanek's words.

"Case closed. That's what she said?"

"Direct quote."

"How often does that happen? I mean, if a kid goes missing, then returns, is it always case closed?"

Vanek swallowed and shook his head. "Usually, we continue our investigation to learn a few key answers. Why did the child go missing? Was she kidnapped? Did she runaway? Was the child harmed? If so, by whom? So on, so forth. Samantha Graves had gone missing on a riverboat for only a few hours. Maybe Ferneau and the parents agreed it was a misunderstanding. No harm, no foul."

"Do you agree with their decision?" Alina's stomach felt empty and fluttery.

Vanek shrugged his pointy shoulders. "I have seven other missing persons cases I'm currently working. I'm happy Samantha found her way home and that she's okay."

"In the short time you worked the case, did you have any working theories about what had happened?"

Vanek glanced toward the cash register before settling his sky-blue eyes on Alina. "Not a one. I kept asking myself one question, though, believing that the answer would help me solve the mystery. How did Samantha get off the boat?" Vanek chuckled. "Apparently, she never did. The search teams just failed to find her."

Alina shook her head. "I don't believe that. I mean, how would they fail? It's a confined, localized space. Was there a trap on the floor beneath the coffin? Was that how the magician made her disappear?"

She thought of Christopher Nolan's modern masterpiece, *The Prestige*. In it, Hugh Jackman appeared to teleport across the stage. He only dropped through a trapdoor before sprinting beneath the platform and returning to the audience a second later. Alina wondered if the mediocre Iniduoh had pulled off a similar act with Samantha. Had he dropped her beneath the stage?

"The responding officers didn't find a trapdoor," Vanek said. "According to them, the stage didn't have a space for her to fall through, either."

"Did you interview Victor Pemberton about the trick?"

Vanek side-eyed Alina, shedding a half-smirk. "He said the coffin had a false wall. My team confirmed it did. When he closed and reopened the lid, it would hide the girl from the audience, creating the illusion of her disappearance. Repeating those steps, she would appear again to the audience's amazement."

"Except Samantha never reappeared on stage."

"No, but she showed at her home this morning, about two hours ago."

"What did she say about the trick?" Alina asked. "Where did she disappear to?"

"I never had the chance to call and ask her. Ferneau dismissed the case."

"You never asked Ferneau?"

"Of course I did," Vanek said. "She told me not to worry about it, to focus on my seven other cases. A case closed in this business is a case closed. I don't have the time or the energy to spend investigating one already concluded."

Alina sucked on her lower lip for a second. Vanek, at least to Alina, didn't seem like a man to forget about this case. Too many unknowns existed, too many questions remained unanswered. Where had Samantha disappeared to? Why had her parents asked Ferneau to dismiss the investigation? Why had Ferneau dismissed it with no follow-up procedures? Vanek, to Alina, seemed like a man who took orders like a well-trained dog, even if he disagreed with them.

So, where did that leave them?

Alina thought she knew.

Vanek hadn't asked her to leave the dining area—he hadn't even asked her to stop eating his fries. He had willingly shared everything he knew about the case after learning Alina was looking into it.

Why?

"You think I have the time and energy to continue looking into this case, don't you?" Alina asked.

Vanek's cold eyes never left hers. His thin lips curled into a devious smile. "Do you?"

I have to find August, she thought. Especially if Samantha had returned home, Alina had to spend all her time and energy finding August. However, her curiosity demanded she make at least two more stops. She had to ask a few follow-up questions about Samantha's strange disappearance and sudden return.

"I need to know your truth," Alina said. "What do you think happened?"

Vanek hesitated. "Before shelving this case, I had the chance to speak with Victor. He answered my questions, but I believe he answered them dishonestly. He's withholding information. Also, I don't like the smell of Samantha's sudden appearance."

"It's fishy, huh?" Alina asked.

"Extremely fishy. Why didn't we find her last night? How did she get off the riverboat and return home? Why would her parents ask Ferneau to drop the case? Why would Ferneau listen? There's a lot of unanswered questions. I'm not sure what happened, but whatever it was, it's not what we're being told."

"Do you think Samantha is in danger?"

Vanek scratched behind his ear. "You said someone hired August Watson to investigate this case? He's the one in charge?"

Alina inhaled, steeling herself for the lie. "He assigned me to speak to you as a liaison between our agency and law enforcement, similar to how he stopped the Vampire of Sacramento by working with Detective Ted Wilson."

Vanek eyed Alina, his eyes slashing and piercing through her fabrication. "You can assure me I'm not sending a teenage girl to investigate this problem?"

"Yes," Alina said.

"If I called Mr. Watson's office, he would corroborate your story?"

Alina nodded. "Yes." She hoped beyond hope the overworked detective wouldn't call that bluff.

"If there's any scent of illegal activity, you will notify me immediately."

"I'll keep you posted," Alina said. Her heart beat so hard and fast, she barely heard herself speak.

"I'm curious," Vanek said. "With Samantha at home and her parents requesting to have us drop the case, who hired you to find her?"

No one.

Alina stood. "Thanks for the fries, Detective. I'll be in touch later this afternoon."

A Detective and a Murderer.
Tuesday, July 25th.
1251hrs.

I INSTRUCTED RITA TO drive past the Butcher's Shoppe (the sandwich shop where Wilson waited) and drop me off a few blocks away. I preferred to play this rendezvous safely, not caring to waltz into a sting operation and have a dozen officers surrounding me with their guns drawn.

It's not that I didn't trust Wilson. I believed he wanted to hear the story from me before pursuing any criminal charges. However, playing the scenario safe and acting cautious mattered more than trust.

"Friday night," Rita said. "Don't forget."

"I'm positive you won't let me," I said.

"I'll text you my address."

"You—" I bit my lip, cutting myself off. I had meant to ask her how she would text me without knowing my cell phone number, but figured she pilfered it from the apartment lease forms. "You do that."

Rita lurched across the center console, leading with her pursed lips. They pressed against my forehead with wet aggression. "I can't wait for Friday to come." She pulled away and winked. "Take that as you will, but I meant it one way."

"Alright." I reached for the door handle and pulled it open, but the door didn't budge.

I frantically searched for the power lock, unable to find it. For a wild, insane second, I thought Rita might have kidnapped me. Then I located the button, pressed it, and the door unlocked. I opened it and spilled out of her SUV. Without glancing back at her, I strolled down the sidewalk to the Butcher's Shoppe.

Everything appeared ordinary. No officers obviously disguised as pedestrians busied the block. No undercover cars parked along the curbs. Everything seemed normal. Halfway satisfied that Wilson's private meeting was legit, I stepped into the sandwich shop.

The big detective sat in the back corner. He wore plain clothes—jeans and a white T-shirt. We made eye contact. He glanced at his watch and brushed a hand across his brow in relief.

I sat across from him.

"Didn't think you would show," he said. "You cut it close."

"I didn't have a ride."

"Left it at the Spirit?" Wilson asked, leaning back in his chair and crossing his arms over his broad chest.

"At the Spirit?" I asked, more to myself than to him. I half-hoped a memory from last night would tumble free of the jam.

"Spirit of Sacramento, off of Garden Highway."

I had heard of the abandoned ship. John Wayne had used it in one of his movies. It was sold after that, renamed to the Spirit of Sacramento, and used to host river cruises for tourists. A fire nearly destroyed the ship, and it never returned to its former glory. The owner docked the vessel on the ground beside the Sacramento River, where it remained, though abandoned.

"I left my ride at the Spirit?" I asked, scratching my neck.

"Did you?" Wilson eyed me with suspicion.

"Why am I here? What's this about?"

"You tell me."

"You'll believe my story?"

Wilson shrugged his broad shoulders. "It beats believing what's currently on the table."

"Which is?"

"Tell me your story first, then I'll decide how to proceed with you."

I told him everything I knew, which was, admittedly, quite little—the meeting with Quinn in the parking garage before waking up in a decrepit bathroom that slowly turned into my apartment.

"That's everything," I said. "I have no recollection of anything else that happened last night. You're going to have to enlighten me."

Wilson sucked on his teeth. He rapped his knuckles against the table. Whatever thoughts ran through his mind, he warred with them. "Sacramento Police Department has an APB for your arrest. You're the primary suspect in a multiple homicide from last night."

Dread chilled down my spine. I thought of Aaron Brooks lying dead on the hot summer asphalt, of the gun smoking in my hand. My stomach roiled, sick with the idea of Quinn murdering and framing me for committing those homicides. More though, I was terrified of the alternative. That Quinn had poisoned my mind, had controlled my actions.

Gerry had fought giant chickens that were only children. What if I had retaliated against—

A group of zombies abducted my friend.

—a group of zombies? What if I had murdered innocent people, believing they were undead monsters?

I stared directly at Wilson. "Why am I the primary suspect? I have to know. If I killed them, Ted, arrest me now. Quinn won't stop using me. If I'm in jail, though, I can't hurt anyone else. What happened last night?"

Wilson licked his lips. "You really have no memory after the parking garage?"

I shook my head. "Zero."

Wilson nodded. "Alright then. Earlier this morning, an anonymous call came into the department, reporting the discovery of three dead bodies and a fourth person in critical condition."

My heart rate sped up to an impossible speed. I didn't interrupt Ted, though.

"We responded, and we confirmed what the tip reported. Three dead, one in critical condition. He's currently at UC Davis in a medically induced coma. While investigating the scene, we found a white van about a hundred yards away from the Spirit of Sacramento. That's where we found the bodies. Inside the boat. The van had a dash-cam attached to it." Wilson sniffled and ran an arm across his nose. "August, it showed you stepping out of the van and walking directly to the Spirit."

"It didn't show me attack anyone, though? It didn't show me returning to the van covered in blood?"

"No." Wilson cleared his throat. "The victims, all three of them, died of blunt-force trauma." The detective's gaze dropped. My hands rested on the tabletop. "Your knuckles," he said.

"I tried to punch through the locked bathroom door. I didn't beat anyone to death with them."

"You can say that with certainty?"

I chewed on my cheeks. I could only say with certainty that I had tried to pummel my way free of the bathroom prison.

"Who were the victims?"

Wilson sighed and shook his head. "I know you, August. I know you don't have it in you to kill someone."

The proceeding silence screamed at us as the impact of his statement settled. I spoke into existence about what I knew we both thought. "I have killed before."

"Not like this."

"Who were they?" I asked again. "Do I know them?"

"Yes."

I wanted to explode to my feet and throw my chair across the sandwich shop. Instead, I remained seated. My entire body vibrated, though. My anger and pain and fear couldn't remain contained forever. They needed an escape.

"Who?" I asked, the question low and cold.

Wilson blew air through his lips. "Eddie Denier. Greta Tonyan. Christopher Steele."

I slumped in my seat as a weight lifted off my chest. He hadn't named my family. He hadn't named Maya, Alina, or Fred. The relief only lasted for a few seconds as the victims' names fell into place.

Eddie Denier was the Voodoo Killer from one of my first cases. Greta Tonyan was married to Gilbert Tonyan, whose death the Voodoo Killer had used to enact a premeditated murder. Christopher Steele was having an affair with Gilbert. Greta and Christopher had recently gone missing, and we had assumed Quinn was involved with their disappearances.

I swallowed. "Who survived?"

It was an answer I needed to hear, though I thought of his name as Wilson uttered it.

"Randall Fincher."

Another person related to the Voodoo Killer.

"They're all connected to my previous case," I said, though Wilson already knew that.

He had responded to the death of Muriel Fincher, Randall's mom. We had also discussed the sudden disappearances. More people connected to my past cases had vanished along with those discovered last night, including Glacia. Nearly everyone directly related to my prior investigation had gone missing.

"We know," Wilson said.

We know, not *I* know. The meaning reverberated through my core. Sacramento Police Department had connected the victims to me; they saw me on camera walking toward the scene of the crime near the exact hour the murders probably occurred.

I popped my neck and allowed my thoughts to spiral. They funneled directly to Quinn's story from earlier. *I have a friend who went missing. A group of zombies abducted my friend. He was moving to his new home when he stopped his vehicle to investigate something strange. I saw the dash-cam video.*

"Every word was a puzzle piece," I said, verbalizing my thoughts.

"What?"

"Quinn called me earlier, right before you did, when I was locked in the bathroom."

"Locked in the unlocked bathroom?"

I nodded, brushing aside his slight. "He inquired about my services, asked me to solve a case for him. His friend went missing, abducted by a zombie."

"I'm not following."

I raised my index finger and shushed the detective. "It's a clue."

"Catch me up, please. I'm in the dark, and I'm the only person who you don't want in the dark right now, as I'm the only one who can help you."

"Zombies, as we know them, are a new-ish invention by Hollywood. The original zombie sprouted from the voodoo religion." I looked at Wilson. "You caught up?"

"No."

"Zombies took Quinn's friend, right?"

"Sure."

"It was a clue alluding to Eddie, the Voodoo Killer. Not only that, Quinn mentioned that three zombies attacked his friend. We have three victims of the Voodoo Killer, leaving Eddie as the friend who needed saving." I planted my elbows on the table and leaned forward, feeling the familiar sense of excitement as I pieced the puzzle of a case together. "Quinn said his friend was moving. Eddie, his friend in the story, was being transported from prison, right? That's when he escaped. Quinn said he watched the dash-cam video of his friend getting ambushed."

"Maybe he meant you," Wilson said.

"Now I'm not following."

"Did he say three zombies?"

I thought back on the conversation with Quinn. "He said something like three, but possibly more."

"So," Wilson said, shrugging, "maybe the friend was you. You drove the van, stepped out of it, as seen by the dash-cam footage, and fought four zombies. Maybe he meant you." Wilson cleared his throat. "Neither theory, whether it's you or Denier who Quinn referred to as his friend, answers a very important question, though."

"Who murdered them?"

"Bingo."

"Before showering and changing, I had blood on my clothes, my hands, my face," I said. "This morning, when I came to my senses in the bathroom, there was blood all over me. Not my blood, either. No fresh injuries on my body."

Wilson rubbed his eyes. "Why did you tell me that?"

"I have nothing to hide. Glacia's life—"

"I don't know Glacia. Never met her. You knew her for what? For a week? You're risking your life, your career, everything for a girl you knew only a week? Forget her, man. Forget Quinn." Wilson's chest deflated as he exhaled. "That's what I should've told you yesterday. Now it's too late. You're in this now. You're a part of his game."

I nodded, biting my cheeks and choosing my next words carefully. "It's not only Glacia. It's all the people Quinn took. He's already responsible for Cambria's death, for the three people killed last night, and Randall being in the hospital. We can't let him kill again. That's your job, right? To take murderers off the street?"

"And what if you murdered those people last night? Even if you don't remember it, what if you committed the actual murders? I'm responsible for holding you accountable, too."

"Then hold me accountable. I'll accept the consequences. But first, if you want Quinn, you need me to play his game. He messed up, and he messed up big time. He wanted me scared of him and of the police. He overlooked you, though. Make him pay for his oversight. Once he's dealt with, you can focus on me."

Wilson rolled his shoulders and sat straighter in the chair. He raised his chin and stared down at me. "If I help you, it's by the book. I'm reporting your involvement to my superiors. If you act contrary to anything I say, the deal crumbles. Once we catch Quinn, we're no longer friends. I'm a detective, and you're a potential murderer."

"I understand," I said.

Wilson exhaled, pitching a childish smile across his face. "What now?"

"Well," I said, glancing over my shoulder. "I'm starving. Also, I need to charge my phone."

The Three Labors.
Tuesday, July 25th.
1329hrs.

Wilson retrieved a phone cable from his vehicle and paid for my lunch, seeing that I didn't have a wallet.

I thanked him and offered to Venmo some money back as soon as my phone had a decent charge. He waved it off, told me I had more pressing matters to worry about. Seeing that I did indeed have a mountain of other worries, I heeded his advice and ate lunch on his dime.

He left shortly thereafter. I guess he didn't much care to linger with a murder suspect for too long.

I found an outlet and plugged in my phone. I chose not to turn the device on until after eating, though. My food arrived quickly, and I scarfed it down. With the meal finished, my stomach satisfied, and my mind firing for the first time all day, I turned on the cell phone.

A million missed calls, voicemails, and text messages from Alina, Maya, and Fred popped up on the screen. I scrolled past their names, searching for the number Quinn had called me from. It appeared as a Blocked Number right before Wilson's call earlier that morning.

I wiped my mouth and considered my next move. As my thoughts churned to create a plan, my phone vibrated in my hand. I glanced at the screen.

Maya.

With a sigh, I answered. "Hey."

"What the actual fu—"

"Before you—"

"Don't you dare *before you this* or *before you that* with me," Maya said, her words hot as fire, her voice popping like trapped steam bursting from wood against a flame. "Fred beat you into the office today. Did you know that?"

"It doesn't count."

"Do you understand the implications of that? It's not that he wins, and we'll never hear the end. It's not that you have to go on a date of his choosing, and it'll be miserable for you, and we'll never hear the end of that. It's the fact that he beat you to work, which is impossible. Which shouldn't ever happen. Which has me worried sick to my stomach about your health, well-being, and life."

"Those are all more or less different words for the same thing."

"If you talk again, August Allan Watson, I will rip your tongue from your mouth. You've done enough damage today, and your dumb voice with your stupid words won't make matters any better." Maya breathed. "What happened?"

"Is that a real question?"

"Is what happened a real question? Yes, of course, it's a real question."

"I'm a little confused because you told me not to talk, then you immediately asked me a question."

"I'm glad you're not dead. I really am. That means I can kill you with my bare hands. I want to watch the life leave your eyes."

I bit my lip, utterly confused. "Maya."

"Don't *Maya* me."

"Are you okay?"

"No. I'm not okay. You had me terrified today. Scared out of my wits. I'm half crazy with worry. Fred beat you into the office, August. Where were you? Why didn't you answer our calls? What happened with Quinn?"

I licked my lips, understanding dawning. They figured out I had met with Quinn last night. Of course they had. After drawing that conclusion and after me not showing at the office that morning, my absence had them panic-stricken.

"I'm sorry," I said. "It's just—"

Another call came through, chirping in my ear.

I pulled my phone from my face and checked the caller ID. Blocked, which either meant Quinn or a representative from the Sacramento Police Department. Wilson had left twenty minutes ago, and he meant to share our meeting and my involvement with their investigation into Quinn with his superiors. I doubted any number, especially a blocked number, apart from Wilson's, would contact me from the police department.

That left Quinn.

"Just what?" Maya asked.

"I have to go."

"August, if you—"

I switched the line. "Hello," I said, holding my breath.

"I need an update," Quinn said.

I cracked the knuckles, collecting my calm before responding. "I found your friend."

Quinn chuckled. "Now you understand the gist of the game."

"Where's Glacia?"

An incoming call chirped in my ear as Maya called me back.

I ignored her.

"You're a relatively educated man, Mr. Watson," Quinn said. "You graduated from a four-year university with a degree in English. With honors, if I'm not mistaken. That's an accomplishment to be proud of."

"What do you want me to do next?" I asked.

"Is it a stretch for me to assume that you've heard of the Twelve Labors of Hercules?"

"I'm familiar with them." I had spent a summer session studying Greek mythology.

However, I was more familiar with the myth in question through the *Hercules* Disney movie our professor showed instead of assigning a final.

"Well, in case you've forgotten the details, allow me a moment to refresh your memory. The goddess Hera despised our hero, Hercules. In an act of abhorrent evil, she drove him mad. He lost his mind, becoming confused and angry. In his enraged state, he murdered his wife and children. After awaking from his temporary insanity, Hercules realized the horror he had committed." Quinn paused for a beat. "Does that sound familiar?"

I swallowed back bile as Quinn's retelling crashed onto me. He had poisoned my mind last night, drove me into a fugue state, and I had possibly murdered three people while temporarily out of my mind.

"To atone for his sin," Quinn said, continuing with his lesson, "Hercules prayed to Apollo through an oracle. The oracle instructed Hercules to serve the king of Mycenae for twelve years, as a punishment for his crime. I wonder what punishment you will receive for your crime? I think twelve years is a pipe dream for you." He cackled. "Anyway, as part of his service to the king, Hercules had to complete twelve impossible labors. Quite a haunting story, no?"

I gritted my teeth. Maya's incoming call beeped in my ear again.

"Mr. Watson, I found twelve labors quite tedious. Instead, to atone for your crime, you will complete three labors. Failure means death, and not for you."

"What's my first labor?" I asked without a second's hesitation.

"Hercules fought the Nemean Lion for his first labor. After defeating it, he wore its impenetrable fur like a hooded cloak. Since you're a monster hunter, though, a lion feels too tame. You must defeat the manticore. You have three hours until the party is eaten alive." Quinn saw himself off the phone.

I stared out the window at the afternoon, at the people walking or driving past the sandwich shop, stopping at the intersection, singing in their cars, talking on their phones, living their lives. I envied them, but I only allowed my coveting to stretch for a few seconds.

Quinn wouldn't have ended the call if he hadn't provided me with enough clues to solve the newest case. I needed to parse through our conversation to find directions to whoever he meant to harm next.

Knowing I couldn't head to the office or my house, I remained in the sandwich shop to piece the puzzle together.

Maya called again, but I silenced my phone and placed it facedown. I didn't have the time or the mental energy for her lectures. I had to focus.

Standing, I padded over to the register and asked the attendant for a pen and blank paper. The employee handed them to me without question, and I returned to my table. I had to make a visual list to help me organize my thoughts.

- Hercules' Twelve Labors.

- I'm Hercules in this scenario.

- The Spirit of Sacramento—an abandoned boat—was where I lost my mind and *murdered (?)* three people. Why there? What did it mean? Did Quinn allude to breaking my spirit?

- Zombies regarding voodoo. Eddie Denier found dead at the scene.

I tapped the pen against the counter, studying my notes. I had to find the pattern between his references earlier to what he referenced now. Grabbing my phone, I Googled the first labor of Hercules to refresh my memory. As I reread the myth, I jotted down anything that seemed relevant.

- Hercules fought the Nemean Lion by luring it into a cave. He defeated it by strangling it, and he used its claws to skin the hide.

- Quinn replaced the lion with a manticore, though he didn't change any of the other details of the myth.

- Quinn said I had three hours until the party was eaten.

I underlined party. It was a strange word to use. Why not say victims, or they, or people, or anything? Why party?

I leaned back in the chair and crossed my arms, staring at my sloppy handwriting scribbled on the notepad.

"Party was eaten," I said, feeling the words on my tongue.

It made no sense. How did I identify victims, determine their location, and save them from whatever torture Quinn had planned if nothing made any sense?

Hercules killed the lion in a cave. Would I find the manticore in a cave?

I wanted to slam my head against the table. Instead, I squeezed my eyes shut and lowered my head.

Quinn would have provided me with all the answers. I needed to find them.

Zombies related to the Voodoo Killer. Quinn gave me a manticore this time. I Googled the legendary creature, pulled up its Wikipedia page, and skimmed through the information, hoping to find something that stood out.

It's name translated to 'man eater.'

"Party," I said, snapping my eyes open and sitting straight.

The answer stood right on the periphery of my mind.

"Party, party, party. Why use that word? Three hours until the party is eaten. Eaten... man eater." I slapped the table, frustrated, drawing a few skeptical stares from the other patrons. I had the answer, I just couldn't quite form it into something definitive. "Cave. Tunnel. Mine."

I bolted to my feet and raked my hand through my hair.

"Donner Pass!"

It made sense. It had to make sense. Party, as in the Donner party.

In the winter of some nineteenth century year, the Donners had migrated to California from a Midwest state. They spent the winter stuck in the Sierra Nevada mountains, and some of the party resorted to cannibalism to survive.

Manticore—man eater.

Party—Donner Party.

The lion's cave, I had little doubt, meant the Donner Historic Tunnel—a train tunnel long ago abandoned. Abandoned like the Spirit of Sacramento.

I had a location. One which would take me approximately ninety minutes to drive to, and I didn't have a car to drive there. When Quinn said three hours, he most likely meant someone would die at 1630hrs. The time on my phone read 1331hrs.

I had two-and-a-half hours to find a car and drive eighty miles into the mountains to save...

Save who?

I shook the thought aside.

It didn't matter who. I could figure that out during the drive. What mattered was me arriving in time to save them.

Where did I come up with a car, though? If I had driven the van to the Spirit of Sacramento last night, did that mean my car remained in the parking garage? It was only a fifteen-minute walk from my location.

Did I risk it?

I didn't have my keys, which meant I had either left them in the van or at the crime scene, or I had left them in my car, the least likely of those scenarios. I had no other avenues to explore.

I walked toward Butcher Shoppe's exit, knowing I had to do something. Retrieving my car from the garage was the only proper solution available.

Spinning in Circles. Tuesday, July 25th. 1331hrs.

ALINA DIDN'T RETURN TO the Blue Moon office after surprising Detective Vanek. She didn't dare head to Maya's house, either. Instead, she used her spare key to unlock August's home and hide in the spare bedroom he had allotted to her.

It smelled like Gerry, like stale cigarette smoke and foul body odor.

Gerry, on the advice of a judge, temporarily lived with August. August had yet to make a home of the house, and it severely lacked the basics, such as a bed in the master bedroom, let alone a bed in a guest room. So Gerry slept on the floor of Alina's furniture-less room.

Alina hadn't noticed Gerry in the kitchen or living room as she walked through the house, and he wasn't in the bedroom. She hadn't noticed Bagley, August's new puppy, either. Alina decided Gerry had taken the dog for a walk, and she pushed the two of them from her mind.

More pressing concerns needled her, such as her dad's whereabouts.

Stephen Moore, Alina's father, bunked in a hotel room during his temporary stay in California. Alina didn't know the hotel he stayed at, but information like that was easy to come by if you knew where and how to look. She could have called and asked him, but she preferred to spring an unannounced visit on her father.

Maya might know where he stayed, but Alina's aunt would have far too many questions—questions Alina didn't have any intention of answering, at least not truthfully. Why lie when you could avoid it?

Instead of seeking help, Alina hacked into Stephen's bank account. The night before, while on the riverboat, he had used a Bank of America credit card. Alina downloaded the banking app on her phone and went to work at guessing his username and password.

Stephen always used the same login for his Facebook account as he did for everything else in his life—his Netflix, his email, his OnlyFans, his FanDuel. The login was his Yahoo email address. The passwords were some variation of BOOBIES, usually B00B!e5., with the period at the end to satisfy the eight-character requirement most websites suggested.

Alina gained access to his bank account on her second attempt at the password.

The first thing she noticed was that Stephen had no money in the account. Zero dollars. Not a single penny. It didn't surprise her much. Stephen had always preached about the dangers of keeping money in a bank. He believed in cold, hard cash. Him having a credit card linked to a bank account had shocked Alina, but she chalked that up to him being employed, buying a car, and renting a house. Credit history mattered for those kinds of things.

She navigated to his transaction history, searching for evidence of the hotel where he stayed.

Stephen hadn't made a single payment to any hotel.

Duh, Alina thought, feeling dumb for having wasted the time.

The hotel would only charge him after his stay. Still, transactions should exist that provided proof of food purchases in or around the hotel.

Alina scrolled through his transaction history, pausing with confusion after the screen stopped moving. She refreshed the page and scrolled through the list again and again. The screen didn't move. Her eyes drifted to the purchase dates, and she realized the three showing transactions only went back two weeks.

Three credit purchases in two weeks.

One for the riverboat dinner. One for plane tickets to fly into Sacramento. One for an Uber in Indiana on the day of his flight.

Baffled, Alina navigated across his various accounts. She looked at his checking and saving accounts, his credit card history, and debit card transactions. No proof existed of him paying any rent, as he claimed, of him paying for gas or food, of him receiving an income from a stable job, or of him living beyond the three purchases bringing him to Sacramento.

Alina leaned her head against the wall and stared at the ceiling. She hummed a nameless tune beneath her breath and thought. After a few minutes without drawing any conclusions, she surrendered and dialed Maya's number.

"Well, well, well," Maya answered, sounding high strung. "Look who's deciding to show her face, or rather, her voice. Where have you been? I'm over here, absolutely sick with worry about August and about you. I hate feeling worried. It's my least favorite emotion. My least favorite. I prefer hate, love, annoyance, or frustration because with every other emotion, I can do something about it. That's not a luxury with worry. I just sit around and feel beyond helpless, lost in my dark imagination. You know my imagination. It's a terrible place at the best of times."

Alina rolled her eyes. "Where's my dad staying?"

"Did you not listen to a word I said? Why would you even care about him?"

Could Alina admit the truth, that she had sidestepped searching for August to pursue the mystery of Samantha Graves' disappearance? That confession felt wrong to think about, and it would feel worse to say aloud. Maya would let her know how wrong it was, too.

I should just pay a surprise visit to Samantha's house, Alina thought, not for the first time since learning she had returned to her home that morning. *Show up and ask her what happened.*

Alina dismissed the idea each time it surfaced in her mind. If she could satiate her curiosity without having to speak to Samantha, she preferred that method—work from the shadows and keep her investigation off the record. Once she had her answers, she would spill all her energy to finding August.

"I wanted to surprise him with lunch," Alina said, scrambling for a lie. "Thank him for last night, you know?"

Maya clicked her tongue. "You're lying to me."

"What?"

"Usually, when you speak, it's like anything you utter is absolute gold, and anyone who's listening should cherish every word. When you lie, though, you hesitate before responding. Only for a second, but you hesitate. A brief, half-second pause. Then you speak slower than usual, as if trying on a new outfit and evaluating how it looks in the mirror. It's minor, and I'm sure you fool most everyone you lie to, because you're good at it. But you don't fool me." Maya inhaled. "I'm smarter, wiser, more experienced than you. You can't ever fool me."

"Where is he?"

"Tell me why you want to know."

"I need to speak to him."

"About?"

Alina huffed, frustrated by her aunt's gatekeeping.

"What have you learned about August's disappearance?" Maya asked.

"Nothing."

"Nothing?"

"I've been looking into Samantha Graves' disappearance. My dad knows something about it, and I want to ask him face-to-face. Now, where is he staying?"

"You won't let this go, will you?"

"Not until I have an answer," Alina said.

"Why? August is missing, in case you missed that memo."

"No matter how much effort we put into finding August, we won't find him." Alina frowned. "We don't know who Quinn really is. We couldn't locate where he brought the other missing people, and that was with August's help. I hate to say it—it physically hurts to admit it—but we won't find August. I can do something about Samantha, though. I can help her."

"I spoke to August," Maya said.

The confession hit Alina in the chest and stole her breath. "What?" she asked, gasping.

"I spoke to him on the phone, but he hung up on me."

"Was he okay?"

"He sounded like he wasn't wearing any clothes and running around in public."

"Stressed?"

"More than stressed. Lost, like he didn't know what to do next. I could hear the uncertainty in his tone."

"He didn't tell you where he was?"

"No," Maya said. "I'll find him, though. Don't tell me some lunatic like Quinn can make two dozen people vanish without a trace. I'll find August, and I'll help save him, along with Vincent, Glacia, and all the rest."

"I know you will. That's why I'm doing this. Because I can help elsewhere. Now, where's my dad?"

"Motel 6, downtown Sacramento," Maya said. She hung up the phone, leaving Alina alone in the silence of the empty bedroom.

The ceiling fan spun in a blurred movement, barely perceptible. Alina laid on the floor and watched it whirl.

What was her dad thinking, starting the custody battle with her mother? Wouldn't the court ask for his financial records? Wouldn't he have to prove he had an income, that he paid rent on a house? Unless he had another bank than the one Alina hacked into (which she doubted), he had lied about everything.

You're going up on that stage... Alina, do what I say... I brought you all the way out here, tipped the magician to select you. Now go up there.

Alina had refused, though. Samantha had volunteered instead, and she vanished.

Why had Stephen pushed Alina so hard? Because of a measly tip he offered? Maybe. That didn't sit outside of her father's character. But Alina doubted that being the reason. He had appeared frustrated with her when she refused to volunteer, but beyond that, he had reeked of fear. The way his eyes bulged, the way he fidgeted, the way he spoke in a whispered voice.

Alina kicked to her feet from her prone position, collected her belongings from the bedroom, and called an Uber to take her to downtown Sacramento.

Fatherly Advice. Tuesday, July 25th. 1413hrs.

THE UBER DROPPED ALINA off at the Motel 6—a rundown establishment where horny high schoolers, horny older men, and druggies rented their rooms by the hour.

Alina marched into the front lobby. The reception counter had a billboard attached to the siding, advertising the Motel 6 brand. 'We'll leave the light on for you,' it read, the white block letter punched against an exotic landscape. The wall behind the counter was a burnt orange. An old flat-screen television hung too high, its power chord snaking down the orange paint to an outlet. On the screen played a muted rerun of an old sitcom not even Alina recognized.

A middle-aged woman with a graying bob haircut and a narrow face stood behind the front desk. She wore an Amish-gray dress and glared over the monitor as Alina approached. "How can I help you?" the woman asked, her tone bordering on annoyed, as if she wanted nothing less to do than her job.

Alina practiced her best smile. "I'm here to meet my dad. Well, not meet him. I've met him before. I'm here to meet with him. He's divorcing my mom, and they're in a custody battle, and—"

The woman raised a wrinkled, arthritic hand and pursed her mouth. "How can I help you?"

"He told me his room number over the phone, but I didn't really listen. I was flipping through a magazine, reading an article about…" Alina leaned over the counter and whispered, "bedroom activities. See, I have this boyfriend, and I think he's the one. Not to marry or anything, but to… well, give my flower to." The words made her cringe, but she had a role to play. "Anyway, the magazine had an article, and I—"

"I don't care," the woman interrupted.

"Well, I don't remember what room he said." Alina curled her lips inward and smirked, an expression that placed her in the light of a careless teenager. Hopefully, the woman's uncaring demeanor prevented her from thinking too hard, because Alina's story would unravel with a single question. Why not call him back?

"I can't share a customer's room without their permission," the woman said.

"He's my dad."

"I'm sorry. Why don't you call him and ask?"

Alina exhaled, stealing a second to come up with another lie. "Sure," Alina said, "I'll call my dad." She winked. "How do you know I'm not calling my boyfriend, though, having him pretend he's my father to trick you into providing me with the information I need? Great operation you have here. Can we skirt all the nonsense? I'm Stephen Moore's daughter, and I brought him his lunch." Alina mentally scolded herself for the added detail.

First rule of lying, don't add unnecessary information.

The woman rose on tiptoe and glanced over the counter at Alina's empty hands. She frowned.

"DoorDash," Alina said, answering the question before the woman could ask it. "It'll arrive in twenty minutes. I showed up a little early."

"Fine." The woman grunted, shook her head, and turned to the computer. Her fingers poked at the keyboard at a snail's pace. At one point, for about an eternity, her index finger searched the buttons for the right letter.

Alina picked at her nail and silently hummed as she waited.

"Room 223."

"Thanks." Alina snagged an orange-wrapped hard candy from a ceramic bowl on the front counter and turned her back to the lady.

The hotel only had two levels. To get up to the second floor, Alina had to walk outside the lobby and climb an outdoor set of cement stairs covered with bird droppings. An outdoor balcony wrapped around the face of the building. Alina followed it to her father's door.

She rolled her shoulders, breathed deeply, and knocked.

A few heartbeats later, the door unlatched, clicked, and opened.

Stephen stood shirtless inside the dark hotel room. Surprise sketched across his face. "Mylene." He had always called his daughter by her middle name. Apparently, Wanda preferred Alina and Stephen preferred Mylene. They had settled to give their daughter both names.

Alina pushed past her father and entered his room without an invitation. She strode to the back window and ripped open the curtains. Sunlight flooded inward, hot and bright. The room provided a view of the leaf-swamped swimming pool and the parking lot to the apartment complex beyond.

"What are you doing here?" Stephen asked, shutting the front door.

Alina turned and scoured the room. An unmade bed. A crumpled pack of cigarettes tossed on a desk, along with a couple of joints. Clothes lay in a pile on a chair sitting before the window, and on the table beside it was an empty bottle of Jack Daniels. Alina removed her phone and photographed the empty Jack Daniels bottle and the smoked joints.

She turned to her father with a winning smile. "Sober, huh? I'm sure the judge will enjoy this picture."

"It's not mine."

"And every prison is full of innocent men."

Stephen sighed and sat on the edge of the bed. "I had a friend over last night. That's his stuff."

"Believable." Alina exhaled the pent-up tension she harbored about the custody battle. A dark, heavy shadow lifted from her shoulders. With the pictures as evidence, at least she wouldn't have to move to Indiana with her father. "Who's Samantha Graves to you?"

Stephen raised his chin and scratched the scruff on his neck. "Who?"

"The girl from last night. The one who went missing at the magic show. Who is she to you?"

"She's nobody to me."

"You don't know her?"

"No."

"Never seen her before?"

"Never."

"You're sure?"

"Hold on, Mylene." Stephen's flabby stomach hung over his waistband. Scars and faded tattoos covered his torso. "What are you talking about? What's going on?"

"Why did you want me to go on stage?"

Stephen rubbed his eyes and shook his head. "I don't understand what you're asking."

"You insisted I volunteer for Iniduoh. Why?"

"Because, before the show, I tipped him a hundred dollars to pick you from the crowd."

Alina whistled, amazed. Stephen Moore didn't part with a hundred dollars lightly. Tipping a magician was more than light, it was downright foolishness. So... "Why?"

"I thought you would like it," Stephen said.

"Why would I like that?"

"Stop asking why!" He cursed beneath his breath. "I wanted to do something nice for you. Whenever we attended those shows before, you always wanted to volunteer. Don't you remember? As a little girl, you always jumped up and down in your seat, begging to join the magician on stage when he asked for a volunteer. I wanted to give you that."

Alina wanted to believe him. She almost convinced herself to believe him. Instead, she shook her head, shaking away his false charm. "Had I volunteered, I would've vanished like Samantha, right? That was your plan."

"What?"

"That was the trick. Iniduoh made his subject disappear, but for real. You knew that, didn't you?"

"How on Earth would I know that?"

"Because you know Victor Pemberton."

"Who?" Stephen asked. "Mylene, what are you talking about?"

"I'm not sure how well you two know each other. I'm not sure I want to know, either. But I know you two are acquainted, and you schemed to make me disappear."

"You're not making sense."

"Did you plan for him to kidnap me, to take me back to Indiana?"

Stephen coughed out a chuckle. "That makes no sense. Why would that girl disappear if I planned to take you to Indiana?"

"She didn't disappear. She's back at home. If it were me, though, I'd be well on my way to Indiana, wouldn't I?"

"Mylene, that's nonsense. What are you getting at?"

"How did he do it?"

"Do what?"

"Make her disappear? How did he do it?"

Stephen stared at the dark television screen. "You would have to ask him."

"Okay," Alina said, shrugging. "I will."

"What?"

"I want to ask him."

"Mylene, this is crazy. What are you after?"

"Truth." Alina's fingers danced against her thigh. She wanted to throw all of her father's lies into his face, show him the empty transactions on his banking statement, convince him to drop the custody battle and return to Indiana, but she resisted. It wouldn't help anything. It would only make him more angry and possibly defensive.

"Do you know Victor Pemberton?" she asked.

Stephen glanced at the front door. "No."

"You're a liar. Why can't you ever tell me the truth? Why do you always have to dodge and run and avoid what actually matters?"

"And what matters?" he asked.

"Honesty. Responsibility."

"I don't know him." Stephen grabbed a shirt resting on the comforter beside where he sat and pulled it over his head. "I met him before the riverboat dinner."

"Why?"

Stephen's gaze never met Alina's eyes. "To tip him."

Alina still didn't believe he told the entire story. "Do you know where he's at now?"

"How would I know?" Stephen stood and walked to his daughter. He placed his rough hands on her bony shoulders. "You said the girl came home. That's great. So, what are you looking for?"

Alina brushed her father's hands off of her and walked past him. After a few steps, she turned and stared at the back of his head. "Why did you want me on the stage? Why did you want me to disappear? Why did the magician take Samantha?"

"I don't know why he took Samantha, but I didn't want you to disappear. I wanted you to have fun. I wanted to give you something I could never give you before. That's it, Mylene. I just want my daughter to be happy."

Alina shook her head and chuckled. "You know what happens when you consistently disappoint and lie to someone throughout their entire life? They learn to expect everything you say or do to be a lie. So, when you tell me you had nothing to do with what happened last night, I naturally think you had everything to do with what happened last night." Alina pivoted and marched toward the door.

"A little fatherly advice," Stephen said, his voice booming across the room.

Alina paused with her hand on the doorknob, slightly trembling. "Sure, why not? What can a deadbeat father who's good for absolutely nothing other than causing harm and destruction have to say to his daughter? I'm so curious to learn from you, Dad."

"Be careful, Mylene. Curiosity killed the cat."

Alina's stomach plunged to the floor. Her body compressed, and the back of her teeth ached. She opened the door, quickly closed it behind her, and sprinted across the second-story balcony to the stairwell.

The Deal.
Tuesday, July 25th.
1426hrs.

ALINA REACHED THE GROUND level and glanced over her shoulder, up at the balcony, toward her father's room. She half-expected to see him lording over her, but she only saw the rusted metal railing.

A bench rested outside the lobby door beside an Out-of-Order vending machine. Alina sat and watched the street traffic with a listless gaze.

If her father changed his mind and followed her outside, he would be hesitant to harm her. Alina sat in a public location, one visible to the world and safe from him. The thought of having to find refuge from her father gutted her. A child shouldn't have to find safety from their parents.

Alina wiped stray tears from her eyes and thought about Stephen's parting advice. His threat.

Curiosity killed the cat.

Though he had many shortcomings, Stephen had never laid a hand on Alina or Alina's mother. He had abused them in other, more subtle, possibly more dangerous, ways. Despite his history of nonviolence, though, Alina knew that if it protected his best interests, if push came to shove, her father would throw a punch, or worse.

Alina no longer believed the myth that her father had come back to Sacramento to win a custody battle, to bring her back with him to Indiana.

Why had he come back, then? What did he need her for? Why had he insisted she volunteer for the magician's trick? Where had Samantha disappeared to? How had she returned home?

Alina exhaled, momentarily wishing she had a vice—smoking, drinking, anything to help her relax and forget about life for a while. She settled by reaching into her pocket, removing earbuds from their case, and shoving them in her ears. She navigated to a curated playlist and played the music far too loud. The volume helped drown her thoughts and quiet her mind, though.

After three songs blared to completion and she felt a semblance of calm, Alina turned the music down and scrolled through her contacts.

"Vanek speaking," the detective answered on the first ring.

"It's Alina."

"How did you get this number?" he asked. "This is my personal number."

"It's not that hard to uncover unlisted numbers."

"You're too resourceful for your own good."

Alina smirked. "I need some information from you."

Vanek clicked his tongue. "That will be tricky, considering I'm off the case you're looking into."

"Hence the reason I didn't call your business line."

"I don't have any information to give."

"Maybe you don't. I'm going to ask, anyway."

"I'm sure you will."

"Where can I find Victor Pemberton?"

Vanek sighed.

"You guys collected contact information from him, right?" Alina asked. "You know where he's staying?"

Vanek snorted a sharp laugh. "Not happening."

"What's not happening?"

"I'm not giving a sixteen-year-old girl information on how to contact a middle-aged man, so she can approach him and question him. I'm not that irresponsible."

Alina bit her thumbnail. "It's for August, remember?"

"Alina, I'm often dumb, but I'm not stupid. If August wants the information, he can call me."

"Come with me to interview Pemberton," Alina said.

"Sorry, kid. I'm off the case, remember? Samantha found her way home. Ferneau closed the case. I can't involve myself any more. I have no ethical or legal reason to question Victor Pemberton."

"Fine." Alina snapped the word off like breaking a branch in half.

"My hands are tied. You know that."

"I'll keep you posted when I learn something new. With or without your help, my next stop is speaking with the magician."

"Alina," Vanek said, his voice somber. "Please, be safe about this."

"Never learned the definition of the word."

She disconnected the line, immediately navigating to the phone's internet browser and searching Iniduoh into the search engine.

From the previous night's research, Alina had stumbled upon the magician's poorly constructed website. It gave her a headache to look at, but despite its lackluster design, it had a contact page with a contact number.

Alina pieced together a quick backstory for herself and called the magician.

In middle school, she had often taken part in the school plays. She had a natural stage presence, an ability to memorize her lines or improve them through improvisation, and she could sing despite her lack of formal training. Performing came second nature to her.

Victor Pemberton answered immediately. "Iniduoh speaking." He sounded like he just woke up—his voice gruff and ragged, his tone terse.

"Hi," Alina said, impersonating an adult's voice (a mother's voice, if that made sense) as best as she could—tired with a feigned cheeriness. "My name is Colleen." She drew the name at random, not wanting to tip off Victor to his true caller or the intention behind the call.

"Hi Colleen."

"My son turns eight in a week. He stumbled upon your YouTube videos a few months ago. He's obsessed." Not a shot in the dark. Alina had found some low-quality, low-viewed videos of the magician performing his simplistic tricks uploaded onto YouTube. "I would like to book your performance, if possible."

Victor cleared his throat. "Well, Colleen, I'm currently out of the state."

"You're in California, right?"

"I am."

"That's why I called rather than emailed. I needed to speak to you before you left back for Indiana. I know you're in Sacramento. I saw an advertisement for the riverboat show last night. We couldn't make it, unfortunately."

"That's too bad."

"Anyway, I was hoping while you were still in town, you could perform at my son's party on Saturday."

"My flight is on Thursday."

Alina buzzed the air off her lips. "If you could push your flight back, I'll pay any extra costs the airline demands, and I'll cover any inconvenience fees you would charge. Please. This means the world to my son."

Alina held her breath as Victor remained quiet on the other end of the line. She needed two things to happen for her plan to have a shot at succeeding. First, the magician needed to accept the fake gig. Second, she had to convince him to meet with her in person to discuss the details of the fabricated magic show. Was the latter part unusual when booking magic acts? Probably. Alina didn't care, though. She had to meet with Iniduoh.

"Deal," Victor said. "But it will cost more than my usual rates, plus the rebooking fees for the flight, and, as you so kindly mentioned, an inconvenience charge."

"Name the price. Anything."

"Before I agree to the performance, you'll have to sign a contract to guarantee the costs, and I'm going to require that you provide a hefty deposit."

Alina's heart nearly raced up her throat and out of her mouth with excitement. She hadn't needed to do any convincing to meet up with him. He had proposed the idea himself.

"Yeah," she said. "Of course. Could you meet this afternoon?"

"What time?"

"I get off work in the," Alina glanced at the time on her phone, "next thirty minutes. Jared—that's my son—has soccer practice until five this afternoon." Was it even soccer season? "I'm mostly running errands and killing time until I need to pick him up. I can meet you anywhere."

Again, Victor stole a few seconds before responding. "You mind meeting at my hotel?"

Alina's throat tightened to the size of a straw. She could barely breathe.

"I know it's atypical," Victor said, hurrying now as he spoke, "but we can meet at the bar—"

"That's perfect," Alina said, biting her lip and hoping she hadn't sounded too eager. "I could use a drink, anyway. Is the bar open this early?"

"I don't see why it wouldn't be." He chuckled. "I'm at the Motel 6 in downtown Sacramento."

Alina glanced over her shoulder at the motel's entrance, bearing the name and logo. Motel 6. Victor Pemberton stayed in the same spot as her father. Another coincidence? Alina strongly doubted that.

"I'll be there within the hour," Alina said.

"I'll be at the bar. I'm wearing a blue Colts hat."

"See you there." Alina hung up and stared across the street as she caught her breath. Her nerves fired like a blowtorch.

Once she had herself settled, she made one last call.

"Blue Moon Investigative Agency, this is Fred. How may I help you?"

"It's Alina." She stood from the bench and faced the motel entrance. The glass door now appeared like the dark maw of a hungry monster.

"Where are you?" Fred asked, paranoia tinging his voice. "Why aren't you back at the office? You have me worried sick."

"I need your help. And before you respond, know that I'll buy you a week's worth of lunch if you help me."

Fred adopted Victor's annoying tic, and he bided his time to respond, probably weighing the worth of the bribe. "Tell me the task and I'll tell you the price of my participation."

Alina groaned and rolled her eyes. "You need to meet me at the Motel 6 in downtown Sacramento ten minutes ago."

"Why?"

"Because I need your help."

"Help with what?"

"I've scheduled a meeting with Victor Pemberton."

"Who?" Through the receiver, Fred chewed on something crunchy—chips, perhaps, or carrots.

"Stop chewing so loudly. You eat like a dinosaur."

"You don't know how dinosaurs ate. You weren't around when they were." Fred made a point of chewing extra loud into the phone.

"Victor Pemberton is the magician from last night," Alina said, closing her eyes and visualizing her happy place—an empty cinema playing her favorite horror movie. "He's the person responsible for Samantha Graves' disappearance."

"Maya said to forget about that and focus on finding August. The police will take care of Samantha."

Alina ruffled her hair. "Fred, Maya isn't your boss."

"Neither are you."

"Technically, I am."

"How so?"

"Well, with August gone, I'm the only other employee who makes money through the agency, meaning I have rank and superiority over you, thus I'm your boss."

"Interesting. Can you give me a raise?"

"You don't deserve one."

"What do you mean, I don't deserve one?"

"You've done nothing to warrant a raise."

"Please. I went into the field and took down a golem. That deserves a raise. You're asking me to leave the comfort of my desk again. I didn't sign up for field work without pay. I signed up for desk work without pay. I want a raise, fake boss. I want it now."

"Fred, here's the deal," Alina said, tired of Fred's stalling. "I'm meeting with Victor, a possibly dangerous middle-aged man who may have wanted to kidnap me last night. You can accompany and protect me from any potential harm, or you can allow me to meet him alone. It's your call, big boy."

"He's a magician, Alina. What if he uses his magic against us?"

"He can't use magic because it's not real."

Fred sighed. "We're just questioning him, right?"

"Possibly torturing him for information if he doesn't answer our questions."

"What? Alina, no. No torturing. I don't have the stomach for it."

"I'm kidding."

"A raise and two weeks' worth of lunch."

"Two weeks' worth of lunch."

"Deal," Fred said.

"I'm confronting him in ten minutes, with or without you."

No Pain No Gain.
Tuesday, July 25th.
1438hrs.

ALINA ENTERED THE MOTEL 6 once again. She looked away from the front desk, taking in the rest of the small lobby. A single chair stood against the wall opposite the front door beside a floor cabinet with a laminate countertop. An unframed canvas image hung above the station, showing a coffee mug resting in a pool of coffee beans. The picture read, 'Your Morning Charge Up for No Charge.' Except the counter didn't have a coffee maker to make coffee.

Also missing from the small, dingy lobby was the bar where Alina had agreed to meet Victor Pemberton. A cold sweat formed on her brow.

Why had Victor agreed to drinks at the motel, to wait at the bar wearing his blue Colts hat, if a bar didn't actually exist?

"Excuse me, Miss," said a deep voice from behind the front counter. "Can I help you find something?" A tall, gangly young man with sky-blue eyes had replaced the middle-aged, contemptuous woman. He had acne on his pale face, and his hairline receded severely. Though he wore the hotel's uniform, the shirt draped off his shoulders, fitting him like a curtain and squaring him off.

Alina bee-lined to the counter and plucked another hard candy from the bowl—some unknown brand with butterscotch flavoring.

The young man interlaced his long, spider-like fingers together and rested his hands on the countertop. He said nothing as he waited for Alina to voice her concern.

She unwrapped the candy, popped it into her mouth, and crumpled the wrapper, purposefully wasting time to allow Fred a chance to catch up to her. "Do you have a garbage can?" She slid the balled wrapper across the counter to the young man.

"I do." His hand opened. With long and skinny fingers, he swiped the wrapper and dropped it behind the counter, maybe to the floor, maybe into a trash bin. "Is there anything else I could do for you?"

"I'm meeting Victor Pemberton at the bar." Alina flashed her brightest smile. "Don't worry, I'm not drinking. I'm only sixteen."

The young man nodded.

"He's my uncle, and he's in town for a work appointment. My mom sent me to pick him up. Victor asked me to meet him at the bar." Alina glanced over her shoulder. "Except I don't see a bar in here."

"Ah," the young man said, his baritone voice similar to a frog's croak and completely out of place, considering his physique. "If you exit the front door and follow the sidewalk past the stairwell that way," he pointed to the left, "it will lead you to our dining area, which has a small bar in it. He probably meant to meet him in there."

"Thank you." Alina smirked, spun on her heel, and headed to the exit. She paused as she reached the door and glanced back at the pimply faced man. "I'm actually twenty minutes early. I would call my mom to ask for his room number, but she's in a work meeting, hence why she sent me here to pick him up. I already texted Uncle Vic, asking for his room number, but he hasn't responded yet. Do you think you could pull that up for me so I don't have to wait out here alone? This area doesn't seem the safest for girls my age."

The man snaked his long arm behind his head and scratched his thinning hair, creating a flurry of dandruff. "I'm not supposed to give out room numbers."

"I get it." Alina raised her palms and smiled. "I'll wait in the bar for him." She turned away again, mentally counting down from three.

Alina was attractive, and she understood the psyche of men—they wanted, maybe even needed, to save a helpless woman in distress. The gangly man probably didn't receive too many opportunities to impress women. Alina believed he would pounce on this chance to help her.

Three.

Two.

"Wait," he said, his voice a near croak.

One.

Zero.

After the brief hesitation, she turned to face him, splashing a look of concern and anticipation across her face. "Yeah?"

"What's your uncle's name again?"

"Victor Pemberton."

The man's long fingers danced across the keyboard, practiced and lithe, unlike the older woman's stumbling poke. After a few seconds, he sighed and looked at Alina with his soft blue eyes. A flash of realization smacked Alina. Though the young man appeared awkward now, in ten, twenty years, when he turned thirty or forty, he would grow into himself, and he would possess a unique handsomeness.

"Room 224."

Alina lifted her chin. Her lips twitched, quivered into a shy smile. Her father was in 223.

"Thank you," she said.

"Just... tell him that your mom shared the room number with you."

"Why wouldn't I tell him that? She did share the room number with me."

The blue-eyed late bloomer smiled, and again his face boasted of a hidden beauty.

Alina glanced at the front door, hoping to see Fred walking toward her from the parking lot. She had no such luck.

Acting as Colleen, Alina had told Victor she would meet him at the bar before 1530hrs. Alina had no intention of meeting the magician at the bar, though. She had to intercept him before he made his way over there. Surprise him.

Not caring to risk any more time in the lobby, Alina hurried outside and ascended the stairwell once more. She removed her phone and texted Victor's room number to Fred, along with the hotel name, in case he had already forgotten, and drove to the wrong location.

At the top of the stairs, on the second floor, Alina slunk along the balcony, pausing just before her father's window and door. She leaned against the metal railing, waiting for Fred before she approached Victor. If Victor left his room, she would see him. She would follow him, keep him in her sights until Fred finally arrived.

After three minutes of waiting, her phone buzzed.

Just parked, Fred texted. *On my way up.*

Glancing through the slats in the wrought-iron railing, Alina saw Fred and watched as he circled the building, climbed the stairs from the opposite side of where she had gone up, and stomped toward her. He held a bag of Cheetos in his bearish paw.

"Hey," he said, calling across the balcony. "I brought snacks."

Alina stood, bringing a finger to her mouth and shushing him. She crept toward Victor's door in a hunched posture, like a monster in a cartoon lurking in the dark.

Before knocking, she regarded Fred. "Hang off to the side. I don't want him seeing you."

"Aye, Aye." Fred ripped open the chip bag and tipped it bottom's up into his mouth.

Alina raised a fist and knocked. Fred chomped from a few feet away. Alina's nerves fired brilliantly—the smacking sound of the chips, the anticipation of waiting for Victor to open his door, to see him, to speak to him. The thought of her father stepping from his room and catching her. From the second her knuckle rapped against the hotel room door to the instant the deadbolt clicked from the other side, Alina stood in a timeless frame. She became a living photograph.

This is eternity, she thought. Heaven. Hell. This is eternity.

It was a moment that lasted forever, but not quite long enough.

The door cracked open, and Victor's buggy eyes peered through the two-inch wide gap. "Can I help—"

Not planning on it, not realizing she would do it, just acting as the moment and her instincts dictated, Alina kicked the door inward. The heavy wooden door slammed into Victor's face and flew fully open as he stumbled back.

He screamed in pain.

Alina didn't waste time. She filed into the magician's room. Thankfully, Fred had the wherewithal to follow her. Once inside, she closed the door and twisted the deadbolt.

Victor stood in the entry before the bathroom door, holding his face and groaning. Blood poured through his hands, over his hairy, bare chest, and onto the carpet. A single white tooth lay on the ground.

"You broke my nose!" At least Alina thought he mumbled that from behind his hands and the gushing blood. It sounded like, "Oo broe muh oshe, bish." She was sure he added a few colorful words in his surprise.

"Fred," Alina said, "could you escort our friend to the chair by the window?" She stepped past Victor and sashayed to the backend of his room. She pulled the curtains shut, grabbed the desk chair, and dragged it to the middle of the room. Despite her calm demeanor, her body tingled, had mostly gone numb, and her mind screamed one wailing, incessant scream.

Without putting a cheese-stained hand on the bare-chested magician, Fred herded him, like guiding cattle, to the chair.

Victor sat. Fresh blood drenched his bulbous belly, matted his hairy chest. His pudgy hands remained over his mouth and nose. He continued to mumble curses between the moaning.

Alina inspected the dim room. Victor traveled much neater than her father. He had no clothes scattered around the room, and he had taken the time to throw his empty alcohol bottles into the trashcan.

"Do you remember me?" Alina asked, returning her gaze to the magician.

He looked at her with wide, angry eyes, removed his palms from his face, and spat a wad of blood in her direction.

Fred, a man not known for wanton violence—despite his long and successful career as a defensive player in the NFL—smacked Victor across the face with an open palm. The sound cracked like a rifle firing on a crisp winter morning. "Never do something like that again," he said, his voice nearly a growl. "Especially toward a lady."

A bright-red handprint appeared on Victor's left cheek, along with a string of tears. "What do you want?" He mumbled the question. When he spoke, a dark gap appeared where his front teeth should have been.

"Do you remember me?" Alina asked again.

"Should I?"

She shrugged. "I don't know. Do you?"

"No."

"Do you know Stephen Moore?"

"No."

"You're Iniduoh, the magician, right?"

"Yes."

"Do you know Samantha Graves?"

"No."

Alina snickered and paced to the front door. She checked the locks before returning to the magician. "Victor, please, let's not make this difficult. I'm not with any police agency. Understand that. I'm here out of my curiosity. I can't hurt you based on what you tell me, but... I can hurt you based on what you don't tell me." Alina glanced at Fred. "Rather, he can hurt you. You know what they say, right? No pain, no gain."

"What do you want to know?" Victor asked, his eyes wide as he stared at Fred's hulking form. He rubbed his welted cheek.

"What happened to Samantha Graves?"

Victor pulled in his bloody lips and shook his head.

"Stephen Moore, my father, volunteered me to step onto that stage last night. I refused. Samantha took my spot. She disappeared. You made her disappear. What happened?"

"Hello," Fred said.

Alina glanced at him. The small giant had his phone to his face, speaking to someone.

"Yeah, I'm with her. It's getting out of hand fast. What do you know? Okay. I see. Yeah. I'll have her back at the office in twenty minutes." Fred disconnected the line. He looked at Victor with an apologetic frown. "Sir, I can't express how sorry I am for all of this. She called me, claiming she needed my help, but I didn't know she was going to knock out your teeth. I'm not sorry for the slap, though. You deserved that, and I hope you learned from it."

Alina stared at Fred, mouth agape, shocked to the point of not having any words.

Fred faced her. "We have to go."

"What?"

"Well, according to my sources, Samantha Graves, the girl you're tracking, showed up at her house this morning. She's with her parents, happy as a clam and safe from any harm."

"Who told you that?" Alina asked.

"Your aunt."

"How did she learn that information?"

"Supervising detective for missing persons."

"Ferneau?"

"Didn't get a name," Fred said. "Wait, how do you know the supervisor's name? Did you know all this already, that Samantha returned to her house?"

Alina felt hot and cold at the same time. She faced Victor, desperate now. "What happened to her? How did you make her disappear?"

"Magic," Victor said, chuckling. His previous fear and confusion had flushed away, replaced with amusement. "And a magician never reveals his secrets."

"Come on," Fred said. "It's time we leave." He turned to Victor. "Sir, send your dental bill to the Blue Moon Investigative Agency, Sacramento. We'll pay for the damages, along with your stay here at the Motel 6."

"Oh, you'll get more than a bill from me. I'm suing the company for damages. Do you understand? And I'm pressing charges on the girl. If you leave with her right now, remove her from this crime scene, then I'm pressing charges against you as well. Abetting. Conspiracy. Battery."

Fred's face bunched into a tight scowl. "I'll make sure my lawyer isn't on vacation. Come on, Alina." His massive mitt gripped her small shoulder and steered her toward the room's door.

As they walked toward the balcony, Alina glanced at her father's room. He stood framed in his door, wearing a blank expression, as if he had never seen Alina before in his life.

She couldn't meet his nonchalant gaze. Instead, she dropped her head and stared at her feet as Fred led her to the parking lot.

Scolded. Tuesday, July 25th. 1517hrs.

Maya was waiting at the Blue Moon office when Fred and Alina walked in. She leaned back in August's chair, feet kicked up on his desk, arms crossed. Maya's glare was cold and sharp, like an icicle slicing open skin, and her attention fixed squarely on Alina—at least, that's how it felt.

"What were you doing?" Maya asked. "What were you thinking? I thought you had a semblance of intelligence in that thick head. Do you know that August once mentioned you take after me, and you're too smart for your own good? That feels like an insult now." Maya dropped her feet to the ground and sat straighter. "Oh. Speaking of August, he's still missing. Not that you care, but I thought I would update you on our progress."

Alina broke away from Fred and went straight to her space in the office. She sat at her small desk and stared out the window overlooking the alley.

"I spoke to Detective Ferneau," Maya said. "She spoke to Samantha Graves' mother this morning. Guess what? Samantha is at home."

"That was supposed to be me," Alina said. "I want to know why."

Maya snickered. "This is why we never involve ourselves in cases that we're emotionally close to. They blind us. If you were meant to disappear as Samantha did, it was because your deadbeat father planned to kidnap you. It's that simple."

Alina shook her head. "But it's not."

"But it is."

"He might be dumb, but he's not stupid," Alina said, repeating what Vanek had said to her earlier.

"You're wrong. I've known your father longer than you have. He's both dumb and stupid. He's also a moron, an imbecile, and a troglodyte. He has no forethought, and he acts on impulse. He worked with the magician to kidnap you and bring you to Indiana. If you had disappeared as he planned, he could have hidden you away for a few weeks, acted the grieved father, returned to his new home, with his new job, and his new life, along with you."

"It makes no sense."

"It doesn't have to make sense," Maya said. "It's your dad. He does dumb stuff all the time. It probably sounded foolproof to him, a fool, so he ran with it, blind to all the holes in the dumb plan."

"You're wrong."

"Enlighten me. Please. What is running through your mind that convinces you I'm so wrong?"

Alina gathered her thoughts. "I hacked into his bank account."

Maya burst into a mild fit of laughter. "Your dad would rather chop off his hand than create a bank account."

"He has a bank account, and I hacked into it." Alina turned away from the window and glared at Maya. "If he has a job, like he says, he needs a bank account, right? A place to deposit his checks?"

Maya cocked her head back and forth. "Not necessarily."

"Sure. Maybe not. But if he's renting a house, he had to get qualified, right? He needed some kind of credit history and proof of employment?"

"Depends on who he's renting from."

Alina ran a hand through her thick, tangled hair. "Well, he has three transactions in his bank account. Ever. The Uber to the airport, the flight to Sacramento, a purchase on the riverboat. No deposits from his job. Nothing showing he pays rent, gas, utilities, or literally anything."

"What's your point?"

"He's lying about his employment, his home situation, about everything. Once my custody battle hits full swing, you don't think Mom's lawyers will find that information out? He will lose on day one."

Maya lifted her palms and shrugged. "You're proving my point. He meant to kidnap you because he can't win a court battle."

Alina grabbed her head with both hands and squeezed. How did she explain to Maya what her instincts had convinced her of? How did she explain the creepiness of the dinner on the riverboat, the way the Graves' had looked at her with hungry eyes, the way they whispered and glanced at her with tangible anticipation? There was something perceptibly wrong about the riverboat dinner and the magic show, and it revolved around Alina's volunteering for the trick.

Except she hadn't volunteered. Samantha had.

"Ferneau closed the investigation on Samantha Graves," Alina said, her voice rising. "They're not even investigating where she disappeared to for eight hours. Who took her? How? Why? Did they abuse her? They aren't following up with any of that. It's all been dropped. Case closed."

"She probably convinced her mom nothing happened."

"How did she get off the boat?"

"She probably never did," Maya said. "Cops just missed her. That's it. You're seeing things that aren't there, Alina. You're making assumptions based on your emotions. I don't know if it's because you're scared that August went missing, and you don't want to fail saving him, so you won't even try to."

"Really? That's your deduction? Really brilliant you are."

"Or if it's because you can't admit to yourself that your father would kidnap his daughter out of desperation. I don't know. It doesn't matter. You're shooting in the dark, and you're missing the target by a wide margin. Drop this Samantha Graves nonsense. Focus on August. He needs us. Why can't you see that?"

"We won't find August," Alina said, slapping her palms on the desk, bolting to her feet, shouting. Her nerve endings fired, and her emotions ran unchecked. So much filled her cup, and it had just overflowed. "He's on his own. Daniel Quinn, that's a pseudonym. If that was a real name, August would have found him by now. He's using a fake name. Not only that, he has the resources and the power to help convicted felons escape from jail and heavily guarded patients escape from a hospital. They, like a real magic trick, disappeared, and we're not finding any of them. Get that through your thick skull." Alina tapped her forehead with her index finger to emphasize her point. "August was out of his depth with Daniel Quinn, and we're far beyond that."

Maya chewed on her cheeks for a second. "I've never mistaken you for a quitter, or for someone to back down from a challenge. I guess I had always mistaken you, though, as a woman who could fight and persist."

Alina dropped back into the chair and huffed.

"He could use your help, regardless of what you think you can offer. August needs our help. We have to try. Why can't you see that?"

"The cops never interviewed Samantha," Alina said. "Ferneau never spoke to the girl. Detective Vanek never spoke to her. Does that make sense to you? Be honest with me. Does it?"

"No," Maya said.

"I didn't step onto the stage, but Samantha did. I have to make sure she's okay. Please understand that. The police aren't doing their job here, so I have to make sure she's alright. Once I have that confirmation, I'll pour every ounce of energy I have into finding August. Okay?"

Maya glanced at Fred. "What do you think?"

Fred chomped on a full carrot. "Alina knocked out two or three of the magician's teeth. It was a mess. I offered to pay for hotel damages and the damage to his face. He's still threatening to sue the company and press charges against Alina and me. I expect we should have a boy in blue knocking on our door at any moment."

Maya popped her lips. "Alina, do you know what your little stunt cost us? I don't mean financially, either. If we're dealing with an arrest warrant, that's wasted time August probably doesn't have. You're so worried about Samantha taking your place last night and feeling guilty about her disappearing that you went and did some actual harm to our chances of finding August."

Alina stuck a finger into her mouth and chewed on the nail. Her body buzzed with embarrassment, guilt, fear, anger. She couldn't speak if she wanted to, and she wanted nothing less than to speak to Maya.

Unable to contain the pent up energy and emotions burning through her, Alina popped back up to her feet and hurried to the door.

"Where are you going?" Maya asked.

Alina opened the door. Fred stood six feet away, leaning on the reception counter and watching her. He could have taken one step, reached out, and grabbed her, but he didn't budge.

"Alina. Get back here. When the police arrive, you're speaking to them. Fred, grab her."

Alina stepped into the hallway and slammed the door behind her. She didn't dare glance over her shoulder to see if Fred or Maya chased her. Instead, she headed straight to the stairwell, jogging down the steps to ground level.

When she reached the sidewalk, she ran, creating as much distance between her and Maya as possible. When her lungs burned and tightened and a stitch formed in her side, she stopped and leaned against the nearest building, gasping hard and fast.

After a minute, her heart rate slowed, and her breaths came easier and less ragged. Sweat from the hot summer day slicked her skin. It taped her hair across her forehead in little, tight curls, and it grabbed hold of her yellow shirt.

Alina removed her phone and called Detective Vanek.

He answered immediately. "How goes it?"

"Terrible," Alina said, still slightly out of breath from her sprint. "I spoke to Victor, and he's pressing charges for battery."

"You assaulted him?"

"More or less."

"Jesus."

"Yeah, not good, blah, blah, blah. I know all that, believe me." Alina inhaled deeply. "Listen, I need to know Samantha's mother's or father's name."

"I'm sorry, Alina. I can't help you any more. You assaulted a man. I have to step away from this. I probably never should've involved myself to begin with. If this gets back to me..." Vanek trailed off.

"It will never get back to you. I guarantee that."

"Still, I'm backing off. I'm washing my hands of it. Ferneau said drop it, I'm dropping it. For good."

Alina lifted her chin and stared at the blue, cloudless sky. "I understand."

"Thank you for that. Terry and Wendy called Ferneau, convinced her to drop the case, convinced her Samantha was alright. There's nothing more we can do."

Alina's ears perked, and a beat of hope ran through her veins. "Of course. Case closed. I get it. Thank you, Detective Vanek. I'm sorry for any inconvenience I may have caused."

"Goodbye, Alina."

The line went dead.

Alina removed the phone from her face and tapped on the internet browser. Finding a home address wasn't too difficult, especially when you had a first and last name, and a city to type into the search engine.

According to her quick Google search, Terry and Wendy Graves lived in El Dorado Hills, a suburb thirty miles east of Sacramento. Their address showed across Alina's screen. She copied it, pasted it into the Uber application, and requested a driver.

Then she waited.

The First Labor.
Tuesday, July 25th.
1551hrs.

FROM I-80 EAST, I turned onto Donner Pass Road. The borrowed car's GPS showed I had less than four miles until I arrived at my destination—the Historic Summit Tunnel.

I pressed on the gas pedal, ignoring the speed limit signs.

After leaving the Butcher's Shoppe, I dashed to the parking garage where I had parked my car the previous night. My luck ran true to form. My car wasn't there, though the stall where I remembered parking it had another vehicle occupying its space. A red-rusted dinosaur truck, most likely manufactured before the Vietnam War.

Had Quinn planted the truck there? Was it another clue? Or was I about to commandeer an unsuspecting person's antique vehicle?

Only one way to find out.

I glanced around the garage to make sure no one kept tabs on my odd behavior. Satisfied I was alone, I strolled to the truck's driver's door and tried the handle.

Locked.

I laughed with a little too much fervor, like someone slowly and torturously losing his mind. Edgar Allan Poe's words flashed through my head—a chunk of words long ago memorized, long ago stuffed into the recesses of my mind, only to break free at the most convenient of moments.

And have I not told you that what you mistake for madness is but over-acuteness of senses? — now, I say, there came to my ears a low, dull, quick sound, such as a watch makes when enveloped in cotton.

In Poe's *The Tell-Tale Heart*, the narrator hears a heartbeat beneath his floorboards. Much like that heartbeat, more like the watch, I, too, heard a low, dull, quick sound ticking away. The beating away of seconds, of precious time. It formed in my overly aware senses, driving me mad with urgency.

As I considered breaking into the truck, stealing it, and driving to Donner Pass, a young man about twenty strolled up the ramp to the third floor. He had cyclist calves, a slight, athletic frame, and he moved with fluid grace.

Like a spastic insect, I lurched toward him. "Excuse me," I said. The seconds ticked loudly, percussively in my head.

The man turned to me, reaching into his front pocket for his clipped-on pocketknife.

"Wait," I said, reaching out my hand and grabbing his wrist. "I want to offer you money."

He cocked his head.

"I'm grabbing my phone from my pocket. That's all." Slowly, so not to startle him, I removed my phone from my front pocket. I navigated to Venmo. "What's your account?"

"What?"

I scratched my eyebrow. "I need a car. I want to rent yours. If I crash it or can't return it, I'll buy you a new one."

"No way."

"What's your Venmo account?" I asked.

"Are you crazy?"

"I'm getting there." I suffocated another fit of bubbly laughter. "Please, it's an emergency. Someone's life... multiple people's lives are on the line. You can help save them."

He rubbed his face. "You want to rent my car?"

"Yes."

He pondered the proposal for a few seconds. "So what if you pay me a grand up front, right now, but you never come back with my car? I'm out of a car, and at least another thirty-grand to buy a new one."

"I swear to you, I'll bring it back."

"Sorry, man." He stepped forward.

I sidestepped and blocked his passage, scrambling to think of a solution. Should I knock him out, swipe his keys, steal his car? The police already suspected me of a multiple homicide. What did grand theft auto matter?

It matters that I'm not a criminal, no matter how desperate I get.

"How about this?" I asked, switching over to my Chase banking app.

"What?"

I logged into the account and shoved my phone into the young man's chest. "Take it, do with it as you please. Okay? I need your car."

The kid looked at the phone's screen, back at me, frowning. "My car isn't worth what you have in there."

"Can I rent it from you? Please."

"I get to hold on to your phone, with your Venmo and Chase account open?"

I gritted my teeth. The clock ticked louder in my head. "Yes."

"What's your touch screen password, in case the phone goes to sleep?"

"All zeroes."

"Really?" he asked.

"Keys?"

He drove a gleaming-black Acura RSX. Stick shift. I had little experience driving a manual transmission, but I didn't have any other options. The engine roared to life. An icy fear pricked at me.

What if the kid had an illegal exhaust on the car? What if a cop pulled me over because he noticed the custom, probably not road-legal work? I brushed those concerns aside.

All that mattered was that I had a car.

A little over ninety minutes later, I skidded to a stop at the overpass looking at the Historic Summit Tunnel. The dashboard clock showed 1557hrs. Over thirty remained for me to find and save whoever Quinn had planted out there.

I pulled the keys from the ignition and locked the doors before navigating down to the cave entrance. It stretched open like a giant's ravenous mouth. I stepped into the thick darkness.

Up ahead, swaths of light burned through the cold, damp tunnel as natural stone turned into manually framed lumber which allowed sunlight to bleed through. Carefully, muffling my progress as best as I could, I navigated toward the light source.

As I neared the edge of the square of sunlight, I stopped, my body still pitched in the thick shadows.

The sun leaking into the tunnel highlighted two figures. They sat against the wall furthest from the slats in the wooden tunnel. Their heads lolled with their chins against their chests. Both women had dirty-blonde hair draped over their faces, but I didn't need to see their faces to know they looked identical to each other. They wore the same outfit—blue jeans, hiking boots, and a black tank top.

As I studied them and the area, keeping my distance until I had a watertight plan, an alarm blared through the tunnel like a C-4 explosion digging into the side of a mountain. The walls trembled, and loose debris fell from the ceiling.

For a terrible second, I thought Quinn had brought me out here to collapse the tunnel on my head.

Then the chiding alarm quieted, settling like thin ice across a deep lake. The tunnel settled into stillness.

I held my breath and waited for something to happen. The two women, about twenty yards ahead of me, stirred, woken by the thunderous wake up call. Claire Balzan and Trisha Berry looked at each other.

I couldn't see the details of their faces from where I stood, but I watched as they scrambled to their feet and separated themselves from each other. Neither one removed her gazes from the other.

Then, like a scorpion's tail shooting forward, one woman pulled a gun. She held it in front of her body with both hands, feet in a bladed stance, leaning slightly forward. She had experience with holding the weapon.

I stepped forward from my cover, squinting as my vision adjusted from the darkness to the brilliant brightness of the sunshine. I crept forward, keeping quiet, not wanting to startle the woman with a gun aimed at another person.

The second woman brushed her hands against her torso, her hips. She paused for a half-second, removing a kitchen knife from her pocket. The blade glinted from the cascading sunshine.

Information from the case riffled like a slideshow through my head. Trisha Berry, who looked identical to Claire down to the freckles on her nose, had murdered Claire's husband and therapist, framing the murders on Claire.

From where I stood, I could only see the face of the woman holding the knife. It bore a similar expression to the person in Edvard Munch's most famous painting—complete and utter terror.

I crouched and padded forward, stepping into another waterfall of light pouring through a slat. Once the sun touched my skin, I inhaled and exploded forward, charging the woman with the gun. She had her back to me. By the time she sensed my assault, my shoulder slammed into her spine. She bent backward, folding awkwardly over me. Then she snapped forward, her skull smacking against the ground as I tackled her.

She went limp. A bright light flashed, followed by the thunderous report of a gun firing. More debris fell from the tunnel's ceiling.

I shoved one hand into the back of the woman's head (hopefully Trisha's head, but I had no way of knowing), pinning her face to the floor. My knee went into the small of her back. With my free hand, I wrested the gun from her loose grip, punched the safety on, and stowed it in my waistband.

The woman wielding the knife screamed, her piercing battle cry bouncing off the walls of the tunnel. She bulled toward me like a territorial rhinoceros, the gleaming knife leading her assault like the rhino's horn.

To stop the woman with the knife, I sprang from the woman I had momentarily restrained and raised my hands to ward off the attack.

The blade punched through my left palm as I reached out to grab her wrist and twist the weapon away. Hot, fiery pain raced up my arm, back down into my hand, incinerating all my nerve endings. My limb went completely numb.

Using my right hand, I punched across my body, hitting the woman's wrist. Something snapped, and she released the handle of the knife and screamed.

My left palm now held the knife, the hilt pressed into the center of my hand, the blade five inches out the back. I fought to ignore the sight and the pain, keeping my focus on the threats.

Though I had broken the woman's wrist, she glared at me with untamed desperation, like a wounded, cornered animal with no recourse but to fight to survive.

She slightly squatted, loading up before pouncing at me.

I sidestepped, dodging her predictable attack. As she flew past me, I stuck out a foot and shoved her back with my good hand. She tripped and plummeted face-first to the ground, landing with a nasty crunching sound.

Catching my breath, I loomed over both women.

The one who had wielded the gun remained face-down, still dazed or unconscious after I had slammed her to the ground.

The other woman turned onto her back. Blood masked her face, and she hissed and screamed and kicked at me, scrambling away in an awkward crab walk.

For a second, I entertained the idea of pulling the knife from my palm, but I thought better of it. What if I passed out from the pain? Unlikely, but not outside the realm of possibility, and I needed to remain conscious if I cared to live.

"Are you Claire?" I asked.

The woman backed into the wooden slats forming the tunnel wall. A graffitied fish with red eyes and sharp teeth threatened to bite off her head.

"Do you know who I am?" I asked.

"You're... you're a lion, but with wings."

I frowned. I hadn't expected that answer. Did Claire (or Trisha) see a monster instead of me, as Gerald had seen giant chickens instead of kids?

"Am I a manticore?"

"What's that?"

"Body of a lion, tail of scorpion, face of a man?"

"Are you going to kill me?"

"Am I a manticore?"

"Yes," she said.

"What's she?" I nodded to the woman lying facedown, though breathing—her back lifted and fell in a slow rhythm.

"Another one like you," the woman said, tears freely falling from her face. "A manticore."

"Whatever you believe you're seeing, it's not real. Your mind is lying to you."

"No. That's not possible."

"I'm August Watson, a private investigator for the Blue Moon Investigative Agency. I worked with Sarah Herling and helped clear you from all the charges Trisha Berry framed you of. Do you remember me?"

"You're not August." She pawed at her face, scratching it.

"Are you Claire Balzan?"

"Yes."

"It's me. It's August." I closed my eyes and exhaled, putting myself in the glass-walled interview room where I had first met her. "One of the first things you said to me was when you're nervous, you scratch your face. That's why you hated the handcuffs." I opened my eyes again. "Your face itched and you couldn't scratch it. You said that was the worst part. Do you remember?"

Claire brushed her sandy-blonde hair from her eyes and breathed through her mouth, loud and ragged. After a second, she glanced at the other woman—the woman I assumed was Trisha Berry.

"That's her, isn't it? That's Trisha?"

"Yeah."

Claire faced me. "August?"

"It's me."

"Where am I?"

"Donner Pass."

"Why? How did I get here? What happened?"

I considered her question, stacking it beside my memory loss from the previous night. *What had happened?*

"I don't know," I said.

Claire grunted, leaned over, and pushed herself to her feet. As she went through the slow, painstaking process of standing, a necklace fell from within her shirt and rested on her chest. A pendant of a black spider crawled down the thin, white chain made to represent a spider's web.

A memory from the night before crashed into me.

Darkness, except for the pale moon sitting fat and high, casting its pale light over giant, bipedal arachnids (not zombies). They had two legs, but six arms burst from their torsos. Eight green eyes and thick fangs the size of forearms constructed their facial features.

The remembrance ended after the flashing image. No other details informing me of what actually happened, nothing but the recollection of the sinister creatures that appeared half-human, half-spider.

"August? Are you okay?" Claire asked, her small hand touching my arm.

I jerked away, startled by her fingers pressing against me.

A shot of dull pain spread up my arm again, reminding me I had a knife buried into my palm. "We need to get back to Sacramento." I glanced at Trisha Berry, who grunted and stirred. "Can you help me with her?"

A Couple
of Questions.
Tuesday, July 25th.
1613hrs.

THE UBER DROPPED ALINA off in front of the Graves' closed electronic gate. A security shed stood off to the left, but no one occupied the interior. Behind the spiked, black bars of the gate, sprawled a cartoonishly large house, landscaped beyond magazine perfection.

Vincent Dupree's plantation-styled mansion was the biggest home Alina had ever visited, at least until she stood on the outside of the Graves' closed gate. Vincent's property had over forty acres of walnut orchard, a quarter-mile driveway canopied in trees, and a man-made pond in the front yard, complete with a wooden dock and a paddle-boat. The interior of his mansion was just as impressive, if not more so. However, compared to the juggernaut on the other side of the gate, Vincent's house seemed affordable, if not cheap.

The Graves' manor backed into Folsom Lake, making Vincent's front yard pond look like a puddle. The estate nestled into the oaks and granite outcroppings atop a hill, providing an endless skyline view. Though Alina couldn't be sure based on exterior appearance alone, the house had to have doubled the size of Vincent's mansion.

It was beyond gratuitous.

Once the Uber vanished around the corner, Alina cut around the property line, taking refuge in the small forest of oak trees. The sun sat at its peak in the sky, and the heat radiated across the granite soil. The shade of the trees provided a brief respite from the scorching temperature.

When Alina reached the side of the property, she approached the fence and peeked through the wrought-iron slits. As she stared at the estate, she debated how to proceed.

She could work back to the gate, press the call button, create a story to convince Wendy or Terry to allow her access into their home. She could hop the fence and sneak in, breaking yet another law.

Why not? she thought. If she were in trouble already, why not make her trouble worthwhile? It was like eating too much junk food. If her stomach already hurt, why stop? Why not add to the pain with a little more enjoyment?

"Because you're a masochist," Alina muttered, staring through the fence at the incredible home beyond.

Her phone vibrated in her pocket. She removed it, saw Maya's name, and ignored the call. A second later, before she had the chance to click the phone's screen to sleep and slip it back in her pocket, another call came in.

A blocked number.

Alina wiped the sweat off her upper lip and stared at the mysterious caller.

Telemarketer?

Possibly, though Alina doubted as much. A phone number usually showed when they called, or the warning of a Spam Risk flashed across the screen. The identification on the incoming call said, No Caller ID.

That usually meant police.

Vanek?

Alina doubted that, too. It was more likely that an officer or two had showed at the Blue Moon office, responding to Victor Pemberton's complaint. They would have spoken with Maya and Fred, which explained why Maya had called a second before. When Alina had ignored her, the officer gave it a shot.

Alina tapped the red button and shoved her phone into her pocket. She had more important tasks at hand.

How did she get into the mansion and speak to Samantha?

Her phone buzzed once more. Alina grunted and dragged it free.

A text message from the blocked number. *It's easiest if you answer the phone.*

As Alina finished reading the sentence, the No Caller ID popped up again, and her phone vibrated in her hand, signaling yet another incoming call.

She backed away from the fence, into the shade of an oak tree and leaned against the sturdy trunk.

"Hello."

"Please," an assertive, unfamiliar male voice said, "leave the shade of the oak and return to the security shed. I'll escort you into the Graves' house. Don't think about running or causing further incident. It'll only be more difficult for the both of us, and the heat today is nearly overbearing. I would prefer if we could avoid the chase."

Alina swallowed and glanced along the fence line, searching for cameras. She didn't see one positioned anywhere.

"Now," he said. "No more delaying."

"You were expecting me?" Alina asked.

"I'm expecting you at the gate in the next minute. Make it easy on the both of us." The line went dead, pitching Alina in a silence only disturbed by her racing thoughts and the distant engines of ski boats cutting across the lake.

With her phone in her hand, though dangling near her hips, Alina discreetly glanced at the screen and returned Maya's call as she ambled toward the gatehouse. She knew the mysterious man from the other end of the line had his sights on her. So, she tapped the speaker icon, not caring to risk bringing her phone to her ear.

"Alina Mylene Moore," Maya said, her voice edging on panic and fury. "Where did you run off to? Don't lie to me either. I know when you're lying, remember?"

Alina licked her sweaty lips. They tasted like salt and sunshine. "I'm in El Dorado Hills," she said, hopefully loud enough for her voice to reach her hip where she carried the phone.

"What? Did you say El Dorado Hills?"

"Terry and Wendy Graves' house."

"Whose house?"

Alina ended the call and shoved the phone into her front pocket. She picked up her pace by half a stride, coming around the fence line and walking toward the front gate.

A squat man built like SpongeBob SquarePants, including the rail-thin legs, waited near the spiked gate. He was bald, but his dark, bushy eyebrows and thick beard more than made up for his lack of hair. He had sharp, angular features—piercing eyes, a beaked nose, elfish ears, and a cutting grin. Despite the heat, he wore an all-black, long-sleeved, full-pants uniform, along with a kevlar vest. Slung across his back, he carried an assault rifle, and holstered onto his Batman belt was an assortment of tools, including a handgun, handcuffs, a stun gun, and a canister of pepper spray.

Alina stopped fifteen feet from him. "You must be Rooster," she said, nodding at his skinny legs. "Is it tough having a chicken-shaped body? Do you get ridiculed by your more proportionate friends? I wouldn't feel too bad about it. I've heard chickens may have evolved from the Tyrannosaur, an apex predator."

The man's slicing smile cut wider. "Speaking of friends, you're fresh out of them here. If I were you, I would consider a more charming approach."

"If you were me, you wouldn't have skipped leg day." Her heart hammered a thousand-miles-per-hour against her chest, beating so hard, it reverberated in her ears. She couldn't recall having ever been so nervous in her life. "Why am I here, G.I. Joe?"

"To speak with Mr. and Mrs. Graves, right?"

A severe chill ran up Alina's spine. Had they been waiting for her to arrive? Who would have called and warned them? Ferneau? Vanek? Why?

"I... I had a couple questions to ask them." Alina had youthful confidence, hollow and without substance—much like a balloon. It took only the simple prick of a needle to pop and deflate it.

It suddenly struck her with a resounding clarity that she was alone. She had left the comfort of the office and the protection of Fred and Maya. August was gone, vanished. Alina had no one but herself now. Not that it differed much from the rest of her life, but she had grown accustomed to the security of her friends and family. She had become complacent, and she had forgotten what genuine fear—isolation—felt like.

Now, standing in the dead heat of summer, before the security guard armed to his teeth with military-grade weapons, thirty miles from any of her friends or family, Alina realized the peril of her situation.

She stood on an island surrounded by ravenous sharks.

"Questions about their daughter's disappearance?" the man asked.

Alina nodded. "I refused to volunteer for the magician. Samantha went on stage instead of me. That could have—it should've been me. I wanted to ask Samantha questions. That's all."

"Well, you might get to ask her whatever you like." The man's grin stretched across his face, his teeth like the serrated edges of a blade. "Come with me." He turned to the keypad standing before the gate and punched in a code.

The double gates opened wide.

The security guard gestured down the driveway. "After you."

The driveway wasn't as splendid or as long as Vincent Dupree's—the dentist had the Graves beat in that category. It sloped upward for about fifty yards, abruptly turning right at the end.

Alina and the guard held their tongues throughout most of their walk to the estate. Near the end of their trek, nerves claimed the best of Alina, though, and when nervous, her mouth motored.

"What's your name?"

"Jericho."

"How long have you had this gig?"

Jericho's square jaw twitched, and he failed to respond.

"Do you like it?"

Nothing.

"What do you think of Mr. and Mrs. Graves? Are they good people?"

Silence.

"What can you tell me about Samantha? I met—well sat—with the Graves last night. They have a son, too, right? I never caught his name. He was younger than Samantha, though. Anyway, they seemed strange. I don't mean that negatively. But they didn't really engage anyone at the table, least of all me... apart from stealing a few stray glances. Strange glances, you know? Like they were curious about me. Does that make sense? Maybe I'm paranoid, but everything felt so pointed."

Jericho and Alina ascended three steps leading onto the front porch and the ten-foot tall, solid wood double front doors. Jericho opened them and ushered Alina into the mansion.

The interior was like a gymnasium—vast and empty, filled with the echoes of every step and breath. Alina's nerves prevented her from noticing too much of the place, but she couldn't miss the indoor pool through the glass wall to her right.

It was an Olympic-sized pool. Water arced from fountains every ten feet. A floor above, balconies overlooked the pool, and a back wall of windows provided a stunning view of the oak forest and the Folsom Lake.

To Alina, the entire set-up bordered on ridiculous luxury.

Thirty miles west, in downtown Sacramento, humans slept on the streets without access to hot water, three meals, or proper medicine. Alina wasn't blind to the simple fact that the world didn't, and couldn't, solely run off of pure benevolence. She knew people worked hard for their fortunes, and they deserved to spend their money as they saw fit.

Still, after growing up with next to nothing, the excess of the Graves' house seemed like too much for a family of four. Why live like that? What did it accomplish for them, other than allowing them to boast their status?

Yet, Alina only knew one side of the coin—the impoverished side. If she had the money and the opportunity, maybe she would do the same thing. It's easy to judge when you've never experienced or lived or perceived life from someone else's position.

Jericho led Alina through the dwelling, into a sitting room furnished with a sofa and two leather armchairs across from it. Between them was a marble-topped table. A floor-to-ceiling bookshelf stood on the far wall and, positioned before it, was a white grand piano.

Mr. and Mrs. Graves sat on the sofa.

Mr. Graves looked like Pierce Brosnan from James Bond—dark hair slicked back, light, knowing eyes, and a stern, no-nonsense disposition.

Mrs. Graves had a bob haircut, and she looked more Barbie than woman—more plastic than flesh.

Jericho cleared his throat and gestured to the leather armchairs. Alina obeyed without a word, shuffling forward and sitting.

She slouched on purpose, hoping to exude a vibe of confidence and nonchalance, despite the fear raging through her bones. She crossed her arms. If she had gum, she would have blown the world's largest bubble. Instead, she tilted her head and regarded the Graves, waiting for them to incite the conversation.

For quite a while, maybe thirty full seconds, no one said a word. The clock on the wall behind Alina ticked, ticked, ticked. The air conditioning hummed through the vent in the ceiling. Alina's heart pulsed in her head, though it had sunk deep into her stomach, filling her innards with acid.

She couldn't handle the silence any longer. "It's like a real-life doll-house, complete with Ken and Barbie. Incredible. Did you know my aunt's ex-boyfriend bought me a Barbie for my sixteenth birthday? I hated that stupid gift so much. Why would he buy me a Barbie? What about me screams Barbie?"

"Alina Mylene Moore," Terry said, leaning forward. "I understand you're nervous. I can smell your fear." He sniffed the air, like a predator honing in on his prey. "You came to us, did you not? Why, if you now sit before us trembling?"

"I wanted to speak to Samantha," Alina said, hoping she sounded more confident than she felt. How did they know her full name? Why were they waiting for her?

"In due time," Wendy said.

"Why did you drop the investigation into Samantha's disappearance?"

Wendy and Terry shared a glance before turning back to Alina.

Terry spoke. "She's not missing anymore."

"Can I speak to her?" Alina asked.

"In time," Wendy said again.

"What's that even mean? Why can't I speak to her right now? Why do I have to wait?"

"To understand," Wendy said.

"To understand what?" Alina looked back and forth between the husband and wife, growing more and more unsettled.

Terry glanced around the room, gesturing at the bookshelf and piano and furniture. "This... all of this... it's not free."

"Obviously," Alina said.

"It comes with a great price. I don't mean my house, either. I mean my wealth. That comes with an incredible cost."

"What are you talking about?" Alina asked. This meeting had taken a strange turn, and she no longer felt comfortable enough to slouch. She straightened her posture, readying herself. If push came to shove, she wanted to escape in a hurry. "What does that mean?"

"We built our success on sacrifice," Terry said. "Do you understand now?"

"Not at all."

Terry snapped his fingers twice.

Jericho slipped out of the room.

"Last night was a misunderstanding," Terry said. "Samantha knew not to volunteer, yet she did. She's in a rebellious phase." He chuckled. "The magician didn't know better. He only had one bit of information—collect the kid. How was he supposed to know which kid?" Terry's eyes flickered to the door and he smirked. "Ah."

Alina turned her head.

Jericho escorted Samantha Graves into the sitting room. The girl appeared distant, physically standing in the room, but mentally elsewhere. She faced the floor and hugged her arms around her body.

"There she is," Terry said. "Ask of her what you will?"

For a moment, Alina had no words or thoughts. She hadn't expected Samantha to be home.

In a whispered tone, she asked without thinking, "What happened?"

Samantha's gaze lifted, her eyes held Alina's. "You shouldn't have come here."

A scratchy, burlap sack whipped over Alina's face, tightened around her throat so she couldn't breathe. Still, she screamed and writhed, but to no avail. Strong hands grasped her shoulders. A restraint latched around her neck, securing the burlap sack over her head. She could see a star-burst of light pricking through the tiny gaps of the material, but she couldn't see outside of the fabric. It stank, too, like old produce, and her frantic breathing made it unbearably hot.

"I would suggest relaxing," Terry said from across the room. "You will need rest to have all your strength."

Alina was hoisted from the chair and thrown over a broad shoulder—probably Jericho's. He carried her out of the room as she kicked and clawed at him, as she screamed. It didn't matter how hard she fought, her blows landed on cement. He continued forward as if made of stone, unbothered by her attacks.

They ascended a flight of stairs, followed by another flight. A door opened, and the hot summer breeze washed across Alina's body. A few steps later, Jericho tossed her onto the ground—a cold metal floor. He handcuffed her wrists to a steel bar.

Then the percussive, whomping sounds of a helicopter filled the silent summer afternoon.

A Lost Puppy. Tuesday, July 25th. 1621hrs.

"Alina Mylene Moore," Maya answered, her voice edging on panic, flirting with fury. With her free hand, the hand not threatening to crush the phone in its grasp, she gripped a bundle of her graphic T-shirt—a printed cover from *A New Hope*.

After the magic show debacle and August's disappearance, Maya figured Alina felt confused by the overwhelming developments in her life. Her mother had come back from rehab, sober and healthy. That was a great thing, but a change in the young woman's life. Her father had returned, claiming he wanted to take Alina back to Indiana with him. The results had ended in divorce papers and a pending custody battle. August had proved himself the only constant in Alina's life—he had provided her with stability, with a job, with his presence. Now, he had gone missing.

Maya knew Alina had to sort out her thoughts, but she was only sixteen and she still needed guidance. Maya wasn't the person to provide that guidance. She still acted sixteen half the time. Besides, Alina wouldn't listen to her. Alina saw her more like a sister than an authority.

So, when Alina had fled from the office, Maya didn't chase after her. She figured her words would only upset Alina more. Instead, she allowed her niece to run, hide, take a minute to decompress and think.

Five minutes had ticked away. Those minutes quickly turned into ten. Alina didn't return to the office.

Maya and Fred went downstairs and searched the immediate two-block radius. When they finished circling the perimeter, finding no trace of Alina, Maya called her.

Of course, Alina ignored the call.

Maya gnawed on her lip and stared at the summer sky.

"What are you thinking?" Fred asked.

"You should drive to August's house," Maya said, forming a half-baked plan. "See if she's over there."

"And you?"

"I'm going to head to my house to look for her. I'm also going to call her father to see what the scumbag knows." Maya rubbed the top of her head and bit back a primal scream.

First August, now Alina. If Daniel Quinn had anything to do with her niece's disappearance, Maya would inflict so much pain upon the man, medieval torture would seem like a ride at Disneyland.

She had her car, but Fred had to call an Uber to take him to August's house.

As Maya sped from the Blue Moon Office to her house, the phone rang.

Alina Mylene Moore.

"Where did you run off to?" Maya restrained her voice, but the question came out in a raspy, whispery scream. "Don't lie to me to either. I know when you're lying, remember?"

"I'm in El Dorado Hills." Alina's voice was distant and muffled.

"What? Did you say El Dorado Hills?"

"Terry and Wendy Graves' house."

"Whose house?"

Alina didn't respond. The line ended.

Maya's car fell into a shivering silence. Despite the nearly hundred degree temperatures charring the Sacramento Valley, chills covered Maya's entire body. She couldn't remember ever feeling so cold. Her mind was like a block of ice, holding a single thought frozen in place.

Terry and Wendy Graves' house. Terry and Wendy Graves' house.

Maya abruptly jerked on the steering wheel, tugging her car to the shoulder. She parked at a red-curbed space beside a fire hydrant, scrolled through her contacts, and dialed Evan's number.

Maya and Evan had dated since the beginning of May, and Maya really saw no signs of their relationship ending. Evan worked as a tenured professor for UC Davis, and he was an esteemed ornithologist. A bird scientist. Currently, his research had him holed up at the university until Sunday evening.

"I was just thinking about you," Evan answered. "How's your day going?"

Maya coughed, releasing a deep-throated, desperate chuckle. She hadn't spoken to Evan yet that day, and he didn't know August had gone missing. He knew nothing of the erratic behavior Alina displayed, either.

"I need you," Maya said, hating herself for admitting to someone that she needed them, but knowing that she did.

With Alina missing, her entire world had spiraled out of control. If something happened to her niece on Maya's or Wanda's watch, that hiccup could hand Stephen the custody battle.

"What's going on?" Evan asked, his tone growing more serious.

"August went missing."

"Missing? What's that mean?"

"What do you mean, what's it mean? He's gone." Maya teetered, counterbalancing from a point of barely holding it together—with scotch tape and craft glue—to breaking, cracking, crumbling. Tears, fat and full like ticks, crawled down her face. Her throat tightened. "I'm so scared. I just wanted to hear your voice." That wasn't fully true. She needed to hear the voice, the safe and warm voice, of someone she loved. She wiped a sleeve across her nose.

"Do you want me to leave work?" Evan asked.

"No."

"I will."

"I know."

"I'll tell the others to study *these* birds, and then I'll throw up my middle fingers and fly to you, baby."

Maya chuckled and brushed away her tears. "Bird jokes, really?"

"They're funnier in my circle of friends."

She swallowed and inhaled. "Stay at work."

"You're sure?"

"I just... thank you for answering."

"I'm serious. If you need me, I'm there." He said it somberly, with equal steadiness as a judge delivering a sentence.

If you need me, I'm there. Those six words pieced Maya together again.

Evan's career meant everything to him. For him to say he would abandon it for her... it gave her all the strength and backing she needed to carry onward with her day.

"Evan," she said.

"This is he."

Maya thought she would feel scared, or the very least, hesitant about what came next. She had never uttered I love you to a romantic interest. She had never made herself that vulnerable to someone else; had never allowed someone to have that much power over her.

The thought of love had always terrified her. It was the primary reason she had never actively pursued something more than friendship with August. He was a man she could fall in love with, and she didn't want that kind of love.

Evan had snuck up on her, though. He had originally drawn her interest through pure physical attraction and natural charisma, and that had grown and blossomed.

Now, she sat in the front seat of her car, pulled into an illegal parking spot, terrified out of her mind about August and Alina, but not terrified about Evan. In fact, with his voice in her head, she felt warm and safe, and she felt seen and heard. She felt loved.

"I love you," Maya said, articulating each word with conviction. She wanted him to believe her. When he said nothing for half a heartbeat, Maya jumped back into the driver's seat of the conversation. "You don't have to say it back, but please, please, don't make a joke. I'm serious. I wanted you to know how I really felt."

"I love you," Evan said.

Tears formed again and broke down her cheek. Maya couldn't help but smile as she wiped them away.

It was a wild feeling, to love and to be loved back. It was like stepping off a ledge in the dead of night, not having any idea how far down to the bottom, and landing in something warm and fuzzy and worth squealing about.

"I hate the way you make me feel," Maya said.

"Horny?" Evan asked.

Maya snickered and shook her head. "I can't explain it."

"Maya Mylene Adler doesn't have the words to explain something?" Evan whistled. "You've got it bad for me, don't you? What did it for you? Was it my award-winning smile?"

"I can hear you smiling over the phone right now. It's obnoxious."

"You can hear me smile? That makes no sense."

"None of this makes any sense, you dork."

"Dork? Do you know what that means? You just called me a whale's penis."

"Really?"

"That's what dork means."

"No, it doesn't."

"Yes, it does. Some kid in middle school told me that."

Maya smiled. "Dork refers to a certain phallic part of the anatomy, but its not limited to marine mammals."

"So a dork is a penis is a dick?"

Maya furrowed her brow. "Less playful when we break it down, isn't it? I take it back. Your middle school source had it right. You're a whale's penis."

"Incredibly large?" Evan asked.

Maya thought of Fred at the mention of incredibly large. She had to call him to see what he learned from August's house. She also had to find Terry and Wendy Graves's house, drive to El Dorado Hills, and pick up her niece.

"Thanks for answering the phone," Maya said. "I'll call you tonight at the regularly scheduled time."

"I'm looking forward to it. Oh, and Maya."

"Yeah?"

"I love you."

Maya bit her lower lip and smirked. "You don't get it twice in one conversation. Bye, Evan."

She hung up the phone, sighed with a youthful giddiness. The moment of pure bliss quickly dissipated, though. August loomed in her mind, as did Alina.

Before Maya could call Fred, her phone vibrated, and his name appeared on the screen.

"Fred," she said.

"Hey." A pause, followed by subtle chewing.

"Did you find Alina?"

"No. But I found Bagley."

"What do you mean? The puppy?"

"He was in the backyard. Alone. Without Gerry."

Maya stared out her windshield at nothing in particular, mostly looking beyond everything and visualizing August's backyard, seeing the doodle puppy running on the lawn.

"Without Gerry?"

"Gerald," Fred said. "He's staying with August, remember? He's helping with Bagley while August works."

"I remember. What do you mean, without Gerry?"

"Oh. Gerry's gone. I called Sarah Herling, because I didn't think Gerry would leave Bagley alone, especially not outside like some lost puppy. Sarah hasn't seen or heard from him since yesterday."

"Is Bagley okay?"

"He's fine. A little dirty from digging in the garden, but he's not hurt."

"Anything on Alina?"

More chewing filled the line, followed by a loud swallow. "Nothing on her. You?"

"She called me."

"What?" Fred asked. "When?"

"Five minutes ago. She's in El Dorado Hills, at Terry and Wendy Graves' house."

"Why does that sound so familiar?"

"Samantha Graves was the girl who went missing during the magic show, the girl Alina has been chasing all morning."

"Oh." Fred chewed on something again.

"What are you eating?"

"A granola bar."

"Why?"

"I'm hungry."

"It's annoying," Maya said. "Can't you go ten minutes without food, or, I don't know, at the very least, a conversation?"

"She's okay, then?"

"What?" Maya asked.

"Alina is at the Graves' house. You spoke to her. She's okay?"

Maya considered the question. Alina's voice had sounded distant during the strange, brief conversation, as if she spoke with the phone in her pocket. She also had a strange tone, something bordering on...

"She sounded scared," Maya said.

"Alina scared of something? Impossible."

"I can't explain it. But she called to tell me where she was, then she hung up."

"Did she sound... in trouble?"

"I don't know, but my gut says she's in trouble. We have to go to El Dorado Hills."

"I'll call another Uber and meet you back at the office. You want to head straight out?"

"Yeah. I'll see you there."

Maya hung up the phone and pulled back onto the road, turning her car around and rushing to the office. As she drove she dialed Alina's number, but it went straight to voicemail, as if someone had turned off the phone or it had lost service.

Maya shoved a nail into her mouth and chewed on the cuticle, tasting a little blood. August had already vanished. Alina couldn't disappear, too. Maya wouldn't know how to handle it. She would have to go after Alina, right? She would have to abandon searching for August to save Alina.

Maya clenched her jaw and pressed her foot against the gas pedal, building her speed until she nearly doubled the speed limit.

A Warm Welcome. Tuesday, July 25th. 1721hrs.

WENDY GRAVES GREETED MAYA and Fred at the estate's massive front door. She had platinum-blonde hair, dark-red lipstick, and more injections, fillers, and cosmetic alterations than natural appearance. When she smiled, nothing on her face moved—the corners of her lips sort of just stretched a little.

"Welcome," she said, stepping aside and gesturing inside the manor—a house better fit for shooting a music video than actually living in. "Please, come inside."

Fred cleared his throat, drawing the attention of Wendy and Maya. He held a pink leash, which was attached to Bagley's collar. The double-doodle puppy sniffed the front mat as if searching for a location to lift his leg.

"I can't leave him outside," Fred said. "What's the pet policy to your house?"

Wendy jutted her lower jaw forward. "He can come inside."

"Of course. If there's an accident, I'll clean it up, too," Fred said.

"Let's avoid any accidents."

Maya rolled her eyes and stepped into the vast entryway. A glass wall allowed sight of a massive indoor pool. The opposite wall was not glass, but sheet-rocked and painted, fully adorned with gold-framed photographs with intricate trim, and a row of hand-crafted, heavy-looking oak doors. A wall of windows made up the back wall, and they overlooked an oak tree grove and the Folsom Lake.

"Gorgeous home." Maya circled her gaze around the immensity of the hall. "What did you do, sell your soul to the Devil?"

Wendy glanced at Maya, blinking her giant, fake eyelashes. To Maya, the extra weight appeared like an unnecessary, miserable chore. "What if I did?"

"Well, you're ballsier than me. I'll say that. I'm not sure I want anything enough to make a deal with the Devil."

Wendy's plastic smile crinkled across her face for a split second. "You mentioned something about your niece."

At the gate's call pad, while convincing the woman to allow them into her home, Maya had mentioned Alina, that she shared this address with her, and it was the girl's last known location. After that, it took little persuasion for Wendy to allow them onto her property.

"She came here," Maya said.

"Your niece—that's what you said, right? She's your niece?"

"Mmhmm."

"She came here, to my home?"

"She did."

"That's impossible. We have a secure fence and a manned gate, as well as hired security to deal with any trespassers."

Fred stood behind Maya, just inside the front door, giving Bagley a short leash. "Did one of your security guards see Alina sneaking around the property?" he asked. "Maybe they arrested her and have her in some room now."

"I don't think so," Wendy said, scratching the back of her neck.

"What does that mean?" Maya asked.

"I'm unsure."

"You're unsure about what happens at your house?"

"Jericho is the head of my security team. If something happened, he would inform Terry, not me. Dealing with security details is worrisome, and I prefer not to worry. Life is easier."

"So your head of security would have told your husband about a trespasser?" Maya asked.

Wendy shrugged. "Not necessarily. If he found a sixteen-year-old girl snooping around, he may have asked her to get lost. If she complied without trouble, there's nothing to report. He did his job. We pay him to handle the security so we don't have to."

"But not the traffic?" Maya asked.

Wendy frowned, at least whatever excuse her stiff face could form of a frown. "Excuse me."

"The in and out traffic coming through your gate. There wasn't any security manning the shed or anyone near the front gate when we arrived. Do you always have the time to answer all the traffic coming to your house? Or were we lucky for you to answer our call?"

"Jericho usually posts near the front gate. He'll screen most of our visitors against our appointment calendar for the day. If an unexpected guest arrives, he'll phone me."

Maya narrowed her eyes and leaned forward. "My point exactly. He wasn't there, so I tapped the call button on the keypad, and you answered. Where was he?"

"With me," said an unfamiliar voice, which echoed across the vast hall. A tall, handsome man in a fitted suit strode into view. When Terry Graves reached his wife, he placed a hand on her lower back and smiled—a genuine smile—at Maya and Fred. His smile soured when his eyes dropped to the puppy.

"Alina Moore, right? That's who you're here for?"

Chills shot down Maya's spine. She licked her lips. She didn't like that Terry knew Alina's name.

"Jericho was just debriefing me on his encounter with the young girl," Terry said. "That's why he wasn't at the gate."

Adrenaline pumped through Maya, and her body grew hot and sweaty inside the cool interior of the mansion. "She was here then?"

"Was, yes." Terry extended his hand in greeting. "I'm Terry Graves, by the way."

Fred stepped forward, dwarfing the tall man, devouring Terry's rigid hand in his massive paw. "Fred."

"Where's Alina now?" Maya asked.

"We called her an Uber and sent her back to..." he clicked his tongue and looked at the ceiling. "Blue Moon Investigative Agency, is it?"

"You called her an Uber?" Maya asked. "She couldn't call herself an Uber? Or are you always so kind to unwanted guests?"

"An unfortunate accident, according to Jericho." Terry scratched his eye. "Alina, when discovered, attempted to run. Our house sits atop a hill with a severe downslope, one which leads straight into the Folsom Lake. In her retreat, Alina suddenly came to the drop-off point. She abruptly halted, otherwise she would have cascaded a hundred feet into the water. The young woman, in her desperate attempt to remain on higher ground, dropped into a braking slide. Apparently, according to Jericho, her efforts weren't enough to prevent her fall."

Alina fell off the cliff, Maya thought, her mind stuck on that one worry now.

Terry must have noticed the fear written across her face. "Don't worry. Jericho grabbed her before she... well, he saved her. Unfortunately, he failed to save her cell phone. In her panic, she must have dropped it. Jericho looked for it, even tried calling it to see if they could hear it ring, but it went straight to voicemail. I believe it plunged into the water." Terry smirked smugly. "So, Jericho called her an Uber and sent her back to the agency."

"Why was she here?" Maya asked.

"My daughter went missing for a few hours after a magic show last night. According to Alina, she believed her disappearance was supernatural. That's what the Blue Moon agency specializes in, right? The supernatural?"

Maya nodded.

"Jericho mentioned Alina believed the magician used actual magic to make Samantha disappear. I believe she came here to speak to Samantha, but seeing that she didn't have a legitimate reason to be on our property, and seeing Jericho standing before the gate, she planned to sneak into our home. Only Jericho caught her before she could succeed."

Maya scratched the back of her neck, slowly nodding her head.

Believed her disappearance supernatural.

The simple statement echoed through Maya's mind like Terry's initial greeting had bounced around the entryway. Alina, much like August and Maya, didn't believe in the supernatural. She wanted it to exist, entertained the idea of it existing, but she needed tangential, scientific, observable proof of it first.

Besides, Maya knew why Alina had gone to the Graves' estate—not to investigate the supernatural, but to learn how and why Samantha had disappeared, because that disappearance was meant for Alina... or so Alina believed. It had nothing to do with the supernatural, but everything to do with a guilty conscience and the fragility of a child relearning her father sucked.

Terry broke the momentary silence. "The Uber only left five or ten minutes ago, around the time Jericho knocked on my office door to let me know what happened. Had we known you were on the way, we could have served Alina some soda and snacks until you arrived."

"Is Samantha home?" Maya asked, scanning the entry hall.

"Excuse me?" Terry looked taken aback.

"Your daughter, is she home right now?"

"She's in her room," Wendy said.

Maya stroked her chin. "Is she okay?"

"Of course she's okay."

"Well, I mean, saying of course is pretty… superlative, don't you think? She went missing for the entire night."

"She's fine," Wendy said.

"It seemed like a pretty sophisticated ordeal. Cops, from what I heard, combed the boat, but they didn't find a trace of her on board. It doesn't seem like she ran away, does it? It seems like that magician made her disappear. Like he had some, I don't know, nefarious plans. But Samantha came home instead. So, is she okay?"

"She's fine," Terry said, his voice restrained.

"And you're working?" Maya asked.

"What do you mean?"

"Doing whatever it is you do to stay in this house? And you're," she looked at Wendy, "you're what?"

"I'm not following you," Wendy said.

"Neither of you seem to be concerned about your daughter. You're not with her, comforting her, loving her, missing her. It seems strange. I don't have a daughter, so I wouldn't know, but if my daughter went missing, even for a few hours, when she returned, I wouldn't want to leave her side."

"We're dealing with you at the moment," Wendy said.

"It takes the both of you?"

"As mentioned," Terry said, his voice levelling, "I was preoccupied with Jericho. Wendy had to answer your call."

"Right," Maya said. "My mistake." She sucked on her cheeks.

"Is there—"

Maya cut off Wendy. "You dropped the investigation, though. It's just so hard for me to," she waved her hands beside her ears, "wrap my head around. Your daughter went missing, and there's an obvious suspect in the magician, but you dropped the case. Not only that, but the police dropped their follow-up investigation, which isn't protocol. I'm just not comprehending the situation well."

"Samantha returned this morning," Terry said. "She sustained no physical or mental trauma during her time away."

"As confirmed by... whom?"

"She said the magician had a false floor beneath the coffin, which she fell through. There was an assistant beneath the stage who instructed her to climb back into the coffin when the magician prompted the crowd he would bring her back. Samantha, always a rebel, thought it would be funny not to comply with his orders."

The story, at least to Maya, sounded less and less believable the more Terry spoke.

"I'm going to interject," Maya said. "I don't care about what happened. Really. I'm not a part of the Blue Moon Agency. I'm just a worried aunt." Maya spread a smile across her face. "I only care about my niece."

"She's headed back to Sacramento now," Terry said.

"Thank you for taking care of her. For saving her life. We owe you one."

"Don't worry about it."

"One more thing." Fred raised a finger.

"Yes?" Terry gritted his teeth and glared at Fred.

"Could I speak with your daughter?"

"Excuse me?" Wendy asked.

"I would like to speak with her."

"For what reason would that be?" Wendy planted her hands on her hips and glared at the giant.

"I'm an employee for Blue Moon. Alina was assigned to solve Samantha's strange disappearance. I rarely work in the field, but since I'm here, and since Alina came all the way out here and didn't get the chance to speak with Samantha, I figured I could. What would it hurt?"

"Who hired you?" Terry asked.

"I'm not at liberty to share client information," Fred said. "However, I would like to speak with your daughter while here. It would help our investigation tremendously."

"No," Wendy said.

"Well, with all due respect, Ma'am, I'm going to speak with Samantha. It can be now, in your presence and in your home, or it can be when I randomly bump into her at the store."

"Where's your son?" Maya glanced back and forth between Terry and Wendy.

The couple expressed pure annoyance now. Their accommodative posturing had all but evaporated beneath the heat of Maya and Fred's questioning.

"What does Wade have to do with this?" Terry asked.

Nothing, other than Maya wanted to watch them crack. She planned to push, to question until one of them stumbled. She knew the Graves' had provided her with nothing but false stories and lies. She also doubted Alina would be at the office when they returned.

"I'm only curious what his thoughts are about his sister's disappearance and reappearance."

"I think you have overstayed your welcome," Terry said.

"What happens, Mr. Graves, when I get back to the Blue Moon office, and Alina's not there? What happens when I get home tonight, where Alina lives, and she's not there? You're the last known person she had contact with. Maybe I've overstayed my welcome today, but I'm sure my company is much friendlier than that of the police."

Wendy grinned something menacing and knowing, as if the mention of the police entertained her.

"Please, head back to Sacramento now," Terry said. "If the Uber doesn't arrive with Alina in company, call the police. In fact, call Tara Ferneau. She's the supervising detective for the Sacramento Police Department, in charge of the missing persons department. I'm sure she can help you find your niece."

In response, Fred released an explosive fart.

Wendy and Terry shifted their attention to him, eyes wide, mouths snarled back in disgust.

Maya, also startled and turned to him.

He cleared his throat. "It was the dog."

"Fred, what is wrong with you?"

"I thought it was a silent one. I'm sorry."

A rank perfume, like old meat, clouded the immediate area. The Graves' faces soured, as did Maya's.

"What did you eat?" Maya asked. "That's disgusting."

"It's a steak fajita sandwich from this place near our house. They bake their own bread. It's so soft, like biting into cotton candy, but it's bread. They melt fresh pepper jack cheese over the—"

"Fred," Maya said. "No one is going there, not after knowing it digests like that."

"I think you should leave now," Terry said, stepping back a few feet, pulling his wife with him.

Wendy appeared utterly shocked—or maybe her unmoving face always appeared in a state of surprise.

"Mr. and Mrs. Graves," Maya said, "could I speak with Samantha?"

"No," Terry said. "She's been through enough already, and she doesn't have to relive the experience with you."

"I thought she didn't suffer any physical or emotional trauma?"

"Please leave my home and property before I call the police."

"Tara Ferneau, right?" Maya asked. "Is that who you would have me call?"

"Leave." Terry stepped forward into the rank stench. He curled his nose and stepped back again.

"One more question," Maya said, raising a single finger. "Then we'll leave."

Terry snarled, as if he might lash out at her. Then he glanced at Fred, took in his size, and sighed. "Make it quick."

Maya stared at the indoor pool for a second, then at the picture window overlooking the lake. She couldn't leave yet. She needed more from them, so she attempted to stroke Terry's ego a little. Hopefully praise would loosen his lips.

"I've never been inside such an impressive house. Congratulations on your wealth and success."

"Thank you, but that's not a question."

"How did you come by it?"

"Through my business."

"Which is?"

Terry scratched his nose and cleared his throat. "I sell a subscription service."

"Like Netflix?" Fred asked.

"What's the subscription?" Maya asked. "Maybe I'm a target customer."

"Or maybe I am," Fred said.

The corner's of Terry's mouth twitched. "Pictures of my feet."

Fred coughed.

Maya's eyes widened, and she blurted out a restrained laugh. "What did you say?"

"I sell a subscription service that provides the customer with pictures of my feet."

"At higher tiers," Wendy said, her posture and tone proud, "the customers receive shipments of his patented foot lotion and toenail clippers, and at even higher tiers, they receive self-foot massage tips, Terry's patented socks and slippers, and a guided foot bath."

"I'm sorry." Maya raised a hand for Wendy to stop. She needed to catch up. She gestured at the mansion. "You're telling me you afford all this by selling pictures of your feet?"

Wendy stepped forward, pointing a finger at Maya. "Pictures of his feet generate six figures a month for this family. Once you include the higher tiers with the lotions, oils, socks, baths, his feet net us nearly seven figures a month, and that doesn't include his book sales."

"Book sales?" Fred asked. "He wrote a book?"

"A best seller, too," Wendy said.

"Well," Maya interrupted, "that might be the single most ridiculous thing I've heard in my entire life, and I've heard a lifetime's worth of ridiculous stories."

"Goodbye," Terry said, grabbing the front door and attempting to push it shut.

Fred backed out of the house and stood on the porch.

Maya remained in the entryway. "Did you know people broke their bodies laboring in the scorching sun, digging the hard ground to create this beautiful home you live in? Those same people work the entire day, every day of the week, to earn enough money to pay for their families to live. You take pictures of your feet, Mr. Graves, and you live here?" Maya rolled her eyes and chuckled. "You really sold your soul to the Devil, didn't you?"

Feet Finder.
Tuesday, July 25th.
1733hrs.

MAYA CLIMBED INTO THE driver's seat of her car. Her entire body vibrated. She twisted the leather steering wheel as her thoughts twirled—words she should have said, but hadn't considered in the moment, suspicions of what had happened to Alina.

Fred had allowed Bagley to do his business on the front lawn before picking him up and opening the passenger door. He leaned his head into the cab to clamber inside.

"Wait," Maya said. "Wait."

"What?"

"If you fart in my car, I will kindly pull to the side of the road and ask you to exit stage right. You'll leave Bagley with me and walk yourself back to Sacramento."

"It was an accident."

"I don't care."

"Steak always bubbles up my digestive system."

"Bubbles up?"

"Makes me gassy."

"Why do you eat it, then?"

Fred shrugged. "Why do you drink though it gives you a hangover? It's too good to go without, damn the consequences."

Maya couldn't argue with that. "Sure, makes sense. What makes no sense is how Daphne puts up with it? That stench was god-awful."

"She doesn't mind it."

Maya stuck out her tongue and retched. "I hate love. I really, honestly, can't stand the notion of love. How does Daphne not mind that?"

"Can I get in the car or not?" Fred asked.

"No silent farts, either." Maya shifted her attention out the windshield. Her view overlooked the manor's front door, where Terry and Wendy remained standing and glaring at Maya and Fred. "If you feel bubbly, squeeze your butt cheeks and pray nothing seeps out of your sewage site."

"You have a way with words, don't you?"

"Why do you think I write for a living?" Maya gripped the gearshift and put her car in drive.

Fred climbed into the vehicle. Bagley curled into his lap. "Speaking of writing, I came up with a title for your piece on the Vampire of Sacramento."

"Oh, yeah?"

"*Undead Dread*," he said.

Maya chewed on it for a while, rolling down the driveway and onto the street. "Why do all of your titles have a subtle rhyme?"

"I find them catchy."

"They're not."

Fred brought his shoulders to his ears. "You still use them."

"Jonah loves them." Jonah was Maya's editor and boss at the *Here & Now* tabloid she wrote for, where she investigated and wrote about all things paranormal and strange. "I don't have a choice in the matter. I mean, I guess I don't have to mention your dumb title ideas to him..."

"Why would you not mention them?" Fred reached forward and cranked the car's air conditioner. "They're pure gold."

Maya frowned, knowing their time of procrastination had ended. They had to face the grating music.

"What do you think about all this?"

Fred opened the center console, closed it, opened the glove box, closed it. He rolled his window down a few inches, allowing a thumping airflow into the car, before rolling the window back up.

"I'm hungry," he said. "I always think better after eating."

"Alina is missing. August is missing. We don't have time to eat."

"What if Alina is headed to the office in an Uber?"

"Do you really believe that?" Maya asked.

Fred chewed on his lower lip, his cheeks, his tongue, as if willing to devour parts of himself to stave off his hunger. He said nothing, though.

Maya sighed. "I don't believe it for a second."

"What do you think then?"

Maya suspected foul play, especially when she considered Alina's initial concerns about Samantha's disappearance. She couldn't act on her instincts—not legitimately and not without proof.

"I find it strange Terry pushed the idea for me to notify the police. He even provided me with a name. Tara Ferneau."

"You think that's weird?"

"It felt like he meant to plant her name in my head."

Fred pursed his lips. "I think it's strange he makes millions a month on selling pictures of his doggies."

"Doggies?"

"His hounds. I glanced at them hounds, too, just to check out the hype. He was wearing shoes—comfy looking shoes... but shoes. I bet he doesn't let anyone see those dogs unless they pay for the view."

"Why do you keep calling his feet dogs?"

"What do you think the uproar is all about?" Fred asked. "Like, does he have a sixth toe? Are they abnormally big? Small? I thought they looked average." Fred removed his phone and unlocked the screen. "I need to know. What if he has tiny dachshunds, but abnormally big wigglers?"

"I don't know what any of that means." Maya wanted to scream, but she restrained herself. "Why do you keep referring to his feet as dogs?"

"Because they stay yapping, you know?"

"No, I don't know." Maya shook her head. "I have no clue what you mean, and I really don't care for you to explain it right now, either. What I care about is the actual subscription-model business."

"What about it?"

"Terry doesn't make all that money selling pictures of his feet."

"Seven figures. Wendy said so."

"Impossible. There's no way on Earth he nets that much money."

"Ah. Here. Lowest subscription tier, sixty-nine dollars a month." Fred chuckled. "Nice."

"Let's do the math." Maya buzzed, excited they had statistics to work with. "How many customers do they need to reach six figures a month?"

"Hold on," Fred said. "He has three more tiers. Six-hundred-ninety dollars, sixty-nine hundred dollars, and--"

Maya saw the pattern. "Don't even say sixty-nine thousand dollars. That's absurd. No one is paying that much money for his feet."

"That's the third tier. He has an online shop, too. He sells the products as a onetime purchase for those who don't care to subscribe. The lotions and oils, the soaps and socks. The guided baths. He has books."

"Seven figures, though?"

"Liver King makes, like, ten million a month selling nutrition stuff. It's possible."

"Fred, Terry is obviously into illicit activities."

"You think so?"

"It's probably why Samantha went missing, and it's why Alina is now missing. It's also why he name dropped a certain detective. Ferneau is probably someone he has in his pocket."

Fred stared at his phone. After a minute, he said, "I think you're right."

"I know I'm right."

"I mean, they look like your typical mutt from a shelter. Not some pure-bred Doberman."

"Huh?"

Fred held his phone up for Maya to sneak a peek. A picture of someone's feet showed on the screen. An average-looking foot, with average-looking toes, manicured, though, with a few black tufts of hair around the toe knuckles.

"What am I looking at?" Maya asked.

"I bought the sixty-nine dollar membership."

"You're supporting him?"

"I had to see what the people were raving about."

"No one is raving about his feet, Fred! It's a laundering scheme!"

"You really think Terry is a criminal?"

"No, I don't think that. I know that. It's the only explanation."

"Not the only."

Maya slammed the wheel with the heel of her palm. "He doesn't make money off his feet. Now cancel your subscription and focus."

"I already paid for the month, though. Should I cancel it now, or before the next payment cycle?"

"If we can uncover his criminal ties," Maya said, "we'll have a foothold into locating Alina."

"She's in an Uber."

"Fred," Maya said, taking her eyes off the road to glare at him with pure fury and impatience, "keep up, please."

"I'm hungry. Food is brain power. Food. I need food." He said it like a zombie crooning for brains.

"I want to meet with this Tara Ferneau detective."

"Right now?"

"As soon as possible. Google her name, see if you can't come up with a phone number."

Fred obeyed, though he made a decent show of his malcontent by grunting and groaning.

Maya stared at the highway as she sped along in the fast lane, passing cars as if they stood still. She had a tendency for a lead foot, a contrasting behavior from August. He drove like a granny on a lazy Sunday afternoon.

"Got it," Fred said. "Tara Ferneau, supervising detective of the missing persons division. I have her office number right here."

Maya glanced at the dashboard clock. 1746hrs.

She gritted her teeth, doubting that a supervising detective would still be in her office that late into the evening. They had to give it a shot, though.

"Call the number and put the phone on speaker. I'll do the talking."

"Alina always says that, too. Why can't I ever talk?"

"Because you're always hungry. I'd hate for you to embarrass yourself because... because you can't think straight from starvation."

Fred made a quiet mocking protest, but pressed the screen on his phone to call Ferneau. He tapped the speakerphone icon.

A tired male voice answered on the third ring. "Detective Ferneau's office, this is Jenkins, how may I help you?"

"Jenkins," Maya said, nearly shouting his name. She hadn't expected an answer. "I would like to speak with Detective Ferneau."

"She's currently out of the office. I can take a message."

"When will she be back in the office? I'd like to speak with her, preferably meet with her in person."

Lazy keyboard typing filled the momentary quiet. "There's a fifteen-minute opening tomorrow at 1100hrs. What is this meeting about?"

"My niece went missing," Maya said. "I was told to contact Ferneau because she's the best at finding missing children."

Jenkins clicked his tongue. "Contact the police department directly. They'll dispatch a unit to ask you questions and determine the nature and severity of your niece's absence."

"What do you think I'm doing? Are you not the police department?"

"I'm part of an individual office within the police department. I am not the police department. I don't have the authority to dispatch units or coordinate searches. Neither does Ferneau, at least until a case gets assigned to her division. A missing person doesn't deem Ferneau's involvement in an investigation. If we suspect drugs, we contact our narcotics team. If we suspect a murder, we contact homicide. I would recommend for you to contact an officer or Sergeant and report your concern to them."

Maya closed her eyes and breathed to calm her temper.

Fred must have noticed her practicing on-the-fly meditation practices. "Hey! You're driving."

Maya's eyes shot open. "Mr. Jenkins, my niece knows Samantha Graves, the girl who went missing during the magic show on the riverboat last night. Coincidentally, my niece is now missing. Ferneau had the final say in the Graves' investigation, so I would like to speak with her to understand why she closed the case."

"1100hrs tomorrow," Jenkins said. "She's not in the office this evening."

"Can you share her direct contact number with me?"

"I can't."

Maya clenched her jaw. "Fine. Schedule me for tomorrow, Mr. Receptionist."

Jenkins provided Maya with an address.

She didn't thank him before prompting Fred to end the call.

After dropping his phone back into the cupholder, Fred said, "That wasn't cool."

"What wasn't cool?" Maya asked, annoyed.

"Your insult."

"What insult? I was trying my hardest to be kind."

"Mr. Receptionist. Like it's below a man to be a receptionist. I'm a receptionist, you know that, right?"

Maya glanced at him, mouth agape. She exhaled. "If you were to eat something, would that also ebb your sensitivity? I'm operating on fumes here. I can't filter what I say to protect your feelings. I'm sorry, but I can barely handle my feelings right now."

"Was that an apology?"

"Nope," Maya said. "I don't apologize for things I'm not sorry for. If it wipes the tears from your eyes, though, let's grab some food. It's almost dinnertime."

"We've spent very little time alone, haven't we?" Fred asked.

"What?"

"You are a little mean."

"The craziest part, I'm being friendly right now," Maya said.

"The scary part is, I believe you." Fred sucked in air through his teeth and slowly exhaled. "Should we call the cops before grabbing a bite to eat? Maybe head to the office to confirm Alina didn't show up in an Uber?"

Maya narrowed her eyes and pressed her foot down on the accelerator.

Back at the Office. Tuesday, July 25th. 1806hrs.

WHEN THEY ARRIVED AT the Blue Moon office, a Sacramento Police Officer waited by the front door. She had dark eyes and a tight ponytail. The name tag on her breast pocket read, Gillespie.

"Evening," Maya said. "I hope you're here about Alina."

"Matter of fact, I am." She had a strange drawl in her voice—not southern, but almost forced, as if she had taught herself to speak with the accent. "For him as well." She nodded at Fred.

The giant man pressed his thumb against his chest. "Me?"

"Breaking and entering. Assault. Does that sound familiar?"

Maya stepped between Fred and Officer Gillespie. "Alina has gone missing."

"When?"

Maya shared the complete story, going back to the previous night at the magic show.

Officer Gillespie placed her hands on her hips. "Well, that's quite the situation now. I'll report her status back to the department, and hopefully we can get a detective looking into her whereabouts. Though, you should know Alina has a warrant out for her arrest."

Fred gulped, not bothering to hide his nerves. "And me?"

Officer Gillespie turned to Fred and smirked. "It's your lucky day. The assailed didn't file any formal charges against you. Out of curiosity, why were you attending a minor in a felonious crime?"

Maya stared at Fred, watching as his eyes shifted every which way. "Yeah, Fred. Why?"

"Don't make this worse than it is," he said. "She's persuasive. She said nothing about breaking and entering or hurting him. She said she meant to knock on his door and talk to him about Samantha. That's all."

"But you slapped the man held prisoner in his hotel room?"

"He spit at Alina. I would've smacked him regardless of the situation for doing something like that."

"Well," Officer Gillespie said, "the department issued the arrest warrant earlier this afternoon. You and Alina are on a security camera at the scene of the crime, at the time of the crime."

"No one cares they beat up a man who attempted to kidnap young girls," Maya said. "We only care that you do your job and find Alina, whether that's through detectives assigned to fugitives or to missing persons."

"I just want you to know that we'll most likely perceive her disappearance as an attempt to escape custody."

"Do your job. Find my niece."

"We'll perform a proper investigation into her disappearance. Our goal aligns with your goal. Find and recover Alina."

"Thank you," Maya said. "Now, I'm going to work on doing the same thing because I don't trust a word you have to say. Please, step away from the door and kindly report back to your superiors."

Officer Gillespie reluctantly stepped aside and returned to her police cruiser.

Maya and Fred went upstairs to the Blue Moon office. They found no trace of Alina's presence there. Still, they waited thirty minutes for her to arrive.

In that time, Maya called Alina's phone roughly five-hundred times. Her phone went straight to voicemail every time.

As each minute passed, Maya's stomach twisted into a dark, dreaded confirmation—Alina had gone missing, and the Graves had something to do with her disappearance.

Alina had suspected her father played a role in the magic show co-nundrum, so Maya leaned to believing her niece's instincts. She called Stephen Moore. He didn't answer. Maya called the motel where he stayed. The front desk transferred her to Stephen's room landline phone. He didn't answer that, either.

"I just got off the phone with Daphne," Fred said. He leaned against the wall near the door. "She said she'll have dinner ready in thirty minutes. Enchiladas. Guacamole. Homemade salsa. It's one of my favorite dishes."

"We're eating at your house?" Maya asked.

"There's booze there."

Maya bit her lip and nodded. "I'm not drinking tonight. There's too much going on." She sighed and shook her head. "I won't turn down a Daphne Rogers meal, though... as long as it's not steak."

Fred chuckled.

Guilt seeped into Maya's stomach. She knew she should work tirelessly on finding Alina and August, but tirelessly worked better in movies. Her stomach rumbled, as she had skipped all her other meals working tirelessly. Her head ached, and her mind was fuzzy with fatigue. To help Alina and August, she had to keep herself sharp. She doubted sleep would be possible until they were found, but at the very least, she needed to eat something.

Maya wrote a note for Alina and left it on the office door, in case she showed. She also sent her niece a few text messages, telling her they went to Fred's for dinner.

Not that it mattered. Alina, Maya knew, was gone.

Dinner and Drinks. Tuesday, July 25th. 1904hrs.

FRED AND DAPHNE LIVED in a suburb fifteen minutes outside of Sacramento. They had a quaint, two-story home nestled into a grouping of similar-styled homes along the labyrinth of crisscrossing streets.

Cracks marred their driveway, but dirt and debris remained clear of the cement. They kept the front lawn manicured to perfection, the flowerbeds weeded, the plants vibrant. Stocky, white-bearded yard gnomes busied themselves around the mulch, between the rose bushes and a Japanese maple.

"This is nice," Maya said.

She followed Fred to the wreath-adorned front door. A welcome mat lay on the concrete, the words HI, I'M MAT, stenciled across the rough material.

The house was more than nice. Maya rented her place, living there with temporary flashing in bright neon. Fred and Daphne's house was the spitting-definition of a home—worn, loved, accepted as it was. He and Daphne hadn't painted over the rust, but they had allowed it to shine.

Fred unlocked the front door with one hand. Bagley rested in the crook of his other arm.

The hinges creaked as they stepped inside. Fred scratched his ear and chuckled. "Daphne has asked me to fix that squeak for over three years now. Her dad said to spray some cooking oil on it—works as well as WD40. It would probably take either of us less than thirty seconds to quiet those hinges." He chuckled again, not finishing his thought.

He didn't need to, though. Daphne, as much as Fred, didn't really care to fix the creak. It, along with Daphne's gentle reminders to oil the hinges, were part of the warmth permeating throughout the home.

The inside smelled like fresh-baked cookies, like vanilla, like a warm, safe place on a harsh, winter night.

Fred kicked off his shoes and slipped on a pair of slippers set off to the side of the entry. He turned to Maya. "You can keep your shoes on. Daphne wears hers. I just like the feel of a bed for my puppies to rest on, you know?"

Maya shook her head, and she elected to toe off her sneakers.

Fred led her into the kitchen—a cozy nook just around the corner of the entryway. It had little counter space, lacked an island, and missed a walk-in pantry, but it smelled like a kitchen should smell. It felt warm and used.

Daphne leaned against the counter, scrolling through her phone. From a speaker on a shelf beside the sink window, a country song played at a low volume.

"Daph," Fred said, dropping his keys on the dining table. He circled the counter and kissed his wife.

Maya didn't think of Evan in that moment, but of August. She thought of creating a home—not a house, but a home—with him. One that was warm and cozy. One where he greeted her with a kiss.

What would that kind of love feel like? Not the fast and furious love or infatuation of a new, shiny relationship, but the love of toil and work and pain; a love hardened through life. A love where a single forehead kiss said everything.

Daphne glanced up from her phone and looked at Maya. She broke into a light laugh. "Maya, welcome. Please, help yourself to anything. Nothing is off limits to you... except my husband."

Maybe it was August vanishing, or Alina's disappearance, or maybe it was telling Evan she loved him, but a thick, acidic lump formed in Maya's throat. She couldn't think of anything to say as tears stung her eyes.

A painful reminder crashed into her. She had never had a home, a place where she felt safe and loved without question. As a child, she had only ever felt alone and scared.

Maya swallowed the sharp and sudden pain, and she burped out a tight chuckle. "After our afternoon, your husband is safe from me."

"Uh, oh." Daphne glanced at Fred. "What did you do?"

"The steak fajitas," he said, scrunching his face.

Daphne covered her mouth and giggled. "Every single time, huh?" She turned to Maya. "I'm sorry you had to experience that. Luckily for everyone, I'm making vegetable enchiladas for dinner. No meat involved."

"That sounds amazing," Maya said.

"Also, there's homemade ice cream for dessert."

"I can't wait."

"How do you feel about a light tequila cocktail as the pairing?"

"I'm going to refrain from the cocktail." Maya stepped to the counter and planted her hands on the cool marble. "Can I help you with anything?"

Daphne glared at Maya. A flash of annoyance shadowed her face. "Don't insult me by coming into my house, stepping into my kitchen, and asking to help me. You're a guest. Sit. Eat. Drink. That's how you can help, by enjoying yourself."

Maya raised both hands in surrender. She grabbed a chair and sat, a hefty smile bursting across her face. "That's a responsibility I can handle."

Maya hadn't spent too much time alone with Daphne and Fred. She mostly knew them through August, and she only saw them with August around. He acted as the buffer, as the intermediary. With him gone, their commonalities drifted into obscurity. A tight silence filled the otherwise cozy home.

"How's work?" Maya asked after a few seconds, cringing and hating herself for asking such a lame question. Before Daphne could respond, Maya hurried into the follow up. "I mean, have you thought any more about starting your own restaurant?"

Daphne had the talent of a world-class chef. She had prepared meals for the group while vacationing in Santa Cruz, and Maya had never eaten better in her entire life. A few weeks ago, while getting together at August's house, Evan had prompted Daphne to open her own restaurant, claiming the world needed her cuisine.

Daphne absent-mindedly prepared a cocktail, garnished with jalapeños and a lime wedge. She brought it to Fred, who sat at the table across from Maya.

He thanked his wife and sipped.

Daphne pulled out a chair and sat. She looked at Maya. "I have thought more about it."

"You have?" Maya leaned forward. "And?"

"Don't laugh."

"Never."

"I really like the idea of a food truck."

"A food truck?"

"It will have a rotating menu, along with a rotating dessert list, and it will only be open during select dates and times." Daphne frowned. "When I'm not at my day job. So, some evenings and most weekends."

Maya stroked her chin and pressed her tongue into the roof of her mouth. "I... I freaking love it. It's genius. Limitedness will create urgency, especially with how incredible your food is. I can see it now." Maya spoke with her hands—the momentary distraction from August and Alina helping to free her thoughts. "Customers lined down the block, around the corner. You're taping signs on the window, informing them you're out of ingredients, because they're selling like gosh-darn hotcakes. Fred, forget about feet, this is your hundred-million-dollar endeavor."

"Feet?" Daphne asked, glancing at her husband's slippered feet. Bagley bounced around, chewing on a string.

Fred brushed away her question. "Work stuff."

Those two words acted as gravity to Maya's temporary flight, and she dive-bombed back to the ground.

She glanced at Fred, waiting for him to share.

"Work stuff, huh?" Daphne asked.

Fred spilled. He went into a full explanation of their day.

Maya bit her tongue, not wanting to speak their experience into existence, not wanting to hear the words, not wanting to convince herself that all that had happened had actually happened.

When Fred finished his uninterrupted tale, Daphne asked, "Do you think Daniel Quinn took them both?"

Maya slowly shook her head. "No. I think we have two separate missing persons' cases, and we have to decide who to go after first. We have to decide who to save. Alina or August."

The three of them exchanged concerned, but knowing looks. They all knew the answer, but not one of them spoke it. They had to find Alina, and they had to hope August could help himself.

The Recruit.
Tuesday, July 25th.
1905hrs.

A FIFTY-SOMETHING WOMAN ANSWERED the door. She had heavy eyes, dark and puffy, and a mop of messy gray hair tied in a loose bun. Her clothes were too big and covered in splotches of dried paint. She leaned a shoulder against the doorjamb and greeted me with a frown.

"Hi," I said, fully aware of how I appeared. Where paint stained her oversized overalls, blood freckled my outfit. I had a bandage wrapped around my left hand, also dark with blood.

"Can I help you?" she asked.

I glanced over my shoulder and nodded at the Acura RSX I had borrowed. I parked it beside the curb in front of her house.

"Timothy Tilton offered me his car, in exchange for my cell phone."

Her face stretched, but she didn't say a word.

"I promised to return the car if possible, but in my haste earlier, I never asked for an address. I searched through the glove box, found his name and this address on the car's registration." I smiled, hoping it appeared sincere rather than predatory. "I'm here to return it and collect my phone."

The woman glanced over her shoulder into the house. "Timmy! Someone at the door for you." She eyed me. "He'll come down in a second."

I pumped my cheeks up with air and slowly released it. The silence didn't bother me, but the woman fidgeted more and more with each passing second.

"Where is he?" She turned her head to look into the house. "Timmy!"

"Calm down, Mom!" The voice came from upstairs. "I'm coming." A couple of seconds later, a figure appeared at the top of the stairwell, quickly descending the steps. He hopped down the last three, landing in the entry before noticing me. "You."

"Hiya." I waved in a rainbow arc. "Brought your car back in one piece. I would've filled it with gas, too, but I'm a little short on cash."

Timothy's mom backed away and disappeared around the corner of the entry without another word. Timothy backfilled her place, standing in the doorframe. "Did you save the people?" He craned his head, glancing over my shoulder to the car. "I don't see anyone with you."

"I saved them," I said. "Dropped them off at a hospital before coming here."

Before heading to Timothy's house, I dropped off Claire Balzan and Trisha Berry at the hospital, unsure of where else to leave them.

Earlier, Detective Wilson mentioned the cops had eyes on my office and house. I couldn't bring the two women to either location. I wasn't sure if Quinn kept tabs on my comings and goings, either. I couldn't take the risk, though.

I didn't want to put Claire's and Trisha's lives in further danger by dropping them off at an unsafe place. I definitely couldn't leave the two of them alone anywhere. Not willing to endanger my friends or family by asking them to help, I picked the hospital as the safest option. Besides, Quinn had drugged the two women, probably by some experimental concoction of his design. The doctors could best handle any adverse side effects.

While at the hospital, I convinced someone in the waiting room to let me borrow their cell phone.

Wilson had, thankfully, answered. I informed him of the latest developments, and I shared the hospital name with him. Trisha Berry was a convicted felon, charged with two counts of premeditated murder, and she had escaped from prison. Claire Balzan, though innocent of any crimes, could use police protection until the dust settled. So, I shifted responsibility over to Wilson, trusting he would handle the situation with discretion.

I also stole some gauze to wrap my hand. It slowed the bleeding, but it did nothing for the throbbing pain.

"You took them to the hospital?" Timothy asked. "Them? How many?"

"Two women."

"What happened?"

I shook my head. "That's a long story, and I'm not exactly sure."

"You saved them, though?"

"Do you have my phone?"

He dug into his front pocket and removed my cell phone, handing it over to me. "I exited out of the money apps. I didn't steal a dime from you. Man, I'm just stoked to have helped save their lives."

I placed the phone in my pocket and reached out my hand. "You didn't just help, you were the catalyst. You saved the lives of those two women. Feel proud of what you did."

Timothy grabbed my hand and shook it. "Can I know their names?"

"Sorry, buddy. I'll share your name with them. They'll reach out if they choose to."

"Thank you. Oh, also... I almost forgot. I charged your phone, too. I saw it was almost dead."

I chuckled. "Timothy, I owe you the world. Thank you."

"I'm happy to help." He knocked on the door frame with his knuckle. "Um, so... seeing that you don't have a car anymore... do you need a ride anywhere?"

I considered his offer. I definitely needed a ride. However, could I involve another person in Quinn's twisted games? What if Timothy's help put him in danger?

The echoes of so many people who I tried to protect whispered in my mind. Glacia. Cambria. Maya. They had all delivered the same message. *It's not your choice to decide how others go about their lives.*

I needed his help, too. I couldn't afford to turn him down, but I would allow him to decide for himself.

"Tim, this could get dangerous. Deadly."

Fear flashed across his face, quickly chased away by excitement. Timothy held a beaming grin. "Listen, the most dangerous thing I've ever done is battle Tiamat in my D&D campaign. I didn't even do that. My fake character in a fake world did that. I'm twenty-three years old, a college graduate with a part-time job at a coffee shop, single, and living with my mom. I could do with a little danger in my life."

"Deadly," I said.

Timothy shrugged. "If I die, well, at least I'll die actually living." He stepped by me and headed toward his Acura.

I grabbed the handle to the open front door and gently closed it. Turning, I called after him. "I'll pay for the gas!"

"I know you will. Now, where's our destination?"

The Hydra.
Tuesday, July 25th.
1911hrs.

I LOOKED AT TIMOTHY and burst into a hearty laugh. Honestly, the random outburst acted like a hold for my negative emotions to drain from. A surge of warm energy filled me.

"Are you okay, Mister... what's your name?"

"August. And I'm fine." I stole a few seconds to catch my breath. "I just realized I don't know, I don't have the slightest clue, where we need to go."

Timothy regarded me as if I had lost my mind, and maybe I had.

I wiped a few stray tears from my eyes. "I need to make a call to know what we do next."

Timothy nodded. "Yeah, okay. Do your thing, Man. Want me to step out of the car and allow you some privacy?"

"That would be great."

The young man hopped out of the driver's seat. "I'm going inside to collect a few items. You need anything from the house? Water, food, weapons?" He nodded at my bandaged hand. "Hydrogen peroxide? Painkillers? Anything at all?"

I scratched my nose. "A wet cloth," I said. "Alcohol or hydrogen peroxide. Antiseptic or antibiotic cream, and some painkillers."

"What happened, if you don't mind me asking?"

"I'll tell you after the phone call."

"Anything else?"

I clicked my tongue and thought. "A clean bandage."

Timothy nodded, tapped the roof of his car, and headed back toward the house, leaving me alone in the car.

I scrolled through the missed calls and messages on my phone, ignoring Fred, Maya, and my mom, who had called three times. I hoped beyond hope no one had told her about my absence. I searched the notifications for Blocked or Unknown callers.

Of the five-dozen unread messages, I noticed a number I didn't have stored. *Call when you can*, it read.

I tapped on the unsaved number.

The phone rang once before disconnecting. I glanced at my screen to confirm the call had gone through. Before I could try dialing back, an incoming call came from a Blocked number.

I answered. "Quinn."

"August, sorry about hanging up on you. I had to destroy the burner phone and call back on a secure line. You had me worried from your extended silence."

"I forgot my phone in Sacramento."

"Well, you defeated the Manticore. You completed the first of your three labors. Congratulations."

"I want to speak to Glacia. I want to hear her voice and make sure she's okay."

"That's not an option."

I licked my lips, knowing I had no leverage to convince him otherwise. I changed course. "What happened last night?"

"According to what I've gathered from my sources, you murdered three people, and you sent one person to the ER in critical condition. You must have thought they were demons."

"Arachnids," I said. "Spiders, oddly enough, are one of my greatest fears. It's strange, because chickens are one of Gerald's biggest fears. I don't believe for a second that's coincidence."

Quinn snickered. "Coincidence or not, demons or arachnids, you killed three people to protect yourself from harm."

"I didn't kill them." I said it with little conviction.

"The police disagree."

My jaw ached from grinding my teeth. "Let's get this over with. What's my next labor?"

"The hydra, of course."

I swallowed, recalling the creature from my Greek mythology class.

"For every head Hercules removed from the hydra, another grew in its place. Some accounts mention two more heads grew back."

"I'm familiar with the creature."

"Then slay the hydra, as Hercules slayed the hydra." He inhaled sharply. "Keep in mind, the multiple heads don't always get along. If you don't intervene in time, they might kill themselves."

"Where can I find it?"

"With the saber-toothed, the wooly mammoth, and the dire wolf."

"What does that mean?"

"You have until 2100hrs. When the clock strikes nine, the hydra will feast, even if that means feasting on itself." Quinn burst into peals of laughter before ending the call.

I lowered the phone to my lap and pulled on my lower lip as I stared blankly out the windshield. A line of large trees obscured my view of the neighboring homes on the wide-set street. Not that it mattered. I barely saw what I looked directly at. My eyes glossed over as I became lost in thought.

Drawing from Quinn's previous tasks with the ship and the tunnel, I searched for commonalities. He set the stage for each event in abandoned locations. Also, he always said just enough to provide me with the answers to his riddles.

So, what had he said?

He had me reenacting Hercules' second labor, where he fought the hydra.

What else did I know?

If remembering the myth correctly, Hercules cauterized the stumps of the decapitated heads to prevent another from respawning.

Did Quinn hint at the fire, then? Had any of my cases dealt with fire?

Not that I recalled.

Quinn had also, randomly, listed three extinct mammals—the saber-toothed tiger, the wooly mammoth, and the dire wolf. Specifically, he said I would find the hydra with them.

Where could I find those animals? A museum?

I struggled to think of an abandoned museum off the top of my head.

I glanced at the time on my phone. 1918hrs. I had less than two hours to solve this riddle. What if I had to drive ninety miles again? What if I had to drive further?

That gave me no slack. I had to solve the puzzle right then.

I ran a hand through my messy hair. "Think. Think."

The driver's door popped opened and Timothy appeared. He climbed back into the driver's seat and tossed a backpack into the backseat. "Is it cool if I come back in? I saw you hang up the phone."

I nodded. "You know anything about Greek mythology?"

"Only that Thor is my favorite demigod."

I exhaled, deciding not to ask Timothy for his thoughts on the matter. "What about local history?"

"Like Sacramento stuff?"

"Like Sacramento stuff."

"I know about the Kings, the basketball team here. I know a little about the gold rush—that old people came here to find gold. Why? What's up?"

I hated to admit it, but Timothy's knowledge was a dead end. I had to phone a friend.

Maya answered before one full ring finished. "Where the—"

"Maya, I need your help."

"Where are you? Are you okay? What's going on?"

"Quinn has me on a monster-themed scavenger hunt to find him and Glacia. Other than annoyed, I'm fine." My left hand screamed at me otherwise.

"Why won't you pick up your phone?"

"I haven't had it on me."

"Where has it—?"

"Maya, I need you to listen to me! I'm on a timer here."

"Okay. Shoot."

"Saber-toothed tiger. Wooly Mammoth. Dire wolf. Do those mean anything to you?"

"They're prehistoric animals that have gone extinct."

"Regarding the Sacramento area," I said. "Is there some kind of abandoned museum or old zoo that features those creatures?"

Maya sucked on her tongue. "Not that I'm aware of. You said abandoned?"

"Yeah. It has to be abandoned."

"Give me a few minutes to research it."

"I don't have a few minutes. I have now."

"What do you want from me, then? To summon the correct answer from the depths of my mind? Give me some time, and I'll get back to you with an actual, legitimate response."

"Who's that?" Fred's unmistakable voice asked from the background.

"It's August," Maya said.

"What? Give me the phone."

"Stop it. Fred!"

"August," Fred said, his voice booming into the receiver, "where are you?"

"Sacramento."

"You're alive."

"No, I'm dead, though a ghost now and speaking to you from the other side."

"Don't say things like that."

"Don't ask dumb questions, then."

"Where have you been?"

"Dancing as Quinn shoots at my feet. Put me on speakerphone."

"You're on it," Fred said.

"Maya, narrow your search to these specifics: an abandoned location that has something to do with the prehistoric animals." I drilled deeper into my memory, trying to draw forth more details about Hercules' second labor. "It's probably in a cave or a tunnel."

"August, quick question."

I wanted to scream at her. Instead, I bit my tongue.

"When you find Quinn, what will you do?"

Kill him was the first thought that popped into my head.

I drowned that idea and considered Cambria. Quinn held full responsibility for her death. I thought of Greta Tonyan and Christopher Steele, both now dead because of Quinn. I thought of Randall Fincher in critical condition in the intensive care unit. I thought of all those who he had taken, who suffered at his whim. He had hurt so many people. Quinn deserved the same, if not worse.

"I'm going to give him what he deserves," I said, tempering the anger coursing through my body.

"Which is what?" Maya asked. "Death? Are you going to give him death?"

"If it comes to that, if I have the chance, I won't hesitate to..." I paused, having nearly said pull the trigger. Aaron Brooks crossed my mind, as he so often did. "To kill him."

For an eternity, no one said anything on the other end of the line. Silence met me, and it was loud. I could hear Fred's and Maya's thoughts in that quiet, and they begged me not to kill Quinn, despite all that Quinn had done.

I broke the spell. "Eddie is dead."

"What did you say?" Maya asked. She had dated Eddie Denier for a few months, only breaking it off with him once he tried to kill her.

"Eddie Denier is dead."

"Did Quinn kill him?"

I killed him, I thought.

"I don't know," I said.

"You don't know? How don't you know?" Maya sounded panicked, on the edge of screaming. Her voice quivered with each word.

"I'll explain everything when this is over. Right now, we need to focus. Find me an abandoned cave or tunnel that has something to do with saber-toothed tigers."

"With what?" Daphne said, her voice appearing on the line.

I briefly wondered how Maya had ended up with Fred and Daphne. Probably a double date with Evan. A pang of jealousy stabbed at me, but I ignored the feeling. I didn't have the emotional bandwidth to feel jealous.

"Did August say saber-toothed tigers?" Daphne asked.

"Yeah," Fred said. "And wooly mammoth and dire wolf."

"There was an old limestone mine in Auburn," Daphne said. "Some dentist—I think he was a dentist—discovered the remains of prehistoric animals, such as the saber-toothed tiger, mammoths, some sloths, even a few humans."

"In Auburn?" I asked, my heart racing. "What's the mine called?"

"I'm looking it up now," Fred said. "Hold on."

I glanced at Timothy and showed him my teeth—not a smile, but something bordering on one.

"Quarry Trail to Hawver Cave," Fred said.

"That's it!" Daphne chuckled. "I had a picnic out there once..."

As she rambled with her story, her voice slow and slurred, probably from indulging in one too many cocktails, I muted the call and shared the destination with Timothy.

He typed the location into his phone. It was forty miles away, and about the same time to drive there.

"We need to go now," I said.

Timothy put the car in drive and merged onto the street.

"Daphne, finish your story in a minute. I need to tell August something."

"I'm telling August something," Daphne said.

"But I have to tell him something important."

"Uh, oh," Maya said.

"Important?" Daphne asked. "My story isn't important?"

"August, before I die," Fred said, speaking loudly and quickly, "the mine is a little over a mile from the trailhead. I'm sending you the electronic guide."

I unmuted the phone. "Thank you."

I rested my head on the warm glass of the passenger window with a sense of relief. If the location ended up being correct, I would arrive an hour before Quinn planned to unleash the chaos. That revelation brought a genuine smile to my face. It was the first time I felt hope in a while.

"You get it?" Fred asked.

I glanced at my messages to confirm it had come through. "Got it. I have one more question."

"Go ahead," Maya said.

I thought about last night, of the murders Wilson had accused me of, and I thought of earlier, of Claire claiming she saw me and Trisha as manticores. I thought of the arachnids hazy in my memory.

"If possible, can you find out about any marketable or off-market drugs that incite fear-based hallucinations and prevent the brain from forming concrete memories? It should also have the capability of being deployed through an aerosol."

"You want me to identify a drug?" Maya asked.

"I need to know how to negate its effects."

"August." Something lived within her voice—despair, maybe, or fear. She remained quiet for a handful of seconds, before saying in a whisper, "I can't."

I glanced at my feet. "What do you mean you can't?"

"Do you trust me?"

"Yes," I said without hesitation.

"We can't... we can't waste any more time on your behalf." The words spilled off her tongue in broken fragments.

"What do you mean?"

"I can't tell you, otherwise I risk distracting you."

"Maya, you're scaring me. What happened?"

"If the opportunity arises, and you have a shot at Quinn, don't take it." Maya hung up the phone.

I held the phone to my ear, frozen with confusion at what had happened.

Maya, Fred, and Daphne had refused to help me. Why? Had Quinn got to them? Did he have their hands tied? I doubted that. Maya would've pushed a coded message through the line, much like Quinn had spoken in riddles about his tasks for me. She hadn't, though. She had flatly refused to help me.

Why?

Do you trust me?

I nodded my head. I trusted her, and I had to allow that trust to remain strong. That left me alone, though.

Well, nearly alone.

Timothy stole a look at me as he drove. "We have to stop for gas."

"I'll cover the cost."

"You okay?"

I stared out the passenger window, considering his question, but I didn't answer him.

Next Step.
Tuesday, July 25th.
1927hrs.

MAYA GENTLY PLACED HER cell phone on the kitchen table beside her half-eaten dinner plate.

The enchiladas had tasted fresh and light, worthy of a fistful of cash for a bite, but Maya's appetite had slipped away with each lingering minute, lost like Alina and August.

She stared at the dark screen of her phone and swallowed back a mouthful of guilt.

Had she really just told a desperate, pleading August that she couldn't help him? That he had to fend for himself?

She placed her trembling hands flat on her chair's seat and sat on them to keep them still. Her eyes lifted, peered across the table to Fred.

The giant man wore a grimace, as he, too, sat in a considerable amount of pain and mental turmoil. Daphne placed her hand on his. The size difference looked like a child grabbing the hand of her father.

"What's the next step?" Maya asked, unable to sit and self-loathe for too long.

"I don't know," Fred said.

"We have to do something. Alina needs us. August needs us. Yet, we're sitting around a table, eating a delicious meal like nothing is wrong. What are we doing here?"

"We needed to eat."

Maya eyed Fred with skepticism. "Why did you have me come here? We could have been in and out of a Taco Bell drive-thru, finished with our meal, back at work already. We can't afford to be doing this right now."

Fred glanced at Daphne and sighed. "You and August are very much the same person." He took a deep breath. "And I'm like you, too. Rather, I was like you."

"What are you talking about?"

"Like you, I had a pretty traumatic childhood. The details don't matter, so I won't go into them. However, I coped with my trauma much like you and August cope with your pasts. I ran and hid from my pain. I buried the hurt by losing myself in football at a young age. It was my only escape, and I made it out."

Maya had never heard Fred speak in such a manner—so deliberately, with pace and thought, as if each word muttered from his lips held immense weight. Enough weight, at least, to hold down her tongue, to prevent her from interrupting.

"After August killed Aaron Brooks, he, too, ran from that pain. He buried himself in alcohol, and we lost him for a while. He never dug himself out of that hole, Maya. He just dug in a different direction. He created a warren, moving from alcohol to exercise to work, but he never climbed upward and outward. He remained in the dark, buried and isolated. You didn't know August before the incident. Did you know he used to smile?"

"He still smiles."

"I mean, he would smile just to smile. We called him Joker, because he always smiled. He also loved pranks." Fred trailed off for a second, as if tripping from his recollection. "Recently, he came close to the surface again. After asking the Brooks' to forgive him, after going to Aaron's gravesite. He has come close, but he's still lost beneath the ground."

"What are you trying to say, Fred?" Maya asked, growing impatient. "We don't have the time for you to ramble."

"You do the same thing as I did, as August does. You run and hide from your pain. You have buried yourself from your past."

Maya considered what he said, and his words hit close to the mark.

Maya, similar to August, distracted herself with her work. She always worked. When she wasn't working, she drank. She wasn't punching in the same drunken weight class that August had punched in during his binging, but she could hold her own in a fight against Jim, Jack, or Jose.

"I know you run and hide," Fred said, "because I did the same thing. I ran, dedicating every waking second to football. It ruined my relationship with my family and friends. It nearly ruined my relationship with Daphne. Football trumped everything, because I made it everything." Fred crossed his tree-trunk arms over his chest.

"I get it," Maya said. "People cope with their past by distracting themselves with other things. So what? We move forward. We live. We do our best. We help our family and friends, which means we have to save August and Alina." Maya stood from her chair. "I'm leaving. I'm going to find Alina. Once I do, I'm switching my sights back to August, and I'll find him."

"There's coping, which is a fancy word for surviving. Then there's conquering. There's defeating your past. There's living in the present and preparing for a future as a victor."

Maya rolled her eyes. "Fred, you've read one too many self-help books." She faced Daphne. "Daphne, thank you for dinner. As always, it was splendid."

"I conquered my past," Fred said. "I confronted my demons and overcame them. You know what, though? I had to stop running first, because running away is exhausting and you can't fight if you're worn out, if your back is to the enemy. I had to rest, build my strength, face my fear, and then fight. Does that make sense?"

"Nothing you ever say makes sense," Maya said.

"I brought you here to rest. To distract yourself from the chase, if only for thirty minutes. To enjoy a warm meal, a cold drink, and a few laughs."

"To waste time."

"To recharge!"

"You've only made me impatient and frustrated."

Fred sighed. "One more example."

"Please, God, no."

"It's like when you're looking for something, and you turn over the entire house searching for it, but it's nowhere to be found. Eventually, you give up."

"I'm giving up on this conversation."

"You sit down and relax." Fred smacked his hands together. "Then it hits you. You remember where you left the lost item."

"In my car, driving away from here to get back to what matters."

"Our lives are like that, too."

"I can't sit here and not do a single thing for them." Maya grabbed her purse and headed to the front door, trembling with anger at Fred for having wasted her time so he could steal a quick bite to eat.

As Maya wrapped her hand around the doorknob, something lost in her mind came into focus and clicked—something Alina had said on the phone earlier.

Daniel Quinn, that's a pseudonym. If that was a real name, August would have found him by now. He's using a fake name.

Maya cursed under her breath, baffled they hadn't looked deeper into the notion before. She hesitated, not wanting to prove Fred's obscure strategy successful, but she swallowed her pride and shuffled back into the kitchen.

"Fred, I hate you."

"Did stepping away from the task work?" He presented a prideful grin.

"I'm an idiot."

Fred cocked his head. "Not an idiot, but you're often a fool."

Maya flexed her hands. "About six months ago, while August and I still worked at the bookstore, a used book arrived. It was titled *The Weird, the Strange, the Impossible in Everyday Life.*"

"A terrible title," Fred said.

"I didn't read it, but I showed it to August. He had just started the paranormal gig, and I was freelancing for *The Here & Now.* Most of our conversations centered on the supernatural. Anyway, neither of us had ever seen the book before. So, we flipped through it. It was a guide on how to create practical effects—costumes, makeup, animatronics, puppets, and other props—to replicate the supernatural world for film. The author marketed it toward amateur film makers with low budgets." Maya spun on her heel and trotted back to the front door.

"Where are you going?" Fred asked. "You didn't finish your story."

"I need to find Alina, which means I need to go speak with Stephen. He knows something, and I'm going to draw that information from him."

"Should I go with you?" Fred asked.

"No." Maya opened the front door and glanced back through the entryway, which had a straight view of the dining room and the table where Fred sat. "You're going to find August."

"How?"

"The author of that book I told you about."

"What about the author?"

"His name was Dan Quincy."

"Dan Quincy?" Fred asked.

"I'm sure it's a pseudonym, just like Daniel Quinn isn't the man's real name. Find the author of that book. That's your job. That's how you save August."

The Hunt.
Tuesday, July 25th.
1947hrs.

"Uh," Alina groaned. She gently touched her head for an injury. Relief and surprise poured into her when her hand came back without a trace of blood, without feeling a hard goose egg.

Despite the lack of physical damage, she had a severe headache; her brain bounced around in a blender spinning at low speed. The grinding, bumping noise didn't ebb and flow, either. It existed in a state of chronic, never-ending pain. It was the headache that had awoken her from the dead, comatose slumber. Still, despite having woken, she refused to open her eyes to face whatever hell awaited her. The blending agony behind her eyes and between her ears couldn't cope.

Not yet.

Instead, she struggled to orient herself. What had happened? Where was she?

The last thing she remembered was Jericho tying a burlap sack around her face, carrying her to the rooftop, and throwing her into a helicopter.

What had happened afterward? Where had they flown her to? Why?

Answers wouldn't pop free from the haziness clouding her thundering mind. She would have to face the truth, eventually. It was just that keeping her eyes closed meant she could remain in the dark, hiding from her pain and from her murky situation. Except Alina had never been one to sit on her laurels, to sit around and allow life to happen to her. She controlled her destiny.

With a deep breath and a force of will against her headache and the terror sweating from her pores, Alina opened her eyes.

A dreary, dark forest sprawled out before her. The trees pierced the cloud-dark sky. A light mist fell over her, and a damp, chilly breeze worked through the tree trunks and across the muddy ground. In the distance, seemingly from every direction, waves crashed onto a shore.

Alina sat and propped herself against the stump of a felled tree. Mud caked the right side of her body, soaking her clothes, matting her hair, sticking to her skin. For a few minutes, she remained seated, breathing, basking in the coolness of the late evening. The wind and wet helped to soften the burning within her head.

She reached into her pocket, mostly out of habit, for her cell phone, coming up empty. She tried her other pockets, none of which had anything in them. Jericho had not only rendered her unconscious for God knew how long, but he had confiscated all her belongings.

When Alina felt ready, she stood. She held the stump for balance as the forest lurched and heaved like a ship caught in a storm on the ocean. For a miserable minute, Alina thought she might vomit, but the sensation passed, and the heat drained from her face. She spit, clearing the taste of bile from her mouth.

Straightening her posture, Alina glanced around the shadow-thick forest.

Where am I? She thought.

Had the helicopter taken her to the coast, somewhere near Santa Cruz, hence the redwood forest and the ocean-salt air? Unlikely. The surrounding trees, though immense and ancient, weren't the renowned redwoods of Santa Cruz... or so she thought. She had only seen the redwoods at a distance during her recent vacation there with August, his family, and the Blue Moon crew, so she wasn't entirely sure.

The sun drooped in the sky, revealing the westward direction. The only location that made sense, given she had arrived at the destination the same day Jericho had flown her out, was somewhere off the Pacific Coast. With the sun setting to the west, Alina turned toward the east—the most probable direction to get back home.

If she headed east, what would she find? A beach? A dock? A boat?

"There's only one way to find out," she said, heading eastward.

Her steps were wobbly, as her nerves still adjusted to the jolting awakening. As she muttered inspiration to herself, an explosive sneeze interrupted her.

Alina froze mid-stride. She focused on the spot where the sudden noise had shot forth. She saw a silhouette crouched behind the tall bushes.

Without removing her eyes from the threat, Alina squatted. Her fingers scraped the muddy ground for a rock or a thick branch. The rough surface of a stone greeted her, and she grabbed it. She stood and crossed toward the figure hiding in the shrubs.

"I see you!" Alina hoped to disguise the fear streaking through her body with a semblance of confidence by raising her voice. "I played pitcher for my high school softball team." A lie. Alina, though athletic enough, never enjoyed the idea of team sports. "I'm as accurate as a marine sniper with a ball in my hand... or, in this case, a ball-shaped rock. You have three seconds to step forward, or I'll throw the rock at you. The last time my coaches clocked my pitch speed, it reached over eighty-miles-per-hour." Another lie, and Alina wasn't even sure if that was impressive or believable. She didn't care, though. "One. Two."

"Okay." A teenage boy emerged with his hands raised above his head. He was tall, maybe six-three, and he had long, shaggy hair that kissed his shoulders. "What's wrong with you, anyway? You were going to throw a rock at me? That could kill someone. We're supposed to be working together out here. Geez Louise."

His carefree attitude nearly disarmed Alina. To counter his demeanor, she cocked the rock over her shoulder, ready to throw it at him, or hit him with it, depending on the circumstance.

"Who are you?" she asked.

"Rhett."

"Rhett who?"

"Hill. Who are you?"

"I'm asking the questions."

"Okay."

"Why were you hiding in the bushes like a pervert?"

He grimaced. "There's a lot to unpack there, and I can see why you connoted my bush prowling with perverted tendencies." Rhett cleared his throat and glanced over his shoulder. "Also, however this unfolds, whatever happens within the next few seconds, trust me, I'm not a pervert."

Alina's grip tightened on the rock. "What does that mean?"

"I'm a captive on this island just like you. I'm running for my life so the monster doesn't kill me."

"Monster?"

"We heard the helicopter, saw it fly away, and we headed here to investigate. I hid, like a pervert, as you unkindly mentioned, because if you were a threat, I didn't want you to notice me."

"Well, great job at not getting noticed."

"That wasn't me," Rhett said, glancing over his shoulder again. "That was her."

"Who?"

"Nora," Rhett said. "It's okay."

For a moment, nothing happened. Then a young girl, no older than ten, appeared from the shrubs. A layer of muck covered the front of her body and face.

Alina couldn't contain her swelling laughter. "Rhett Hill, I don't know what to think of you. You're hiding in the bushes with a ten-year-old girl?"

"Nine," Nora said.

"She hardly talks," Rhett said. "When she does, she has a mild attitude problem."

"I'm stuck with a moron. I have an excuse for poor attitude. I'm going to die."

Rhett smirked at Alina and shrugged. "Do you see what I mean?"

"Who are you?" Nora asked.

"Alina Moore." Alina glanced between the two ragged, worn looking individuals before her. "You said you're captives on this island. What does that mean?"

"Kidnapped," Rhett said. "Brought here on a boat—well, someone brought me here on a boat. Nora, like you, had the first-class transportation of a private helicopter. And people have the audacity to complain about gender equality."

Alina rolled her eyes, not sure if Rhett annoyed or amused her. "You heard and saw the helicopter that dropped me off?"

"We hoped to intercept it, but it flew off like thirty minutes after we first heard it. I thought we should continue to the castle, but Nora figured the chopper had dropped off another one of us."

"Increase our chances of surviving," Nora said.

"You know the old saying," Rhett said. "Two feet can pedal a bike, but six legs can... six hands can row a—"

"He's done that a few times now," Nora said. "He quotes some gibberish he made up on the spot. Do you see why I felt the need to ally with a third person?"

"You said there's a monster hunting us?" Alina asked.

Rhett reached into his pocket and removed a torn, muddy, unreadable note. "Samantha found this before she went missing."

Alina's breath hitched. "Who?"

"Samantha. This other girl who was on the boat with me. She found this note. Next thing I knew, I'm waking up in the forest, and she's gone. I haven't seen her since."

"Was she short?" Alina asked, speaking the first thought that popped into her head as she recovered from what Rhett had said.

"I mean, I guess. She's shorter than you. Probably Nora's height, but stockier, you know? More mature." Rhett cupped his hands a few inches in front of his chest.

Alina curled her face in disgust at the description.

It wasn't a coincidence, though. Rhett referred to Samantha Graves. Samantha had been on this island with him, but she had returned home.

"We'll circle back to Samantha," Alina said, more focused on her current predicament. "What's the note say?"

Rhett clicked his tongue. "Based on memory, it starts with, Greetings. It continues with, we're on a remote island, one not found on a map, and a monster lives on the island. A monster that requires the flesh of humans to live. It chose us as its meal. Lucky us, right?" Rhett chuckled. "Also, it said there's no escaping the island, except through death, obviously." Rhett glanced at the canopied forest ceiling. "What else? The monster's name is Ass-Terry... Ascary... something weird like that. I don't remember. It's some ancient monster with an appetite for kids, though. Only through eating a lot of children on a regular schedule will it stay on this island and not venture into more populated areas.

The note ended with something like we should consider ourselves lucky because we're meaningful sacrifices to prevent a great evil from destroying the world. Then, the writer wished us an expedient death, like a true gentleman would... or gentlewoman. Gender equality." Rhett tapped his temple with an index finger.

"Asterion?" Alina asked.

Rhett popped his lips. "What?"

"A monster who feeds on children as sacrifices. Was the creature's name Asterion?"

"Oh, yeah. That sounds right."

"He's from Greek mythology."

Rhett raised an eyebrow and whistled. "Dude has been here for that long? No, no, no. That's crazy. That's impossible."

Alina brushed her forearm across her nose. "Asterion, the Minotaur, required the sacrifice of Athenian children."

"I'm not Athenian, though," Rhett said. "Wait, what's Athenian. Am I Athenian?"

"The Minotaur isn't real, you moron," Nora said.

"She's right," Alina said.

"About me being a moron? Not you, too."

"The monster haunting this island is some sick person recreating the myth. They're kidnapping children and sending them here as a sacrifice. That's why I was supposed to volunteer," Alina said, more to herself than to Rhett or Nora. "They were going to send me here, but Samantha volunteered and came instead. When Terry learned of the mistake, he must have sent someone to come back for her. Then I walked right through their doors."

"What are you talking about?" Rhett asked. "Who's they? Volunteer for what? Why would they come back for Samantha?"

"They are her parents, and they came back for her because they didn't want to kill their daughter."

Rhett's eyes went wide as saucers. "Samantha's parents are the Minotaur?"

"I don't know." Alina's thoughts jumped to her father.

Stephen had urged her to volunteer—he had tipped the magician to choose her for his trick. Had he known what would happen? Did he know about this island, about the Minotaur? What did Stephen get for selling Alina as a sacrifice to the beast?

"What do we do?" Nora asked, her voice loud against the wind and the tide.

"Have you seen it yet?" Alina asked.

Rhett shook his head. "Not yet. When I woke up—the second time, that is—I was still near the shore. I've been hiking upward most of the day. The helicopter dropped Nora off in a clearing. I ran to it, hoping they meant to save me. They flew off, though, leaving her behind. We continued hiking uphill until we saw your helicopter, and we hurried to it."

"Uphill? Why uphill? Why not to the shore?"

Rhett pursed his lips. "There's a castle at the top of the hill. Who knows, maybe there's a phone or some weapons, too. At the very least, maybe there's food and some water, warmth from the cold out here. Also, I didn't know what else to do. We can't escape from the shore, and we're on an island. There's nowhere to run, unless you want to swim."

"A castle?" Alina asked.

"Like something from a fairytale," Nora said.

Rhett pointed at the young girl and nodded. "She's right. Like something from *Game of Thrones*."

"That's not like a fairytale," Nora said.

"She understood the point."

Alina briefly reviewed her situation. She was on a mysterious island with a seventeen-year-old boy and a grade-school-aged girl, hunted by a mythical creature. Few options presented themselves. Venture off alone, or trust the two strangers enough to stick with them and hopefully work together to get off the island.

Alina sighed, deciding to cast her fate with Nora and Rhett.

"We'll call ourselves the Athenian Three," she said.

"The A*three*nian," Rhett said, chuckling.

Alina couldn't help but share in his amusement.

Rhett might present as a little dull, but he possessed something interesting about him—a light that shined through this pervading darkness. He seemed like the person Alina would want beside her if lost.

As she smiled, spitballing more group names with Rhett and Nora, she hoped her intuition would prove correct.

The Exchange.
Tuesday, July 25th.
1951hrs.

MAYA PARKED AT THE Motel 6 in downtown Sacramento and stared out of her dusty, cracked windshield.

She rubbed her heavy, weary eyes and removed her phone from the cupholder to call her sister—Alina's mom.

Wanda recently finished a rehab program, and she temporarily lived with Maya as the custody battle for Alina waged between her and Stephen.

Wanda's voice sounded heavy, thick with sleep. "My shift at the diner starts at four in the morning. It takes an hour to dress and walk there, which means I set my alarm for two-thirty. I value sleep, and you're cutting into it."

"It's not even nine o'clock," Maya said, rolling her eyes.

"We've lived together almost two weeks now. I go to bed at eight every night to wake up at two-thirty. You should know I need a full night's sleep to function."

Maya furrowed her brow and thought about her sister's pattern. How had she not recognized Wanda went to bed so early every night? Was she really so involved in her research and writing that she failed to notice her recovering sister? Maybe Fred was right. Maybe Maya ran without bothering to stop for anyone else, least of all herself.

"Maya, you there?" Wanda asked.

"I'm here."

"Is everything okay?"

Maya and August had more than just running away from their pasts in common. They believed and practiced one core value. Honesty. Honesty, no matter how brutal or cold or destructive, was always kinder and warmer and more restorative than dishonesty, or so they believed. It's what drew her to August, and most likely him to her.

That and their undeniable attractiveness.

Maya wouldn't subvert her beliefs now, not in the face of conflict. She wouldn't hold her tongue to save her sister's peace of mind. Wanda, of all people, deserved the truth.

Maya swallowed a wad of nerves. "Alina went missing."

"She ran away?"

"Kidnapped."

Wanda exhaled a whirlwind of air. "It's Stephen."

Maya stole a page from August's book. She said nothing; instead, she waited for Wanda to grow weary of the quiet and continue speaking.

The way Wanda said Stephen's name signaled Maya to practice patience. Her sister hadn't casually blamed her husband because he represented everything wrong in their lives. She said his name with sincerity and weight.

With heavy regret.

"You should've seen how he reacted when they first proposed the idea," Wanda said, her voice small and shaky. "I thought he actually might accept their offer." She sniffled. "I don't know what kind of trouble he found in Indiana, but if Alina's missing, I guarantee that's why he came back to Sacramento. He never wanted custody of her. He wanted a way out of his life, and he sold his soul for a key."

Maya shivered. She had used that same expression when stepping foot in the Graves' estate.

What did you do, sell your soul to the Devil?

"Who proposed what idea?" Maya asked. "What happened?"

Wanda took a second before responding. "I'm not sure how long ago this happened. Five years, maybe. Alina wasn't any older than ten or eleven. Stephen and I... our lives had caught up to us. The drugs, gambling debt, retribution payments, rent. We didn't have money, and we owed a lot to powerful people. To survive, we only ate once a day, if we ate at all. We stopped paying utilities—no showers, no heat, no garbage service. We casually searched for employment, but no right-minded business owner cared to hire two junkies who didn't own a car between them. So, Stephen and I resorted to other means to make a dollar. He was my pimp for a time. We robbed people, we burglarized homes. We did what we had to do to repay our debts and buy another high."

Maya bit her tongue, held it clamped between her teeth. She tasted blood. It was the only way to prevent herself from interrupting. Sure, Maya had made her fair share of mistakes, but not with a child to care for.

"Alina was there for some of it," Wanda said after another second. "That's how they noticed her. I remember how the man looked so clearly. He had a harsh face. Not ugly, but... mean. His breath smelled like old coffee, and his body odor stank of something sour, yet he reeked of money. He offered a lot of money to us." Wanda paused again, struggling against the emotions her memories most likely conjured. "Maya, he offered a lot of money. Money our family wouldn't possess for ten generations combined. 'For the girl,' he said, and he glanced at Alina."

Why was Alina in your house when all this transpired? Maya wanted to ask, but the question would only lead to anger and accusation. She had to stay focused, so she remained quiet.

"Stephen pulled me aside, as if he actually wanted to have a conversation about selling our daughter to the man. I shut the idea down immediately, before he even proposed entertaining the idea. I would rather live in an actual pigsty than sell my daughter to the creep."

"Who was the man?" Maya asked.

"I never learned his name."

"What did he look like, apart from having a mean face?"

"I don't know. Middle-aged. Dark hair, clean shaven... big, too. Not just muscular, but beastly."

That didn't provide information to act on.

The next question, Maya preferred not to ask. The answer seemed too obvious. Even though she didn't want to know it as truth, she had to know.

Maya cleared her throat. "Why would he want Alina?"

"You must understand something. Stephen didn't change when he moved to Indiana."

"I understand that."

"If not for me interfering that day, he would have sold Alina to that man. I saw the dollar signs in his eyes when he heard the selling price."

Maya's throat tightened to the size of a straw, yet she forced out the three-word sentence. "She's his daughter."

"Not to him," Wanda said. "Alina, to him, was and is nothing but a burden. To get rid of her for a fortune... that's an answered prayer, a dream turned to reality."

Maya clicked her tongue and glanced at the car's rearview mirror. She thought of what Alina had been trying to tell her all day, and she absent-mindedly spoke her thoughts aloud. "Stephen wanted Alina to volunteer for the magic trick. She refused, and the Graves girl volunteered instead. She went missing."

What did Terry and Wendy Graves have to do with this?

The silent question brought forth a burning-bright answer, like a falling star streaking toward the earth. Maya bolted upright and twisted the steering wheel in her anxious grip.

"I've got to go."

"Go where?" Wanda asked, the worry in her voice obvious. "You won't get yourself in trouble, will you?"

"I live and breathe trouble."

"At least tell me what you're planning."

Maya considered the request.

Alina was missing. Throughout their conversation, though, Wanda had spoken with an unsettling calmness. Sure, she hadn't ever been Mom of the Year, but to not show any emotion at the news seemed odd.

Did Wanda play a role in Alina's disappearance? Maya refused to believe that, but what else could she think?

Wanda had abandoned her daughter many times before—for drugs, for sex, for the simple freedom of not having a child. Yeah, she had recently completed rehab... but, so what?

What if she and Stephen fought so fiercely for custody because they had the same benefactor, the same buyer. Because they both wished to make the same transaction—Alina for enough money to escape their lives.

It made Maya's stomach roil to have such a thought, but she couldn't help her suspicions. Neither could she share her plans with Wanda.

"I have a few stops to make," Maya said, remaining vague. "I plan on finding and saving your daughter, though."

Maya hung up the phone. She pressed her head against the headrest and lifted her gaze to stare out the sunroof at the night sky. She had a simple, impulsive, probably idiotic plan.

Barge unannounced into Stephen's room and demand that he answer her questions. If he refused—

"Then, what?" Maya asked herself, chuckling.

She was five-six and had to weigh only half as much as Stephen.

Throughout the years, she had enrolled in a few combat classes. Eddie Denier, the Voodoo Killer and her ex-boyfriend—apparently now dead—had nudged her to take a self-defense class through the police department. Maya also exercised with weights nearly every day. In a pinch, she could hold her own.

Still, why tempt fate? Why confront Stephen, a desperate man, alone?

To help Alina, Maya had to look out for herself first.

Exhaling, Maya scrolled through her contacts. Her finger hovered over Fred's name. She thought twice, though. He was working on saving August, and August needed someone looking out for him.

Maya considered calling Detective Wilson. That thought had holes enough to leak. While he had helped Blue Moon, specifically August, in the past, the Sacramento Police Department employed Detective Wilson—the department which had dropped their investigation into Samantha Graves' disappearance, and the department who believed Alina had fled town to avoid arrest. Could Maya trust Wilson?

Next, Maya scrolled to Jake Stallings' name, August's brother-in-law. He was working his way through the police academy, hoping to get on with the Stockton Police Department. Would he come up to Sacramento to provide help? Maya chewed on the thought. Essentially, she planned to break into a hotel room to extract information from Stephen in whatever manner she saw most effective. Maya wouldn't risk Jake's career... not if other options were available.

One option remained.

Maya hated herself for considering it. She hated herself all the more for tapping on his name and dialing his number.

"I was just about to call you," Evan answered.

"You busy?"

"Just stepped out of the shower. I missed you in there. It's tough to reach my back while all alone."

"I need you," Maya said.

"You're picturing me standing naked in the steaming bathroom, dripping wet with hot water, aren't you? I would need me, too."

"Evan, I need you in Sacramento. I need your help."

He paused for a beat. "You're asking me for help?" His voice lost the edge of banter, replaced with something more blunt and serious. "What's going on, Maya? Are you okay?"

"Alina went missing."

"Like... what do you mean missing?"

Maya swallowed. "Police think she ran off, but I know better than that."

"What do you think?"

"Somebody took her."

"I'm getting dressed now," Evan said. "Where am I meeting you?"

At his willingness to drop everything and join her, a warmth grew inside of Maya.

"Motel 6, downtown Sacramento."

"I'll be there in thirty minutes."

Evan arrived twenty-six minutes later.

Maya had killed the time by digging into Tara Ferneau. She searched the supervising detective's name into Google and went to work. It wasn't grade-A research, but it skimmed the surface of the woman's illustrious and lucrative career. Ferneau's social media accounts also told the story of a detective with an absurd amount of disposable income—first-class vacations, VIP passes to concerts and sporting events, hunting safaris, and Michelin-star restaurant experiences.

In California, if someone worked for the state, their income showed publicly. Maya looked up Ferneau's income, curious how she supported such an extravagant lifestyle. Ferneau made a detective's salary, give or take a few thousand dollars, most likely based on her overtime hours.

Something, rather, a lot of something, didn't add up.

Maya returned to Ferneau's Facebook account and navigated to her husband's profile. Manson Ferneau. He worked as a pipe welder for the union. As with Tara, he had a solid career, but not one that warranted their celebrity lifestyle. They were both in their early forties, no children, so they could have banked a lot of their income, especially if they worked a lot of overtime hours in their twenties and thirties to splurge in their forties.

"Still," Maya said, clicking through Manson's Facebook pictures, "a private jet?"

Maya didn't think they owned it, but they had pictures of themselves chartering one, drinking expensive Champagne and bourbon.

Maya dug into the public record of their property. Had one of their parents passed away, leaving a massive inheritance? Nope. The Ferneaus had purchased their twenty-acre ranch about two years back. No deaths in the family. No inherited fortune.

Thoughts of the Graves jumped into Maya's mind. He had skyrocketed his income about two years back. They claimed Terry's foot business generated their incredible fortune. Maya had a difficult, if not impossible, time believing that. Now the Graves lived in a home reserved for television shows and movies.

Knuckles rapped on the passenger window, startling Maya from her research.

Evan stood outside the car, hunched over and grinning. He waved, wiggling his fingers.

Maya breathed, calming herself, slowing her heart. She unlocked the car and stepped outside. "Hey," she called over the roof.

"Hey. You look nice."

Maya glanced at her outfit—baggy jeans, combat boots, and the tight-fitting Star Wars-themed T-shirt that belonged to Alina. "I try my best to look sexy."

"It works." Evan flashed a grin and worked around the hood of the car. He embraced Maya, kissed her. "I missed you, and I—"

"Not now," Maya said, putting a finger over his lips.

She couldn't stand to hear him say I love you. Not at that moment. Not until they found Alina and brought her home.

"So, what's with the one-star motel? We hoping to contract lice? I haven't shaved my head in over a decade, so I think it's about time."

"I like bald men," Maya said, breaking away from Evan. She marched toward the stairs leading to the second story.

Evan chased after her. "Is Alina here? What's going on?"

"We're breaking into a room. I need you for muscle."

"For muscle? I don't like what that implies, but I enjoy the compliment."

Maya reached the cement stairwell and turned to Evan. "I don't like that my niece has gone missing, but I enjoy that you're here to help me get her back." She smirked and took the steps two at a time.

The Second Labor. Tuesday, July 25th. 2006hrs.

TIMOTHY PULLED HIS ACURA to the shoulder of Highway 49, just before the turnoff to Quarry Road Trail. I could have asked him to continue to the trail's parking area, which would have saved a hundred yards for my hike, but I preferred he remain covert.

We sat in a moment of pre-battle quiet. The sun sank low in the darkening, orange-hued sky, slowly surrendering to the night. Large hills with a forest of pines growing off the slopes surrounded us. The American River cut through it all. Behind where we had parked, the No Hands Bridge connected one road to another. A hill backdropped the bridge, and the sun dropped below the hillside.

The entire scene was hauntingly beautiful—the eerie silence or the unnatural calm before a disaster.

I inhaled deeply through my nose. "You're going to stay here." I faced Timothy, turning away from the splendor and focusing on the task at hand. "If a cop or a Good Samaritan pulls over to ask if you need help, tell them you're tired or you were afraid to keep driving. You pulled over to calm down. Hopefully, they'll leave you alone with no follow-up questions."

Timothy scrunched his face and tilted his head. "If people are in trouble, don't we want the cops involved? Shouldn't we call the police, send an officer to your location to help?"

"No!" The answer came too quickly, too harshly. I inhaled again, having to be mindful of my firing nerves. "No," I said in a more neutral tone. "No cops. Otherwise we risk the safety of those we're helping."

"Yeah, sure." Timothy scratched his messy hair. "What if something happens to you, though? How will I know? Do I sit here all night? Do I go after you after so much time?"

Quinn had said the fireworks wouldn't begin until 2100hrs, less than an hour from now. That's when our stopwatch began. I mentally calculated the time the labor should take, using the length of the first labor as a marker. I tacked on a handful of minutes for the hike back from the abandoned mine.

"Wait here until midnight," I said, allotting myself way too much time. Honestly, if Timothy didn't hear from me in the next hour, he probably could have considered me dead. Still, I preferred to give myself too much time than too little.

"If you're not back, then what?"

I considered sharing Maya's and Fred's numbers with him, but thought of what Maya had said.

Do you trust me?

I gave him Wilson's number instead. "Call this number directly. Wilson is a detective who's working with me on this. He'll know what to do." I glanced to the backseat where Timothy had tossed his backpack. "Did you grab the first aid?"

"It's in the bag."

I reached back and retrieved the backpack. Timothy had stuffed clean bandages, alcohol wipes, hydrogen peroxide, Neosporin, and painkillers into the pack, along with a fillet knife and a flashlight.

I set the flashlight in the cupholder, pressed the overhead cab lights to turn them on, and went to work at cleaning the puncture wound in my hand.

Timothy picked up the flashlight and investigated it. "This just came in a few days ago." He powered on a high beam—a disorienting light similar to that used by law enforcement. "It's called the StrikeLight. Beautiful, huh?"

I grimaced as I peeled the old bandage from my hand. "What's special about it?"

"It's a three-in-one flashlight. The high beam." Timothy pressed the button again, and the intense light dimmed, representing the brightness of a standard flashlight. "The low beam setting." The light shifted to red. "Red light, for improved night vision. But that's not the coolest feature." Timothy grinned at me.

I clenched my jaw as I poured the hydrogen peroxide over the open wound. The liquid bubbled and fizzed. After a second, I cleaned the gunk away with an alcohol wipe.

"What's the coolest feature?"

Timothy pressed another button, and the unmistakable arc warning of a stun gun sounded. The sudden, threatening noise startled me. Timothy must have noticed me flinch. He chuckled.

"It does more than bark," he said, pressing another button. Electricity flashed between two prongs. "The flashlight is also a close-contact stun gun."

I wrapped the clean bandage around my palm and eyed Timothy. "A StrikeLight?"

"Pretty sweet, huh?"

"Pretty sweet."

Timothy placed it back in the center cupholder. "You'll need it more than me."

I leaned my head against the seat and looked at the young man. "You don't know me," I said. "You don't know what I'm really doing out here. Yet, you're helping me. That makes me slightly suspicious. People rarely do things like that."

Timothy nodded. "Well, I looked through your phone, and I looked you up. You're halfway famous in this area."

"That's an exaggeration."

"August Watson, the paranormal private investigator. Not a quack, either. You solved the Doppelgänger case and proved Claire Balzan's innocence. You caught a serial killer in Santa Cruz. You solved the Voodoo Killer mystery." He chuckled beneath his breath.

"I had a lot of help."

"Well, I wanted a crack at helping you with this case. My only foray into the world of adventure is through fantasy novels and Dungeons and Dragons. Accompanying you, though, I'm on a real-life quest to defeat... what are we after? Vampires? Ghosts? Zombies?"

"I'm hunting mythical monsters."

"Like dragons?"

"A little like that."

"We're on a quest to slay a dragon?"

"A hydra," I said.

Timothy frowned. "That's a type of dragon, right?"

I wasn't sure, but I didn't care which species the hydra fell under. "Listen, if you want to help, you can flex your research skills and look something up for me."

"Anything."

"Find an airborne drug that makes someone hallucinate their fears..." I trailed off, my thoughts jumping to Claire and Trisha.

They hadn't witnessed their greatest fears. They had both seen the manticore. Had Quinn decided what they would hallucinate? That seemed to border on the impossible.

I couldn't leave any stone unturned, though. "Or find an aerosol drug that would force the user's mind to become malleable to suggestion."

Again, my thoughts drifted. I had said aerosol not airborne that time, and it yanked free a new realization. Steven Anderson, the man behind the gargoyle attacks, had used an aerosol to infect his victims. He, like many others directly related to my previous cases, had gone missing over the past few weeks.

Had Anderson and Quinn allied with each other?

That was a terrifying thought.

"Is that it?" Timothy asked.

"The drug won't allow the user to piece together fresh memories, much like alcohol prevents someone drunk from forming memories. Research with the idea of Hera forcing Hercules into a state of madness, with Greek mythology or history as a lens."

"Yeah, okay."

"Midnight," I said. "If I'm not back by then, contact Detective Wilson."

"Will you be back?"

I hadn't expected the question, and I hadn't considered the answer. I took a moment to mull it over, thinking of Hercules' second labor. The hydra's lair was in or near Lake Lerna. According to some sources, Lake Lerna was the entrance to the Underworld. To enter the Underworld meant to die.

"I doubt it." I opened the passenger door. "If you learn anything from your research, call me."

The mile-and-a-half hike took me a little less than thirty minutes. The dark-orange, purple sky guided my steps. Still, I carried the Strikelight, thumb on the button, in case something popped out at me. My trek went without interference, though, at least until I arrived at a rusted steel gate preventing access into the mine.

Three posted signs adorned the gate.

The center one screamed NO TRESSPASSING. THE AREA BEYOND THIS SIGN IS OWNED BY THE BUREAU of RECLAMATION.

Another sign, more of a placard, provided information on the history of the mine, including sketches of a black-and-white woolly mammoth, saber-toothed tiger, sloth, and other prehistoric animals.

A smaller sign warned of video surveillance.

I gripped the flashlight tighter. My body tingled. A cold draft from within the bowels of the mine rose and greeted me at the gate. I reached for the chain holding the iron bars, and the links slid free, dropping to the rocky earth and coiling in a mound.

I pushed the rusted gate. The hinges whined and creaked, opening into the heavy darkness beyond.

Before entering, I glanced up at the stenciled letters burned across the steel frame. Where it usually read MOUNTAIN QUARRIES MINE, someone had struck a red line through the title, writing LAKE LERNA in dripping-wet, block letters.

I reached up and touched the red paint. It smeared against my finger. Fresh.

Standing in the entrance, I collected my thoughts and nerves. I clicked to the red light setting on the flashlight and stepped fully into the mine.

With light strides, I navigated through the darkness. Loose rocks the size of footballs and splintered lumber paved the uneven ground. As I moved at a near crawl, I strained to listen for sounds. Water droplets smacked the hard ground, and a trickle of water moved around fallen rocks. A frigid draft howled from deep within the shaft. My heart hammered between my ears.

I pushed deeper.

A few minutes later, the tunnel opened into a large chamber. In the nearest corner to my left, stalactites hung from the ceiling like stony icicles, and stalagmites pointed upward. From the way my flashlight hit the pointed rocks, the meeting of the formations looked like the clenched jaws of a terrible monster.

A dark body of water made up most of the cavern's center. Directly to my right, another tunnel opened and continued into darkness.

"Lake Lerna," I said, ignoring the wayward shaft and continuing to the edge of the underground lake.

I shined the light across the water. Yet another shaft appeared across the lake.

I snickered. "The entrance to the Underworld."

"And to enter the Underworld, one must first die."

I jumped and faced the tunnel to my right. There, leaning against the half-rotted beam built into the shaft wall, stood Daniel Quinn.

Pure rage and fury coursed through my body, through my core, through my entire being and spirit.

The night prior, when he appeared with the van, I hesitated to attack him, hoping my restraint would allow more insight into Glacia's location. My tactic had failed.

I wouldn't repeat the mistake.

I burst in his direction, flying across the open chamber.

Quinn never moved. His arms remained crossed, his left foot over his right, his shoulder leaned against the old lumber.

I was twenty feet away, ten feet, five. I never slowed down. In my head, I envisioned lowering my shoulder and crunching him between my momentum and the immoveable cavern wall.

We collided. Bones snapped.

White light exploded behind my eyes, followed by red-hot pain. Everything went numb and dark for a beat.

When my senses returned, I lay on the damp, hard ground. My left shoulder and arm were numb with debilitating pain. I couldn't move the limb. Shining the light at the injury, I saw my arm hanging at an odd angle. A bump had formed where my collarbone had most definitely fractured and threatened to punch through the skin.

Shifting my gaze to where Quinn had stood, I saw no one. Nothing.

I scrambled to my feet and spun a circle, assessing my surroundings. A shadow moved in my periphery. I cut the light through the darkness, settling it where I had noticed the blur.

Two saber-toothed tigers, thick with muscle, pawed toward me, crouched like lions on the hunt and ready to pounce.

A rock skittered across the ground.

I pivoted to face the noise.

Four dire wolves, slightly smaller than the saber-toothed tigers, stalked toward me from the rear.

Quinn's hyenic laughter reverberated through the chamber. I frantically searched for where it originated. He leaned against the shaft opening across the lake. He had his arms crossed, left foot over his right. He had somehow moved fifty feet across the lake without the water touching his dry clothing.

The water rippled and splashed. Then, from its dark depths, one, two, six serpentine heads rose ten feet into the air. The hydra glared at me with twelve leaf-green eyes, and it roared—a terrible sound that rattled my bones.

I backed away, toward the tunnel I had come in through. The shaft remained open for me to turn and flee. That's all I could do. Run away. How else would I fight two saber-toothed tigers, two dire wolves, and a six-headed hydra?

Except, I had come all this way to find Glacia and to stop Quinn.

I was tired of running. It felt like I constantly ran, without pause—ran away from my feelings, problems, friends, family. I ran and hid and forgot. Running away was so easy. Running, hiding, losing myself in alcohol, work, exercise.

To stand and face my demons, the threats as they surrounded me, that was terrifying and hard. It hurt to fight, to get punched, to get defeated. Why experience the fear and the pain when I could run?

Because running is exhausting, I thought. I wanted to rest. I wanted to experience peace again. To do that, I had to stop running from my past, from my fears, from me.

I glanced at the open tunnel, then I faced the hydra as it rose from the dark water, from Lerna Lake.

The myth flashed through my mind. Hercules shot flaming arrows in the hydra's lair to lure it out of the cave. Once it had emerged, Hercules seized the creature.

A tight smile fought against my clenched jaw. I would run away and hide, but only once more. Only so I could finally turn around, face the monsters, and fight.

"If you want me," I screamed at the hydra, at the tigers and wolves, "you'll have to catch me!"

I spun on my heel and did what I did best. I tore through the chamber at full speed. Halfway to the shaft, my foot caught uneven ground. I tripped and flew forward, landing on my fractured shoulder, scraping my body across the rough cavern floor. Adrenaline disguised the pain, though. I scrambled to my feet and spared a glance over my shoulder.

The creatures bounded after me, though uncoordinated in their pursuit. One of the saber-toothed tigers stumbled and fell. A dire wolf posed a slight limp and barely moved beyond a brisk walk.

Only the hydra seemed coordinated in its attention and efforts. It burst from the lake, splashing water in every direction. Its six heads stretched toward me. At full height, the monster stood near fifteen-feet, big as a school bus.

I glanced at Quinn, who remained in the same position. He smiled at me.

I flipped him off and launched into a full-out sprint once more. As I ran, dodging jutting stones and fallen lumber, my mind raced to draw details from the myth.

Hercules had brought the hydra from its lair. He then fought it, using the help of his nephew, and they decapitated the creature, cauterizing the stumps to prevent the heads from growing back.

I was missing something, though. Something important. An over-looked detail that carried an abundance of weight.

The night air met me like hot breath. I stumbled through the gate, nearly falling face-first once more. I kept my balance and turned, climbing up the hill and into a thicket of dead bushes and skinny trees.

I turned off the flashlight, set it on the ground near my feet, and removed my cell phone.

"Hey," Timothy said.

"Call Wilson now. Tell him to get here twenty minutes ago with as much backup and weapons as he can muster."

A moment of silence passed.

"Tim, you there?"

"I already called him."

I swallowed back anger. He had disobeyed what I had asked of him, but he had also made the right call.

"How long ago?" I asked.

"When you headed off. I'm sorry, but it felt irresponsible not to. I had to do it. About three minutes ago, he drove past me onto Quarry Trail."

As Timothy spoke, as if on cue, a car door slammed in the near distance, followed by another and another. A din of voices filled the night.

"Don't apologize. You did good, kid. Now go home."

"What?"

I hung up and stared down at the gate leading into the mine.

The hydra's head snaked through, then its body emerged—though I'm unsure how the massive creature fit through the man-sized gate.

I remained hidden on the slope above it, behind a scant covering of foliage.

The hydra lumbered forward, scanning the landscape, but not turning back and looking upward. It focused on the police officers, led by Detective Wilson.

They were no longer disembodied voices, but their silhouettes appeared around a corner less than thirty yards away.

When they saw the looming threat, they came to a sliding halt. The hydra roared.

Chaos ensued.

A Dead End.
Tuesday, July 25th.
2029hrs.

MAYA STOOD BEFORE THE door bearing the numbers 224. She glanced back at Evan. He had his hands shoved deep in his sweatpants, and he kept glancing down at the parking lot.

"You okay?" Maya asked.

"You're sure about this? I mean, there's no other action beyond breaking a law?"

"If Stephen opens the door, we're not breaking the law."

"So we're going to knock?"

"No."

"How will he open the door?"

"That's what happened, right? He opened the door." Maya felt slimy, but she didn't know what else to do.

"I have a bad feeling about this."

"Yeah, well, I have a bad feeling about Alina's disappearance."

"You can't keep throwing that in my face. You can't keep using it to act recklessly."

"I act recklessly. It's who I am." Maya surveyed the area for any on-lookers and confirmed the area deserted. "If this doesn't work, we'll steal a master key from maintenance. I don't believe that will be as easy."

"As what? Lock picking a hotel door? An electronic hotel room door? Is that even possible?"

"It's criminally easy. I'm surprised it doesn't happen more often." Maya winked at Evan. "Remember this trick next time you purchase a room at a fancy hotel."

"How do you know something like this?"

Maya pulled in her lips and shared a coy smile.

She had paid her college and medical school tuition as a sex worker. Apart from the clients' vehicles, hotel rooms were her business office. She had become quite familiar with the ins and outs of the hotel industry's dark secrets.

"For the sake of brevity, let's say I lost my keycard a few times. Re-sourcefulness and self-learning is beneficial to thriving."

"I'm not sure what that means. So we're both on the same page... we're breaking into Stephen's room. That's the plan?"

"I'm glad we're on the same page. Stephen's probably snoring through a drunken fog right now. I'd prefer if we caught him while he's snoozing. It's ingrained in my nature to spring surprises onto unsuspecting people."

"You don't say?"

Maya stared at the door. After a second, she removed an expired credit card from her wallet and snatched the DO NOT DISTURB sign off the door's handle. She slid the credit card in the quarter-inch space between the jamb and the door, wedging it against the latch. She fiddled and pressed, pushing on the door to create a fraction more space to work with.

After about twenty seconds, it popped open.

However, Stephen was a careful, if not paranoid man. A life of crime does that to someone. He latched the swing bar on the inside. Maya used the DO NOT DISTURB sign to lift the bar.

After another twenty seconds, it unlatched. The heavy door glided open without a creak.

"Ladies first." Maya gestured for Evan to enter.

Evan glanced at the door, at Maya, back at the door.

"As you're keenly aware," Maya said, "I have many talents."

Evan smirked and chuckled nervously, but he strolled into the hotel room. He lifted his hands to a defensive gesture, and he tiptoed into the dark room.

Maya wasn't as discreet or cautious. She slammed the door, pulled the swing bar back into place, flipped on the entry light, and whistled a nonsensical tune as she marched to the bed. She jumped onto the edge.

Stephen lay with his head beneath the pillow.

Sober my ass, Maya thought, removing the pillow from his head and patting the back of his skull with an open palm.

"Stephen, Stephen, Stephen," she said in a singsong voice. "I have dreamed of this moment."

He made no response, not even to move.

Not to breathe.

Maya grabbed his shoulder and pulled him onto his side. She rolled him to his back. Her hands shot to her mouth, covering an involuntary gasp.

Stephen's eyes were wide open, staring unblinkingly at the ceiling. Dried saliva and vomit stuck to his chin and stringed across his cheek.

An empty bottle of prescription pills lay on the nightstand, along with an empty bottle of whiskey, an empty baggie with powder residue sticking to the plastic, a spoon, and a lighter. Maya glanced at the crumpled sheets. A belt and an empty syringe lay beside Stephen.

A sickening, sour sensation rushed from Maya's groin to her mouth like burning-hot acid. She burped. Her only thought was not to lose her breakfast on Stephen's corpse.

Wheeling around, Maya projectile vomited all over Evan.

"Oh my God," she said, tears burning her eyes. "Oh, my God. He's dead."

Evan stood stock still, hands raised in a combat-ready pose. His mouth moved, but no words formed from his lips. If they did, Maya couldn't hear him.

Her head rang—a constant, high-pitched wail. Alina filled her thoughts. As much as Maya despised Stephen, the man was Alina's father. His death would shatter the girl, or at least a part of her.

Maya thought of the day her father up and left her life. He moved to another state without providing her a forwarding address. She was sure she could find him if she looked hard enough, but she didn't want to look. She wanted the nightmare of his influence over her to end. So, she had treated his departure like a death. He hadn't been any more of a father or a husband or a man than Stephen. He had abused, in every meaning of the word, his wife and his daughters.

Yet, when Maya decided he was dead to her, it still hurt. She remembered being a little girl, shouting songs at the top of her lungs and crazy dancing with him in the kitchen, feeling so secure when he held her.

He was her dad, and she was his baby girl.

He was alive, though, and Maya could seek him out and try to build a new relationship with him. Alina's father was gone forever. Maya felt sick thinking how Alina would handle the news.

If she returns home, Maya thought, staring at Stephen's waxen face.

"Maya," Evan said, his voice on the edge of breaking into sheer panic. "What the actual—"

"There's a shower in the bathroom." Maya's voice bordered on annoyance. "It's right there, three steps away." She pointed, moving her arm like a light marshaler directing a plane. "Just go clean up."

"No apology?"

"For what?"

"For what?" Evan presented the mess splashed across his body. "For what?"

Maya rolled her eyes, incapable of processing Evan's desire for an apology. She hadn't done it on purpose, and it was a natural response to witnessing death. "Just go clean up. You and Stephen are about the same size. When you're done showering, find some of his clothes to wear."

"You're kidding me?" Evan asked, incredulous. "You're actually joking, right? This is all a joke?"

"You can't wear your vomit-covered clothes. I mean, you can, but why would you?"

"He's dead, Maya. If I wear his clothes, if a cop happens to—"

"A cop happens to what? Pull you over? What's he going to do, ask why you're wearing clothes that fit you? Tell me, Evan, in this purely panic-stricken, made-up scenario, does the cop know about Stephen's death? If so, and if he pulls you over, would he know you were wearing Stephen's clothes? Does he have, like, an inventory of everything Stephen owns? Or maybe, more realistically, he has an inventory of everything you own. That's why he questions you, isn't it? He wants to know why you're not wearing your clothes."

"You're a head case," Evan said, turning his back to her and opening the bathroom door.

"Excuse me?" Maya asked, leaping off the bed. "What did you say?"

Evan rubbed his eyes with the heels of his hands and groaned. "Just... leave me alone, okay? I'm going to shower with the door locked. Please, don't use your criminal skills to break into the bathroom. I want a little privacy to think this over."

"Think what over?"

"Think what over?" Evan asked. "Think all of this over."

"Alina is missing. What's there to think over?"

"Her father is dead. We broke into his room. I'm going to wear his clothes. There's a lot to think over." He slammed the door. A second later, the shower turned on, creating a static white noise.

Maya leaned against the entryway wall and slid to the floor. She sat with her knees hugged to her chest and fought against tears, against the idea of defeat, against the thoughts of losing Alina forever.

She had to do something, she just didn't know what that something was. One of her only reliable leads had turned out to be a dead end.

Door Number Two. Tuesday, July 25th. 2037hrs.

THE SHOWER WATER FILLED the dead-silent hotel room. That and the high-pitched ring in Maya's head.

She stood from her seated position and paced the room, careful not to direct her eyes toward Stephen's corpse. As she completed her first lap, reaching the back window, her phone buzzed in her pocket. Maya fished it free with a trembling hand and nearly dropped it.

An unknown caller showed on the screen.

Police, she figured.

Her heart kicked into a higher gear. Had one of the staff from the motel reported Maya breaking into Stephen's room?

"No," she hissed, annoyed with her paranoia. How would they have identified her so quickly?

Why are the police calling me then? She thought.

Only one way to find out. Maya accepted the incoming call.

"Hello."

The owner of the voice cleared his throat. "Uh, who am I speaking with?"

"You called me. Who are you?"

"I, uh... um, I'm Detective Kyle Vanek of Sacramento Police Department. Is this Maya Adler?"

"This is she." Why was a detective calling her? "To what do I owe this pleasure?"

"Your niece is Alina Moore, correct?"

"Correct."

"You reported her missing."

"I did."

"Officer Gillespie took the report from you?"

"She did," Maya said, irked at Vanek's insistence at asking questions he obviously knew the answers to.

"Did Gillespie seem willing to help?"

That inquiry piqued Maya's curiosity. Why wouldn't a cop be willing to help?

"She seemed willing to do her job—finding Alina." A half-truth. Gillespie had wanted to find Alina, but she believed her a fugitive, not a missing person.

"Gillespie considered her a fugitive, right?" Vanek asked, as if reading Maya's thoughts. "Do you think Alina ran because of the arrest warrant?"

Maya recalled her niece fleeing from the Blue Moon office earlier. She also thought of Stephen, of the Graves, of Samantha going missing during the magic show.

"No," Maya said.

"Alina and I spoke a few times earlier today."

To Maya, Vanek sounded worn and ragged. More than that, though, he sounded nervous.

The detective continued speaking. "If she's missing, truly missing, Ms. Adler, I'm afraid I'm to blame."

Maya froze. "What do you mean?"

"I subtly provided her with confidential information about the Samantha Graves investigation, which prompted your niece to—"

"Investigate on her own," Maya said, finishing the detective's sentence. "Are you an imbecile?"

"Some might argue that."

Maya cursed under her breath. "What did you do?"

"I dropped Samantha's parents' names in a conversation. I'm sure Alina, bright as she is, could have figured who they were eventually, but I expedited the process." He cleared his throat. "I looked up Alina after our meeting."

"You met with her?"

"She bombarded me with a visit I couldn't prevent. Anyway, I looked up her name in our database. She's been through the court system."

Maya remained quiet.

The detective must have deduced what had happened, or why. It was his job after all, right? Alina, during one of her stints in a foster home, while Wanda and Stephen disappeared on a bender, stole a thousand dollars and ran away from her temporary parents. An officer caught her three days later, five-hundred miles away.

"I'm aware the court dismissed the case," Vanek said. "Still, Alina has a history of running, and she has a warrant for her arrest. The department will look for her, but they will look in all the wrong places. Even if they caught a whiff of her trail, Ferneau would sidetrack the investigation."

Maya's stomach opened, and gravity grabbed everything from within and dragged it to the dirty, motel floor.

Vanek had all but admitted Ferneau was dirty, or at least connected to Alina's disappearance.

"Anyway, I looked up her name. I looked up her mom—Wanda Moore. Her dad, Stephen Moore."

Maya bit her lip and reflexively glanced at Stephen's dead body.

"Wanda and Stephen have a checkered past. I didn't much care to contact them. Your name showed on Alina's file as an alternate guardian. Your name also appeared as the person who reported Alina's disappearance earlier. That's why I'm calling you. I believe I can trust you."

"Okay," Maya said.

"Victor Pemberton has attempted a similar kidnapping before. The charges fell through, but the arrest tarnished his reputation as a magician. He earns a living moonlighting at a movie theater and performing his magic in the streets."

"Wait," Maya said, closing her eyes, reeling to catch up. "Who?"

"Iniduoh. The magician from the riverboat."

"The one who took Samantha Graves?"

"Yes."

"He kidnapped someone before?"

"Conspiracy to kidnap, but never convicted."

"How did he get the riverboat gig?"

"I have my theories, but I'm going to keep them close to my chest for now," Vanek said. "Despite his background, we didn't have enough evidence to pursue him last night. After Samantha returned home and her parents dropped the case, we have no reason at all to speak to him."

"But Alina spoke to him. She knocked out his teeth, and he pressed the charges against her. He's responsible for the arrest warrant."

Vanek confirmed with a grunt.

Maya chuckled as she realized the detective's game. "You think I should question him."

"You spoke with Terry and Wendy already, didn't you?" Before Maya could ask how he knew that, Vanek continued speaking. "They contacted Ferneau and requested a restraining order against you. They believe you and Alina are harassing them."

"Seriously?"

Vanek ignored her question. "I searched you up, too. No criminal record, but your name was easy enough to Google. You work for the Here & Now as a journalist."

Maya bit her lip.

"You're familiar with investigation techniques, and you're investigating Alina's disappearance on your own, as Alina investigated Samantha Graves' investigation on her own."

"With your help, apparently."

"I want to help you now."

"Oh, yeah?" Maya asked, snickering. "You sending me somewhere to vanish, as well?"

"I'm sending you to Victor Pemberton's hotel room."

"Why don't you knock on his door?"

"I'm a cop. I have no legal standing to knock on his door and ask him questions unless he's a witness to a crime or a person of interest, neither of which he is."

"You want me to speak to Victor Pemberton, the magician with the tooth knocked out of his mouth, courtesy of my niece?"

"I believe he's lucky to have only three missing teeth."

The bathroom door opened. Evan stepped into the entryway wearing nothing but his boxers.

Maya shared a half-hearted smirk with him. She nodded at Stephen's open suitcase, which overflowed with clothes.

"You still there?" Vanek asked.

"Where can I find the magician?" Maya asked, turning her back to Evan and staring at the drawn curtains.

"Motel 6 in downtown Sacramento. Room 223."

Maya couldn't believe it. Victor roomed next door to Stephen. Coincidence? Doubtful. According to Vanek, the magician lived in Indiana, the state where Stephen had moved to.

"We interviewed Victor last night, after the vanishing act. When we asked for a place to contact him, that's what he gave us."

Maya held her tongue for a second, weighing the proposal. "Am I going to walk into a trap, Detective Vanek?"

The man on the other end of the phone sighed. "Alina trusted me."

"That's what I'm afraid of." She hung up the phone and turned to Evan with an embarrassed grin. "You look good."

He had stepped into a pair of Stephen's pants, and he wore Stephen's sweatshirt. They fit him in a baggy, boxy manner. Stephen had a robust physique. Evan had narrower shoulders and hips, but possessed more of an athlete's muscular frame. The two men, though probably close to the same weight, fit into very different sized clothes.

"I look like a college kid before finding a steady girlfriend," Evan said. "No sense of style, fit, or awareness of how dirty my clothes are."

"They do smell like..." Maya trailed off and sniffed. "What is that? Mold?"

"Very musky, huh?"

"It's repugnant, but I'm sure it's not any worse than my dinner." Maya's lips flickered into a soft smirk.

"That's debatable," Evan said.

"Daphne made enchiladas. I bet a regurgitated meal prepared by her is still better than half the food you could get anywhere else."

Evan chuckled, but without amusement. His face was strained, his humor restrained. "There's a dead man ten feet from us, and we're carrying on like nothing is wrong. I don't like that. I'm wearing his clothes, and I like that even less."

Maya scanned the bed and nightstand, regarding the instruments used in his death—drugs and alcohol.

Stephen had decided he wanted to die, and he carried it out himself.

Maya wondered what had propelled him into the act. Had he learned of Alina's fate? Had that knowledge driven him off the ledge? Sure, maybe, Maya thought. If selling his daughter for an absurd profit would inspire his suicide, why sell Alina?

"Do you think someone murdered him?" Maya asked.

Evan rubbed his palms on the too-big pants. "Do you?"

"I don't know. It's possible, right? They murdered him and scattered pills, booze, all the paraphernalia to make it look like an overdose."

"Maybe that's all it was... an overdose. Accidental."

Maya pursed her lips, contemplative. Maybe guilt had driven him to the high. He hadn't meant to kill himself, but had accidentally done so.

"There's only one way to find out." Maya blew past Evan, her shoulder brushing against his, and she opened the door.

She glanced to her left and right, located Victor Pemberton's room, and walked to it. For a second, she entertained the idea of knocking, of kicking the door into his face when he opened it, just as Alina had done. Instead, she opted for surprise.

Maya grabbed her credit card and went through breaking into a hotel room again.

"What are you doing now?" Evan stood framed within the front door leading into Stephen's room.

"Seeing what's behind door number two."

"You can't break into these rooms. It's illegal."

"This motel is so cheap, these doors so insecure, they're practically inviting us inside."

"That's not how it works, Maya."

The latch clicked.

Maya brushed hair out of her face, sighed, and looked over at Evan. "The man in here was one of the last people to see Alina before she vanished."

"Not the last, though."

Maya grunted in annoyance. "Not the last, but one of the last. He has something to do with her disappearance."

"You don't know that. You're desperate for answers and afraid. You're not thinking rationally. I mean, look at you... you're breaking into a hotel room. A second hotel room. The first room had a dead man waiting for us, and I'm wearing his clothes. Where's the line? Where do we stop and step back and reconsider? At what point do we involve the police?"

Maya glared at Evan. "There's a potentially dangerous man in this room. I'm going in, with or without you, and I'll do whatever it takes to find my niece." She wriggled the swing bar free of its hold and pushed the door open.

"Except call the police."

Maya chuckled under her breath and shook her head. How did she explain to Evan the police wouldn't do a thing? Ferneau would make sure Alina was good and gone without a semblance of a proper investigation. Vanek had said as much, and he had said as much while off duty, as a citizen.

That told Maya one thing: Vanek feared contradicting Ferneau while on the job.

"Sorry I bothered you tonight," Maya said. "Go back to Davis." With that, she grabbed her phone, tapped the voice record application, and stepped into the magician's motel room.

294

The Clown.
Tuesday, July 25th.
2048hrs.

DARKNESS COLORED THE MAGICIAN'S cheap motel room. Maya didn't care to navigate through it, so she flicked the entryway switch. Dull yellow light flooded through the room, casting shadows to hide along the walls and in the corners.

The magician, Iniduoh, Victor Pemberton, sat on a chair beside the far window. He was stark naked. One pale, hairy leg crossed over the other. A book rested in his lap, in a conveniently placed location. He held a glass filled with whiskey. The half-empty bottle stood on the table beside him. The middle-aged man had a bulbous, soft build, and his pale, nearly translucent skin told a story of a life spent avoiding the sunshine.

In the sickly yellow light and the dark shadows dancing along the edges of the room, the man almost appeared like the ghost of John Wayne Gacy.

"What do a clown and a magician have in common?" Maya kept her voice level, authoritative. Confident.

The magician appeared unconcerned by her unannounced visit. He remained seated, naked legs crossed. He brought the whiskey to his swollen, cracked lips and sipped. His face was a mess of bruises from Alina throwing the heavy door into it.

"What do they have in common, Ms. Adler?"

Chills sprinted up and down Maya's spine as he uttered her name. He expected her appearance. Had Ferneau called him? The Graves? Stephen... before the incident?

Maya forced a smile, putting on an arrogant mask to hide her nerves. She wanted, instinctually needed—and she fought hard against the urge—to look back to see if Evan stood behind her. The simple action would show fear, though. She refused to allow the magician the satisfaction of seeing her fearful.

"They're both jokes," Maya said.

Victor chuckled. He placed the whiskey glass on the table, uncrossed his legs, and stood. "I heard from Stephen that you're for sale... your body, at least. I heard you're expensive, but well worth the cost of admission." His stubby legs carried him nearer to Maya. "I know why you're here. You want something from me. Information, right?" He paused two feet from Maya and leaned forward, sniffing at her. His thick, sausage fingers reached out and touched her arm. "Well, the information you seek is for sale."

Repulsion engulfed Maya. It took everything in her not to strike the man's swollen, bruised face, or to pivot and flee from his room.

She closed her eyes, though, falling back into the persona of her old practice. She swallowed her pride and stepped a foot closer to Victor. She looped her arms around his neck. He stank from wearing too much cologne, and his hot breath was rancid. Maya had experienced greasier, though. Maya leaned forward and kissed his stubbly cheek up to his ear. Her fingers traced intricate patterns over his furry back.

"I want half the information up front."

"I'll answer three questions," he said, breathless. His hands looped around her hips, pulling her body against his. "What do you want to know?"

Maya stayed in character, remaining patient with the process despite the horror spreading through her veins. If she could solve this case without resorting to violence, she would.

The question was, how far would she go to save Alina?

Kissing his face and pressing her body firmly against him, she glided her lips to his other ear. Maya wanted to know where Alina was, but she was concerned the magician didn't have a clue, and she didn't want to waste a precious question.

So, she laid the groundwork with a simpler question, one she believed he would know. They would go from there.

"Who hired you to kidnap Alina?" Maya's hand slid down his back. Her fingernails scraped his skin.

"Terry Graves."

Though Maya had all but known he would utter the name, the confirmation made her feel cold and hot at the same time. The answer also solidified another truth—Alina had gone to the Graves' estate, and they had finished what the magician couldn't do the previous night.

Before Maya could think through her second question, she heard herself asking, "Where did they take her?"

"A place you'll never find."

"That's not how this game works,." Maya drew away from the man. "You answer my questions."

"I answered it."

"I asked where they took her, not if I would ever find her. Where did they take her?"

"I'm bored with foreplay," Victor said. His hand struck upward like a spring-loaded snake and grabbed Maya around the throat, cutting off her airflow. The other palm released from her hip and pressed against her face, shoved back her head, smeared her nose and lips off base.

Maya still had her arms wrapped around him. She stood with her body mostly pressing against his. It took little thought to execute her escape, to gain the dominant position.

Her knee drove. One, two, three hard and fast strikes to his testicles.

Victor released her and yelped. He leaned to the side and folded to the ground, holding his sensitive area.

Maya backed away, gaining a foot of separation. She cocked back her foot and kicked him square in the face, adding to the dark, swollen mess of it.

He groaned and raised a hand to his bleeding nose.

Maya desperately searched for a weapon. She settled for stepping over the magician and grabbing his half empty bottle of Jack Daniels. She kicked him again, right on the hand gripping his frank and beans.

Victor coughed out a hiss of pain.

"Since you ruined what we had going, here's the new deal. If you don't cooperate with me and answer my questions, you'll have to change your name to Victoria. Do you understand what I'm saying?"

"Yes," he said, his voice surfing on sobs.

"Just so we're crystal clear. If you do anything more than hold your tiny, little balls while lying there in tears, I'll break this bottle over your kneecap. Then I'll use the jagged edges to perform an operation reserved for newborn baby boys. Are we crystal clear?"

He vehemently nodded his head.

"Say it. Say we're crystal clear."

"We're... crystal clear."

"Good." Maya held most of her weight on her left leg, her right propped back eighteen inches in case she needed to kick him again. "Let's return to my previous question. Where is Alina?"

"Please," Victor said. "Please. They'll kill me."

"I'll castrate you. I'll leave you without your manhood to bleed out on a dirty motel floor. Maybe you die, maybe you don't. Still, that's what I'll do. So, I'll give you three seconds to decide if you want to answer my questions. One. Two. Th—"

"An island!"

"An island?"

"A private island. Remote. It's not on any maps that I know of."

"Where?"

"I don't know. I've never been there."

"Where's the general area? We talking Hawaii? Africa?"

"San Francisco."

Maya clicked her tongue. The answer did nothing for her. How many private or remote islands existed out of San Francisco? Maya could think of three off the top of her head, and she figured at least three times that number existed, if not more.

"Terry Graves took her?" Maya asked.

"Yes."

"Why?"

"That's what he does. He's paid to find, take, and send children to the island."

"Children?"

"Ages ten to seventeen."

"What do they do on the island?" She wasn't sure she wanted to hear the answer, but she had to know.

"I don't know." Tears ran freely down Victor's bruised, stubbly face.

"How are you involved?"

"This is my first time."

Maya kicked the magician in the stomach, then reset her foot in the ready position. "Don't lie to me, clown. I know it's not your first rodeo."

"It's the first time with Terry Graves."

"That's not what I asked," Maya said. "How are you involved?"

"I orchestrated the initial disappearance."

"Through magic?"

"Yes."

Victor gasped for breath. "Trap floor in the stage. It dropped her straight into the river. Someone was waiting, assisted her to a rowboat, which transported her elsewhere. That's all I know."

"Strange. The police didn't find a trap floor. Neither did the security on the riverboat."

It was easy enough for Maya to deduce, especially considering Graves had Ferneau (supervising detective of missing persons) in his pocket. Someone had paid the guards to not find anything; someone had paid off the police to overlook the trap floor.

"And Stephen?" Maya asked. "What role did he play?"

"He commissioned the deal."

Maya had figured as much, but the truth still hit her like a punch to the throat. She briefly lost her ability to breathe, to think coherently.

The magician must have had experience with sticky situations, and he must have noticed her deflated body language. He rolled across the floor, away from her, and jumped to his feet. Without hesitation, he charged Maya, slamming into her with his full weight. They tumbled to the ground. Though they stood about the same height, he weighed fifty pounds more than her, probably heavier. The magician overpowered Maya. He mounted her, centering his weight on her stomach.

Maya struggled to breathe. Panic filled her lungs, burning and suffocating. She used the Jack Daniels bottle like a club, beating on his shoulders and battered face. With him so close, though, she had little power to her hits, and he deflected most of the weakened blows.

Once fully settled on top of her, Victor wrested the bottle from her grip. With one stubby hand, he wrapped his thick fingers around her throat, leaning his weight into his outstretched arm, crushing her windpipe.

Maya's breath stopped at the base of her neck. She croaked and wheezed. The room faded in and out of her vision, pulsing. The thick shadows lashed at the dull yellow light, reaching for her.

As if in a dream where time ceases to exist, Maya watched Victor cock the bottle over his shoulder. A half second could have passed, or a lifetime. Maybe both.

Victor screamed something, but Maya didn't hear him, and she couldn't read his lips. He screamed, though. His puffy and bruised face contorted into something despicable, something filled with hate and anger.

Then, as if time all crashed back into place, skipped forward to catch up, Victor's jaw unhinged and sat sideways on his face.

Oxygen rushed back into Maya's body. She inhaled sharply, with desperation, and coughed from swallowing too much air too quickly.

The magician lay on his side, a few feet away from her, howling in agony through his broken jaw. He dropped the bottle to push himself to his hands and knees, and he crawled toward the back window.

Evan stalked him. He kicked Victor in the ribs, flipping him back onto the ground. He collected the bottle.

"I'll shove the bottle down your throat," Evan said, his voice hard and raspy. "If you dare do anything more than blink, I'll shove this bottle down your throat, then I'll kick you so hard, it'll shatter inside your body."

Victor must have shown his compliance. Evan turned away and tended to Maya. He stepped over her, never turning his back on the magician, and he crouched beside her.

"Thanks for saving me," she rasped, her throat raw with pain. She touched her neck and scooted up against the edge of the bed. After taking a few seconds to build the courage, she spoke in a ragged, worn tone. "Victor, I'm a journalist. I recorded our entire conversation." It pained her to speak, but she powered through. "Drop the charges against Alina and Blue Moon. I know you're thinking we broke into your room. My recording won't hold up in court. I don't need it to. I only need to release it to the public. To send it to a determined detective. They'll see to the rest. They'll build a legitimate case against you. Against the Graves. Against Ferneau." Maya winced. She wanted to grab the bottle of bourbon from Evan and chug it to wet her throat, but she thought that might be more painful.

"What do we do?" Evan asked.

"Call an ambulance," Maya said. "I'll call a trusted cop to handle it from there."

"Then what?"

"We go to Terry's house."

Evan chuckled and shook his head. "What does that mean? We break into his house, too? Maybe beat him up for information?"

"No, no, no. Nothing that crazy. We'll knock."

The Distraction.
Tuesday, July 25th.
2107hrs.

Detective Wilson advanced on the hydra. He signaled for the three other officers accompanying him to fan out. Ten yards from the monster, they came to a stop and fixed their firearms on the hydra.

From above the scene, up on the hillside, I peeked through the leaves and watched. Four police officers squared off against a six-headed monster and six prehistoric predators.

They're not real, I thought. Or, rather, they were real, but they weren't as I saw them. The police wouldn't suffer from my hallucinogenic affliction, though. They would see the creatures as they really were—as human—and respond appropriately.

Except, what if the creatures (the afflicted humans) saw the officers as some form of attacking monsters? What if Quinn's creations attacked Wilson and the other three cops? Would the response then be to incapacitate the threat? Would the police officers shoot whoever I saw as the monsters?

A new fear drowned me.

What if Glacia or Vincent were down there? What if they hallucinated the police as monstrous threats? What if they attacked? What if the officers responded with deadly force to protect themselves from harm?

If I appeared, though, what would happen? Or, what wouldn't happen?

I knew one thing: Quinn hid himself in the Underworld. By crossing out the name of the mine, replacing it with Lake Lerna, he had all but announced where he waited for me—in the realm of the dead.

I had to defeat the hydra, return to the mine, cross the lake, and enter the Underworld to confront him. If I revealed myself to the police, would I lose my chance at reaching Quinn?

I hunched down and waited for the scene to develop.

Wilson barked a string of curses before raising his handgun and aiming it directly at the hydra's stomach—not at any of its six heads, but at its body.

"Don't move!" he said.

Two saber-toothed tigers emerged from the gate. One of the three officers shifted his aim to the massive cats.

Wilson kept his sights on the hydra.

Fresh blood matted the saber-toothed tigers' fur. They growled at the uniformed men.

For a tenth of a second, reality cut through the hallucination. Instead of the prehistoric cats, I saw two humans screaming at the cops.

"I need every single one of you to get on your bellies and kiss the ground," Wilson said. "If your mouths aren't full of mud from making out with the dirt, I'll see that you eat a pound of mud-pie for dessert later tonight. On the ground, now!"

One of the hydra heads lunged forward like a striking cobra. It went straight for Wilson.

Again, a moment of clarity sliced through my mind. Not a head but a person sprinted toward the detective.

Wilson stood in a firm stance. He held his firearm with both hands, and he didn't hesitate or waver. The gun's report thundered through the night three explosive times in rapid succession.

Boom!

Boom!

Boom!

I flinched after each shot, as if the round had struck me.

The rogue hydra head jerked and wavered. It fell limp—dead weight on the shared torso.

"In case you're hard of hearing, I'll repeat myself once. Unless you want to end up like him, lick the ground!"

Him? I thought. Who had he killed?

"Get on the ground!"

Three of the four dire wolves exploded from the gate and slammed into the saber-toothed tigers. They rolled and thrashed and fought, biting and slashing and howling.

In the sudden distraction, two more of the hydra heads lashed out.

Wilson fired six more shots.

From my vantage, I saw only three of them hit their marks, but three were enough. The two heads dropped a couple of yards in front of the detective's feet. He steadied his gun on the hydra's body.

I kept waiting for the fallen heads to respawn, but nothing happened.

Two of the officers had stepped into the brawl between the saber-toothed tigers and the dire wolves—two average-sized men wedging themselves into a predatory battle between two legendary creatures. It took a few seconds, but they separated the combatants, thankfully without firing a single shot from their pistols.

After the officers physically interfered, the predators laid on the ground, their faces in the dirt.

One of the uniformed men kept his gun fixed on the prone creatures, while the other officer brought their front limbs behind their backs and handcuffed their paws.

Glimpses of clarity appeared through the hallucination, but they were fleeting. Still, I understood the officers worked to handcuff the five men and women who shifted between saber-toothed, dire wolf, and human.

I squinted and focused on the scene, convincing myself of the hallucinations, forcing my senses to perceive reality. Slowly the clarity and detail faded.

Five people lay on the ground where the saber-toothed tigers and dire wolves had surrendered. Three other people lay in bloody pools where Wilson had shot them down. The three remaining hydra heads shifted into three more people.

From where I crouched, I couldn't discern who Wilson had shot, who had surrendered, and who remained a potential threat.

I also realized the incident could continue for hours. Back up would eventually arrive. A careful search of the area would occur. They would find me, meaning I wouldn't find Quinn, and he would likely escape once again, possibly murdering Glacia.

That couldn't happen. I needed to get back into the mine.

But how?

I hid directly behind the monsters, directly in front of the officers. How could I slip back into the mine without them noticing me? I couldn't afford to have them stop, question, and possibly arrest me. Wilson couldn't follow me into the mine, either.

If Quinn caught scent of someone tagging along with me, especially a police officer, I wouldn't put it past the maniac to kill Glacia out of spite for me ruining his precious game.

Whatever Quinn had in store for the third and final task, I had to go about it alone. And I had to do it soon.

I removed my phone and called Timothy.

"Did they show?" he asked.

"They showed. Listen, I need your help."

"The cops can't help you?"

"No," I said. "Not with this. I need you, okay?"

"Yeah, sure."

I glanced down the hill. The gate stood beneath me. I needed to descend the slight slope with no one noticing me.

"I need a diversion," I took a deep breath.

Wilson continued barking orders at the three remaining people standing upright, his gun and his attention fully focused on them, as was one of the three officers. The other two cops dealt only with the individuals lying on the ground, making sure they didn't decide to make a run for it.

"A diversion?" Timothy asked. "What do you mean?"

"Blare your horn," I said. "Hit your horn and hold it for ten seconds. A slow-count ten seconds."

"You're serious?"

"Do it now."

A full breath of time passed. "Oh, crap."

"What?"

"I removed the horn."

My mouth moved, but no words emitted.

"My job... I'm a part-time mechanic at this shop. They let me stay after work to mess around with my car. I removed the horn because I wanted to put something louder in it. I thought it would be funny to have, like, a train horn coming from my little Acura, you know?"

"Hilarious."

"Anyway, sorry."

I hung up the phone, picked up the StrikeLight. and tapped the butt against my skull to jar an idea loose. A desperate, idiotic thought popped into my head. I almost threw it away, but I held it in my mind's eyes. It grew more enticing as I had no other recourse.

Pocketing the flashlight, I reached to the ground and grabbed three stones the size of tennis balls. In rapid succession, I threw them. They slapped against the ground in a loud, clattering report, crashing like a lot of pots and pans.

I held my breath and watched every head turn to the source of the noise.

Exhaling, I exploded upward and skipped down the hill. My left shoulder screamed at the sudden, jerky movement, but I pushed away the pain, not having time to consider it.

As I reached the bottom, I dove through the gate.

Blood pounded in my head. Heat poured into my face. My hands trembled.

I stood in the darkness and glanced through the gate's slits. For a second, I thought Wilson stared right back at me. The detective quickly refocused on the three threats standing before him, all of whom, now that I was nearer, I recognized.

Shannon Dupree, Vincent's wife. Susan Owning, the real estate agent who helped haunt Glacia's Nana's house, which I now lived in. Miguel Luna, Glacia's uncle, who had worked with Susan Owning and Glacia's mom in the haunting.

Miette Verdin, the woman who had a Changeling assume her identity and take over her life, lay beside her brother, Zachary Verdin. Blood bathed their faces. They had initially been the saber-toothed tigers.

Johnny Lantz, the lone survivor from the dream demon case lay beside them, as did Jackson Armstead, the kid who was nearly turned into a flesh golem to recreate a woman's dead daughter. Janet Vasquez, Glacia's mom, made up the third dire wolf.

Across the way, a few yards in front of Detective Wilson, were those he had shot when they ran at him.

Vanessa Snow, the Changeling.

David Shaye, the dream demon.

Armando Lopez, the man who wished to turn Jackson into his dead daughter.

Not a one of them moved. Wilson had killed them.

I bit my cheeks and pulled myself away from the scene. I had to continue forward to what mattered most—stopping Quinn and saving Glacia. Everything else could wait until afterward.

As I hobbled through the mine shaft, the left side of my body completely numb, I came across another body lying off to the side. I dropped beside the person, turned him over, and gasped.

James Connors, the man who had hired me to solve the Rabid Sasquatch case, rested in a raggedy crumple of loose limbs and oversized clothes. I'm not a medical examiner, but it didn't take years of training to know Connors was beaten to death.

I closed my eyes and pictured Miette and Zachary Verdin, the two saber-toothed tigers, covered in blood. Quinn had infected their minds, and they had believed Connors was a threat. They had acted out of self defense. I had to believe it. They wouldn't have harmed anyone otherwise.

Lying on the dirt outside the mine, did they even know what they had done?

It broke me to stand and leave Connors where he lay, but I had to continue forward.

I reentered the open chamber. The dark water sat before me like a pool of blood.

Without thinking twice, allowing fury hot as an inferno to guide me, I waded into its freezing depths. I swam to the other side, climbed onto the ledge, and walked through the tunnel leading into the Underworld.

The Underworld.
Tuesday, July 25th.
2119hrs.

I DESCENDED A MIST-FILLED, downward-sloping tunnel into the Underworld. The haze obscured my sight, forcing me to walk with my hands outstretched.

I'm not sure how long I went on like that, walking down the slight gradient at a shuffling speed. Eventually, though, I stepped into another chamber.

The Underworld.

Daniel Quinn hadn't disappointed with his recreation of the legendary afterlife.

He populated the realm with hundreds of ghostly spirits. They were nearly translucent and insubstantial. One of them phased right through me as it hovered inches off the foggy ground.

I clenched my jaw when I recognized a spirit. My entire body tensed with anger as I recognized another. As they wandered throughout the gymnasium-sized cavern, I recognized nearly all of them. Those I failed to identify, I had a feeling I had known at some point—high school peers, police academy cadets, dates whose names and faces I had long forgotten.

I saw the victims randomly killed and exploited by Eddie Denier in the voodoo doll case; the victims murdered by Trisha Berry to frame Callie Balzan in the doppelgänger case; those murdered by the dream demon in Santa Cruz; the victims the Vampire of Sacramento had brutally murdered; those killed by Clara Lopez during her mad attempt to recreate her deceased daughter.

The spirits of those who had died during my investigations filled the cavern.

Along with the spirit of Cambria Parker. She stood apart from the crowd as if a spotlight had shined on her. She raised a hand and waved in my direction, sending my heart into a series of mad flutters, and my mind into a state of pure confusion and shock.

I bit hard on my cheeks until I tasted blood. I couldn't allow Quinn's illusions to trick me in the end. I had to remain focused.

Shifting my gaze, I settled on the elephant in the room, or rather the monster in the chamber. A three-headed hellhound the size of a backyard shed stood in the center. Cerberus, if my memory served me correctly—Hades' pet instructed to prevent the dead from leaving. The creature glared at me with dark-red eyes. Jagged, yellow teeth appeared as it snarled, and saliva stretched toward the stony floor in goopy tendrils.

Two arachnids stood on either side of the hellhound. As I had briefly remembered them from the previous night, they bore the bodies of humans, though they had six arms instead of two, and their faces resembled a horrific spider. Sixteen eyes joined Cerberus' gaze, staring at me with ravenous intent. Instead of a tendril of drool, the arachnids dripped venom from their thick fangs.

Behind the Hellhound, on a throne atop a raised ledge, sat Daniel Quinn. He was dressed in all black—pants, jacket, boots. He bore a bright, amused grin.

As I entered his realm, he stood, his arms stretched outward. "August Allan Watson." His radio-host voice ricocheted off the cavern walls.

I blinked hard, allowing my eyes to remain shut for a second. I had to reestablish my bearings after what I had walked into. I had literally walked into the Underworld, inhabited by creatures of myth and the spirts of the dead.

It's not real, I thought. *None of this is real.*

I recalled the saber-toothed tigers, the dire wolves, the hydra.

When Detective Wilson had shot the multi-headed monster, when the other officers had handcuffed the beasts, their actions hadn't aligned with what I perceived as truth. That rift in reality, that inconsistency, helped me bridge the gap.

Quinn had drugged me. I saw the illusions he planted into my head.

I allowed that knowledge to cement itself in my mind, hoping it helped me see through the haze muddling my reality. I would see Cerberus for what it really was, the arachnids for who they really were. The spirits would vanish. Because none of that existed. Spirits weren't real. Arachnids the size of humans weren't real. Massive hellhounds with three heads weren't real.

I opened my eyes after the long, hard blink and saw...

... everything exactly the same.

Creatures of myth and of my nightmares staring at me.

Quinn still stood, his arms outstretched, grinning at me.

I shivered as a spiral of fear burrowed through my body.

Then, like a guiding light, Glacia entered my mind. I had entered another world to save her, not to allow a few hallucinations to turn me away. I shrugged off my fear and confusion, replacing those emotions with pure, fiery fury. I glared past the hellhound and the arachnids, directly at Quinn.

"I'm here. I played your game, and I won. I made it to the end. Now, I demand the promised reward. Glacia's freedom. Where is she?"

Quinn stared at me in a state of a pure excitement for a half-second, then he simmered and bubbled over with hyenic laughter. He grabbed his knees and leaned forward, howling like the maniac he was.

The spirits chorused and echoed his mania.

The hellhound coughed out smoke through its six nostrils.

The arachnids made a terrible, skittering noise.

After what felt like an infuriating eternity, Quinn hiccuped into silence. He plopped onto his throne and slouched, crossing his left leg over his right.

"Why so hasty, Mr. Watson? We've so much to discuss, do we not? I'm sure you have many questions for me."

"I have one question for you."

Quinn wanted me to feed his ego by asking how he did this and that?

Explain your genius to me, oh great King Quinn.

Well, unfortunately for him, I refused. His explanations and answers meant nothing to me. I didn't care how he planted illusions into my head. I didn't care to know how he corralled all the people related to my previous cases, including those who escaped prison. I didn't care to know why or how or what. I only had one concern that demanded an answer.

"Where's Glacia?"

Quinn yawned, patting his open mouth with his palm. "You bore me, Mr. Waston. I grow weary of hearing the same question over... and over... and over. Where's Glacia? Where's Glacia? Where's Glacia?" He clapped his hands together with each emphatic question.

I gritted my teeth and restrained myself with nothing more than bubble gum and string.

"I'm a teacher at heart," Quinn said. "It stands against my nature to... to just gift you the answer. I've provided you with all the clues and hints to arrive at the proper conclusion on your own. If you wish to rescue Glacia, you'll have to do more than ask me to bring her out."

"What then? What do I do? Fight you? Fight your little circus show?" As I posed the question, my shoulder and collarbone shot a pulse of pain through my body. My hand quietly ached where the knife had punched through my palm. I stood straighter and taller to hide my doubt from Quinn. "I'll fight whatever you throw at me."

He snickered and held up a finger. "You must understand something. The game hasn't ended yet. You're on the last level, though."

"No more riddles!"

"You've descended into the Underworld, a feat only accomplished by the dead. Once someone enters this realm, they don't return to the world of the living."

"Hercules went into the Underworld and returned. Odysseus. Theseus."

Quinn chuckled. "You've done your homework. Bravo! You should know only those of heroic status have ever returned—those exceptional from the rest. Mr. Watson, are you exceptional?"

"What's the rest of the game?" I asked.

Quinn's chuckle grew into a full guffaw. He pointed at me. No, not at me. Beyond me. "We were waiting for the last player to join us. Go on. Take a peek at the last participant."

I didn't want to turn and see whoever had entered the chamber. I wasn't sure I could bear the realization of seeing someone I knew and trusted working with Daniel Quinn.

With a substantial force of will, I turned my body.

My fear prove justified.

Detective Wilson strutted through the tunnel. He wore a respirator, but I could see his smile in his eyes.

Unmasked. Tuesday, July 25th. 2117hrs.

MAYA STOMPED ON THE gas pedal. Her car, an old, beat up Toyota from the dinosaur era, worked beyond its capabilities—it had made a career of pushing beyond its limits with Maya behind the wheel, though.

In the passenger seat, Evan white-knuckled the grab bar and stared unblinkingly out the windshield, hissing and grunting as Maya weaved in and out of traffic.

"You're going to kill us. What good are we to anyone if we're dead?"

"I'm going to kill you if you don't stop whining." Maya clenched her jaw so tight, her teeth ached.

Maya immediately regretted her words, but she didn't have the bandwidth to spare for an apology. Brake lights appeared in front of her.

Her attention fixed solely on driving. She swerved to the highway's shoulder, bypassing the traffic.

"You're driving on the shoulder!"

"Evan, enough!" Maya wheeled back into the legal lanes after passing the culprits slogging along at the speed limit. "Happy?"

"Terrified. Not happy. Definitely not happy."

Maya's phone buzzed in the cupholder. She reached for it and answered without looking at the caller.

"Go for Maya," she said.

"It's Fred."

"Please tell me you found something on Quinn."

"It pains me to admit it, but you were right."

"Goes without saying."

"His real name isn't Daniel Quinn," Fred said.

Maya gnashed her teeth. "Did you learn that from the book I mentioned?"

"Yeah."

Maya cussed. "I can't believe I missed it. It was right there the entire time. He left us a clue before he even inserted himself into our lives.

Jesus. We could've figured this all out from the beginning." Maya twisted her hand around the steering wheel. "What's his real name?"

"Jack Schaefer."

"Jack Schaefer? Do we know him?"

"Are you an *X-Files* fan?"

"Alina loves the show. She always has it on in the background, like study music. It helps her focus, I guess. I don't know. A few years back, we spent the summer watching the entire series. Why?"

"Jack Schaeffer was a character in an episode, played by the actor Daniel Quinn."

Maya pursed her lips, jerked the Toyota into the slow lane to pass a string of cars traveling at a turtle's pace in the passing lane. "I'm confused."

"Daniel Quinn, our Daniel Quinn... his real name is Schaefer. Jack Schaefer. He must have watched the *X-Files* episode, heard his name used for a character in the show, and looked up the actor. I don't know. That's conjecture and doesn't matter. Schaefer is Quinn."

"You're sure?"

"I Googled Dan Quincy, the author of the book, and it brought back Jack Schaefer. Dan Quincy is a pseudonym."

"So what of Jack Schaefer, then? What did you learn?"

Fred cleared his throat. "He grew up in Sacramento, but he moved to Los Angeles to pursue a career in film."

"As an actor?"

"He had aspirations, but his true talent came in special and practical effects. He was a makeup, animatronics, CGI genius. USC contracted him to teach a few classes, and he authored the book you mentioned to further his authority on the subject. His credentials are impressive within the field."

"Do you know why he's here, what he has against August?"

Fred took a second to respond, as if collecting his thoughts. He sighed into the receiver—a whirlwind of air crashing into Maya's ear. "Quinn—"

"Schaefer," Maya said.

"Either way, he grew up with Ted Wilson's older brother. Jayden Wilson. They were inseparable, at least based on what I gathered."

"Jayden Wilson. Why does that name sound so familiar?"

"A cop shot and killed him almost twenty years ago. He was no older than Alina at the time of his death."

Maya instantly recalled the infamous incident. She had only been eight or nine when it happened, but she could still feel the anger and frustration in the crowd when her dad and mom brought her to the march in front of the capital building. She could smell the sweat of strangers, hear their chanting voices, see the pain screwed tightly in their eyes and across their faces.

The shooting had occurred in Sacramento, near Oak Park, and the story made national news... at least until the next tragedy happened, and the news wore off.

"Wasn't it a traffic stop or something?" Maya asked.

"Jayden stole his dad's car. The cop flagged him for speeding," Fred said, his voice somber.

Maya glanced at her speedometer. Ninety-two miles-per-hour.

"Jayden drove. Schaefer sat in the passenger seat. Our Detective Ted Wilson was in the backseat."

"What did you say?" Maya's entire body shivered with a deep-set chill. "Wilson and Schaeffer know each other?"

"The cop hit his siren to pull the kids over, but Jayden had other plans. The incident turned into a pursuit. He wasn't any older than Alina when it happened. The police herded the stolen car off the road. Officers surrounded the kids with their guns drawn."

"They shot and killed him."

"Ted Wilson sat in the backseat when it happened. In a proceeding interview, he claimed his brother put both hands on the wheel when the officer approached. That's what their parents always instructed them to do if the police pulled them over. Hands on the wheel; hands always present, always within sight of the officer. Ted said his brother would've had his hands on the wheel. Schaefer corroborated that."

Maya struggled to connect Wilson and Schaeffer. What did that mean for August? Were Wilson and Quinn in cahoots?

Fred cleared his throat. "I don't know what the officer perceived as a threat, but he shot until he dry fired. Every round hit its mark. Jayden died in the stolen car."

"So, what?" Maya asked, her mind churning. "They're exacting revenge on August for shooting Aaron Brooks, as if he stands in place for what the other cop did to Wilson's brother? Wilson is a cop. He should understand the pressure and fear August felt that day."

"I don't know their motivation," Fred said. "You wanted a connection, and I found one. Schaefer left Hollywood about seven months ago. Finished working on a movie, which concluded his last contract, and no one has heard a word from him since."

"That's the exact time August created the business."

"Yup."

"Is every cop we know corrupt?" Maya blurted, not really asking anyone in particular, just stating her frustrations.

First Ferneau had been complicit in Alina's disappearance, now Wilson had worked in tandem with Quinn.

Was that how Eddie Denier, and the other convicts related to August's past cases, escaped their imprisonment? Had Wilson worked from the inside, coordinating with Schaefer?

"We have to tell August," Maya said.

"I tried a few times before calling you," Fred said. "I can't get a hold of him."

Maya's phone chirped, signaling an incoming call.

"Fred, I'm headed to Terry and Wendy Graves' estate. I have Evan with me. If you don't hear from one of us in the next thirty minutes, contact Detective Kyle Vanek. I think he's about the only law enforcement officer we can trust right now."

"You're sure we can trust him?"

Maya glanced at the phone's screen, at the name of the new caller.

A blocked number.

"We can trust him." She hung up on Fred and switched over. "Vanek."

"Tis I," he said. "I'm on my way to the hospital to visit a Victor Pemberton." He went quiet for a second. "You're sure about his guilt? You're absolutely positive? Once I step into his room, there's no turning back for either of us."

Before leaving the motel, Maya had sent Vanek the file of her recording of Victor, of him incriminating the Graves' in the plot to kidnap Alina.

If Vanek could pursue them and Ferneau, he could uncover a lot of corruption and crime within the political echelon of society. Vanek and Maya would incur a swarm of powerful enemies with deep pockets and wide influence, though.

What would that do for her investigative career? What would happen to Vanek and his career?

In the end, it didn't matter, as long as they did the right thing at the right time.

"I'm sure," Maya said. "Do you know anything about the island he mentioned?"

"Not yet," Vanek said. "Where are you now?"

"I'm headed to Terry and Wendy's estate to ask if they know anything about the island's location."

"Maya."

"Don't worry. I'll ask nicely. With a smile even."

"They're dangerous people," Detective Vanek said. "I'm advising you to stand down. I'll call the El Dorado Police Department, have them send a unit to the Graves' house."

"No!" Maya all but screamed. She lowered her voice. "No. We can't. We don't know which cops they own. This is something Evan and I will handle."

Vanek sighed. "I can't condone that."

"I don't need your permission, Detective. I'm saving my niece, no matter what it costs me." Maya ended the call. She glanced at Evan, who sat rigidly beside her. "You alright?"

"What's the plan, Maya?"

"Knock on their door."

"Then what?"

Maya shrugged and merged the car three lanes across traffic, barely making the offramp. "Take a page out of Alina's book, kick the door into their teeth."

"That's breaking and entering. That's assault."

"It's Alina's life we're talking about, Evan. You didn't have to show up at the motel. You didn't have to kick the magician in the face. You don't have to tag along right now."

"Someone has to look out for you since you're incapable of taking care of yourself."

"I was doing just fine."

"He was going to kill you."

"Better dead than having this conversation."

"God, Maya!" Evan half-screamed. "What was that earlier, anyway, about you being for sale?"

Maya chuckled and shook her head.

"He said your body was for sale, and he'd purchase it for information. What did he mean by that?"

"It doesn't take a genius to figure out what it means."

"That you're a whore?"

The words struck Maya like a powerful slap. Her cheeks burned. Her breath hitched. "Sex worker."

"So you screw desperate, old men for cash?"

"Screwed, past tense."

"You're a whore, and you never thought to tell me that?"

"Evan—"

"I mean, honestly, Maya, how irresponsible are you? What STDs am I infected with now? All of them?"

"You're something special."

He chuckled. "I'm the special one? How many men?"

"What?"

"How many men have you serviced?"

"Serviced?"

"That's what you do, right? You work in the service industry."

"Worked."

"Is that the correct way to say it these days, since whore and prostitute and slut are too offensive? Seriously, Maya. Do I have herpes? Warts? What was the cost of me sleeping with you?"

Tears burned Maya's eyes, but she refused to cry in front of Evan. "I shouldn't have to explain myself."

"But you should!" Evan slapped the dashboard with his palm. "That's something I deserved to know before we first sleep together. You don't think that's shareable information?"

Maya navigated up the hill, working through the crisscrossing streets leading to the Graves' estate.

"I don't have any STDs. I'm clean."

Evan smiled, snickering. "You have a loose definition of clean."

"What does it matter right now? We're trying to save Alina. That's why we're here. Once she's safely home, we can discuss anything you want. I'm an open book."

"Alina ran away. She ran away to whore around like her crackhead mom... and like you."

Maya had sat where Evan now sat many times in her past—in a state of pure, eclectic terror.

He had stumbled upon a dead body, wore the dead man's clothing. He had broken into a hotel room and assaulted a man—broke his jaw. He had learned that his girlfriend, the one he had confessed his love to only hours before, had once provided sexual services for money. He now sat in a car heading toward another place they planned to break into and assault the owners for information.

Maya knew Evan was terrified beyond his understanding. She also knew confusion and raw terror led a person to say miserable, uncharacteristic things.

Maya swallowed her pain, her retort, her tears, and she pulled off to the curb a hundred yards before the Graves' estate.

She faced Evan after turning off the car and cutting the headlights. "I won't ask you to come with me. The Graves took Alina. They know where she is. If I have to murder Wendy in front of Terry to find my niece, I will. I won't ask you to join, though."

Without another word, Maya opened the car door and stepped into the night.

An Act of Revenge.
Tuesday, July 25th.
2127hrs.

DETECTIVE TED WILSON AND I had gone through the police academy together. We hadn't clicked then, and we hadn't stayed in touch. Galt Police Department hired me, and he went with the Sacramento Police Department. Not until I joined with Tempest Michaels did Wilson and I cross paths again.

For the past few months, we have worked closely on a few strange cases. Naturally, a trust formed between us... or so I believed.

Wilson removed the respirator from his face. The smile beaming in his eyes showed in a broad, proud grin. He held his service gun—the gun he had used to shoot and kill David Shaye, Armando Lopez, and Vanessa Snow—though he pointed it at the ground.

"Did you figure that one?" Wilson asked.

There wasn't a Sherlock Holmes moment, where everything fell into place and made perfect sense. In fact, confusion constricted me.

When Wilson first emerged from the tunnel, a surge of excitement and relief poured through me. I nearly laughed with victory. Turned out, I laughed anyway, though a defeated, deflated chortle.

Certain gray areas made more sense with Wilson's involvement. Quinn had helped imprisoned criminals slip away from police custody. Wilson had probably worked behind the scenes to orchestrate the transfers and subsequent escapes.

A measure of silence impregnated the chamber.

Quinn broke the spell by clearing his throat. "No snarky remark?"

"I'm not the type," I said, glaring at Wilson, scrambling to fit the pieces together.

How did he and Quinn know each other? Why had they preyed on me? What could they possibly gain by these games? Despite my mightiest efforts, I fell short of the answers.

"I don't understand." I faced Wilson and ignored Quinn, hoping it would sting his pride. "We shared meals together. You trusted me, and I trusted you."

A flicker of regret, or maybe guilt, passed over the detective's eyes, but I couldn't be sure. The lighting wasn't great in the chamber—bright in certain sections, dark and thick with shadows in others.

The realization brought another thought to mind. Had Quinn installed lights in strategic positioning, and to what end? Obviously, so we could all see each other's bright, smiling faces. But the elaborate setup was for more than illumination.

It enhances the scene, I thought. Quinn organized the lighting to create vagueness, pockets of gray within the cavern. The positioning of the lights allowed the hellhound, the arachnids, the spirits to appear realistic.

No, not quite, I thought. *That's part of it, but not all of it.*

I recalled the bathroom I had awoken in earlier that day—my apartment's bathroom. It had appeared decrepit. I had perceived my cell phone as a bar of soap. He had hidden the truth of the bathroom from me.

Quinn had organized the lighting in the cavern to hide its features more than show them.

That begged the question, what was Quinn hiding?

As my thoughts raced through the deductions, Wilson raised his pistol and pointed it at me.

"So, what?" I asked with a knowing smirk. "All the theatrics just to kill me?" I shook my head, turned my back on Wilson, and looked at Quinn. "That's not the script. What happens next? What am I missing?"

Quinn tapped his knuckles on the throne's armrest. "I provided all the clues. You could've learned my name, my true name. You could've stopped me before any of this began. But you didn't. You couldn't. Do you know why?"

"I'm sure you'll enlighten me."

"You saw nothing beyond the stained reflection in the mirror."

"Enough with the vagueness," I said. "Speak your mind."

"You noticed only your pain, only your suffering. You lived in the shadow of your past. You could've stepped into the light. You could've used your experience to help others."

"What experience?" I asked, but I knew the answer.

He meant my encounter with Aaron Brooks—the nineteen-year-old kid I shot and killed.

"He was innocent," Quinn said.

He pointed a gun at me, my mind screamed. The words nearly jumped off my tongue, but I had grown accustomed to swallowing the excuse.

Aaron Brooks had pointed a gun at me. I responded by shooting him. I couldn't know he had an airsoft gun. How would I have known?

The Galt Police Department, the police union, the court system, and the public, for once, all agreed on something—my shooting was justified.

The excuse fit, but it tasted so sour.

"I know he was," I said.

"Yet, you shot him dead," Quinn said.

"That's what this is about? Me shooting Aaron Brooks."

"You're finally catching up, Mr. Watson. It's about time."

I exhaled and faced Wilson. The detective aimed his firearm at my chest.

"You're a cop," I said. "You worked the night when Officer Bronson died in the line of duty."

Wilson clenched his jaw.

"I went to work the next day, angry and afraid. You know what I felt when I responded to the call. You know that fear and that anger. We all had itchy, sensitive fingers after Bronson went down. You can't tell me you didn't want to exact your brand of justice when you clocked in. We all did."

"You don't know me like that," Wilson said.

"I'm not saying that what happened was right or justified. I'd go back, if I could. I'd gladly change places with Aaron. I'd gladly be dead right now instead of him."

"Then why aren't you?"

"Because I allowed my emotions to dictate my actions." I took a calming breath. "I've regretted it ever since. You of all people should understand the fear an officer faces every time they put on the badge."

Wilson spat on the ground. "We make a conscious decision every time we wear it, sure. But when we put it on, it shields our fear and anger from lashing out. It protects the public from us as much as it protects the public from criminals. Yes, we might feel a little afraid, but once it's on, that fear hides behind it. No matter what. It has to." Wilson huffed and his hands trembled. "You allowed your colors to bleed, and they painted a coward."

I didn't have an argument. Wilson was right, of course.

"What now?" I asked. "What's the endgame here? Do I die?"

Quinn chuckled. "Nothing like that. You get to experience what I experienced because of your cowardice. What Wilson experienced because of your cowardice. You get to experience someone, someone you care for, die unjustly."

I closed my eyes and breathed, fighting to keep myself in control. It was a Herculean task.

"You knew Aaron Brooks?" I asked.

"No," Quinn said. "But I knew Jayden Wilson. He was like a brother to me."

The name rang a distant, but familiar bell.

"Jayden Wilson." I spoke it aloud, trying it on for size. The familiarity bled into recognition.

Fifteen years ago, an officer shot a kid in Sacramento at the end of a vehicle pursuit. The kid, Jayden Wilson, didn't have any weapons on him. According to the two kids in the car during the incident, Jayden had complied with the officer, hadn't acted in an aggressive or defiant manner.

The officer spooked at some point, though, and emptied his clip at point-blank range.

I said his name again, staring at Wilson with heavy eyes. "Jayden Wilson. Your brother."

Wilson shared a single nod to affirm my assumption. "I was in that car when he died."

"I'm sorry."

"That's why I joined law enforcement. To be better than the officer who murdered my brother. To be better than you. To help, to serve, and to protect. To change the system from the inside."

I couldn't help my response, and I chuckled. "That's a noble speech for someone playing vigilante to every cop who makes a mistake. It holds a lot of water."

"What would you propose, then? How would you make a change?"

"Come on, Wilson. You're not dumb. What are you going to do? Kill an innocent person to call it even between you and me? That makes no sense. I had nothing to do with your brother's death."

"You had everything to do with it!" Wilson roared. "You're a cop. We wear the same uniform. We carry the same weapons. We follow the same set of rules and guidelines. We are but different parts of the same body. Do you understand? When one cop does something, we all do it."

"You're wearing that uniform right now," I said. "Yet, you plan to kill an innocent person, not protect them."

"I'm making a difference. I'm removing a cancer."

"I'm already gone," I said. "I removed myself."

"You're in the same business. You just don't carry a badge or a gun anymore."

Quinn yawned loudly. "It doesn't matter. I, too, was in the car when Chris died. I, too, swore to exact justice in his name. Blah, blah, blah. There's people who die every day by cops. That's not what this is about."

I turned to Quinn. "Enlighten me, then."

"You are different, August. Wilson knew you personally. You were from the area. Something tragic happens in Los Angeles, what do I care? It happens in my hometown, though, on my soil." Quinn clicked his tongue and shook his head. "An innocent kid shot by an officer in Sacramento... not again. Not after Jayden."

I shook my head, coming to a terrifying conclusion. Sure, Quinn wished to avenge Jayden by tormenting me, but I don't that was his true motivation. I think he used the incident as a poor excuse for his crimes. Quinn had provided the answer during one of our first encounters.

August, we're the next Batman and Joker. Clarice and Hannibal. Holmes and Moriarty.

Quinn's motivation was more chaotic and undefinable. He tormented me because he enjoyed it, just as the Joker or Moriarty enjoyed destroying Batman's or Holmes' lives. It wasn't about revenge, it was about pure selfishness.

I clenched my jaw. "I'm done playing along. I'm done talking."

Before Quinn could respond, I pivoted and darted toward Wilson. I slammed into his body with my functioning shoulder. Still, my other shoulder detonated with fireworks. I ground my teeth and swallowed the stifling pain.

Wilson hadn't expected my suicidal charge. I hit him full force, and my momentum carried us hard to the rocky ground. Though his enormous body cushioned my fall, I bit through my tongue. Blood filled my mouth.

I rolled away and scrambled into a crouch. My left arm dangled uselessly, bright with pain. My tongue burned at a low simmer.

Before allowing Wilson to recover, I burst forward again. I wielded the StrikeLight, clicking the setting to stun. Wilson was a large man and trained in combat. To incapacitate him in my broken state (in any state, really) I had one shot.

Otherwise, he would overpower and kill me.

No one was coming to save me, Maya had made that clear. Hell, no one knew where I was, except Timothy, and he had already called the cops. He had watched them drive past him. Why would he call again? The kid didn't know the officers worked against me.

I feinted toward his body. In his attempt to recover from my sucker punch, Wilson responded as I had hoped. He motioned to block my stunning strike, raising both arms in a warding gesture.

At the very last second, I redirected the trajectory of my attack. The prongs of the flashlight discharged a white, electric current, and it kissed the detective's oaken neck.

His body went rigid as the electricity pulsed through it. I had a five-second window before the incapacitating pain vanished.

I released the charge.

Wilson fell to his knees. He dropped his sidearm.

I hurriedly collected it before backpedaling, putting as much distance between me and the detective as possible.

Wilson panted, and his limbs loosened. He dropped to all fours and spit tendrils of saliva. After three seconds, he glared up at me. "I'm going to kill you."

I pointed the detective's gun at him. My hands shook. "Wilson, re-move the handcuffs from your belt."

"You won't shoot me." He climbed to his feet, still a little wobbly from the shock.

"Wilson! Handcuff yourself. I don't want to shoot you, but I will." My face scrunched as I struggled to fight away the tears. "You know I will!"

Wilson glared at me. I thought he would call my bluff and burst toward me. Instead, he placed his hands on his head, kneeling onto the ground.

My heart thumped hard against my chest cavity, so hard a dull ache seeped throughout my torso. A metallic taste filled my mouth. My breaths came in shallow, staccato blasts.

"Handcuff," I said. "Now."

Wilson obeyed, removing the handcuffs from his belt and clicking them over his wrists.

"Feet." I pointed the gun at his thighs. "I don't need you mobile."

Wilson sighed, but complied. He removed a pair of zip tie cuffs from his belt, sat on his butt, and tightened the plastic manacles around his ankles.

Feeling confident the detective couldn't interfere, I stepped away from him and faced Quinn.

Endgame. Tuesday, July 25th. 2133hrs.

My heart, already working overtime, stopped beating and dropped into my stomach like a hot coal.

During my scuffle, the scene Quinn created had changed.

The hellhound remained in the center of the chamber, obedient and patient.

The spirits ceased their wandering. They stood in a large circle, spectating the next event.

The arachnid standing to the right of the hellhound wrapped its six arms around Vincent Dupree's body, holding him tight. The creature set its venomous fangs to Vincent's taut throat.

Aaron Brooks stood to the left of the hellhound. He held a pistol, and he pressed it tightly against the second arachnid's head.

I blinked, trying to erase the fuzz from my head, convincing myself that nothing I saw was real. It was all a hallucination.

Like a few minutes prior, the monsters remained unchanged.

"They're not real," I said. "They're not real. They're not real. It's all an illusion."

Acting desperate, I prodded my broken collarbone with my finger. Pain exploded through my body. I held it, though. That was real. The pain was real. I focused on it, using it like a chisel to chip away the hallucination.

Little by little, my vision cleared.

Though the spirits and the hellhound remained static, the arachnids' forms shifted. They never quite disappeared, but the illusion slightly faded for me to discern the scene.

The arachnid behind Vincent was Gerald. Instead of pressing thick fangs against Vincent's neck, he held a knife to his throat. Foam bubbling from his lips, and he wore a crazed look in his eyes. Muck smudged his face, greased his wiry, unkempt hair, emphasizing his mania.

Aaron Brooks (the same Aaron Brooks I had shot and killed that life-shattering summer afternoon) held a gun to the second arachnid's head.

Aaron was Aaron. He hadn't changed. He wasn't an illusion.

He held his gun to Glacia's skull. Grime matted her hair, held it at odd, knotted angles. Her jeans and her shirt had ripped. Her face a myriad of bruises and swelling and small lacerations. She had her eyes wide open, staring straight at me, her lips curled into despair.

"Do you see now?" Quinn asked.

He hopped off the pedestal which his throne sat atop of, and he skipped his way around the hellhound, stopping five yards from where I stood.

I could have raised Wilson's gun and killed the man with no effort. I would have, too. I almost did, but a thought shined through my dark mind.

What would happen to Glacia if I killed Quinn?

I swallowed my emotions to play his game a little longer. Without saying a word, I waited for him to speak. That's what he wanted anyway, to hear his own voice and self-perceived brilliance.

"This is how the end of the game plays out, August Allan Watson." Quinn grinned like the Devil. "First, there's Vincent Dupree. You were his best man for his wedding. You have a loose sense of camaraderie, right?" Without waiting for me to respond, he continued speaking. "There's also, of course, the lovely Glacia."

I growled beneath my breath.

"Here in the Underworld," Quinn said, "Aaron Brooks' spirit has made a surprising and material comeback. I'm sure he would love to enact his revenge against you by killing someone you care for."

I inhaled, pushing back my rage. My hand had a mind of its own, and it trembled as I fought against its will to raise the gun, take aim, pull the trigger, and eliminate Quinn from this world.

"If I'm correct," Quinn said. "Wilson has a single round remaining in his weapon. Check."

I went numb as understanding dawned.

They had planned for everything. Quinn must have predicted I'd go for Wilson first to eliminate the most pressing threat—the man with a gun. He most likely instructed Wilson to fight back a little, but to ultimately allow me the victory.

To allow me to confiscate his weapon. They wanted me to have the gun, and that realization terrified me.

My hands worked the Glock with an alarming remembrance. I hadn't owned a gun for five years, and I had only shot once in that time--at Eddie Denier, the Voodoo Killer. Yet, checking the rounds was like riding a bicycle.

Quinn had predicted the scenario correctly; only one bullet remained in the chamber.

"You will make a choice," Quinn said. "I will count down from three. In that time, you will choose to save Vincent by shooting Gerald. To save Glacia by…" Quinn lengthened his grin, showcasing his proud amusement, "by killing Aaron Brooks… again. Or you can allow both of them to die and shoot me." The man extended his arms in a Christ pose.

My eyes stung and blurred with tears.

I wanted, more than anything I had ever wanted in my life, to punch a hole directly between Quinn's eyes. He had orchestrated the chaos and turmoil of the last four months. He was solely responsible for multiple deaths, including that of Cambria.

If anyone deserved to eat lead, Quinn stood first in line.

"One," he said.

My eyes shifted to Vincent.

His back arched, as if he tried to pull away from the knife digging into his throat. Tendrils of blood leaked down his neck. Tears spilled down his face.

I hadn't known Vincent for too long. He had asked for my help on a case, and I had solved it. Afterward, he asked me to serve as the best man in his wedding to the woman who had haunted him—it's all a confusing, messy affair. Over the past few months, we had become something like friends.

To save him, I would have to shoot Gerald.

"Two."

An inconceivable tableau presented to the left.

Aaron Brooks held a gun to Glacia's head. To save Glacia, I would have to shoot Aaron Brooks... again. That seemed too emotionally and physically overwhelming to even consider. To aim a gun at the kid and pull the trigger felt more impossible than him standing before me.

Unlike Vincent, Gerald, and Glacia, where the illusion had vanished as I convinced my mind they weren't real, Aaron remained fully in focus.

"Thr—"

I pulled the trigger.

The shot thundered through the cavern in a deafening, shattering report. The entire cave system rumbled and shook. I thought it might just go on trembling forever. Then I realized it wasn't shaking and about to cave in, but I was. My entire body shivered, and I thought I might collapse.

Quinn's head turned to where I aimed and fired the weapon.

With his attention distracted, I pulled the shattered remains of myself together and sprinted toward him. I cocked the gun behind my shoulder and struck forward as I reached him.

The weapon connected with his cheekbone, scraped across his face to his chin, leaving a deep, bloody furrow.

He screamed, bringing his hands to the gash.

I instantly reloaded another strike. I brought the gun straight down on his head, splitting the front of his skull. He dropped, boneless, and lay on the ground in an awkward heap.

Before I could catch my breath or even confirm my shot, I bolted toward Gerald and Vincent.

Gerald was rigid, stiff as a board. Vincent wasn't any more lively. Fear had most likely short wired their functioning, cemented them where they stood.

I shoved the gun into my waistband and, with a little effort, pried the knife from Gerald's hand.

The captive spirits remained where they stood, watching as everything unfolded.

I walked to Cerberus, straight through the massive hellhound with no resistance, and out the other side to Glacia and Aaron Brooks.

Though I had shot at Aaron, he remained standing, the gun still in his hand, pressing against Glacia's head.

I shuffled to him and touched his shoulder. My hand passed through his body.

"He's not real," I said, looking at Glacia with soft eyes. I placed a gentle hand on her arm. "He's a hologram, a projection. That's it. I know it appears real, but it's not." I chuckled, realizing she might see me as some nightmare, too. "Glacia, it's me. August. I came for you. Do you trust me?"

She blinked.

"We're going to get out of here, okay?" I peered over my shoulder.

All the spirits stood and observed the interaction—all but one. It looked awfully familiar. I squinted my eyes to focus through the distorted lighting, and I recognized him. Steven Anderson. He peeled away from the crowd of other spirits, moving toward the side of the cavern.

"Hold on," I said to Glacia, releasing her hand.

I chased after Steven, wielding the knife Gerald had held against Vincent's throat. I was too late in my pursuit.

He phased through a stone wall.

Much like my bathroom from earlier, I figured the entrances and exits all had a disguise around them. Steven had simply walked through a hidden door, an exit that I couldn't see. I continued after him, but skidded to a stop and slowly backed away.

Steven Anderson reemerged from the wall, though he now sprinted back toward me.

Hot on his tail, a flood of SWAT officers poured into the chamber.

I dropped the knife, placed my hands behind my head, and went down to my knees. A chilling victory spread throughout my body.

Despite the odds, I had defeated Daniel Quinn.

Breaking and Entering. Tuesday, July 25th. 2134hrs

A light burned through the window of the security shed by the front gate. Maya stopped ten yards away from it and crouched in the shadow of an oak tree.

She had to sneak past the guardhouse and through the gate to earn a knock on the front door.

I probably should have thought of a plan beforehand, she thought.

Evan had infuriated her, though. Her anger and hurt distracted her from creating a viable plan. Instead, she forgot about the stupid gate and the dumb security shed.

A powerful hand gripped her arm.

Maya spun around. She cocked back her free arm to throw a punch at the intruder.

Evan released her and raised his hands. "Easy," he said.

"What the hell?"

"Sorry I scared you... and, well, sorry for being an ass." He sighed. "I'm sorry."

"We don't have time for your apologies," Maya said, though her heart warmed from the sentiment.

"Actions speak louder than words, anyway, right?" Evan asked.

"What are you talking about?"

"Wait here." He must have noticed the defiance in Maya's eyes. "It's not up for debate. You're too emotionally tied to this case, and you're not thinking straight. I'm not thinking right, and I'm degrees away from the situation... emotionally speaking, of course. Physically, I'm sitting in the oven."

"What's your plan?"

Evan told her what he had scotch taped and craft glued together—a toothpick bridge that would snap and collapse with the slightest amount of pressure.

"It's ridiculous," Maya said. "There's no way it'll work."

"Do you have a better idea?"

Maya chewed on her cheeks and stared at the star-bright sky. "You're going to get yourself killed."

Evan shrugged and turned away from Maya.

She had a fleeting impulse to grab his wrist and twist him around, to kiss him and tell him she loved him. Instead, she bit her tongue and watched him walk toward her car. Her heart jittered, moving so fast she thought it would burn out and quit any second. Her head hurt. Her hands felt numb, and her feet were heavy.

Evan climbed into the driver's seat. A second later, the engine purred. The headlights burned a conical beam through the night.

Nearly a decade ago, Maya had stolen the car—which she named Betty—from one of her first clients.

The man had sweat stains on his white undershirt and greasy, stinky skin. He had purchased her company for the night, but he didn't ask for sex. Instead, he wanted someone to sleep with; he wanted someone to lie with in bed, to snuggle and fall asleep beside.

As they laid there, Maya adopted the big-spoon role. She held him, and he mumbled to her as he cried. His sweaty, rancid back trembled against her chest.

He told stories about his life, but she didn't listen. Not after the first story, at least. Arrested for sexual assault, the man dodged jail time on a technicality, a loophole in the system.

As the allotted time for the session expired, Maya woke the man and demanded payment for her business.

He refused, claiming she had done nothing. If she wanted his money, she would have to perform her actual duties. Maya said that would cost him an additional session. The man dug in his heels, refusing her proposition. He grew angry, and Maya recognized violence in his beady eyes.

She fled the motel room, cutting her losses to keep her skin. On her way out, she snatched his car keys from off the nightstand. He hadn't noticed. It took Maya ten minutes to match the keys to Betty, to find the car in the parking lot.

With some help from her street-savvy friends, Maya switched the plates and registration, and the old Toyota belonged to her.

For ten years the beat-up Toyota had been a foundational pillar in Maya's life. It represented so much, though it mostly represented freedom.

It was also the first thing she had ever owned. Though she hadn't bought it, she had labored for it. She had earned it.

Betty's engine purred for a second, before rising into a cranky, disturbed yelp. The tires screamed against the pavement. The old girl shimmied and shook in the rear, before bursting forward like a bullet from a gun, a stone from a catapult. It built speed as it raced toward the front gate.

A guard jumped from the security shed, waving his arms and shouting at Evan to stop. At the last second, the guard dove back into the shed.

Evan steered Betty straight into the gate.

A terrible thought crossed Maya's mind a fraction before impact. *What if the gate doesn't budge? What if Betty gets smashed, Evan gets killed, and everything was for nothing?*

The thought shattered as Betty smashed through the center of the gate.

Evan lost control.

The car bounced and swerved to the left, into the gravel divide, and directly into a tree.

As it came to a stop, the security guard rushed from the shed toward the accident. He barked into a radio positioned on his shoulder.

Maya stole a deep breath and moved forward. She stuck to the shadows of the oak forest surrounding the house. As she neared the mangled gate, she stopped.

A second security guard had responded, as if from thin air. He and the initial guard wrestled on the ground with Evan. Fighting against two trained and armed men after just being in a violent car accident, Evan held his own—at least long enough for Maya to slip through the gate unnoticed.

She dipped to the opposite side of the driveway. Moving slowly, so as not to make a noise or garner notice, she made her way up to the estate.

Initially, she believed she would waltz up to the front door and knock. As Maya stalked into the front yard, she noticed a car parked in a guest-allocated parking area.

Did the Graves have a visitor at half-past nine on a Tuesday night? Was that normal for them?

Maybe a camera crew to shoot pictures of Terry's feet, Maya thought with a grin.

The SUV had government plates, though, which film crews rarely had the luxury of possessing.

Maya patted her hair absentmindedly as she fit the pieces together. With a little critical thinking, the probable answer came fast.

Tara Ferneau paid a late-night visit to the Graves' household.

Maya inhaled, weighing her situation. She stood alone, most likely against Terry and Wendy Graves, Jericho, and Detective Tara Ferneau. With Evan indisposed, with Detective Vanek at the hospital in Sacramento with Victor Pemberton, with August missing and Fred working on bringing him back home, Maya had no one to turn to.

She was completely on her own. Outnumbered. On enemy turf.

She didn't even have the element of surprise anymore. With Evan's likely capture, that advantage leaked away, too. Soon, they would come looking for her, if they hadn't already spotted her on a security camera.

"I need another distraction," she muttered, her eyes cemented to the SUV with government plates.

A wild idea struck, one nearly as crazy as Evan's plan. But crazy was difficult to predict and harder to pin down. If Maya stood a chance, she had to employ a little crazy.

She hurried across the driveway to the SUV. The passenger side faced the house, so she went to the driver's side and found the door unlocked.

Maya hopped into the front seat. A shotgun and an assault rifle stood mounted against the mesh barrier separating the front from the back.

"That's a start," Maya said, unclasping the assault rifle and slinging the strap over her shoulder. She grabbed the shotgun and set it outside the vehicle, leaning it against the side panel.

With weapons in tow, Maya scrambled to find the buttons that controlled the sirens. Though it was an undercover vehicle, it still had flashing lights and sirens.

When she and Eddie dated, he brought her along on a ride. He showed her how to work all the buttons and gadgets on his cruiser.

Maya summoned the memory. The SUV had a different setup from the sedan, but the buttons were more or less the same.

"There it is," she said, her voice bright with excitement. "Now, what else is in here?"

She opened the glove box, found a six-shooter pistol, grabbed it without a second thought, and wedged it in her waistband.

Maya sat back against the driver's seat and exhaled, her eyes skimming the cab.

Another offbeat idea jumped into her mind.

What if I pull an Evan and ram the car into the home? Maya snickered at the thought, but her gaze lowered to confirm the credibility of the idea. Ferneau left the keys in the ignition. From the keychain dangled a tactical Kubotan.

"Well, at least one thing went right."

Maya pulled the keys from the ignition and stuffed them into her pocket, feeling the comforting weight of the Kubotan.

She breathed and thought of Alina. "Here goes nothing."

Maya flipped the siren switch. Blue lights flashed in the darkness. The siren screamed a deafening wail.

She leaped from the driver's seat, landed on the cement, whipped the assault rifle around her back, and clicked off the safety. She aimed into the sky, at the stars and the moon, and she pulled the trigger, emptying the thirty rounds into the night.

Once the assault rifle dry fired, Maya dropped it to the ground and sprinted around the side of the house, around to the backyard.

She had to hurry. Based on her best guess, Ferneau and Jericho, both trained for high-stress situations, would respond to the sirens and the rapid fire from the assault weapon.

Which was what Maya intended to happen.

She didn't fear Mrs. Plastic or Mr. Soft-Feet.

Maya tried the glass slider at the back of the estate. It didn't budge. She scanned the exterior wall, searching for an open window. No luck.

Pure panic screamed into her ears, flashed across her eyes, rendering her nearly senseless.

If she couldn't get into the house before Jericho and Ferneau returned, or before someone confronted her, she wouldn't have a chance of rescuing Alina.

"I need a way in. I need a way in." The muted, muffled sound of her voice drowned her surfacing anxiety. "Screw it. If you can't find a way, create a way." Who said that, Maya wondered as she hurried to a wooden lattice. "Probably Warren Buffett."

She looped the shotgun's strap over her shoulder and climbed the ivy-wrapped lattice to the second floor. The brittle, crisscrossing wood held her weight.

When she reached the second-story window, she removed her T-shirt and wrapped the cloth around a fist. With her other hand, she fished into her pocket for the Kubotan. She moved the instrument into her wrapped hand so the end prodded an inch from her grasp.

Maya made three quick, jabbing motions to the corner of the window. The glass webbed and crinkled near the impact.

She returned the Kubotan to her pocket. With her wrapped arm, she punched through the damaged window and cleared away any of the lingering, jagged shards.

Maya climbed through and came into a dark, empty room.

She allowed her glass-filled shirt to fall to the floor. She didn't care to risk putting it back on and getting a thousand small lacerations.

She removed the six-shooter from her waistband and held it in front of her body. Maya had plenty of practice with a pistol. She had a concealed weapon in her purse for emergency situations, and she frequently went to the range to keep her skill sharp.

Creeping forward, careful not to make a sound, Maya came into a hallway. About a thousand doors ran the length of the wall. She sighed, wondering when something would come easily.

Not leaving a stone unturned, she stopped at each door and peered into the rooms.

Eventually, as she worked her way into the far wing, she opened a door to a teenager's bedroom. Pictures of shirtless men adorned the walls, along with a body-length mirror, a dresser covered in make-up, and laundry strewn over every surface.

Sprawled across the bed, lying on her back with a laptop resting on her stomach, was Samantha. She wore highlighter green headphones.

Maya returned the sidearm to her waistband and slung the shotgun forward. With the nose of the Remington 12-gauge, Maya pressed the door fully open and entered Samantha's room.

Graves' Encounter. Tuesday, July 25th. 2143hrs

MAYA SUDDENLY SAW THE many holes in her hasty plan. She had announced her arrival by blaring the siren and firing the assault rifle into the sky. Surely the Graves would have responded to the potential threat by assigning one of the security guards to protect their children.

With a quick glance over her shoulder, Maya scanned the hallway for an incoming threat. It was empty and silent, apart from the sirens halfway muted from the other side of the home.

Maya returned her attention to Samantha's bedroom and adjusted her grip to balance the shotgun in one hand. She placed a finger to her lips and signaled for Samantha to remain quiet.

Maya stepped into the room, closed, and locked the door.

"Remove your headphones," she said, keeping her voice quiet.

Samantha complied.

"Hi," Maya said. "I don't want to hurt you, Samantha. I definitely don't want to kill you. I wouldn't mind killing your parents, if that were legal and I could get away with it."

"Who are you?"

Maya readjusted the shotgun into both her hands. She held it loose, though, not quite aiming at the young woman.

"I'm Alina Moore's aunt." She studied the girl, watching for a reaction.

Samantha blinked a few times and rubbed her hands on the sheets.

"Do you know Alina?" Maya asked.

"No."

"You're sure?"

"I mean, yes."

"Which is it?"

"I don't know her, you know? But I know her."

"You're going to have to explain that one."

"She was at the dinner last night. We didn't talk or anything, but she was there."

"How did you know it was her?"

"I didn't until this afternoon."

Pinpricks of ice poked from Maya's body. Her finger tightened on the trigger. "This afternoon?"

"She came here to see my parents. Jericho came to my room, told me someone wanted to see me." Samantha wiped a tear from her eye. "There's no internet in my room."

Maya cocked her head. "What?"

Samantha glanced at the computer on her lap. "I'm not a bad person. I would've called the police if I could have. I swear it. But there's no internet. This computer only works offline. Look." Samantha turned the screen. "It's some movie my dad downloaded. I don't even like movies. There's nothing else to do, though. My parents took my phone. They locked me in here."

"Your door wasn't locked."

"I'm locked in the house, more or less," Samantha said, closing the laptop screen. "I can't leave. I can't go on the internet. I can't use a phone."

"Why?"

Samantha swallowed. "They'll hurt you."

"They'll hurt Alina unless you help her."

"But they're my parents."

"That doesn't excuse them from accountability. My parents sucked. Alina's parents sucked. Yours suck, too. It's a rite of passage to learn your parents are flawed."

"I can't do that to them. It wasn't always like this. We were happier before." Tears slipped down her cheeks. "We can't go back to that life, though. That's what they always tell me. We can't go back."

Maya did not know what Samantha went on about. She figured her brain was a little rattled from staring down the barrel of a shotgun. Maya refocused the conversation.

"You disappeared last night. Where did you go?"

"I don't know. I was on a boat. When I woke up, we had washed ashore on some island."

"What island?"

"I don't know."

"We? Who else was there?"

"A boy. Uh, Rhett was his name."

"Another captive?"

Samantha nodded. "They took Alina to the island."

"I know. You don't know what the island is called?"

Samantha subtly shook her head. "No, but there's a Minotaur."

"Like a half-bull, half-man kind of deal from the myths?"

"Like the Theseus myth, the Minotaur's name is Asterion. I saw him. I saw the creature. They feed children to the Minotaur." Samantha squeezed her eyes shut. "My parents do."

Maya couldn't decide if Samantha had temporarily lost her mind, or if she told an odd truth. Either way, it didn't lead Maya any closer to Alina.

"I need to get to the island. How can I find it?"

"I don't know."

"Stand up."

"What?"

"Stand up." Maya pressed the butt of the shotgun against her shoulder and leaned into it. "Stand up."

Samantha complied.

What am I doing taking a hostage? Maya thought. *I'm pointing a 12-gauge shotgun at a girl no older than Alina.*

Maya exhaled and lowered the weapon. "Think, Samantha. Please. Is there a map in the house, or something that might help me learn the location of the island. I don't want to hurt anyone. I just want to save my niece."

"There's a map in the sitting room where I saw them with Alina earlier. It's of the coastline. There are islands on it, islands that don't appear on any other map."

"Where's the room?"

"Downstairs. I can take you there."

"No," Maya said, her voice blunt. "Stay up here."

"Will you hurt them?" Samantha stared at the shotgun.

"If anything, they'll hurt me. I need to see the map, take a picture, send it to a friend. That's all. My friend will handle the rest."

"I can do it for you." Samantha spoke with pure sincerity.

Maya almost believed her, allowed her to go through with the task, but she pulled back at the last second. Samantha had been in the room when they took Alina. What if the girl went downstairs, warned her parents of Maya's presence, and sent Jericho and Ferneau up the stairs? Maya couldn't risk it.

"I have to do this," Maya said. "Where's the room?"

Samantha pointed out where the guards were patrolling, the locations of security cameras and what they recorded and what they missed. She provided Maya with a step-by-step route to follow. She even sketched on college-ruled paper with a pencil—the girl had a semblance of artistic talent, too.

After providing Maya with the pertinent details, she glanced at her. "Does any of that help?"

"All of it." Maya regarded the girl and recognized something in her demeanor, her body language, the careful way in which she spoke.

Samantha wanted out from her parents' rule. She hated her life, and she was using Maya as much as Maya was using her.

Licking her lips, Maya spoke. "You need to know something."

"I think I know," Samantha said, her voice shy. "If you go down there and succeed…" She stared beyond Maya. Her eyes filmed and her lips moved, though words didn't spill forth.

"If all goes well, they'll get arrested."

Samantha nodded.

Maya, understanding the pain of being a teenaged girl and not having a father to protect her or a mother to guide her, understanding the turmoil raging through Samantha's mind, reached out and touched the girl's arm.

She had to say something. She had to share words of encouragement. But what? That everything would be okay? That was ridiculous. Samantha would survive, would probably move forward with her life, but would she be okay?

Was Maya okay, though? Had she survived and moved forward from her past?

"What will happen to me and Wade?" Samantha asked. "Afterward?"

"I don't know."

"What would you do right now, if you were me?"

Maya didn't need Samantha to clarify her question. Despite what her parents had become and what they had done, should she betray blood?

"Whatever happens," Maya said, "you're not the bad guy. Do what you know is right. There's pain, sure, but there's never regret doing the right thing."

"That's not an answer. What would you do if you were me?"

"I'd run away," Maya said without hesitation. "I'd hide. I'd avoid the problem. Pretend it didn't exist until it screamed in my face and forced me to confront it. But you're not me. You're stronger and better."

Before Samantha could question her role, Maya crossed the room, opened the door, and checked the hallway before confronting her problems.

Maya followed the map Samantha had drawn her, doing her best to stay in the areas blind to guards and cameras. When she reached the bottom of the stairwell, she hurried to a niche across the hall, flattening her back against the wall and allowing her heart a second to slow down.

Voices chorused from a few doors away, loud and argumentative.

According to Samantha's directions, Maya figured the voices came from the sitting room where the map hung on the wall.

Great.

"I only need a picture, and a few seconds to send it to Vanek and Fred," she said, mumbling to herself. "A picture and a text. That's it. Five seconds. Ten max."

Maya exhaled and snagged the cell phone from her pocket. She created a group message with herself, Fred, and Vanek, and she clicked on the camera option.

After a few deep breaths, she emerged from the niche and hustled to the sitting room's door. It was open, which accounted for the din of voices spilling from it. Maya considered that a blessing. She flattened her body against the wall beside the door and leaned slightly to the right, enough to peek into the room.

Terry Graves paced back and forth. Blood covered his shirt and speckled his face, and he had his long sleeves rolled halfway up his forearms. He barked at his wife.

Wendy sat in an armchair, one leg crossed over the other, holding a glass of whiskey. She glared at Terry, yelling back at him.

Beside Wendy sat a woman Maya didn't recognize, but whom she assumed was Tara Ferneau.

Maya cursed under her breath, realizing another hole in her rash plan. Why would Ferneau or Jericho sprint to the trouble? They would have stayed to protect the Graves, and they would have sent their grunts to assess the threat.

The woman, presumably Ferneau, was in her mid-to-late forties, and she had a hard, weather-worn face. Despite the harshness of her features, she had soft blue eyes that almost made her look beautiful. With subtle amusement, she watched Terry and Wendy bicker. A slight smile cut across her stony face.

Jericho stood behind a wooden chair, both hands on the backrest.

Evan sat in the chair. His face was a swollen, pulpy mess of bruises and blood. His hands were bound beneath the seat, his ankles tied to the chair legs. His head lolled forward.

Maya pulled back. Amidst the commotion and arguing, she doubted anyone noticed her. Even if no one had seen her, she stood in the direct line of a security camera and in the heart of a security guard's patrol route.

When she first arrived at the spot, she hadn't been too worried about the guard or the camera. Snap the picture, send it to Vanek and Fred, and try to escape. If someone caught her committing the deed, they caught her. All that mattered was the picture getting sent.

Now, though, the situation had changed.

They not only had Evan, but they put a pretty decent beating on him. Maya wasn't sure what information they wanted from him, but whether he provided it probably didn't matter to their endgame.

"Kill him now," Wendy said, her voice shrill. "He doesn't want to talk, why waste our time."

Maya's journalist impulses took over. She swiped out of the text message and navigated to the voice recorder, tapping the big red button.

"We're not killing him now," Terry said, his tone growing impatient.

"Why? The car's registration belongs to Maya Adler. We know who he's working with. We know why he's here. Why keep him alive?"

"You're so shortsighted, it's amazing. Really, it's a feat to be as dumb as you."

"Well, enlighten me," Wendy said. "Help me understand. Why are we keeping him alive?"

"Enough!" Ferneau shouted. "You're both idiots, and it's barely worth the money to work with either of you. I don't know why Corvis ever went into business with you. I told him you would bring his empire down. I warned him."

The heated conversation continued, but Maya lost track of it. Her mind fixated on a single word, or rather a name.

Corvis.

Not stopping the recording, Maya switched back to the group message. She typed the name with a trembling thumb and sent it to Vanek and Fred. *He's the head of the bull. Find an island he or his company owns within a hundred miles off the coast. That's where she is.*

Eric Corvis, if that's who Ferneau referenced, was a major figure in Northern California. Corvis Construction developed a majority of big residential neighborhoods and tract housing. His name constantly appeared in political funding campaigns and charitable work in Sacramento, mostly dealing with youth programs. He had at least three parks subsidized by his company, an after-school program, and a foster home service. Corvis Construction also provided a hefty donation to the Sacramento Police Department every year.

Not only was he a financial, philanthropic, and societal giant, he was a giant—nearly seven-feet tall, broad, and muscular. What had Wanda said?

Middle-aged. Dark hair, clean shaven... big, too. Not just muscular, but beastly.

Without Corvis' name, the description meant nothing. With his name, though, it meant everything.

Still, Maya couldn't leave the estate. She needed the picture as a reference to help them locate the island, and she needed to help Evan. She couldn't run away and hide. She couldn't avoid the problem. Not this time. She had to charge forward and fight.

Footsteps echoed through the vast hallway of the estate.

Maya had to act, otherwise the security guard would happen upon her.

With a deep breath, she rolled off the wall and bounced into the open doorway. She faced the phone's camera toward the wall where Samantha said the picture hung, and she snapped a picture, hoping it turned out, and she sent it.

"Everyone, sit down!" Maya spoke with authority and command.

Terry Graves ceased to pace. He glanced around himself for a second, then he sat directly on the floor where he had stood.

Ferneau acted contrarian, though. She raised her hands above her head and slowly stood. "Maya Adler," she said, her voice calm.

"Uh, uh. Nope. You don't get to keep control of this situation." Maya slid her phone into her pocket and brought the shotgun back around. She pointed the weapon in Wendy and Ferneau's direction. "Sit your bony butt back in the seat. I know how to shoot a gun, and I'm not afraid to pull this trigger. Prison sounds oddly comforting to me—the routine, the structure, the predictability. Three square meals, a bed, hot water, television, books, all the free time I could imagine. So, sit down."

Ferneau must have read Maya's expression and concluded Maya spoke truthfully. The detective sat on the couch.

"Let's make this simple, shall we?" Maya asked. "Badda bing, Badda boom. We do the exchange. We're happy. Alive. We go our separate ways. I, of course, being an upstanding citizen, tell an honest cop everything. They show up and arrest you. You live my dream life in prison, hiding from the world and reading all the books at your disposal." Maya nodded at Jericho. "You're still not sitting, big boy. Why don't you rest your weary feet before I make my dreams come true?"

"No one has to die," Ferneau said.

Maya chuckled. "See me laughing? I'm laughing because that's funny. Thirty-two seconds ago, you were all pretty set on enlightening my friend to what awaits on the other side of life."

"Friend?" Evan asked, his voice broken and nearly muted.

"I thought with my past and everything, you wanted... you know what? It doesn't matter right now." Maya glared at Jericho. "Why don't we avoid the small-talk. Untie Evan, sit your bootylicious booty on the ground—yeah, I'm talking to you, Jericho. You have sweet cheeks, and I'm not a girl to let a compliment pass her by. You should know what God has given you."

"Maya," Evan croaked. "Stop talking so much."

"Sorry. I'm nervous, and when I'm nervous, it's hard to stop speaking whatever pops into my head. Jericho, untie him, or I shoot in five... four... three..."

"Untie him, Jericho!" Wendy said, her voice teetering on hysteria. "Now!"

"No," Jericho said. He stared at Maya with a bored expression. "I don't think I will."

"You will!" Wendy's voice pitched into a shriek. "Untie him!"

"Or what? You'll fire me? I don't work for you, remember? I work for Corvis. I'm protecting his assets, his name, even if that means allowing you to die... which I don't think you will." He narrowed his eyes and glared at Maya. "She doesn't have the guts to pull the trigger, at least not unless we scare her into doing so. I think we should all stay right where we are, relaxed, enjoying each other's company. Right, Maya? We'll essentially starve you out—starve your confidence, your patience, your anger." He smirked. "Starve your awareness."

At that moment, movement blurred in Maya's periphery.

A tingle, almost like a malfunctioning Spidey-Sense triggered too late. Before Maya could respond, a blunt force connected hard, with a dull crack, against the side of her skull.

The floor rolled unsteadily. Maya struggled to keep her balance on the shifting hardwood. She reached out for the wall to support herself, but the wall jumped back, away from her, and she stumbled forward, crashing into it rather than leaning on it.

The floor hiccuped again, and Maya tumbled onto the ground, lying on her side. The shotgun sprinted away into the far corner.

Hands gripped Maya's arm, bent it behind her back, cranked it upward at an awkward angle. The sharpness of the pain drove away the haze filling Maya's head.

The room snapped back into focus.

Someone new, the patrol guard, Maya assumed, kneeled atop her, cranking her arm high against her back. Her shoulder tendons stretched to their limits, screaming for respite. Like a newborn baby on their stomach, Maya raised her head to peer around the room.

Terry had climbed to his feet and positioned himself behind an armchair. He crouched, only his cowardly face appearing above the backrest.

Wendy had done likewise, jumping behind the other chair, though she didn't dare risk stealing a glance at the unfolding situation.

Jericho removed a sidearm. He snugged the barrel tightly against Evan's temple.

Ferneau strolled toward the shotgun in the far corner of the room. She leaned over, whistling as she did so, and picked up the weapon. "I thought this looked familiar," she said. "So you're the one who set off the siren? You also stole weapons from my vehicle. You know, that's a lofty prison sentence, to steal from an officer of the law?"

Maya's heart quickened as she remembered the revolver stuffed into her waistband. Had they noticed that? She could feel the weight of it, the steel against her skin. It rested just below the guard's knee, which dug into her spine. His leg most likely (*hopefully*) covered the revolver from view.

"The shotgun and the assault rifle," Ferneau continued. "That's a hefty prison sentence. Though, seeing that you would enjoy incarceration so much, I don't think an arrest fits this crime."

The guard shoved Maya's arm a little closer to the top of her head. She winced. Tears filled her eyes.

"Here's what will happen," Ferneau said, walking across the room and kneeling before Maya. "We'll kill him first." She nodded back at Evan. "You'll watch it happen. Then we'll wait until we hear from Corvis. Maybe he'll call in an hour, maybe three days. I don't know. Sometimes he likes to play with his prey." Ferneau snickered. "Only when we hear Alina is dead will we kill you."

Maya hissed as the pain in her shoulder radiated through her arm and neck.

Ferneau glanced at Jericho and nodded.

That's when the room imploded with chaos.

Family Feud.
Tuesday, July 25th.
2154hrs

AN EXPLOSION FORCED MAYA to squeeze her eyes shut hard enough to hurt her head. She screamed with immutable pain of knowing someone you loved has died.

The room went gravely silent, apart from Maya's staccato gasps.

She didn't want to open her eyes and bear witness to what had happened to Evan, but she forced herself to look, anyway.

Evan remained seated in the chair, sobbing silently—his face twisted into an unnatural display of terror and relief. Jericho stood behind him, gun still planted against Evan's temple, but he hadn't pulled the trigger.

Maya hyperventilated a few quick breaths. The weight of the guard's knee remained rooted to her back. Ferneau still kneeled in front of her, holding the shotgun with both hands, though not in a readied position.

Terry and Wendy Graves popped their gopher heads from their hidey-holes. They appeared more terrified than Evan. They both raised their hands, palms forward—a gesture to signal someone to stop. The two of them babbled, stuttering and tripping over their words, making no sense at all, mostly saying, "No, no, no, no," on repeat.

Maya turned her head as far as the awkward position allowed.

Samantha Graves stood in the doorway. She held a handgun, and she must have fired a warning shot into the ceiling. Now, she firmly pressed the gun against the bottom of her jaw with both hands. They trembled violently. Tears streamed down her broken face.

"Shut up!" Samantha focused her voice toward her parents.

They immediately silenced.

"You've taken everything from me over these past two years. My friends. My home. You're different now, so you took away the parents I loved and trusted and felt safe around. Wade has changed, and you don't even notice him. You don't notice the trouble he's having in school and in his personal life. You took away my brother. What would it matter if I took away my life? Would you even care? Would you?"

"Sammy, please," Terry said. "Lower the gun."

"No! I'm done listening to you. You're a... a murderer."

"Sammy, that's not true," Terry said. "We've murdered no one."

"You're paid to kidnap children and send them to their deaths. What difference is there? I could deny the truth before this morning. I can't anymore, though. Not when I was a part of that truth. How many kids have you sent off to die? To get hunted by that monster?"

"You don't understand," Wendy said. "We did it for you. To give you everything you could ever want."

Samantha exhaled a shattered laugh. "All I could ever want is you, Mom. Is dad. Is a family that's semi-sane. Not this. What is this?" She reached out her hand, signaling the estate. "No one relates to me. I don't have friends because... because they can't relate to this. If someone hangs out with me, it's because of the money, not because of me." She breathed hard for a few seconds, her labored panting the only sound in the room. "You want to kill children and get away with it, well you can do that without me." Samantha pressed the gun tighter against her jaw, shutting her mouth.

"Sammy, listen to me," Terry said.

She shook her head.

"What do you want us to do?"

"Turn yourselves in."

"We'll spend the rest of our lives in prison," Wendy said.

The girl chuckled. "So what? That's the best you deserve after what you took from all those kids and their families."

"You don't mean that."

"Stop it, Mom. Stop! I mean it. Why can't you see what you've done? You've ripped families apart for what? Money? It's the most disgusting thing I've ever heard."

"I can't handle this anymore," Ferneau said, rising to her feet. "Samantha, go on and get it over with. Make it easy for us all."

"What?" Terry asked. He snapped his attention to the detective. "You're encouraging her?"

"I mean, realistically, how does this end, Terry? She either blows out her brains, and we move forward killing Maya and Evan, ending this entire debacle for good. Or you guys take her side, agree to turn yourselves in, which leaves me with little choice but to kill everyone in this room but myself and Jericho. Either way, Sammy dies. The question is, do you join her?"

As the conversation between Samantha and her parents happened, and as Ferneau spoke, the guard atop Maya relaxed his hold. He slightly lifted his knee, providing her with slack.

Maya rolled, not caring if she broke her arm with the lurching motion. Her free hand reached for the gun at her waist.

The guard tightened his grip on her wrist, but too late.

Maya snatched the revolver and pulled the trigger.

The man—he appeared young, no older than twenty-five—released his grip and grabbed his shoulder, screaming as fell over.

Maya jumped to her feet and fired a second shot before Ferneau could raise the shotgun.

The detective screamed harshly, collapsing to the floor and gripping her knee. The shotgun dropped beside her.

Maya stamped forward and kicked the weapon away before turning to Jericho.

"It's over, big boy. There's no need for you to add a murder charge to your resume."

Jericho licked his lips like a snake tasting the air. After a second, he dropped the gun to the floor, raised his hands above his head, and stepped away from Evan, snickering.

"There are twelve security guards, all ex-military, on duty," he said. "I'm sure they'll arrive on scene soon enough. You can't shoot your way out of this. Even if you could..." Jericho lowered his arm a few inches and glanced at his watch. "Well, even if you could, Alina is dead by now. Asterion is efficient in his work."

Maya aimed the gun at Jericho's chest. "Release Evan. Now. No stalling. As you said, twelve trained men are responding to this situation. What are the odds we escape before they capture us? The least you can do before killing us is provide a little hope, right?"

Jericho rolled his eyes. "If it shuts you up." He stepped forward and drew a six-inch blade from a sheath.

"Don't let me think you're going to hurt him. I'll shoot you if I see more blood."

"Yeah, yeah, yeah. I get it." Jericho dropped to one knee, reached under the chair, and cut Evan's legs and hands free.

Evan erupted from the chair, moving to stand beside Maya. "You're pretty badass, you know?"

"I was going to leave, but since you saved my life earlier, I owed you the favor."

"What now?" Jericho asked.

Before Maya could respond, turn and run, do anything, a handful of uniformed men with assault rifles filed into the room from the hallway outside the open door.

Their voices chorused and blended together, all of them barking the same, explicit commands. "Drop your weapons! On the ground!"

Maya stared at Jericho. She watched his arrogance dissipate into panic then defeat. After placing the revolver on the floor, she arrested Jericho's attention and smirked at him, sharing her most winning smile. To emphasize her victory, Maya saluted the ex-military man with both of her middle fingers.

As she lay prone on the ground, the SWAT team filed into the room and took care of the rest.

The Castle.
Tuesday, July 25th.
2158hrs.

ALINA TRAILED RHETT AS they reached the peak and neared the castle. Nora kept pace with Alina, or rather, Alina kept pace with the slow, younger girl.

Nora grimaced as she walked. If she felt anything like Alina, her entire body ached, her head pounded, and her legs strained with each step.

Rhett hardly bothered to glance back to confirm the two followed him. He talked, incessantly, about nothing.

It grated on Alina's nerves to the point of self-reflection. *Is that how I come across to everyone? Obnoxious? Blabbering on about nothing of relevance?*

A tinge of embarrassment seeped through her bones. No. Not embarrassment, though that existed, but regret. Alina regretted the idea of dying on the remote island, believing her friends and family would remember her as that annoying, bratty girl who knew everything about everything.

"I'm not kidding, either," Rhett said, turning his head so his voice actually traveled down to Alina and Nora. His hands touched his chest and extended outward, as if containing an expanding balloon. "That big. I nearly died, believe it or not. Suffocated. My friends nearly died, too, though from laughter. You should have seen them bent over, lying on the ground, all curled up and howling like a bunch of monkeys, while I drowned in her—"

"Shut up!" Alina snapped.

"Woah. Wow. Sorry. I didn't realize my story offended you."

"You don't have the power to offend me. You have the power to run your mouth at an excessive volume, incessantly, as if we're not trying to remain stealthy and hidden from the Minotaur."

They stopped at the base of the castle. It was dark as a tomb. No lights or torches illuminated the innumerable windows covering the stone-faced wall.

"We're here," Rhett said, speaking in a lowered tone. "What now? Do we split up?"

Alina shook her head, recalling most horror movies she had seen. The group split up, and the bad guy picked them off one by one.

"We stick together." She glanced at Nora, resolved not to leave the girl, no matter what. "We get through this together."

Rhett brushed a hand through his tangle of hair. "Alright then. What's the plan?"

"Well, the Minotaur lived in a labyrinth, right?"

"Sure."

"Theseus and a group of kids went into the labyrinth as sacrifices to the creature." Alina stared at the towers and crenelations and turrets. Her eyes moved over the littering of windows and arrow slits. "I believe the castle is his labyrinth."

"So we don't enter," Rhett said. "We stay outside, maybe head back to the beach."

"We're taking the fight to the creature," Alina said.

"We're doing what?"

Alina stepped forward. "We're entering that castle, and we're going to hunt the Minotaur."

Rhett stared at her with incredulity, then he burst into a fit of laughter. "You're funny. Has anyone told you that? You're also pretty. I could you see on stage, the audience eating out of your hands."

"She's right," Nora said, the girl's voice quiet.

Rhett sighed and turned to face the castle. "Yeah, I know. But it's so much nicer to avoid reality, isn't it? Imagine if we went back to the beach and fell asleep under the stars, to the crashing water. That's how I would want to die. Not fighting a bloodthirsty monster while paralyzed with fear."

"Everything you want is on the other side of fear."

Rhett snickered. "Teddy Roosevelt?"

Alina couldn't help but laugh. "No, you moron. Jack Canfield, the author of the *Chicken Soup* books."

"Never read them."

"Have you ever read anything?" Nora asked.

"Woah," Rhett said, a giant smile exploding across his haggard features. "What's this? Now I'm getting reamed from every angle? Nora, I thought you were on my side."

The little girl giggled.

Alina bit her lip and grinned out the corner of her mouth. Rhett—handsome, obnoxious, calming, charming. Despite everything, his humor and bright nature still shined like a constant light.

"Besides, I've read before," he said. "I've read plenty."

"The back of the cereal box doesn't count," Nora said.

"Ha. Ha. You think you're being funny, but I learned to count from the back of a cereal box."

Alina wished the escapism fun could continue, but they had to remain focused if they wished to survive. She stepped forward and cleared her throat. "I believe Asterion left the front door open for guests to walk through."

"A fly buzzing right into a spider's web," Rhett said.

The analogy fit too appropriately. Alina ignored it. "We're going to walk right through, expecting trouble. We'll have weapons."

"Oh, really? What weapon do you have? A bazooka? A sniper rifle?"

Alina leaned over and collected a stone the size of a baseball, though not as round or smooth.

Rhett curled his lip into a sneer. "Oh, gross. No way. Not happening."

"You prefer dying?"

"I prefer not bashing in brains with a rock. I'm not a caveman."

"You had me fooled," Nora said.

Alina smirked and glanced at the tree they stood beneath. "What about a thick, sturdy branch? You could use it like a baseball bat."

Rhett shrugged. "Sure. I guess if I had to choose between a rock and a stick, I would go stick." He turned and began searching the area for an appropriate club.

"What about me?" Nora asked.

Alina hated the thought of asking the young girl to take part in the carnage, but they needed all hands on deck, and Alina needed to show she trusted Nora's capabilities.

"Rhett," Alina said.

"What?" He held up a four-foot long branch, about as thick as a thumb and index finger forming a circle.

"Take off your shirt."

"Listen, gorgeous, the thought ran through my mind, too. There's an undeniable physical attraction between us. But doesn't it feel a little inappropriate considering the circumstances?" He nodded at Nora. "Her being right here and all."

"Gross," Nora said.

"Take off your shirt and give it to me," Alina said.

"Why?"

"Just do it."

"Fine." Rhett leaned the stick against the trunk and removed his shirt. He handed it to Alina. "It's my favorite shirt, so don't ruin it."

Alina rolled her eyes and tore it in half.

"What did I just say?"

"I don't know." Alina shrugged her shoulders to her ears. "You say a lot, and I listen to so little of it." She tied the shirt around Nora's neck like a sling or satchel, picked rocks the sizes of tennis balls and golf balls from the ground, and filled the shirt. "If we end up in a fight, you'll hang back and serve as our range fighter, okay? Do you know how to throw a ball?"

"Yeah," Nora said.

"Do that, but with a rock. Throw it at whoever—or whatever—we're fighting."

Nora averted her eyes from Alina, staring at her feet, or possibly the satchel filled with stones—her prior bravado wavering in the face of a fight. "Okay."

"So, plan," Rhett said. He held up a finger. "We waltz right through the front door, explore the castle until we find a Minotaur, and fight it until... what? How far do we take it? Do we kill the monster?"

The man, Alina thought.

As August liked to remind them before every case, the supernatural didn't exist. If that again proved true, they couldn't kill a human, no matter how despicable he was. They weren't vigilantes. They weren't arbiters of justice. They were scared, desperate kids, hoping to escape from the nightmare they currently lived.

"Unless absolutely necessary, we don't kill him," Alina said. "Our goal is to restrain him."

"With what?" Rhett asked. "The handcuffs I conveniently carry around in my pocket just for situations like this?"

"We'll keep our eyes open for rope or... or something."

"Brilliant plan." Rhett quietly clapped. "Incredibly detail-oriented. At least we're using sticks and stones, because they break bones. Words would never hurt the Minotaur."

"Do you have a better idea? Would you like to kill him?"

"It's a man-eating monster, right? I would love to kill the monster if it meant saving our lives."

"I remember you feeling queasy three minutes ago when I picked up the rock."

"That's downright brutal. I wasn't expecting it."

"All murder is brutal, even when expecting it."

"Eh," Rhett said, making a throwaway gesture with his hand. "You're a murder expert now?"

"What if it's not a monster?" Alina asked.

"It kills children," Rhett said. "Man. Vampire. Minotaur. It's a monster."

"We can debate the morality of murder another time," Alina said. "Right now, let's get this over with."

"Another time? As in, if we live and escape this island... you mean a date?"

Alina eyed him with refusal. "I think I'd rather die."

"Don't say things like that. You'll jinx us. The universe listens."

Alina glanced at Nora. "You ready?"

"I think so."

"Let's go, then."

Alina took lead as they marched toward the castle. Rhett and Nora padded behind her. Thankfully, neither of them spoke. She spared a glance back as they made it halfway across no-man's-land.

Rhett wore a tight expression across his face, and he used his club as a walking stick. Nora trickled along beside him. She cradled her sack of stones so they didn't clang and clatter as she moved.

Neither of them appeared ready for a life-or-death battle.

But who was?

They could prepare as much as they wished, but when the fighting happened, and the first punch landed, all preparation went out the window. In that moment, survival took over.

It happened repeatedly in Alina's life—maybe not physical battles, but mental and emotional wars with her parents, with her teachers, with herself. She prepared for the custody battle. Still, when it happened, when the notion of divorce and separation and divide became a reality, it shredded apart everything she braced for. It hit her hard and fast, and she had to backpedal, reel, recover... at least until she could see clearly enough to advance.

Alina's hand touched the double front door's cool-metal handle. The doors were wide, four feet each, and arched at the top. A car could have driven into the castle's foyer. She leaned her weight into the door and pushed with her shoulder.

The door had to weigh a ton when off the hinges. It felt like it weighed near as much while on them. With a grunt and a forceful exhale, the door nudged open, inch by inch, until it stood wide enough for Alina to slip through. She stepped into the castle.

Nora popped inside after her, her slender form silhouetted in the darkness.

Rhett shouldered the door open another foot, joining them in the entry hall.

"I can't see a thing," he said in a whisper. "How do we move around?"

Alina patted her pockets, though they had confiscated her phone. It wasn't worth asking Rhett or Nora if they had a phone with them. She knew the answer. The castle had rows of windows; however, dark clouds covered the moon, preventing any productive light from illuminating the interior.

"We move forward," Alina said. "Nora, hold on to the back of my shirt. Rhett, keep a hand on Nora. We stick together no matter what."

"You're going to lead the way?" Rhett asked.

"I'll take charge," Alina said.

"I'll protect from the back."

"Sounds good."

"Before we move forward."

"Yeah?"

"What's your favorite kind of food?"

"What?"

"Your favorite food... what is it?" Rhett asked.

"Why?"

"I'm planning our date for when we're back in Sacramento."

Alina bit back a sharp rejection. If they wanted to see this through, if they meant to survive, they needed hope. If Rhett found hope from Alina accepting his date, what would it hurt?

"Sushi."

"I can't afford sushi. What's your second favorite?"

Alina snickered, despite herself. "Mexican."

"I know the perfect food truck. It's right next to the Sacramento River, and it's open pretty late. There's a park where we can set up a night picnic. The view isn't great, you know, but it's not terrible, either. If we get bored from looking at water, there's usually some night life. We can people watch. I don't know. I'm still working out the kinks."

"That sounds wonderful," Alina said.

"Really?"

"Really. But let's survive this first. We have to keep moving."

"Lead the way, captain."

Nora's small hand gripped the back of Alina's shirt, pulling on it a little.

Alina shuffled forward, arms stretched like a zombie, hoping not to trip or run face-first into something. After a few feet, her hands pressed into a stone wall. She turned left at random. One hand remained out-stretched, the other grazed along the wall, feeling for a space discerning a doorway.

After another dozen seconds of dragging her feet, moving slowly and cautiously, Alina's fingers brushed across a protrusion in the wall—a familiar protrusion. She stopped.

Nora bumped into her, and Rhett into her.

"What happened?" Rhett asked. "Why didn't you tell us to stop?"

"And Alina said, let there be light." Alina flicked the switch.

Sconces instantly powered on. They had orange, flame-shaped bulbs, that emitted torchlight, though they ran from electricity.

"And it was good," Alina said.

"Did you just compare yourself to God?" Rhett asked.

"God is a woman."

"We'll save that conversation for the date."

"There's no conversation," Alina said. "*He* is a woman."

"That makes no sense! You literally just said he is a woman."

"I know what I said."

Rhett groaned. "You're so frustrating."

Nora gasped. Her hand released Alina's shirt, and she stared wide-eyed—like a child first stepping into a haunted house—at the interior of the castle.

They stood in a thirty-by-thirty foyer, now dimly illuminated by torchlight. Between the sconces holding the electric torches, heads mounted the walls.

Not animal heads either.

Alina grabbed Nora's head and guided the young girl's face against her body. "Don't look," she said, wishing she could turn her head away, bury her face against someone safe.

The army of faces stared back at her. Their features contorted into something haunting—a picture of their last horrible moments of life. A preview of what awaited Nora, Rhett, and Alina if they continued forward.

A single door stood in the center of the interior walls. On either side of each door, taxidermy minotaurs stood guard. Youthful bodies bearing the heads of bulls. They held a spear in one hand, a shield in the other.

"What is this place?" Rhett's voice threatened to break.

"The entrance to the labyrinth," Alina said. "The monster wants to frighten us."

"It's working. Can we go back outside now?"

"If we move through its maze, or if we flee through the forest, he will hunt us." Alina glanced around, focusing on the electrical torches. "This place has electricity. I would bet anything the monster installed cameras throughout the entire island. I bet he's watching us right now. He'll watch us navigate through the maze, or he'll watch us run through the forest. The monster has always known and will always know where we are and what we're doing."

"You don't know that for sure, though," Rhett said.

"Prepare for the worst, hope for the best," Alina said. "We have to assume..." she trailed off as her attention flickered to the minotaurs standing guard, to the heads mounted on the walls. "We have to assume Asterion has done this before, that he's... he's perfected the game. We've never played it. We don't know the rules. We lost the second we stepped foot on this island."

"What are you saying?" Rhett asked. "We give up?"

So much for inspiring hope.

Alina closed her eyes, forcing herself to think, to draw on all the horror movies she had ever seen, hoping to evoke inspiration.

Her eyes shot open, and she stared directly at Rhett with a bright smile. An idea, a semblance of optimism, popped into her mind. "I could kiss you right now, you little genius."

"Uh... I dare you to."

"You were right."

"I was?" Rhett scratched the back of his neck. "I mean, yeah, I was."

"We need to run."

"We do?"

"I need you to look scared. For the cameras."

"That's not too difficult. I currently need a new pair of pants... and underwear."

"Gross," Nora said.

"Anyway... look scared," Alina said, "like right this second. We're going to back away slowly and move toward the front door." Alina followed her own advice, and she reversed her progress, moving toward massive doors leading outside the castle. Rhett and Nora followed her. As she moved, she spoke. "When we reach the front door, we'll turn and run."

"That's exactly what I proposed from the get-go," Rhett said. "When we're interviewed for this daring escape, you better not take credit for my plan."

"Shut up! I already said you were right."

"Oh, yeah."

"The monster will chase us when we run. He'll know where we are, because I'm sure he placed cameras throughout the forest. Even if he doesn't know, he'll hunt us. He knows the island. We don't."

"That's an inspiring plan."

"Except, we're hunting him, remember?"

"I don't get it," Rhett said.

"We know he's after us. We'll listen for him as we flee. When he appears, we'll be ready." Alina reached the front door.

"I have a lot of questions about this plan," Rhett said.

"Run!" Alina screamed, turning tail, grabbing Nora's hand, and flying through the forest.

The Minotaur
Tuesday, July 25th. 2209hrs.

ALINA'S SPRINT THROUGH THE forest to the rocky beach proved treacherous, even without the Minotaur chasing them. The clouds darkened her passage, creating a guesswork of where to place her next step. Alina tripped more than once on exposed roots or loose stones. Her falls cut up her arms, dinged up her legs, scraped her skin, drawing blood. Luckily, she eluded a broken bone or sprained ankle.

Rhett and Nora trailed Alina, but they fared better as they stepped where she succeeded, and they avoided where she failed. Rhett kept Nora's slower pace, too, which probably saved them from injury.

As Alina picked herself up for the fifth or sixth time, she placed her hands on her knees, acting more tired than she felt. Running downhill was less taxing on the cardiovascular system than trudging uphill.

However, she wanted to present an exhausted appearance to lure out the monster.

Also, perceiving her surroundings while running was inefficient and difficult. A quick pause allowed her to take an inventory of the forest.

"We have to keep moving," Rhett said.

Alina glanced at him and nodded. "We're going to walk for a bit, though. It's too dangerous to run across this terrain."

"You're sure?"

"Slow is smooth, and smooth is fast, right?"

"I don't know what that means."

"If we walk, I'm less likely to break my leg. If I don't have a broken leg, we can move far more efficiently than if I have a broken leg."

"I see."

"So, we walk."

The three of them continued their blind retreat down the mountain, though at a much more contained speed. Alina believed their pace would still appear realistic to the Minotaur. The three kids had stumbled into the entry of the labyrinth, had discovered the mounted heads, had panicked and fled. Once they built some separation, regained their wits, they had slowed to proceed more cautiously.

Alina glanced over her shoulder and looked at Nora. "How are you doing?"

Nora nodded. "I'm okay."

A warrior, Alina thought. *I couldn't have done this, held it all together, at nine. I would have curled into a ball and cried, hoping someone would swoop in and save me.*

"Shh," Rhett said, grabbing Alina's wrist and squeezing. "Did you hear that?"

Alina leaned forward, leading with her right ear. She closed her eyes and listened.

Heavy, plodding footsteps slapped against the muddy ground—a rampaging bull charging its prey. It came from the right.

Alina opened her eyes in time to see a massive figure burst from behind the trees and appear before them. In the heavy darkness of the night, she could only discern the monster's silhouette, but it appeared exactly as a Minotaur would. The creature dwarfed Fred. It was tall, maybe seven feet, maybe more. Broad and rippling with muscle. It had a bull's head with thick, sharp horns protruding from its skull.

The Minotaur stood before the three children like a behemoth before a litter of kittens. It laughed, its voice deep and rumbling, like earth shifting, like a mountain collapsing.

"Now you join my collection."

Alina held the softball-sized rock in her right hand. For all it's worth, though, she could have held a cotton ball. What was she thinking? A stone to take out a Minotaur?

She backed away and bumped into Rhett.

His body trembled against hers. "I was joking before," he said into her ear. "But not now. I definitely need new underpants."

A pincer grip grabbed Alina's shirt. Nora. The young girl whimpered as she held onto Alina.

The Minotaur moved forward, slowly and deliberately, as if basking in the fear of his prey, enjoying their terror before he snuffed out their lights and mounted their heads on his wall of horror.

Nora's grip tightened, bunching up more of Alina's shirt.

Rhett's feet remained rooted, and his body shook like a tree caught in a storm.

Alina realized one simple truth. Her two companions relied on her bravery and leadership. They needed her. If she wished for them to survive, she had to step forward and meet the monster.

Biting down on her lip hard enough to taste blood, Alina matched the Minotaur's progress, stepping forward as he stepped toward her.

"It's over," she said, struggling to keep her voice level and confident.

Without a word, the Minotaur stormed forward.

Alina squeezed the stone in her hand and screamed. She lunged at the bulldozing monster. She didn't stand a chance, not against its power and speed and size.

The Minotaur crashed into her.

Ribs snapped like dried branches. Her breath expelled from her body, and she labored to draw more air back in. White-hot pain exploded behind her eyes, it burned throughout her like a rampaging wild fire.

She barely clung to consciousness.

Shifting into survival mode and acting without thought, only reacting on pure instinct, Alina raised her hand and smashed the stone into the Minotaur's rock-hard skull.

She did it again.

Again.

Again.

Each successive strike grew weaker and weaker... and weaker, until Alina knew nothing more.

Opened Eyes. Wednesday, July 26th. 0824hrs.

ALINA SLOWLY AWOKE TO a tidal wave of pain as it crashed against her head. Chills cascaded down her body, followed by a surging rise of heat into her face. Sour bile and a flood of saliva filled her mouth, and she turned her head, but the sensation dwindled as quick as it had come.

She kept her eyes shut, though she had fully awakened. She had deduced, based on the scratchy fabric of the pillowcase, the flat pillow, and the subtle beeping of a heart rate monitor, she lay in a hospital bed.

I survived the island, she thought.

It didn't bring her relief, though. More fear as unanswered questions piled onto her. What had happened to Rhett and Nora? What had happened to Asterion? Had someone saved them, saved her, or did she rest in a private room, under the care of Asterion until she healed enough for him to hunt her again?

If she opened her eyes, she might learn the truth. Alina wasn't sure if she could handle the truth.

More, though, Alina was terrified of what she wouldn't see if she opened her eyes.

Throughout her life, she had only known loneliness and isolation—at least until recently. Though she had loving, positive memories of her father, he had never been there when she needed him. Unfortunately, her mother had provided little in the way of a constant presence, either. Alina had bounced from foster home to grandma's home to Maya's home, back to her parents' home to repeat the vicious, never-ending cycle.

If Alina opened her eyes and saw an empty chair sitting in the empty hospital room, her heart would shatter irreconcilably. She would be forever lost in a dark, confusing, lonely world.

Or she could keep her eyes shut, ignore reality, pretend someone cared enough to sit with her.

No, she thought, clenching her jaw. *I don't care how much it hurts, even if it kills me, I'll not hide from the truth.*

She had survived Eddie Denier. She had survived the Minotaur. She had survived her parents' constant disappointing behavior. Alina, if she was anything, was a survivor. That's what she told herself, and that's the armor she wore. It was chipped and bloodied, but it had kept her alive so far.

With incredible effort, Alina opened her eyes.

An empty chair sat beside an open window. The morning sunshine spilled through the glass, flooding across the room's tile floor, stopping halfway up her bed.

Shallow, yet heavy breaths rattled inside Alina's throat. She couldn't remove her gaze from the green-clothed empty chair. Her eyes stung, her nostrils burned. A greasy lump clogged her throat, making it difficult to breathe.

A chomping sound, like crunching chips, sounded over her other shoulder.

To Alina, it was the single most incredible noise she had ever heard in her life. She turned her head, pulled her lips to suppress a vocal sob, but she didn't combat her tears. They streaked freely down her face.

Fred sat in a chair beside the closed pink curtain separating Alina's bed from the other bed. He snacked on trail mix and watched *Gilmore Girls* on the small, mounted television. The behemoth man didn't know Alina had come back to her senses.

She was okay with that, too. She stared at him silently, basking in his warm, calm, goofy presence.

Maybe a second elapsed, maybe ten minutes, but after a time, Fred glanced at Alina. His eyes shifted back to the TV, and he tossed another handful of trail mix into his mouth. Then he spat it out, jumped from his chair, and stared directly at Alina with buggy eyes and oval lips.

"You're awake," he said. "Holy smokes. You're awake." He grabbed the pink curtain and ripped it open. Daphne lay on the neighboring bed, reading a book. "She's awake!"

Daphne glanced over, set her book down, and stood. She hurried to the room's door, opened it, and yelled down the hall. "She's awake! Alina's awake!"

Before any nurse or doctor arrived, Alina's mother walked through the door. She wore her work outfit—a maroon apron with her name pinned to the strap. Her hair fell loosely from a high bun, and dark circles weighed down her puffy eyes. As she entered the room, though, a visible transformation occurred. Wanda aged backwards, and the darkness that clung to her aura burned away from a surging radiance.

She rushed across the room and kneeled before Alina's bed. She touched Alina with her trembling hands. "My baby. You're okay."

Alina swallowed and nodded. She didn't have the strength to speak. Instead, she nuzzled her head against her mom's forearm, allowing her mother to hold her, to keep her, to protect her.

The doctor came and asked Alina a few questions, and the nurse came to make sure Alina was comfortable.

When the tears and the traffic slowed, and the gears in her head churned once more, Alina pulled away and stared at her mother. For the first time in Alina's life, Wanda looked beautiful. Not in a societal sense, but in a real, tangible way. Wanda wore a genuine smile that melted years off of her face. She no longer appeared skeletal and stank of sour body odor and cigarette smoke and marijuana. She had put on a healthy amount of weight, and she smelled clean.

"Just a concussion, huh?" Alina asked, her voice a little raspy. "Pretty lucky, all things considered."

"I'd say you're lucky," Fred said. "Based on the old kisser," Fred twirled his finger around his face, "you look like a half-rotten banana."

Wanda turned to face Fred and Daphne. "I want to do this now. Can you give us a minute of privacy?"

"I'm running low on snacks, anyway," Fred said. "We'll be back in a few minutes."

Alina suddenly felt terrified again. What did her mother want to do? Why did Fred and Daphne have to leave the room?

Wanda grabbed Alina's hand and squeezed. "I have some... hard news."

August, Alina thought. Maya never found him—or she had, but she hadn't found him alive.

"Just say it."

"Okay." Wanda inhaled. "Your father committed suicide." Her face collapsed. She lowered her head and sobbed. "I'm so sorry."

Alina went numb. She didn't really feel anything. She didn't compre-hend it.

"Is he dead?"

Wanda nodded, incapable of speaking through her cries.

Alina turned her head and stared at the fluorescent light fixture on the ceiling. A chronic chime rang in her ears, and she had no feeling in her body, no thoughts in her head. She felt completely empty, like a husk, like someone had scooped out what made her Alina—her pain and her emotions.

"How?" she asked.

"Overdose. They think it was accidental."

Her molars ached. For a second, she considered tapping the call button on her bed and asking the nurse if she could speak to a dentist.

"Accidental?"

Wanda only nodded.

The ringing in her ears continued. Alina couldn't pinpoint her emo-tions. Her father had served as a fixture of suffering in her life, but she didn't feel relief or joy from the news. Neither did she feel sad. Was that normal? Should she have felt something more? Should she have laughed with joy, or wept with her mother?

Alina responded by staring at the ceiling, feeling empty and cold.

A knock rapped against the door a few minutes later. Fred poked his head into the room. "You have a visitor. What should I tell him? To kick rocks, come back never?"

"Who is it?" Alina asked, her voice distant as her memories stole her far from the hospital.

Stephen pushed the kitchen table to the corner, stacked the chairs atop it to make more room, and turned the Bob Seger album to maximum volume. He grabbed Alina's small, seven-year-old hand and led her onto the kitchen dance floor. He sang, terribly, but loud and proud, with a sideways smile across his face. He twirled his daughter around, danced off-rhythm, but with energy and excitement. Alina could smell the beer on his breath, the nicotine sweating out of his skin. She could see his pupils dilated. Yet, she screamed with laughter.

"Detective Vanek," Fred said.

Alina's mind swiped like a slideshow, dropping her into another time and place. That same seven-year-old girl sat on the curb outside a low-rent bar in the dead of winter. The owner couldn't afford to get caught with a minor inside his establishment. Stephen's buddies drank there, and they shot up in the bathrooms or the back alley, so that's where he drank. Wanda worked that night. Alina tagged along with her father, and she sat on the curb until two in the morning, waiting for him to stumble, drunk and high, onto the sidewalk. They didn't have a car, so they had to hike through the city, Alina praying to whatever god might listen that he didn't pass out on the street again.

"Let him in," Alina said.

The memories flashed through her head. Stephen shouting out 38 Special songs in the truck with Alina; Stephen shouting out curses and ridicules at Wanda; Stephen holding Alina's hand as they walked across the street to grab ice cream; Stephen stumbling as they navigated through the worst parts of town; Stephen introducing Alina to horror movies; Stephen ripping away her innocence, her childhood, her sense of security.

What did Alina make of her father's death?

As Alina struggled to process the news, Wanda had descended to the empty bed, replaced by Detective Vanek. He wore a formal, on-duty uniform, complete with a badge and a gun.

"This is a business meeting?" Alina asked.

The corner of Vanek's lips slightly lifted. "You doing okay?"

"No."

"You have a strong cast of support around you. We'll take care of you."

Stephen always around to make things worse; Stephen never around to make anything better.

"I know," Alina said. "You have questions for me?"

"When you're ready to answer them."

"I'm ready."

"What happened yesterday?"

Alina shared everything from when she arrived at the Graves' house to when the Minotaur knocked her unconscious. When she finished the retelling, she reached for the rolling tray beside her bed and grabbed a cup of ice water, drinking from the bendy straw. "Nora and Rhett?"

"They're okay... better than you."

A warmth spread through Alina's body. She pawed at her eyes, annoyed at how much she had cried already.

Not for my dad, though, she thought. *I haven't shed a tear for him.*

"The Minotaur?"

"A man in a costume," Vanek said. "We have him, though. He won't hurt anyone ever again."

"And August?"

Vanek chuckled, but he didn't push the topic. Alina had lied to him about August assigning her to investigate Samantha's disappearance, and Vanek had most likely learned the truth by then.

"He's on the floor above you."

Alina coughed out a sob she struggled to hold back. Her eyes welled. Guilt as hot as coal formed in her throat and dripped like acid into her stomach. Why did she feel so much emotion for Rhett and Nora and August, but she felt nothing but numbness for her father?

"We'll see if we can get you up to visit with him in a little while, but for now you can settle to speak with Rhett and Nora."

"They're here?"

"They haven't left the waiting room. Not even when their parents showed to pick them up, they refused to leave until they saw you."

"Yeah, of course. Bring them in now."

Vanek stood, reached out, and touched Alina's hand. "He would have killed for a long, long time. You stopped him. You saved a lot of lives."

"Come on now, Detective," Fred said. "Her head is already so inflated it barely fits through the office door. There's no need to put more air in it."

Daphne punched his shoulder. "Fred!"

He shrugged. "What? She's constantly mean to me."

Daphne shook her head and rolled her eyes.

"Good work," Vanek said, squeezing Alina's hand. "I'm proud of you."

With that, he turned and headed toward the door, leaving Alina stuck once more with her conflicting, confusing thoughts. Less than a minute passed before the door opened again.

Rhett had his hands on Nora's shoulders, and he steered her slowly to the bed.

Nora smiled as only a child can smile. It amazed Alina, because most children feared the hospital, they became nervous around seeing people in such battered conditions. But not the courageous firecracker that Nora was. She smiled, and her smile lit up the room, warmed Alina's soul, and melted her pain.

"I bought... well, my mom gave me the money, but I bought you this." Nora raised a candy bar and handed it to Alina. "It's my favorite."

"Thank you," Alina said.

"You won't cry, will you?" Rhett asked. "Because if you cry, I'll cry, and I'm, like, the ugliest crier in the world... probably in history. If you see me crying, you're going to call off our date for Friday night. So, please, don't cry."

Alina found herself, despite everything that had happened, giggling. "I won't cry."

"Thank you."

Nora wore a clean outfit, and she had washed herself, too. No more mud caked the front of her body. She didn't sport any obvious physical injuries.

Rhett also appeared in a renewed state. He had found himself a new T-shirt, too.

"I'm sorry about ripping your favorite shirt," Alina said.

"Oh." Rhett brushed away the question with a pawing gesture. "I was wrong. I actually hated that shirt. It's funny, though. Hate and love have such a thin border, they're easy to confuse. My favorite shirt is under my bed, or in the trunk of my mom's car... or maybe, though

I'm not sure because I'll never have the bravery to check, in a dresser drawer."

Alina couldn't have flushed the smile from her face had she tried. "What happened?"

Rhett looked down at Nora and mussed her hair, much like a big brother might do to annoy a little sister. "Why don't you tell her? You're better at it than I am."

"Okay." She sniffled and ran her arm across her nostrils. "Well, Alina, you ran at the monster. He tackled you and began punching you in the face."

"It was pretty brutal," Rhett said. "I'll admit, it was terrifying. I froze. I would have stood there and watched that creature beat you to death. Because of this little warrior, though, you're alive." He gave Nora a noogie.

"I thought I was telling the story?" Nora asked, ducking away from Rhett's assault.

"Yeah, well, you can't tell that part. It makes you look arrogant. If I tell it, though, you look courageous."

Nora sighed. "I didn't think about it, I just did it. Rather, my hands did it. They grabbed a rock from the sling, and I threw it and hit the monster."

"Right in the back of the head," Rhett said. "Freaking inspired me, too. A wave of idiocy—"

"You said bravery earlier," Nora said.

"They're the same thing. A wave of idiotic bravery overcame me. I grabbed my stick and charged the monster. I played baseball—tee ball, for one game before realizing I hated it and quitting the team... mid-game. None of those details matter. I remembered how to swing a bat. I struck the Minotaur across the head. Smack!" Rhett clapped his hands, causing Alina to jump. "Cocked back, smacked him again. Again. All the while, rocks are pelting him in the body, the face. He's no longer paying attention to you. That's when I throw all my fear and anger into the swing. I connected with his dumb bull nose, twisted his head completely around so it faced backward."

Rhett glanced at Nora, as if they rehearsed the cadence of their story, and it was her turn to speak.

She must have caught the cue, because she picked up where he left off. "The monster grabbed its backwards head and pulled it off its shoulders."

"He was wearing a mask," Rhett said.

"No," Fred said, shocked. "You guys had me there for a minute. I wasn't expecting a mask."

Alina glanced at Fred and curled her lip. What had he expected, then? That the Minotaur removed its head like the headless horseman?

"I threw another rock," Nora said, "just as the mask came off. Hit the man right in the head."

"I saw him dazed after that hit," Rhett said. He held an invisible bat and swung it as he spoke. "I aimed for the temple, and I hit a grand slam, baby. Out of the ballpark, sending Nora all the way home!"

"We used the shirt to tie him up."

"I guarded him, though, in case he tried something funny."

"That's it," Nora said. "A helicopter arrived thirty minutes later."

"Without you, and without her," Rhett said, motioning to Alina and Nora, "we'd all be dead. I didn't have the balls to act without you two showing me how. So, to make it up, at least to you, Alina, I'll pay for our entire date. No going dutch. It's on me. You earned it."

Nora punched Rhett in the ribs. "You're a moron."

"I'm serious. You saved my life."

"Why do you ruin every nice thing you say with something stupid, though?"

"Why are you always so mean to me?"

"Guys," Alina said. "Thank you both, so much, for everything. Mostly, thank you for being here."

"Well, as they say," Rhett said, "availability is the best ability. That's why I'm always available."

"It's because you have no life," Nora said.

"She's so mean!"

Alina chuckled, but her mind once more separated her from the room. Her father filled her thoughts, and memories stacked one on top of the other. Stephen the energetic, rambunctious man. Stephen the absent, icy man. He hadn't ever been an ideal father or husband. He had been cruel and negligent and abusive. He had sold her to a murderous monster.

Yet, he had been her father, and she had loved him, and she felt numb processing his loss.

But she no longer felt empty. As everyone gathered around Alina's bed, a strange warmth filled her soul, a bright hope that she was no longer, and would never again be, alone.

The Road Less Traveled. Wednesday, July 26th. 0831hrs.

MAYA USUALLY PREFERRED HER coffee black, but it tasted bitter and old. She poured two packs of sugar into the steaming-hot liquid. That did little to help with the taste. Her omelet had tasted bitter, too, as had her hash browns.

The entire morning tasted bitter.

Across the diner table sat Evan. He sported a split lip, a swollen eye, a laceration across his cheek, and a slightly crooked nose. That wasn't the worst of it, though. He bore a defeated expression. Not a frown, but worse. The brokenness lingered in his eyes. Evan, the man who tattooed a smile across his face and replayed his laughter like a broken record, had a dark pallor burdening his eyes. Humor or amusement no longer existed.

Only bitterness, Maya thought, stirring more sugar—though she doubted it would help—into her coffee. *I stole his joy.*

"I don't know where to begin," Evan said.

They met for breakfast at a cafe at eight o'clock. After a European-styled kiss on the cheek, they sat, ordered their food, and ate in silence. Apart from the "Do you know what you're getting" and the "How's your meal," they barely exchanged words.

Maya had spent the night bouncing between August's, Alina's, and Evan's rooms, waiting for one to wake up. Evan had come to first. Though he had received a pretty hefty beating from Terry and Jericho, he hadn't suffered anything more serious than a mild concussion.

The doctors discharged him while Maya sat beside August's bed. Evan snuck out of the hospital, leaving only a simple note for a nurse to share with Maya.

Breakfast at 8? Orphan Cafe.

Maya sighed, staring across the table at Evan. She knew exactly where to begin... or more appropriately, where to end.

Right now, she thought.

Their relationship had run its course. Despite the love she felt for him, the love he reciprocated, too much had happened the night before.

He said words she could forgive him for, but wouldn't ever forget him saying.

"You always seem to have something to say," Evan said, moving the remnants of his breakfast around with a fork. "But not now?"

"What do you want me to say?"

Evan shrugged. "I don't know."

The words sat on the tip of her tongue. I think we should end this. But she couldn't find the strength to speak them. They had dated for a few months, and she had fallen in love with him. He was smart, loyal, thoughtful, and joyful. Most of all, his joy was infectious, and he made Maya feel beyond happy.

She didn't want their relationship to end.

Yet, a hate existed now—a bitterness that no amount of sugar could sweeten away. He had called her ugly names. Maybe he hadn't fully meant what he said, but a seed of honesty existed within his insults. Maya would always know how he truly felt. That she was a dirty, diseased whore.

"My AirPods are at your house," Evan said. "You can have them. I've been needing to buy new ones, anyway."

There it was.

He hadn't outright ended their relationship, but he'd implied enough for Maya to deduce his intent. At least they stood on the same ship, sailing toward the same sunset.

"Say it," Maya said, steeling herself to remain strong.

She feared if the relationship-ending words were never uttered and agreed on, they wouldn't accept the implication of the meeting. They would come back together, break each other's hearts all over again.

Evan scratched the corner of his swollen eye. "Is that what you want?"

"No," Maya said.

A tear crawled down her face. She didn't care if Evan saw her cry. He knew she loved him; this hurt him as much as it hurt her.

"What do you want?"

"To go back in time," she said.

He shook his head. "That's not possible."

"Did you mean any of it?"

Evan hesitated, slightly nodding. "I meant it when I said I loved you."

"Not that."

"I know."

"Did you mean it?"

"It scared me, your past. It still does. I was terrified and shocked about what we had done and gone through—breaking into the motel room, seeing Stephen's body, wearing his clothes." He shivered. "It's not an excuse. I shouldn't have said any of it. I shouldn't have allowed my emotions to speak for me."

"But you did," Maya said.

"But I did."

They were dancing now, swaying in circles and avoiding the inevitable.

"I'm sorry," Maya said.

"I thought you don't apologize?" Evan's bruised face crinkled from a slight grin.

Maya snickered. "I don't apologize for things I'm not sorry for. But I'm sorry for calling you yesterday. I was sorry the second I dialed your number." Maya reached across the table and held Evan's hands. His wrists bore the chaffing marks from the rope. "I needed help, and I didn't know who else to turn to with..." She trailed off.

"With August missing," Evan said, retracting his hands from the table and setting them in his lap.

Maya nodded.

A tense silence built around them. "You were with him when I woke up."

Maya nodded.

"Do you love him?"

Maya pulled in her lips, and she nodded. "It's different, though."

Evan scratched his eyebrow and exhaled. "I think it's time."

"I don't want this to end."

"I don't either, but we both know it has to end." Evan reached for his wallet, dropped a few twenties on the table, and stood. "I don't know what else to say."

It took her a few seconds to build her courage, but she finally spoke. "Goodbye, Evan."

Maya wanted to stand and hug him, to feel his body pressed against hers one last time; she wanted to kiss him, to grab his hand and leave the cafe with him. Instead she remained seated, knowing if she stood, the desired progression would follow, and she would leave with him.

"On the record," Evan said, glancing up at the ceiling and rapidly blinking, "you're the most interesting woman I've ever had the pleasure of knowing. Never change. You deserve someone who accepts you as you are—for your past, present, and future." The light from his smile touched his eyes. "Maybe we'll meet again in another life."

Maya watched him leave.

She would miss Evan's gentle nature, his constant smile and breathy laugh. She would miss their conversations, both intellectual and silly. As she focused on what she would miss, Maya nearly leaped from the table and chased him. She didn't have to miss any of it. They could forgive each other and move forward.

Couldn't they?

Doubt trickled throughout Maya. Whenever she closed her eyes and pictured her future, she never imagined Evan standing beside her. If anything, she saw August.

A couple months ago, she willingly told August about her past. Evan had learned of it through Victor Pemberton. Otherwise, Maya never would have shared that part of her life with Evan, for fear of how he might respond.

It hurt the most that Evan proved her fears warranted.

What now? she thought, sitting alone in the cafe.

Maya was single, and August was single. Did the two of them finally make the jump?

No!

The answer shouted loud and clear across her soul.

Maya always had a boyfriend, or at least someone to keep her busy. The thought of dating again suddenly felt tiresome and arresting. Evan had shown her the brighter side of relationships and romance, and she didn't want to dive into something cheap and shallow. Not that dating August would be cheap and shallow, but if she ran to him now, she feared it would be under the pretext of a rebound. Not only that, she would provide him with all the power in the relationship. She needed him; she had run to him. They wouldn't stand on equal ground.

Maya realized she required time for herself to grow and mature. Once recovered from the brokenness Evan left her with, then maybe she and August could have their shot at that little thing called love.

Until then, Maya would focus on the road less traveled, at least less traveled to her. Single and no longer available to mingle.

Maya glanced at her cell phone to check the time, but noticed a handful of missed calls and messages, most of which were from Fred stating Alina had woken up.

Another message came from Jonah, the editor from the *Here & Now*. It prompted Maya to investigate a potential story in South Sacramento. According to Jonah's source, an elderly woman witnessed fairy-like creatures in her backyard.

After staring at the message for nearly a minute, Maya called Jonah.

She had no intention of following up with the fairy sighting, and she had no intention of working for Jonah Daniels and his tabloid any longer. She had dreamed of becoming a bona fide investigative journalist. Though she treated the *Here & Now* as a stepping stone, it now felt like a stone tied to her ankles, dragging her deeper and deeper beneath the surface.

"Hello," Jonah answered.

Maya inhaled, closed her eyes, and once again turned onto the road less traveled.

As she hung the phone up on her screaming ex-boss, another call came through.

"Sammy," Maya said, smiling despite losing her boyfriend and only source of income.

"Hi," Samantha Graves said.

Maya stood from her seat and headed to the cafe's exit. She placed Samantha on speakerphone, tapping on her screen to call an Uber to take her back to the hospital.

"How are you?"

"Keeping it together," Samantha said. "I have to for Wade. He's a wreck."

"Where are you staying?"

"With our grandma and grandpa, but I don't know how long they'll keep us. Wade already punched through their wall and broke a bathroom mirror. He's angry, and I don't know how to calm him down other than keep myself together and set an example."

The Sacramento Police had coordinated with the El Dorado Police to raid the Graves' residence. Vanek had organized the operation, using Maya's texts to get the ball rolling. The officers arrested Tara Ferneau, Jericho, Wendy Graves, and Terry Graves, along with the other guards stationed around the property.

Maya wasn't sure if they had formally charged anyone with any specific crimes yet, but she knew they faced a litany of felonies, including multiple kidnappings and conspiracy to multiple homicides.

"Well, for what it's worth," Maya said, "you have me. Call whenever you need to talk to someone." It wasn't an empty promise, Maya would pick up the phone if Samantha ever called, but she doubted the young woman would ever dial her number again.

Maya waited on the curb for her ride to arrive, listening to Samantha breathe into the phone. A silence stretched between them, and Maya realized Samantha had only called for a simple reason: she needed something.

"What's going on?" Maya asked.

She wouldn't ever know.

Samantha ended the call.

Maya toyed with calling her back, but opted against it. The morning sunshine bathed her with rejuvenating, revitalizing warmth. She didn't know what stood on the horizon of her life, but it was bright and promising, and Maya couldn't wait to step into the new day.

Land of the Living. Wednesday, July 26th. 0948hrs.

I SAT IN A wheelchair and turned my ear to the closed door. A swarm of voices buzzed from inside Alina's room. I wanted to visit with her, to check on her, to hear from her what had happened on the island, but not with a crowd to interfere with our conversation.

Besides, no one knew I had returned to the land of the living, that I had awoken from my healing slumber.

The doctor had come into my room an hour ago, checked my vitals, my splint, my bandages, before a nurse replaced her.

The nurse, Angel Garcia, asked me a few questions. I asked him if I could move around the hospital. Reluctantly, he agreed, but only if I sat in a wheelchair and he pushed me to my desired destinations.

We went to Alina's room first.

"Do you wish to go inside?" Angel asked. He reminded me of a teddy bear—big with an innate softness about him.

"Not yet," I said, wanting to wait until Alina's room cleared.

I asked to see someone else instead.

The room behind Randall Fincher's door was silent. I reached up and rapped my knuckles against the wood. After a few seconds, I asked Angel to wheel me inside.

Wilson had lied to me about Randall during our meeting in the sandwich shop. Randall hadn't slipped into a coma. He had remained aware enough to share his story about what happened at the Spirit of Sacramento. Wilson withheld and altered that information to control my actions, to build trust between him and me, to tarnish the trust between me and all other law enforcement. He wished to establish himself as my sole source of survival.

The Sacramento Police Department never meant to arrest me for the multiple homicides. Randall had provided them with the full story the day after his hospitalization.

He, along with Eddie Denier, Greta Tonyan, and Christopher Steele, had awoken inside the Spirit of Sacramento ship. When Randall saw the other people, he didn't see them for who they were. He saw his deceased mother and father in their faces. He wasn't sure what the others saw, but based on the way they responded, they saw something equally terrifying to them.

The police connected the threads of the story, and they told me what actually happened, not Randall's hallucinated nightmare.

Eddie Denier had a gun. He fired, shooting Randall in the stomach. Greta and Christopher attacked him, and they all fought, but Eddie prevailed, shooting them both dead. As they skirmished, Randall took the time to find a thick block of splintered lumber. He snuck up behind Eddie—"My mother," he had said to the police; he snuck up on his mother. He broke it over his skull. Eddie dropped the gun, dazed. Randall scrambled to pick the weapon up, and he fired until the weapon dry clicked, then he used it like a club.

"I killed my mother," Randall told the officers. "I killed her."

When I showed up an hour later, I discovered the bodies and fled. In my drugged state, I hadn't seen Randall or Eddie, but I saw my greatest fear—humanoid spiders.

After my sudden departure, the police department received an anonymous call about arachnids at the Spirit of Sacramento. They thought the call was a hoax, but they investigated anyway. Finding Randall still alive, they sent him to the hospital.

Randall's beady eyes stared at me. His throat bobbed as he swallowed.

"Hey, Randall," I said.

"Hi."

"You doing okay?"

He shrugged. "I guess."

The man had killed Eddie Denier. Though Eddie probably didn't deserve to live after all the horror he inflicted throughout his life, Randall had killed another human. The weight showed on his grimacing face. It was a weight I understood.

"Do you believe in God?" Randall asked.

"No," I said.

"Neither do I. Not anymore."

I nodded, not sure what to say.

"Do you think if I prayed to Him, He might listen?"

I shrugged. "I think so."

"Me, too. I don't know what to say, though. Could you maybe speak to Him for me?"

I licked my lips. "Sure." I reached out and grabbed his trembling hand.

When was the last time I prayed? I couldn't remember.

"God," I said, collecting my thoughts.

I didn't know what to say, and if God existed, I doubted He cared much about what I said. Still, I knew my words impacted Randall, so I considered them carefully before speaking. My thoughts swirled. Aaron, Cambria, Quinn, Glacia, my family, my friends, those who contacted me to help them, and those I stopped from hurting others crossed my mind. Pain, guilt, anger, love, joy coalesced and burned within me.

"Forgive us our sins," I said. "Teach us to forgive ourselves of our sins, but not to forget them. Never to forget them. Instead, help us learn from them, grow from them, and become better because of them. Take the weight of our burdens from us. Show us to love, for, if I'm not mistaken, love is all that matters."

I opened my eyes and looked at Randall.

Tears streamed down his ghostly face.

"Amen."

Shortly after the prayer, I left his room and asked Angel to wheel me into another room—a room I had meant to avoid.

Former Detective Ted Wilson sat upright in the hospital bed, eating peaches from a plastic container. His face grew tight when I entered the room. He didn't look angry, only embarrassed and guilty. He was in good condition, better than me at least. I wasn't sure why the hospital held him, unless they waited for corrections to release Wilson into their care.

"Why are you here?" he asked.

I stared out the open window overlooking a rooftop and the blue morning sky. At first, I considered forgiving him, but I decided against it, at least until he asked.

In the end, I had nothing to say to him. I only wanted to see his face.

We sat in violent silence for a few minutes. Angel was fidgety behind the wheelchair, probably sensing the animosity. When my time expired, I glanced back at the nurse and nodded. He wheeled me out of Wilson's room, a few doors down the hallway, to another room guarded by two officers.

Daniel Quinn, or rather Jack Schaeffer, didn't grimace when he saw me. The man beamed with joy, smiling ear to ear. He had a bandage around his head where I had struck him with the butt of the gun.

"August Watson." He sat up in his bed, placing a book without a dustcover on his lap. I couldn't discern the title. "I hoped you might visit me, if only to gloat."

I blinked at him.

His smile waned.

"You shot Aaron Brooks," Quinn said, forcing the grin back into place. "Why?"

"Because you're not as clever as you believe. Despite the illusions and the holograms, I saw through your deceptions. I knew Aaron was nothing more than a projection."

Quinn's lips twitched. "Do you know how I did it?" The egomaniac wanted to exploit his genius one last time.

I stole even that small joy from him. "You're a Hollywood special-effects artist. You planted holograms around the tunnel and the mine, same as you planted the hologram of the ghost on Highway 1 in Santa Cruz. You had Steven Anderson concoct a fear toxin, most likely using the BZ chemical compound as a foundation. It wasn't predictable enough for your needs, so you added the projections to enhance the hallucinations, making sure your victims saw exactly what you wanted them to see."

Quinn's smile faded as I laid out the facts.

After I suspected a fear-based drug, I had asked Fred to look into it. He reported his findings through an email, which I read after waking. In it, he detailed Quinn's actual identity and previous career.

Even if I had a few details wrong in my deductions, my conjecture was close enough to correct to deflate Quinn's ego.

He choked out a forced chuckle. "Daniel Quinn is a mask," he said, uncertainty rising in his tone. "A costume. A mantle. You brought down Jack Schaeffer, but Daniel Quinn remains free and dangerous. You haven't seen the last of Daniel Quinn."

"I've seen the last of Jack Schaeffer, though." I nodded at Angel.

The nurse wheeled me out of Schaeffer's room, and he stopped in the hallway. "We should get you back to your bed."

I still wanted to visit Vincent, and I had to speak with Alina.

"One more stop," I said. "Then I'll rest."

Reluctantly, Angel agreed. He wheeled me through the hospital floor, past the elevators, onto another wing, stopping before the door.

"This is your last visit before we head back to your room," he said. "I'm not even supposed to let anyone in here, so we'll make this quick."

"Of course."

Angel opened the door and wheeled me into Glacia's room.

The nurses had helped clean her up—the blood wiped from her skin and hair, the dirt from her face. Still, bruises covered her body. Somehow, she had the strength to smile at me when I entered.

"Hey you," she said, her voice hoarse. "You look terrible."

"You should see the other guy."

Glacia put on a placating smile, but I couldn't find any humor behind her dark eyes. "How are you?"

I glanced back at Angel. The subtle twisting movement set my upper half on fire. "Could you give us five minutes alone?"

"Three," he said.

"Thank you."

"It's the detectives," Glacia said once Angel stepped outside her room. "They requested no one visits until they've interviewed me fully about what happened."

I could have asked her what she remembered about the experience, what she saw from the toxin and the hologram concoction, but I swallowed back my curiosity, content just to sit with her in silence.

"You haven't answered my question," Glacia said. "How are you?"

"In a wheelchair."

"You know what I mean."

Quinn had forced me to relive my most haunting moment—shooting Aaron Brooks. In a reversal, the act hadn't destroyed me as he had probably hoped. Instead, it served as a moment of healing. Symbolically, I shot the spirit that shadowed the lens I saw the world through, that dictated my every decision. I faced and overcame my greatest demon.

"I feel... light."

"Light?"

"There's no longer a dark cloud hovering over me. I stopped running away. I stopped hiding. I stepped into the open, faced my fear, and won. I feel stronger, at least strong enough to bear the weight of my past now." I spoke freely to her, spilling my thoughts as they touched upon my mind.

"And Cambria?"

"What about her?"

"Have you faced her death, or are you still running away from it? Have you mourned her?"

I scratched the scruff on my cheek and considered her question. "I don't know how to," I said. "Does that sound terrible? I've cried, and I've been angry, and I went after Quinn... but have I mourned her? I don't know. Her loss still hurts me, still haunts my conscience. I know I'm not to blame, but... but I know I am."

Glacia frowned. "I have a friend in Sacramento you could speak with. He's a talented therapist and a better person. I'll put you two in touch, and he can help you process these past few years. Who knows, maybe he'll pull you out from the cave and back into the light."

I nodded, chewing on her suggestion for a minute. She was right. I needed professional help—not the gym, not work, not a psychotic rival to distract me from my pain. I needed a professional to guide me.

"What about you?" I asked.

Glacia smirked. "Once I'm excused from the investigation into Jack Schaeffer's crimes, I'm headed back to Oregon." She reached out and touched my hand. "Thank you for saving me."

I shook my head. "Thank you for saving me," I said. "Will we see each other again?"

"If you're ever in Oregon, let me know." Glacia rested her head on the pillow and closed her eyes. "I'm going to steal some sleep now."

A few seconds later, Angel crept back in. He grabbed the handles on my chair and wheeled me back to my room.

"Do you need anything?" he asked once he had me back in bed.

I glanced at the rolling tray standing bedside. My cell phone rested near the giant cup of iced water. "No, thank you. Maybe later this afternoon, you'll wheel me to Vincent Dupree's room and Alina Moore's room, if they're still here."

"Rest first, then we'll discuss that."

"Thank you."

Angel padded out of the room.

I reached for my cell phone, ignored the hundreds of notifications, and called my mom.

"Gussy!"

I had to pull the phone from my ear to avoid damage.

"Fred called me and told me everything fifteen minutes ago. Your dad and I are on the way to the hospital now."

"Hey," my dad said.

I nearly told them not to worry, to turn the car around, that I would be okay. Maybe the old August would have pushed them away, but I couldn't. "The hospital food tastes like cheese-covered cardboard. Could you pick me up some lunch?"

"Of course," my mom said. She took my order. "How are you feeling?"

"Beat up, but okay. They say I'll live."

"I don't like that you keep ending up at the hospital from this job of yours. You were stabbed and shot only a few months ago, and now... what? Fred said you have a fractured collarbone."

"And a stab wound through my hand," I said, smiling.

"You need to find a new job, something safer and healthier."

The conversation continued like that for a half-dozen minutes—my mom voicing her concern, recommending other career and life paths, me listening but not agreeing—before we ended the call.

A warmth built inside my stomach and leaked outward, filling me with a soft fire, something bordering on true happiness.

I thought about Aaron Brooks and Cambria Parker; I thought about Quinn's victims, the ones I had failed to save, and I thought of the ones whom I had saved. I thought about my friends and my family. I thought about how best to honor those who died and those who lived.

Before, I drank myself into oblivion, and that had proved more than ineffective.

I had lost myself in exercise and work, hiding from my emotions and the weight of all I carried internally.

I had pushed people I cared for away to create the facade of protecting them.

So, what did I do? Did I call Tempest Michaels, shut down my branch of his Blue Moon franchise? Should I move on with my life, listen to my mom's advice, and find a safe, simple career?

I had started my quest to prove the supernatural existed so I could reach out and speak to Aaron Brooks, so I could apologize to him. I had achieved those goals, though not in the ways I had expected—I had made amends with his parents, visited his grave, and faced his spirit in the Underworld. Still, I had reached what I set out to do.

So, with my goal complete, what now? What happened next?

A New Beginning. Thursday, July 27th. 1901hrs.

I SAT ON THE couch in Daphne and Fred's living room. The heavenly aromas from the kitchen drifted to where we gathered for the first time since Monday night.

I spent all of Wednesday and most of Thursday in the hospital. Fred picked me up and drove me to my house, where I showered and changed clothes. Once I was ready, we went to his house.

Bagley greeted me at the front door, jumping on my shins, whining, peeing all over the floor from excitement.

Maya stood in the dining room without Evan at her side. She appeared pensive and unsettled. Whenever she sat, it didn't take her too long to stand. She paced the living room, entered the kitchen, opened the fridge just to close it again, and returned to the couch.

"You okay?" I asked at one point.

"No," she said in a tone that conveyed she didn't really want to talk about it right then.

I dropped the subject.

Alina was the last to arrive, and she showed up with Gerald.

My heart shattered when I saw her. She had bruises across her entire face, around her throat. Her left eye had swollen shut. A laceration stretched from the bottom of her eye down to the edge of her jaw. A medical adhesive held the wound together.

When she saw me, her darkened face illuminated. She dove into my outstretched arms.

I held her as she sobbed into my chest. I melted into her, crying on her shoulder.

We migrated to the living room, planting ourselves on couches and recliners.

Maya sat beside me, and she remained seated, though her legs fidgeted, bouncing up and down. She twisted her hands in tight circles.

For a moment, no one said a word.

Then, Maya—always Maya—broke the silence with a exasperated laugh. The barrier between us shattered. We all joined her, chuckling, laughing, howling.

I wiped tears from my eyes. My face ached from smiling, my shoulder barked in a subtle complaint. But I hadn't felt better in weeks.

When I caught my breath, I turned to Maya. "You go first."

"Okay. Yeah. I'll go first." She cleared her throat and wiped tears from her cheeks. In what felt like a single breath, Maya rehashed her experience.

"Anyway." She glanced at her niece. "Alina, you're next."

We all knew the aftermath of what happened on the island, but we had yet to hear Alina's entire story.

The national and local news channels ran coverage on the incident twenty-four-seven. Eric Corvis, the richest man in the Sacramento area, had purchased a private island about fifty miles off the coast of San Francisco, where he constructed a castle atop the forested, stony hill. The interior of the castle was a labyrinth. A series of narrow hallways created a maze throughout.

Corvis used his influence and connections with youth programs to kidnap children and ship them out to his island, where he dressed as a Minotaur and hunted the kids. To satiate his sick appetite without risking prison, Corvis reached into his deep wallet. He paid Ferneau handsomely, asking her to tamper with any missing children's investigations. To cover her tracks, Ferneau bribed a few of the officers to help her efforts. Corvis had also created a middleman (the Graves) to arrange the kidnappings and ship the children to the island. He paid them well for their service and silence, and he also promoted Terry's foot career.

Alina rubbed her palms on her jeans. "We fought back," she said, looking at Fred, at Maya, landing on me. "That's what we do, right? That's what you all taught me. We fight." She shared her story, and we all sat on the edge of our seats. When she finished, Alina licked her lips and glanced at Maya.

Maya returned her gaze with a shy smirk, and she turned to me. "And what happened to you, Mr. Watson?"

I smiled. "I'm still figuring it out, but Daniel Quinn was a pseudonym. His real name was Jack Schaefer, a special and practical effects genius. Despite his expertise, he had a slimy reputation, and most of the directors in the industry blacklisted him." I stopped and swallowed, still hurt that Wilson had actively worked against me. "They worked together to exact a personal vendetta against their past demon, using my face as its mask."

"What's that mean?" Maya asked.

"A cop killed their brother. They couldn't do anything about it back then, but they could avenge his death by getting back at me—another cop who killed an innocent kid."

"All that to get back at you?" Maya asked. "It seems like a lot, doesn't it?"

I nodded.

"How did Wilson, you know, work his detective gig and coordinate with Quinn?"

I shrugged, not quite of the logistics behind their madness. Though the police department had spoken with me, they hadn't share a lot of information. I would venture to say Wilson provided Quinn with inside information and protection, allowing the madman to wreak havoc as he saw fit.

"Where did they keep them?" Maya asked.

She meant where had they housed the kidnapped victims? Again, I didn't have a definitive answer.

"I've heard unsubstantiated rumblings of a gutted apartment complex owned by a certain Jack Schaeffer."

Maya sighed. "Well, that's it, huh?"

"What?" I asked.

"That's all she wrote."

"That's all who wrote?"

"The fat lady."

"What are you talking about?"

"We brought down a child-murdering operation. Corvis, Ferneau, the Graves are in prison. We stopped Quinn's—freaking-A! Can I just call him Quinn?"

"Call him whatever you want," I said.

"We stopped Quinn's reign of terror. Cops arrested him, along with Wilson and Anderson and the other fugitives who... survived." She spoke the last word with an ominous tone.

I'm sure we all thought the same thing.

People died because of Quinn. More people than necessary. James Connors. Greta Tonyan and Christopher Steele. Even the fugitives, as she had mentioned, died unnecessarily. Quinn had poisoned their minds.

"You don't have any pending cases," Maya said.

"Fred?"

"Nothing at the moment," Fred said.

"What's your next step?" Maya asked.

I scratched my neck and considered her question. Before I could answer, Daphne's voice carried into the living room from the kitchen.

"Dinner is ready!"

Fred popped up from his seat and rushed into the dining room. Alina trudged after him, followed by Maya.

I sat on the couch, staring at the dark television screen.

I had never felt more secure or clear about who I was and wanted to be. Quinn had created illusions, a false reality for me to wade through. In the end, he had provided me with clarity into myself. He had dragged all my past demons to the surface, forced me to face them, to defeat them.

Now, I stood weightless, having conquered my fears and doubts. I had ventured into the Underworld and returned to the land of the living.

I had a new beginning.

The End

(August and friends will return. In the meantime, check the next page for more books)

Blue Moon Boston

A coven of witches bent on murder, a cult of hidden figures raising a leviathan to smite the city ... sound like a regular Wednesday morning for Boston PD's supernatural division.

Chloe Mayfield is a career cop, but when a high-profile bust goes spectacularly wrong, she finds herself assigned to the losers in Blue Moon ...

... and discovers a world she never knew existed.

The Original Series

Fight a demon, investigate a werewolf biker gang, have tea with mum ... it's all in a day's work for England's #1 paranormal P.I.

When a master vampire starts killing people in his hometown, paranormal investigator, Tempest Michaels, takes it personally ...... and soon a race against time turns into a battle for his life. He doesn't believe in the paranormal but has a steady stream of clients with cases too weird for the police.

Mostly it's all nonsense, but when a third victim turns up with bite marks in her lifeless throat, can he really dismiss the possibility that this time the monster is real?

Joined by an ex-army buddy, a disillusioned cop, his friends from the pub, his dogs, and his mother (why are there no grandchildren, Tempest?), our paranormal investigator is going to stop the murders if it kills him ......

but when his probing draws the creature's attention, his family and friends become the hunted.

More by Alex Gates

Dead Awake

Dorian Miller, a private detective specializing in the supernatural, investigates a blackmail conspiracy involving the daughter of one of Sacramento's elite families who partook in a satanic ritual.

But the simple assignment soon turns un-deadly.

Zombies and golems rise around the city. The corpses of vampires are found slaughtered in a horrific manner. And rumors warn that a

Revenant—the spirit of a dead Necromancer summoned back to this world—stands behind all the mayhem.

How much longer can Dorian run from Death before it catches up to him?

More by Alex Gates

Inherent Magic

Once struggling to make rent, Skylar must now use her budding magic to save the world…

As a child of abuse, Skylar Neveah knows desperation and terror from firsthand experience. But nothing in her past prepared her for a date ending with her getting sacrificed to a fallen angel. By blind luck and a touch of magic, Skylar escaped with her life. To do so, she murdered two wealthy, influential men.

On the run from the police and the supernatural world, a man approaches Skylar. He offers her refuge at a secret university for humans like her with magical powers. She hesitantly accepts his offer. But her problems aren't solved... far from it.

A cosmic war has kicked off. Somehow, Skylar landed in the middle of it. And the fallen angel has fixed his attention on her. He will stop at nothing to see her killed. Will Skylar stop running, learn to control her magic, and fight back?

More Books By Steve Higgs

Blue Moon Investigations

Paranormal Nonsense
The Phantom of Barker Mill
Amanda Harper Paranormal Detective
The Klowns of Kent
Dead Pirates of Cawsand
In the Doodoo With Voodoo
The Witches of East Malling
Crop Circles, Cows and Crazy Aliens
Whispers in the Rigging
Bloodlust Blonde – a short story
Paws of the Yeti
Under a Blue Moon – A Paranormal
Detective Origin Story
Night Work
Lord Hale's Monster
The Herne Bay Howlers
Undead Incorporated
The Ghoul of Christmas Past
The Sandman
Jailhouse Golem
Shadow in the Mine
Ghost Writer

Felicity Philips Investigates

To Love and to Perish
Tying the Noose
Aisle Kill Him
A Dress to Die For
Wedding Ceremony Woes

Patricia Fisher Cruise Mysteries

The Missing Sapphire of Zangrabar
The Kidnapped Bride
The Director's Cut
The Couple in Cabin 2124
Doctor Death
Murder on the Dancefloor
Mission for the Maharaja
A Sleuth and her Dachshund in Athens
The Maltese Parrot
No Place Like Home

Patricia Fisher Mystery Adventures

What Sam Knew
Solstice Goat
Recipe for Murder
A Banshee and a Bookshop
Diamonds, Dinner Jackets, and Death
Frozen Vengeance
Mug Shot
The Godmother
Murder is an Artform
Wonderful Weddings and Deadly
Divorces
Dangerous Creatures

Patricia Fisher: Ship's Detective Series

The Ship's Detective
Fitness Can Kill
Death by Pirates
First Dig Two Graves

Albert Smith Culinary Capers

Pork Pie Pandemonium
Bakewell Tart Bludgeoning
Stilton Slaughter
Bedfordshire Clanger Calamity
Death of a Yorkshire Pudding
Cumberland Sausage Shocker
Arbroath Smokie Slaying
Dundee Cake Dispatch
Lancashire Hotpot Peril
Blackpool Rock Bloodshed
Kent Coast Oyster Obliteration
Eton Mess Massacre
Cornish Pasty Conspiracy

Realm of False Gods

Untethered magic
Unleashed Magic
Early Shift
Damaged but Powerful
Demon Bound
Familiar Territory
The Armour of God
Live and Die by Magic
Terrible Secrets

About the Authors

Alex and Steve met online through their mutual love of urban fantasy. Both established writers with their own successful series, they chose to collaborate on a spin-off of Steve's Blue Moon Investigation stories.

They duo hope to meet in person one day when pandemics and other global dramas allow, but one of them will need to cross the Atlantic first. Until then, they will continue to churn out thrilling fantasy tales.

Read on and enjoy.